To Anatasia;

I hope you can

Characters, George

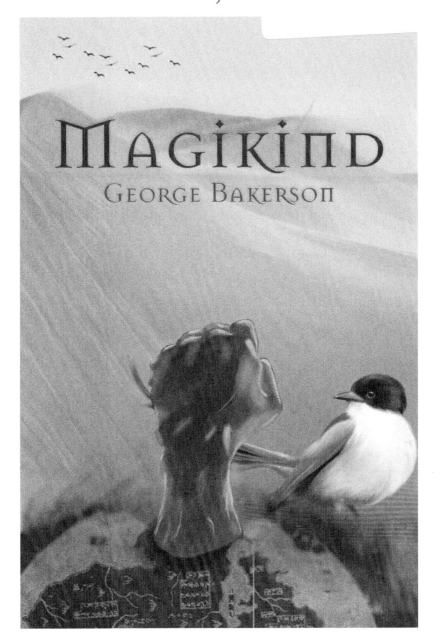

Magikind

George Bakerson

MAGIKIND

GEORGE BAKERSON

CREATIVE NOVELS LLC

Creativenovels.com

CREATIVE NOVELS

Published by Creative Novels LLC

99 Wall Street #1383, New York, NY 10005, United States

ISBNs: 978-1-7344956-0-7 (trade paperback), 978-1-7344956-1-4 (eBook)

ACKNOWLEDGMENTS

"

To my friends and fans who have been there from the very beginning. Without you guys, I wouldn't have even started this journey as an author.

"

1

A Simple Test

As she double-checked the documents, Maria Anasta sighed, placing the papers on her desk before taking a long, hard look at the man in front of her. Something about his appearance felt off. It wasn't his tanned skin, nor his short stature, but rather the peculiar way his facial hair he possessed grew. It was trimmed as if it was just for show. It didn't leave any impression that it could be used for an ability of sorts. However, she couldn't be sure due to the spiralling pattern his beard made around the cheekbones.

'Gin Julius Gale,' she addressed the man. 'In all the eighty years that I've been the colonel of squadron W, I have never seen an application as empty as this. Did you make a mistake somewhere?'

The man leaned closer. He inspected the very documents he gave to Maria in the first place, rolling his eyes as he did so. He assessed his application again then leaned back in his chair, satisfied with what he had written on the pieces of paper. The silence that ensued prompted Maria to clarify.

'All you put down is your name and age,' she said.

'That is correct,' he confirmed without a hint of hesitation.

'So, your magi classification?'

'Technically doesn't apply to me.'

'Your magi rank?'

'Don't have one.'

'Location of breeding.'

'Applicable *if* I was bred.'

'Right,' Maria concluded as she sifted through the application form once more. 'I get the feeling asking about the other questions would be pointless too.'

'But that doesn't matter in the end, right?' Gin spoke out. 'I was told squadron W was the only one that accepted people through a test, rather than their application.'

'That is true. With this sort of application, we're the only ones you could go to. Which division did you want to apply to anyway? Your test will depend on that.'

'Offence,' Gin said, again without hesitation.

'Is that so?' Maria replied, eyebrow raised before speaking again. 'You wrote down that your Date of Breeding is twenty-third March, forty-nine-hundred-and-thirty-nine. That means you're only twenty-nine. You shouldn't be any more than a child going through puberty. Are you sure you want to be on the frontlines?'

'I'm certain.'

'Stand up.'

Gin got up with the colonel following suit. She walked around the desk and inspected the mysterious applicant once more. She noted that she stood a few inches over him, forcing Gin to look up, his expression as calm as ever.

'Here I thought that I was short,' Maria commented. 'Then again, you said you're twenty-nine. You're still a child. You've got several decades to grow.'

'I'm a fully-grown man, I'll have you know. I won't grow beyond my current six-feet-ten. So, about this test...'

'Follow me.'

Maria led Gin out of her office, through several wooden corridors, carved out of the Rezah tree the whole of Squadron W lived in. The bark of the Rezah allowed for torches to be lined up on the sides without catching fire. They flickered, illuminating the path to the testing room. A few of them had run out of fuel but it wasn't too problematic, as the fire elementals would get around replacing it.

'Look,' Maria said at last, breaking the silence. 'I still don't want to involve a child. Do you know what the test is?'

'Yes. Just survive a one v one for a designated time period. Should be simple enough,' he answered, again with an air of confident arrogance.

Maria rolled her eyes at his brashness. She didn't like the tone he was using and decided to change her original plans.

'On second thought,' Maria pointed out. 'This way.'

'What? Don't know your way around your own home?' Gin scoffed.

'No. I just realised we got a special invigilator today. With our standard test, your chances of success are around seventy percent but I thought someone of your calibre would enjoy a challenge instead.'

'It's fine with me, I guess. Shouldn't be that hard.'

'You have that much confidence? How do you plan to fight? You have no claws and you lack bulk or any other significant physical trait. Don't tell me you're a poison elemental type.'

'Let's just say my technique is a bit unorthodox compared to you mages.'

'Does it have anything to do with what's on your belt?' Maria said, indicating to the cuboid-shaped objects on Gin's belts, a different coloured hue on each of them.

'You'll see,' Gin assured her.

They entered a room that was split into two. A thin, see-through film separated the two sides. They were built the same way, with dirt flooring and tree bark walls, but differed in cleanliness. Bar the dust and branches merging from the ground, nothing noteworthy existed on the side Maria led Gin into. On the other hand, the opposing side was stained red, green, and brown. The stains were dry. At least most of them were.

'Looks like there's another test before us,' Maria whispered. 'You're quite fortunate, too. You get to see your opponent in action.'

Three people entered the other side: two men and a woman. Of the three, Maria noticed Gin's gaze was fixated on his future opponent, the only person that looked more like a beast than a human. A ten-foot behemoth, wearing nothing but loose shorts. Brown hair sprouted out of every single part of his body. His nose looked more like a snout, elongated and rounded off with canine-like nostrils at the end. His eyes were fierce; one that showed experience in both killing and being on the brink of death. His legs were packed with muscle and, combined with their bent posture, were ready to pounce at any moment. On the top of this beast's head were dark black horns, a few centimetres in height. Three thousand years ago, he would have been called Lucifer; El Chupacabra; Evil incarnate; Satan. However, he was none of them, but rather a creation of mankind. He was a human being.

'Um, Colonel?' Gin asked, a hint of fear in his voice.

'Yes, child?' Maria answered.

'Just how low is the success rate against that beast?'

'I see you have your eyes on Varunel,' Maria commented, giving the Gin a wry smile. 'He's one of the MBP's finest creations. He's been in Eurasia's service for nearly a hundred-and-forty years. Let's just say your chances have dropped significantly.'

'The Mage Breeding Programme, huh?' Gin replied in an inquisitive tone to mask his true emotions. 'They really do breed monsters there, don't they?'

'You have good taste, child.'

'I'm actually fascinated by all three. I can't tell if the other man will take the test though.'

Gin referred to the one clad in heavy, brown armour, even covering his mouth, that made him bulkier than he really was. He was chatting with the other two. The others nodded at whatever he was saying. Then, once done, he looked through the film and gave Maria a thumbs-up.

'No, he'll be invigilating the fight,' Maria cleared up.

The man left the room, only to return to Maria's side. Maria nodded at the man. She watched the duel that was about to ensue while keeping Gin in her peripheral vision. He was attentive as well, leading to Maria changing her thought that he wasn't as reckless as he first appeared.

The man told Maria and Gin to step back. He then reached to his side where several twigs stuck to his armour. Each of them had red marks engraved on them. Despite the varying lengths of the twigs, the intervals the marks appeared were uniform. He picked out one of the small ones with five markings.

'Like I said, you have five minutes to survive, Whyte. Varunel, you have the same time to kill her. Is that clear?' he addressed the two, getting a nod from both of them. 'Once I light this, the test will begin. Once it is completely burnt up, the test is over.'

He walked over to a torch and pressed one end of the twig into the flames. The twig caught fire. The test had begun.

The woman's dark skin began to glisten. The liquid that formed rolled down onto the palms of her hands. It collected into a globule. Her middle finger and thumb coupled together. She clicked her fingers. The rough grooves on them rubbed together, creating a spark that fell on the globules, lighting her hands into a fiery blaze.

Varunel was unfazed. On the contrary, he was inviting Whyte on. His arms were relaxed, both hanging by his sides. His face contained the widest grin. He kept himself wide open for an attack.

Whyte didn't hesitate to take the initiative. She hurled the ball of fire. Her aim was perfect, hitting Varunel directly on his torso. Whyte smiled, as the fire began to spread, but it didn't last long. The fire fizzled out on Varunel's fur, reducing in size second by second, until it was snuffed out without a trace. Whyte's face turned into one of horror as she knew what it meant.

In desperation, Whyte smothered her hands with more of the oily substance. However, Maria noticed the liquid had a different texture. It burned but, instead of the orange flames from before, it turned into thick, black smoke that impaired everyone's vision of the fight.

A sharp shriek filled the room.

'How long did I take?' a gruff voice called out.

'Done already?' Maria replied.

'Yes.'

'Not your best time, but forty-seven seconds.'

The smoke cleared via shafts in the ceiling. As they did, a conjoined figure formed. In the middle of the room stood Whyte; her ribs broken, lungs bleeding out, mouth agape, unable to make a single sound; her heart destroyed and Varunel's fist in its place.

'Whyte has failed the test!' the man in armour announced as he put out the fire on the twig.

Varunel let go of Whyte. Her lifeless body made a thud as it hit the floor. By her leg, Varunel dragged her out of the room, smearing the pool of blood she left behind.

'You're next, child,' Maria said. 'You've got thirty minutes, while the room is cleaned up. Please take your time preparing. After all, you might share the same fate as the girl.'

Gin didn't respond. His thumb was propped under his upper teeth. He was mumbling something under his breath. Maria could see he was deep in thought. She listened to what he was saying, trying to understand his thought process.

'-which means that the technique she used was a 'fireball'. It's a common technique for fire elementals, so I shouldn't be surprised she could use it. But why didn't it work on Varunel? Hmm. Does Varunel's fur have fire-resistant properties? No wonder she looked distraught after her failed attack. He literally is the worst matchup for those types of mages. But why didn't he finish her off earlier? What if – Yes, If that's the case, then maybe I can–'

'Gin!' Maria called out, causing Gin to jump. She had enough of listening to his ramblings.

'Huh?'

'Time is up. Go to the other side. We're about to begin.'

'What?!' Gin exclaimed. 'You said I had thirty minutes. It's barely been five!'

'I lied. Please proceed to the testing room.'

Gin's eyes widened. Maria knew that look he gave her. It was one of minimal battle experience. The look one had when they knew they were facing their death. *It's what you deserve,* Maria thought. She had no tolerance for those who act mighty, only to falter when faced with danger.

'Give me a minute more. I need more time to prepare,' Gin pleaded.

'When faced with someone much stronger, it is natural to feel afraid, to panic and to begin to beg. It's only human nature. I understand your sentiments, child, I really do. However, imagine you were allied with Whyte and a mage, on the power level of Varunel, attacks you. Given that she tells you she's going to stall, only to last for not even a minute, do you think the enemy will wait thirty minutes for you to prepare? I will repeat again. Your time is up. Please proceed to the testing room.'

'Guess there's nothing I can do to change your mind then,' Gin said with a shrug as he walked into the room with a swagger in his stride.

'Was your begging an act?' Maria asked, taken aback by his response.

'Who knows? I've come up with a plan anyway.'

Gin entered the testing room. Varunel joined him soon after. The bloodstain remained wet, but Maria's main focus wasn't on that. She watched Gin take off two of the cuboid-shaped objects he had on his belt – one red, one green – and wrapped his hands around them, one in each hand. His fingers entered holes in the cuboids.

At first, Maria thought they were just for grip, but then his index fingers moved further into the chambers. From the red cuboid erupted a thin, yet long, blade that was pointed at the end. From the green one emerged a circular plate that Gin held up in front of his chest.

'Is this the 'unorthodox technique' you were talking about before?' Maria questioned.

'Yep. Custom made by me.'

'AHAHA,' Varunel guffawed.

'What's so funny?' Gin queried. 'Something wrong with my sword and shield?'

'You're that weak that you rely on these objects? You're worse than the Afro-Australian Alliance!'

'Varunel!' Maria snapped. 'We don't have time for idle banter. Let's begin this test.'

'Yes, ma'am,' Varunel obeyed.

'Are you both ready?' Maria asked, with Gin and Varunel both affirming.

Another twig with five marks was lit up. The test had begun.

Gin stepped closer towards Varunel, staying cautious. Their difference in size was apparent. Even with his hind legs bent, Varunel towered at least a metre over his opponent. But instead of making the first move, he kept himself open for an attack.

The invitation wasn't taken though. Gin continued to tease an attack, only to withdraw.

Snap!

The one-minute mark had been reached. Neither side made a move in this strange dance. As time went on, Varunel grew agitated. He growled, causing Gin to stop. A temporary truce was made.

'You do realise I am deliberately letting you get a direct attack on me, which is why I haven't killed you yet,' Varunel grunted. 'But you're wasting too much time now. Attack me before the two-minute mark or I'll end it.'

Gin paused for a moment, looking at the twig that was burning. He kept a watch on it, biding his time until it hit the second mark. Right before the flames reached that point, Gin charged.

Snap!

He struck out with his sword, aiming for Varunel's heart. Varunel stuck true to his words and allowed the direct attack. The sword connected, piercing through his skin.

The sword stopped moving. Gin couldn't go farther.

Varunel looked at his opponent in the eyes. His grin showed an array of sharpened teeth as if the bleeding around his chest was irrelevant. His muscles tensed around the blade, nullifying any further threat from Gin's attack. He didn't act, allowing Gin to struggle.

But Gin wasn't done yet. He pressed his middle finger through the second chamber of his sword, then into the third. The metal began to glisten then ignited into flames. The fire burned Varunel's insides, causing him to howl in pain. He had enough.

Varunel sent a right hook at Gin. Gin raised his shield in response but it didn't help. An almighty clang echoed through the room as flew through the air, crashing into the wall behind him. His arm dislocated. He was winded. His legs refused to get up. He switched the shield to his working arm and raised it above him, pressing into the second chamber.

In his rage, Varunel broke the blade in two. One metallic half remained in his body, but the flames stopped. He chucked the other half to the side. He took deep forceful breaths as he took out the blade that remained. The wound began to close and Varunel's focus was on Gin once more. But his opponent had already made his move.

Snap!

A metallic dome surrounded the area where Gin lay. Varunel hurled a fist at the dome but all that did was make a clank upon impact.

With two minutes left, he didn't have time to mess about. Fist after fist, punch after punch, he battered the dome. His knuckles bled from the constant flurry of attacks that was deflected. Each attack dented the dome but it wasn't enough.

Snap!

'You've got one minute left, Varunel,' Maria warned.

'Shut up!' the beast growled.

The dent in the dome got larger. Varunel was getting through. Time was burning down. The constant clanking spurred him to go faster. Each dent made him hit harder.

Then he got his breakthrough.

Varunel punched through the dome. He tore off the sides of the hole he created. He still had time.

He didn't hesitate to pick out the prize inside, lifting Gin out of the dome. With his free hand, he smashed through Gin's chest, crushing his heart.

Snap!

The test was over.

'Finally!' Varunel gave a triumphant roar, dropping Gin's body onto the floor and turning towards Maria. 'That was more annoying than challenging.'

'His tactic was to waste time and hide in a corner all this time,' Maria commented. 'And here I thought he was going to show off his fighting prowess. Turned out he had none!'

'It almost worked in the end though.'

'So, did I pass?' a familiar voice said.

'What?!' Varunel exclaimed, turning around to see Gin, lying in his own blood with a smile. 'How are you alive?!'

'Did you know that the human body can still function for a few minutes, even after the heart stops working?' Gin replied before continuing, 'It takes quite a lot of willpower, but one can even stay conscious for a bit as well. The task was to survive for five minutes and I managed to do that, so do I pass the test or not? Don't worry, I will still survive. Probably. Maybe. I hope.'

Maria began laughing. What a peculiar person. She wouldn't mind having him in her squadron and technically he did pass the test, albeit without a heart (though she didn't know how he was going to survive).

'Yes, child, you pass. Welcome to squadron W.'

Gin chuckled to himself. 'Good,' he said with his final breath before losing consciousness.

'You're dismissed too, Varunel. Oh, and leave Gin's body behind. I'll go get someone else to tend to him. If he lives, that is.'

'Tsk. Fine,' Varunel obeyed with reluctance.

'Maria,' the armoured man whispered. 'Mind if I take him under my wing?'

'What?' Maria scoffed. 'You really believe he's going to survive without a heart?'

'Not really, but just in case.'

'He does use the same unusual fighting style as you. Alright. Permission granted.'

'Thank you. I'll be taking my leave then,' the man said before allowing Maria to be by herself.

She scratched her head. Now for the troublesome part: Explaining to the higher-ups how she had admitted an unknown person into her squadron.

2

Recovery

Gin opened his eyes, blinked, then closed them again. He wanted to rub his eyes but his arms refused to listen. They remained motionless by his side. He tried the same for the rest of his body, but it gave the same result. He could make slight neck movements but felt a sharp pain in his chest that stopped him from continuing further. The pain meant he was alive at least.

The brown, wooden ceiling he saw, before losing consciousness, had become a metallic grey. The dirt and blood-stained floor had become a comfy bed. *Where am I?* he wondered.

'Finally awake!' someone cheered. It was a woman's voice and it sounded like a relieved one at that. 'Who would have thought it was possible to live without a heart? Funny thing is, here I am, a rank B utility medic, and I still have no idea what's going on with your body. I've got so many questions to ask you. Mind explaining?'

Gin wanted the person to keep it down. He wasn't in the mood to hear a monologue from anyone. He forced himself to open his mouth ajar, then focused on trying to speak.

Nothing.

'Can't talk? No surprise there. Can you hear me at least?'

Gin nodded, but at the expense of suffering a sharp pain in his chest again.

'Good. I'm going to do my dailies now. Try not to move too much.'

I wasn't planning to, Gin thought.

He could hear the clink of glass followed by the feeling of something pricking his arm. From the corner of his eyes, he saw his arm outstretched at a perpendicular angle. A pale finger rested on top of it with a long, thin nail digging into Gin's skin. He guessed it belonged to the woman that spoke.

An orange fluid ran through the nail into Gin's body. Once done, the woman retracted the nail, leaving a circular hole. A gel surrounded the wound, causing it to neither bleed nor close up. Instead, it allowed the nail to return with a new serum to inject. The process repeated itself until she spoke up again,

'OK. Last one.'

She inserted her nail into the wound once more, this time injecting a grey liquid. Afterwards, she removed the original gel and replaced it with a different one. It stung but the skin around the wound began to grow, enveloping it until no trace of it remained.

'That should do it. I'll head off now, but I'll be back tomorrow. Glad you're awake though. At one point, I feared I was vaccinating a dead body.'

Gin heard footsteps that led into the sound of a door closing. He closed his eyes. As he drifted off to sleep, the door opened again.

'Oh, I'm Joan by the way. I'll be taking care of you from now on.'

****

Gin woke up, his head aching as much as his body. He tried to move again. He worked through each part of his body in a systematic fashion. Apart from his head and fingers, he still couldn't move. At this rate, he was going to be bedridden for much longer than he had anticipated. Damn. Where's my INS when I need it? he thought.

'Good morning!' a familiar voice sounded. 'Awake again I see.'

Gin tilted his head, causing a satisfying click in his neck from its lack of use. On his arm was a nail, closing the wound he didn't know he had. The wound began to irritate, like a mosquito bite when you first see it, but Gin's attention was on the medic herself.

His new position allowed him to see Joan for the first time. She was a slender brunette woman, with pale white skin which contrasted with the black t-shirt and trousers she wore. Her nails, that wrapped around his arm, each varied in length from finger to finger, each with different coloured pigments. Even though she didn't strike Gin as someone who was spectacular, she was pretty in her own regard.

'Want to try and talk?' she asked, giving a warm smile as she closed the lids on some jars.

Gin opened his mouth, uttering a single 'ah' as a test, like a baby checking its capabilities. His chest burned as he did so, prompting him to stop. He knew he could talk, but decided it wasn't worth it and closed his eyes to show his intentions to the medic.

'At least you managed to make a sound,' Joan commented. 'At this rate, it's going to take another two weeks for you to recover fully.'

Gin's eyes flashed open. Two weeks?! he exclaimed in his mind. It was far too long for his liking. For him, that was precious time that could be used for valuable research, not for lying in bed!

'Give. INS,' he said, a lengthy pause between each word.

'Huh? I don't understand. INS?' Joan replied, an eyebrow raised in confusion.

'Integrated. Nanobot. System.'

'Nanobot? I can't really help if you keep using made up words.'

Frustrated by the effort he had to put in to speak, Gin thought for a moment. From her reaction, and from his first impressions of squadron W, Gin concluded that the mages didn't have anything as sophisticated as his nanobots. Either that or they had a different name for them.

'Cuboid. Metallic. Silver,' he oversimplified. She must understand that, surely?

'Oh! Those weird objects you used for the test. Yeah, they're over there.'

Joan headed towards a desk where she picked up a basket containing several cuboids and a belt with its slots emptied out. She picked out the silver coloured cuboid, as instructed. She inspected it, wondering what it was, before turning back to Gin.

'This one, right?' she asked.

'Mm,' Gin confirmed, the sound hurting less than actual words.

Joan placed the (what Gin called) the INS in the palm of Gin's hand. She stood there for a few moments, expecting for something to happen but, when both Gin and the INS stood motionless, she wondered if she did something wrong.

'Now what do I do?' Joan queried.

'Leave,' Gin responded.

'Wow. Rude much?' she retorted.

It wasn't that Gin was trying to be rude. However, the single word was much more efficient, considering the pain that arose with each word he spoke. He wanted to be alone. The faster that happened the better.

Joan listened, grabbing her medicine and left the room. She didn't harbour any resentment towards Gin's attitude, or at least she didn't show it. It allowed Gin to carry on without feeling any guilt.

He fitted his finger inside the first slot of the INS, pressing a button at the bottom of the chamber. A needle emerged from one end, facing away from him. In one swift motion, as if second nature to him, Gin twisted the INS, stabbed his arm and activated the mechanism in the second chamber.

He could feel the contents coursing through his veins. It put him at ease. From his calculations, his recovery rate should rise exponentially. All he had to do now was rest.

****

Gin woke up, his head aching as much as his body. He tried to move again. Even though he felt continuous pins and needles as he moved, he managed to lift his body into a sitting position. He noticed that his old clothes were gone and replaced with a vest and shorts, both made up of some sort of tanned leather. He looked around for some better clothing, his neck clicking with every turn, but couldn't find any.

The room was spacious. Despite the metallic plating on the ceiling, the walls were made up of dirt and tree roots. To his side was a desk with some paper and stationery with a basket placed on top of it. Its cover prevented Gin from seeing what was inside. His curiosity got the better of him and he attempted to stand up.

The sharp pain in his chest returned. He collapsed back onto his bed under the stress. The muscles in his leg constricted, refusing to move, leaving him helpless, unable to get up again. His heart fluttered in his moment of weakness.

Eh? Heart?

Gin placed his hand on his chest. A continuous beating echoed through his palms. He grinned at the new revelations. Something was beating inside there. What was beating he didn't know yet, so Gin made a mental note to find out sooner or later.

When his legs relaxed, he sat up once more. Satisfied with the progress so far, he looked around for the INS he used yesterday. He went through the same procedure of activating a needle then piercing his skin to inject the contents.

'Looks like sitting is all I can do for now,' he noted, realising that speaking was tolerable now.

'What is going on?!'

Gin turned around to see Joan holding the usual tray of medicine. He finished injecting the serum before extending his arm out for his daily treatment. When he didn't hear her footsteps, he looked back to find that Joan hadn't moved from her position.

'What?' Gin said.

'How are you sitting up, let alone talking properly?' Joan replied, gobsmacked by what she was witnessing.

She didn't wait for Gin's answer, putting down the tray to do an immediate check-up. Her index finger's nail went from white to red then back to white as she emptied the blood into a container. Her middle finger dipped into the container, turning a myriad of colours.

'There's more of those things,' Joan analysed.

'What things?'

'I don't know what they are. It's not organic though.'

'Oh!' Gin realised. 'That's probably because of the nano-booster.'

'Yesterday it was nanobots. Now it's nano-booster. You keep throwing these words around but I still don't understand any of them.'

'Guess you mages don't have them,' Gin said under his breath, not expecting Joan to hear it.

'I'm lost,' Joan said, doing her duties along with her attempt to decipher Gin's language.

'Doesn't matter. Forget about it.'

'No, tell me. As your medic, I need to know what's going on in your body so I can tend to the best of my ability,' Joan commanded, more out of curiosity than necessity.

She stopped the injections, looking at Gin with a stern expression instead. Though Gin wasn't in the mood to give a lengthy explanation, the silence that filled the room created an air of awkwardness that he wanted to dispel. It was better than letting Joan remain in her stubborn state anyway.

'Ok, fine,' Gin conceded, sighing as he did so. 'In my body, there are nanobots: little machines. The ones in my body heighten my bodily functions, recovery rates and, in dire circumstances, can act in their place. I didn't know if the last part was true but, after living through a destroyed heart, it looks like that's the case. Though the rest of my body probably went into standby mode for that to happen.'

'Really?' Joan responded, unsure whether to believe him or not.

'You've seen it too, right? Something's beating in my chest.'

'It's a newly formed heart. I've watched as it grew, though I'm not sure how it grew back.'

'Oh? That's quite the development. My calculations were a bit off,' Gin contemplated while allowing Joan to continue with the dailies. 'Thought I'd be living without a heart.'

'You definitely have one. The problem is, once again, that thing's not fully organic.'

'That part's probably the nanobots I was talking about before.'

'Then the things in your blood?'

'Nanobots.'

'And that– what was it you called it again?' she asked.

'The INS?' Gin responded, pointing to the metal cuboid beside him with his free arm. Joan nodded in response. 'Also, nanobots, but programmable ones this time.'

'Programmable? What? Why do I get the feeling you're mocking me with your made up words?'

'I'm not. It's the truth,' Gin shrugged. 'And all the words I've been using are a hundred percent real. I can guarantee you that.'

'This is the first I heard of it then. Anyway, to be able to regenerate a heart from nothing, they really do breed the most amazing mages in the MBP.'

'Oho,' Gin chuckled. 'I'm not bred.'

'Not bred? You've lost me again.'

Gin leaned closer.

'I'm what you call,' he said, each word a whisper, 'a manush.'

Joan stared at Gin. She blinked several times. Like a machine, she processed what he just said, figuring out how to respond. In the end, she went for a smile that led into a burst of laughter.

'That unevolved extinct race?' she said after she calmed down. 'You must still be delirious from your injuries. Get some rest, Gin.'

'Yeah. I make weird jokes when I'm tired,' he lied.

'I'll leave you to it then,' she agreed, packing up her equipment. 'Oh, almost forgot. Maria wanted to know when you think you'll be ready to join a battalion.'

'At this rate, I'd say four days,' Gin calculated.

'I'll tell her a week to make sure.'

'That's fine,' Gin complied, not wanting to argue further, even if he did think the extra days were a waste of time.

'Well, take care. I'll be back tomorrow like normal,' she waved goodbye, giggling as she did so. 'Manush? As if!'

Gin laid back. He cursed himself for forgetting to ask for a pen and paper. He placed his hands on his chest, the rhythmic beating of his heart calming him down. His mind wandered off, making several mental notes from the conversation he just had.

'Heh. The mages really think we've gone extinct?' Gin thought out loud. 'Well, after what happened back then, we might as well be.'

3

Battalion Leader

Gin eyed the box in front of him, brought to him by Joan. Though he told her his wounds healed up already and had nothing to worry about, she persisted in doing the menial jobs, like collecting his food rations. It peeved him but he overlooked her unwanted actions due to the good intentions.

The box contained a few slices of meat along with vivid blue fruits. Gin couldn't quite pinpoint the origin of the meat (the closest comparison he thought of was veal). The fruit, on the other hand, had a strange taste: a mixture of sweet, sour, and salty, but the water inside it drowned the flavour out somewhat.

With pen in his left hand and food in his right, Gin jotted down various sketches. It took some time getting used to the ink the mages used. It was thicker and took more time to dry than what he was accustomed to. He learned that the hard way, getting an ink-stained hand as a result.

'I see Joan's report was true.'

Recognising the colonel's voice, Gin stood up in response to show his respect. She carried a basket which she handed over to him. Its one-sided weight caused the container tilt, making Gin wonder what it contained.

'Very impressive, child. Very impressive indeed,' she continued, inspecting Gin. 'A broken arm and a missing heart recovered just like that!'

'Thanks for the compliment, but I don't think it was "just like that" as you put it,' Gin scoffed.

'I stand by my statement. Your regeneration is top tier. Even Varunel still has scars from the burns you gave him.'

'Is that so? At least my fight wasn't a complete loss then,' Gin commented as he placed the basket down.

'However, you are severely lacking in your fighting style. If not for Varunel's whims, you wouldn't even have touched him.'

'I know. I know. Which is why I'm trying to come up with ideas to improve that,' Gin indicated to his drawings.

'Ideas are all well and good,' the colonel said, ignoring the sketches, 'but you lack experience, especially someone of your age, child. Fortunately, I know someone who could help.'

'No offence, but I don't think anyone could help with the way I fight,' Gin argued, leaning back into the chair, 'and, judging by how Varunel talked to me when I drew my sword, I don't think the use of weaponry is looked favourably on.'

'Don't worry, child. You'd be surprised the types of people that come out of the MBP. I've given directions to where your battalion leader will be at five pm today. He's a Utility Xernim type mage that uses something like your sword. He's an A rank too so I can assure you he's of high quality. I expect you to meet him on time.'

'I'll see. Can't make any promises.'

'You *will* meet him today,' she said with a piercing glare that straightened Gin's back and corrected his posture.

'Yes, ma'am!'

'You can drop the formalities, child. You're one of us now. You've earned the right to call me Maria.'

'Only if you stop calling me "child."'

'Unfortunately, I cannot do that for one as young as yourself.'

'Then I will continue to show my respect, *Colonel*,' Gin said, stressing the "colonel".

'That's fine by me, *child*,' the colonel replied, stressing the "child".

When she left, Gin had a look inside the basket. The cause of the lop-sidedness was a metal insignia, carved into the shape of a bird with a three-feathered plumage on its tail. From that Gin identified the species as tinoo. He found it ironic how these avian rodents managed to become Eurasia's symbol of unity. The mages used them as couriers, but when the people of the past could communicate from their back pockets, their system of communication felt lacklustre. The most advanced piece of technology he witnessed so far was the pendulum clock on the wall, its weight swinging left to right in a hypnotic rhythm.

As he held the insignia against the flames of the torches, Gin wondered what else was different about the mages. From first impressions, they were evolved physically but primitive in their technology, a complete opposite of the manush lifestyle he was used to back in his village. His curiosity drove him. He wanted to know more; wanted to learn how the various mages ticked.

In a flash of inspiration, as he sat down at his desk, Gin wrote down a few words:

Gin's notes #1 –

He didn't know what to write at first. The plan of writing a book was there but the execution wasn't as well thought out. He rocked the chair backwards, his mind deep in thought. He came up with a few ideas, writing each one down.

Gin cursed his luck. Just as he got into the flow of writing, a project he called 'Gin's notes', his time was up. He needed to meet his battalion leader, so he packed up the notes, equipped the belt full of INS, then headed out using the directions the colonel gave him.

A rough map accompanied the directions, giving a brief overlay of the tree. According to it, there were three staircases that led to all hundred-or-so floors. The upper floors were designated for living while the middle levels were for training. The lowest levels were where all information was gathered and sent out. Gin had to climb down several floors, exiting when he reached the seventy-second.

Gin opened a door beside a flight of stairs, a blast of humid air hit him as he did so. His first step created a squelching sound, followed by his feet getting wet. Water rippled across the room with reeds and brushes sticking out in a sporadic array. Combined with the miniature trees, the whole room felt like it emulated a marsh.

A person sat cross-legged in the middle of the room. From a distance, he looked like the armoured man Gin saw during his test. As he got closer, Gin saw that the armour was twice as thick from before, causing him to doubt whether it really was the same armour fetishist.

'Hello?' Gin called. 'The colonel sent me here.'

The man didn't respond. He remained seated, his helmet covering all but his green eyes that stared into nothingness. Apart from the wooden armour that exhibited intricate markings, that couldn't be noticed from a distance, he held no weaponry let alone anything like a sword. It made Gin wonder if this really was the person the colonel was talking about.

Gin tapped on the man's shoulder. The knocking sound he created was louder than expected, yet the man didn't even budge. Patience running thin, he gave up and went back the way he came from.

'Oi, brat. Where do you think you're going?'

Gin turned around. The man levered himself up. He towered over Gin, who had gotten accustomed to the fact that almost everyone was taller than him.

'First child now brat,' Gin sighed. 'Look. My name is Gin Gale. For future reference, please call me Gin.'

'I'm Alder,' the man boomed in response. 'For future reference, do not disturb my meditation.'

'Alright, I understand. Won't happen again. Can I leave now? I was doing something important and meeting you kinda ruined my flow.'

Alder stepped closer, inspecting Gin, before continuing. 'Let's spar.'

'Spar? I recently recovered and now you want to put me back in a coma? I was told you have the same fighting style as me but you're just a man in a suit. No sword, no shield, no nothing. I'm sorry, but I don't want to waste my time.'

'Well aren't you quite the arrogant brat! Pay attention.'

Gin watched as Alder held his right arm up, perpendicular to his body. At first, nothing happened, but then the wood began to shift. It twisted and turned, growing at the end of his gauntlets. It stopped, taking the form of a hilt. He grabbed the hilt with his free hand, unsheathing a serrated blade from his armour.

'No blade, eh?' Alder showed off.

The hole created from the sheath closed. Alder's armour twisted once more, expanded in width, creating a rectangular block.

'No shield, eh?'

Gin responded with a single 'heh'. He knew he was wrong and now placed his full attention on the man in front of him. The armour he wore intrigued Gin. The desire to find out how it worked lit a spark in his heart.

'Draw your blade, brat,' Alder commanded. 'This is not a request.'

Gin grinned. He didn't need a second invitation. He took out the green and red INS from his belt, activating the mechanisms to create a sword and shield.

'Good,' Alder praised, taking several steps backwards. 'Then let's begin. I'll let you make the first move.'

Gin analysed the situation. Something about Alder's sword unnerved him. He knew his own sword could cut through even most hardened metals. A piece of wood shouldn't pose a problem, yet he couldn't be certain. In all honesty, he just wanted to get this over with and the fastest way was to attack. Getting a bit of data for his notes wouldn't hurt anyway.

Gin charged at the man. Water splashed below him with every stride. As he swung his sword, Alder parried with his own. The meeting of the swords created a thudding sound. To Gin's surprise, the man's sword did not break nor show any cut marks.

Gin took a few steps back then leapt forward again, sending a flurry of attacks at his opponent. However, the man blocked each attack as if he wasn't even trying, treating Gin as if he was a complete amateur failing to make a breakthrough.

Gin managed to get past the man's sword defence and had a chance to attack his body. But Alder had other ideas. He uppercut Gin's sword with his shield, sending it crashing to the floor. Alder then switched to a more offensive stance, swinging his sword. Gin ducked, avoiding the attack, managed to grab his sword and strike a counter-attack on his opponent's armour. It left a mark but it wasn't enough to deal a winning blow just yet.

All of a sudden, Alder picked up the pace.

Gin was forced to take a few steps back. Alder sent out few but deliberate strikes. Gin lifted his shield, feeling the force of the sword. Each blow numbed his arm, but he persevered. After blocking a few more times, he felt the hardness of tree bark behind him. The man took the opportunity to swing his sword, aiming for Gin's neck. Gin saw it in time and ducked and rolled away, dropping the shield in the process. The marsh drenched his clothes, weighing him down.

As Gin regained his balance, he heard a crashing sound. The tree behind him was now on the floor. A diagonal cut remained from where it had been severed from the trunk. In awe of what he had just witnessed, Gin only caught a glimpse of the looming threat behind him. He turned around, grabbed the green INS and activated the shield. He was just in time as his opponent clanged against the shield, forcing Gin to stagger towards the floor.

With his right arm trying to hold himself up, and his left blocking the man's sword, Gin didn't have too many options. The man raised his arm with the shield, the wood twisting again. Gin's eyes widened as he knew what was to come: another sword! Unlike last time when he needed his free arm to unsheathe the blade, this time the sword sprang out. As if he's done it a million times, Alder caught the sword mid-flight and swung it in one motion.

Gin was not in the position to block and was forced to try to leapfrog backwards in an attempted dodge. However, his movements weren't fast enough and the sword nicked the skin on Gin's face. Red streaks ran down his face as he fell flat on his back. The armoured man didn't hesitate to knock Gin's sword away as he planted his boot on Gin's chest, making him lose any hope of getting up.

'You're lacking,' Alder said, letting go of Gin. 'Your strength is poor and your grip on your weaponry is abysmal.'

'Thanks for the confidence boost,' Gin retorted, wiping the blood off his face.

'However, your speed is decent, and your reflexes are excellent.'

'I admit that it was a good fight. Though I did feel like you were trying to kill me at one point.'

'I was,' Alder admitted as he went to pick up the INS he knocked out.

'Really?' Gin laid back into the water. For some reason, he didn't feel surprised.

'I wouldn't be able to see how you coped under pressure otherwise. Now I know how to train you. You use this thing to fight, right?' Alder said, holding up the INS.

'Mhm. I call it the Integrated Nanobot System, INS for short.'

'How does it work? It's just a block now.'

'Just put your finger in the first slot to activate the mechanism. Pretty easy to use, hard to make.'

The wooden armour receded around Alder's hand, revealing a naked finger. He inserted it into the INS, reaching the bottom. Nothing happened.

'Oh, I have it touch sensitive,' Gin realised. 'There's another chamber below that.'

'Is it possible to disable it?'

Gin sat up, bemused by Alder's sudden questioning. 'Why do you ask?'

'I've been thinking, brat,' Alder said pausing for a moment.

'Yes?'

'What do you think about having your weapons equipped permanently. I reckon a certain style of fighting would suit you more. It'll also help deal with your awful grip.'

'Oh?' Gin's curiosity perked up. 'I'm all for self-improvement but mind explaining further?'

'Mmm,' Alder pondered, debating whether to tell Gin or not. 'I'd rather you wait but I can see you're an impatient brat, so I'll tell you the bare minimum. It's called blade boxing.'

Gin thought for a moment. From the name, he could guess what blade boxing entailed. It was also a great opportunity to learn about that strange armour Alder wore first hand.

'Fine,' Gin accepted. 'I'll let you borrow one since I got a spare. Just stop calling me a brat. I don't deserve this.'

'With your arrogant attitude, you deserve every time I call you it.'

Another lost cause, Gin thought.

'I'll train you three times a week and will have you join in with the battalion training by next week too,' Alder commanded.

'Oh, I get to meet my battalion that soon?'

'Most of them, yes. A few are away on a mission though.'

'This three-way war really keeps everyone busy, huh?'

Alder looked up, lost in a train of thought, ignoring Gin's comment. 'I wonder how they're doing right now,' he muttered to himself.

4

Identities

'Rank, magi classification and name please,' a voice bellowed from within the cave.

'Rank D Utility Medic type. Name is Babacla, Tom.'

'Ah! Tom! Long time no see.'

A bald man emerged from the cave, carrying either a set of clothes or boxes full of rations in each of his four arms. He placed them on the counter, counting each item to make sure he got it all correct.

'Sorry, didn't realise it was you at first,' the man apologised. 'You look lighter from when I last saw you. Your voice is a lot deeper than usual too.'

'Work's been draining me. My throat's also a bit hoarse,' Tom replied, rubbing his neck.

'The AAA really does have its hands full, doesn't it?'

'At my expense, yeah.'

'Ha! You know how much us Africans need you medics.'

Tom sighed. 'I wish this three-way war would just end already. Oh, I need to collect the rations for Yanus Temply.'

'It's become more of a two-way war now,' the man corrected as he entered the cave again. 'The Americas haven't made a peep for a while. It's just the Eurasians and the Afro-Australian Alliance battling it out.'

'Probably a good thing. If the other two continents followed TA's lead, then we'd have world peace.'

'It's never that easy, Tom. Have you ever thought about what happens after this war? We have the MBP for the sole reason of breeding mages for warfare. What happens to it if we stop fighting? No one ever thinks about these things,' the man theorised, bringing out more food. 'Anyway, forget about my little drivel. Yanus is your roommate, right?'

'Yeah,' Tom confirmed, scratching his ginger afro, taking what the man said beforehand into account.

'He was always a lazy one, huh?'

'Tell me about it,' Tom agreed, collecting the items.

'Well tell him I said hi,' the man waved.

'Will do,' Tom waved back.

Tom climbed a series of spiral staircases that led to the surface. The barren land felt peaceful, yet he couldn't help but think that it needed some shrubbery. Instead, the dried soil and cloudless skies made it impossible for anything to grow.

'At least the stars are pretty,' he muttered to himself, admiring the blackened sky.

He walked along a vague path made from the continuous footsteps of mages that came for rations. It led to a village marred by numerous holes on the surface. They allowed both light and those above to peer into the hustle and bustle of the streets below.

Making sure he didn't drop anything into these holes, Tom arrived at his destination. He stomped on the floor below him; three quick ones followed by three slows ones. A passageway opened in front of him, revealing stairs to the village.

Stone buildings riddled the village, spanning several kilometres in each direction. In fact, almost everything that could be made from stone was made with stone. The homes? Stone. The facilities? Stone. The barracks? Stone. *The African underground lifestyle sure is different from the Eurasian way of living in trees*, Tom compared.

Tom reached his own home, situated in one corner of the village. He didn't mind its location. It suited him due to the lack of people around the area. Though he found the lock and key mechanism tedious, when the other homes had sliding doors, the real problem with the place was the person living with him.

Tom fumbled in his pockets for his keys, only to tut when he couldn't find it. He knocked on the door, hoping for his roommate to open the door. He received no answer. He knocked once more. Again nothing.

'Oi, Yanus, open up! It's me, Tom,' he shouted but to no avail. 'Can't believe this. Esper! Just wake up already!'

Still, no one opened the door. Was he out? No. He isn't the type, Tom thought. Knowing he had one option left, he took a deep breath.

'I brought food.'

The door opened, and a man appeared at the doorstep, all dreary-eyed. A sheer look of boredom swept across his face. His blonde hair was a mess, his limbs and back drooped and his usual pale skin looked even paler from dwelling in the darkness for too long. Tom could tell his roommate didn't want to get up with the thought of food being his sole motivation to move.

'Oh hey, Jack! What's up, man? Heard someone got food,' he said.

'Yanus...' Tom mumbled with a hint of hostility.

'Hmm? Who's Yanus?'

'Have you forgotten already, Esper? You are not to say my real name outside the house.'

'Man, you are so annoying, you know that Jack? Why are you calling me by my name anyway? Why don't I get a cool name?'

'Because you aren't responding to the name you are meant to be called: Yanus.'

'Oooooooohhh, I get ya. Yanus, right? That's why you have been calling me that lately, Jack. Oops, my bad. I'm not meant to call you Jack either, am I? Tom. Tom. Tom. Tom. Tom. Got it.'

'Please tell me you've at least done the thing I asked you to do,' the irritated Jack pleaded.

'What thing?' Esper responded.

'Why do I have to be paired up with such an imbecile?!'

'Whoa, chill man. I got you covered.'

'If you ruin everything...'

'I said chill! No need to worry about silly little things, let's just go inside.'

Jack handed over the bag of supplies to Esper and entered the house. Darkness filled the home as he shut the door behind him. He could feel his patience running thin.

'You can't even light a torch?' Jack scolded.

'I was sleeping, man,' Esper protested.

'Why am I not surprised? Ugh. Just prepare dinner while I light up the house. You can do that at the very least, right?'

'Yes, boss-man!'

Jack borrowed a torch from outside. He worked from the ground floor up, proceeding up the stairs to the first floor. He poured oil, made from a fire elemental's flammable sweat, into cups stuck to the walls. Using the torch, he lit them up, illuminating the house as he went.

However, as he climbed the stairs to the second floor, a pungent smell filled his nostrils. It got stronger the closer he was to the second floor, which contained a single room.

As Jack pushed the door, it thudded against a squishy object. He squeezed through the gap, the vomit-inducing smell reaching its peak. Jack held the torch against the darkness, he found the cause.

In front of him laid a corpse. Electrical burns tessellated on the body, making the cause of death obvious. Hairs on its ginger afro flaked off, falling onto the floor in a heap. The corpse's dark skin decayed, releasing the foul odour, forcing Jack to cover his nose.

'Esper!' Jack called out.

Knowing his roommate would take his time, Jack created more torches and placed them around the room. He then shifted the body to the centre of the room, away from the windows and any potential prying eyes.

'Yo, Jack. What's up?'

Jack turned and frowned at his roommate. 'You didn't get rid of the evidence like I told you to.'

'Ah, sorry, I just forgot,' Esper replied, putting on a wry smile.

'Just forgot?! Do you realise how important our mission is? If any of the patrollers come by and find the real body of Tom Babacla, lying dead in front of us, we will be executed or even worse enslaved by the Africans.'

'Alright, alright. I'll do it now. Then there won't be any problem, right?'

'It took us a fortnight to kill him in the first place. Burning his body shouldn't have taken a day. All you do is eat sleep and take my rations while having me do all the hard work! Why am I always paired up with the Xernims?' Jack answered furiously.

'Man. Jack. That's low. I am not a Parasite. Well, at least not on the level of a Xernim. Actually, now that I think about it –'

'Just shut up and get rid of him. The smell is unbearable.'

'Woah, chill. See, I'm doing stuff,' Esper defended himself, pouring oil on top of the body, 'I'm not completely useless.'

Esper kneeled on the floor, next to the body, and placed his hand just above it. A small spark of electricity, emitted from Esper's hand, hit the oil-laden body, causing it to catch on fire. As the body burned, both Esper and Jack gazed upon the flames. The evidence of murder melted away.

Jack gave a sigh of relief. He wanted to go back to Eurasia; back to squadron W. His inability to kill let him down, otherwise a solo mission would have sufficed, but he wasn't letting an electricity elemental ruin the mission.

'By the way, you said you needed time to change your appearance to look like this guy,' Esper argued, trying to be the innocent party. 'That's why I left him for you. Don't pin all the blame on me.'

'It literally takes me a day to do that. Burning him would take you a second, yet you left him to almost starve to death. You're lucky he was just a medic, or he could have escaped.'

'Whatever. It's done now. I'll go cook food now with your oil. I used mine to burn this body.'

'Go ahead. It's none of my business. Just leave me alone for the rest of the day. Apparently, Tom was darker than I currently am. I need to rectify that.'

'Man, for someone who can turn invisible in seconds, you like to take your time when changing appearances.'

'Unconscious trait changes and conscious stealth are two separate things. Now shut up and let me do my job.'

'Sure thing,' Esper surrendered.

'Oh, make sure to look into the next person whose identity I'll steal. Right height, right build, right role to get us closer to our assassination target. For once we get lucky. I've also given a plan to subdue him. You *will* read it. I need both of us to be prepared, you hear me?'

'Will do.'

'Today,' Jack sent a piercing stare.

'Alright already. I get it. Sheesh,' Esper rolled his eyes.

The pair split up, with Esper going to the kitchen while Jack went to his room on the first floor, away from the stench. Jack sat down in a meditative stance. He focused, gaining consciousness of his entire body. He pinpointed and changed the pigment of each cell on his skin one at a time. Starting from his head, his skin darkened. He had completed stage one of the mission. Soon he'd be ready for stage two. All for the sake of Eurasia. For squadron W.

5

The Low-Ranked

As Gin waited in the corridor for the room opposite to become vacant, he made a mental note of all the mages that passed him. By now Gin could guess the type of mage someone was based on their traits. The self-imposed classification and terminology the mages possessed seemed random at first but, after his brief stay in squadron W, it began to make sense.

From Gin's understanding, those with enhanced combat strength or animalistic abilities tended to be of the 'bestial' class, while the manipulators of the elements were called 'elementals'. The mages dubbed the remaining people, who belonged to neither category, as 'utility'.

Gin found it simple enough until he realised the categories separated further into several more subclasses. That didn't deter him from trying to learn it all though. Instead, he grinned at the prospect of a challenge. *More research for my notes*, he thought.

The door opened, revealing the group of people using the room. Some had hair that covered their entire body. Others didn't even have a single thread apart from the hair on their heads. The contrast didn't divert Gin's attention from how beefy both the men and women were. He gawked at the absurd size of their muscles, almost ripping into their clothes. When they passed Gin, they gave him a look of disdain, turning his amazement into confusion.

All of a sudden, something grabbed Gin's chest. He looked down to see a person that he'd never seen before embracing him. The person's full-bodied armour, covered with cobbled stone, dug into Gin's body. But the strange thing about him or her (Gin couldn't be quite sure) was that he was shorter than Gin, unlike most of the other mages.

'Play along,' the person said, his voice muffled under his helmet.

'What?' a bewildered Gin responded.

One of the mages leaving the room broke off from the rest. He walked up to Gin, giving him a distasteful glare. Long strands of hair hung from his body like a feral beast that needed to be shaved. He looked just like Varunel but without the canine snout.

'Oi Sam,' he barked at the armoured person. 'What's the meaning of this?

'Uh, I know him. Let me be,' Sam said, pausing mid-sentence, struggling to speak through the armour. 'With him.'

Gin looked at Sam, his hazel eyes pleaded through two round holes in the helmet. Then he looked at the grouching man in front of him.

'I don't know who this is,' Gin said, not bothered by the person's troubles. 'You can take him away.'

'Eh?' Sam whimpered. 'But why?'

'Sam!' the hairy man snapped. 'He's part of Alder's battalion. You know what I told you about those who train under him.'

'B-but. Ok, fine,' Sam conceded before turning to Gin. 'I don't like this you.'

'What was that all about?' Gin mumbled to himself, confused by that last sentence.

With the last of the mages gone, Gin entered the vacant room. The sudden change in temperature took him by surprise. Sand crept into his shoes not a moment after traversing the desert dunes the room emulated. Beads of sweat formed on his skin, the dry, windless air not helping him cool off.

'For an arrogant brat, you sure are punctual.'

'Heh. Alder, being on time is just a habit,' Gin greeted his battalion leader. 'So, this is the room we'll be training in? It's a bit hot. I prefer the marsh for our sparring.'

'This, you presumptive brat, is where we have our battalion training,' Alder clarified.

'Oh. I finally get to meet them? It doesn't seem like a coincidence then,' Gin commented, sitting down only to jump straight up from the blistering heat of the sand.

'What doesn't?' Alder asked, hiding his smirk under his mask.

'I overheard people talking badly about your battalion. Is there something I should know about them?'

'I train those that the Mage Breeding Programme refuses to teach,' Alder began. 'Apart from us, no squadron would accept the F or E ranked mages that come out of the MBP. Without a squadron, these low-ranked mages would simply die of starvation. Squadron W accommodates roughly fifteen-hundred of them, making up most of our roster.'

Alder sighed, sitting down on the sand, his armour protecting his body. He didn't speak but Gin decided not to talk either. The mood didn't allow for it.

'Brat,' Alder said at last. 'I never told you about this before but, now that I have, you can leave my battalion. No one's forcing you to train with the low-ranked. I can file a transfer if you wish.'

'Why would I?' Gin gave an immediate response.

'You're not looking down on them?'

'I haven't met them yet. There's nothing to look down on.'

'Are you sure? You'll be associated with them for your entire stay.'

'I'm certain,' Gin said without hesitation 'I'm interested in how low-ranked mages differ from their higher-ranked counterparts. Surely, there are ways they can improve. Can't do that if I'm never with them, now can I?'

'You're more of a thinker rather than a doer, aren't you?' Alder said, not showing any emotion to Gin's decision and instead thought of the best course of action for him. 'I'll have you sit out for now. I'll be going over formations with the battalion. Learn those and soon you'll be joining them.'

'Fine by me.'

It didn't take long for just over a hundred battalion members to join them. As they walked into the room, Gin couldn't contain his fascination. From the anorexic to those covered in rolls of skin; the silky-skinned to the rough-skinned; the hairy to the bald and so on, how mankind managed to evolve into these beings was beyond Gin's precognition.

However, though each mage differed in appearance, each and every one of them greeted Alder with respect in their eyes and smiles on their faces. Alder greeted them back. Gin could feel a sense of unity amongst them, a contrast to the pair he met earlier on.

Gin picked up on the formations with ease. Alder would call out code, a number or letter, and the battalion arranged themselves into triangles or squares. Some struggled to keep up, due to their physique hindering them, but they managed as instructed, apart from one exception.

During a break, Alder talked to a man with orange slabs of stone strapped to his arms and legs. They weighed his frail body down, bringing him to a standstill whenever a change in formation was required.

Why doesn't he just remove the stone? Gin wondered.

After speaking with Alder, the man moved to the sidelines, away from the others. He unstrapped a stone slab from his arms and sat on the sand, somehow tolerating the heat. He stroked it several times, causing foam to appear on top.

The depressed emotion he failed to hide struck Gin as odd. For all the talk of accepting low ranked when no one else did, the man's exclusion didn't match Alder's words.

'Hey,' Gin said, walking up to the man to find out what happened.

He looked at Gin, forcing a smile. Again, his true emotions showed. 'Hello,' he said in a meek voice.

'Aren't you taking part in the training?' Gin asked, regretting his insensitivity the moment he said it.

'No,' he sighed. 'I'm working on my ability as Alder told me to.'

Gin continued to watch him. The foam melted away at the slab, softening it up. He twisted the stone, creating a horn that hardened within seconds. Gin couldn't comprehend the final product's use, but he found the man's ability to manipulate the stone intriguing.

'That's a cool ability,' Gin commented.

'Huh?' the man replied, astonished.

'Did I say something wrong?'

'Uh, no. I didn't expect you to call my ability "cool". That's all.'

'You literally softened, formed a new object and let it harden. Better than anything I can do.'

The man blinked at Gin then scrunched up his eyebrows as if figuring something out. Gin let the silence go on as he took note of the second half of the training.

'You're the guy who lived without a heart,' the man realised.

'Yep,' Gin affirmed.

'You must be a high-ranked mage then. I think you should avoid me and the others.'

'Alder hinted at something similar literally a few hours ago and I said no, I'm fine. Why would I want to avoid such interesting beings such as you guys? Do you know how much research I'd miss out on if I stayed in my room all day?'

The man blinked at Gin twice more then burst out in laughter. Gin followed suit, laughing alongside the new-found companion.

'You're not like most mages I've come across,' the man said.

'What if I'm not?' Gin hinted at his manush heritage. 'By the way, I'm Gin.'

'Michal,' the man responded.

'Oi, brat!' Alder called out. 'I told you to watch, not to chatter.'

'I have. You just went over formation five, seven and D, making a four-four triangular, six-two square and a cup shape respectively,' Gin replied with confidence.

'Cheeky brat,' Alder cursed before turning to the rest of his battalion for more instructions.

'Just wondering,' Gin said, turning back to Michal with one eye on the training. 'Why did Alder exclude you from training?'

'With my slow speed, my clumsiness, the fact that I can't maintain my foam for long, I'm nothing compared to the other stone elementals,' Michal admitted.

'Why not take off the stone slabs you're wearing? They must be the reason why you can't move as well. You don't look that unfit otherwise.'

'I'm an F ranked stone elemental. Without my stone, I'm even worse than an F rank. I have no purpose. I can't fight like the other bestials or elemental types nor can I do reconnaissance like the utility types. I could tell the others feel the same way. They know they're useless but still try to make something of themselves.'

Gin didn't say anything. He looked at Michal then back at the battalion he joined. Though his time with them was brief, Gin could already see flaws in everyone; inefficiencies that he knew he could eradicate. In Gin's eyes, it would be a fun experiment to conduct. His first subject was the self-loathing mage beside him.

'How about a more support style role?' Gin asked.

'Huh?' Michal responded, confused by the suggestion.

'I want you to make something for me.'

6

Wontiferus Poxim

Gin sidestepped a diagonal swing, keeping his balance, steeling himself for the next barrage of attacks. Alder told him to dodge, not that he had a choice in the matter. With his INS taken away, Gin didn't have a way to defend himself.

Alder picked up the pace. Gin ducked below the first strike then rolled out of the way for the second. The relentless speed kept him on his toes as he leapt back to avoid a guillotine-like attack. He managed to avoid each swing, noticing Alder's repetitive movements.

A sudden lunge threw Gin off, but his reactions didn't fail him. He stepped back, turning just as Alder reached him, allowing the blade to glide past him.

However, despite the dodge, Gin landed on a stray tree root that tripped him up. Alder took the opportunity, knocking him over with the blunt side of his blade.

'Dammit!' Gin exclaimed.

'Cheer up, brat,' Alder consoled. 'Most can't even get past the five-minute mark against me. You achieving eleven minutes this time is very commendable. A major improvement on the three minutes on your first go.'

With his back drenched from the marsh-like floor, Gin took a breather. He clenched his teeth in annoyance. Having done the same exercise for a month, with no deviation, it got to him. Not only that but Alder refused to give the INS back. *What was he doing with them?* Gin wondered. Whatever it was, he had enough. He didn't say anything up till now but he knew he had to speak up sooner or later or he would achieve nothing.

'When are you going to give me my weapons back? It's already been four weeks and all we've been doing is the same thing day after day.'

'You need experience, brat,' Alder explained. 'Repetition enables your body to act instinctively allowing you to think up strategies while your body is in auto-pilot. If the enemy can't touch you, you won't lose.'

'If I can't defeat the enemy, I can't win either. Your point?'

'Have faith. You're improving with each passing day. Everything is being done according to plan.'

'A plan you've never explained to me. Not only have you gone with such mediocre methods for both me and the battalion but you don't even listen to any suggestions I put forward. You've even taken me out of battalion training for some stupid reason of yours. If you really wanted me to improve, I should be joining them! If I knew my month would end up like this, I would have accepted your offer to leave your battalion.'

'Impatient and arrogant as always, brat,' Alder shook his head in disappointment.

Gin didn't respond to the insult. It wasn't anything new, like a catchphrase of sorts. The words became meaningless and easy to drown out. On the other hand, they proved to be a good indicator of whenever Alder got frustrated.

Or maybe that was just Gin's own frustration pouring out. He liked progress and efficiency. When neither existed, he found no point in continuing. A month of dodging practice just to gain eight minutes of survival against Alder? It almost made Gin laugh at how pitiful his improvement was. What made things worse was how Alder didn't tell him a thing about what he's doing with his INS.

'You remind me a lot like myself two hundred years ago,' Alder said, sitting down beside Gin.

'Alder. Don't you think it's too soon to open up to me?' Gin interrupted. 'Do you normally talk about your past for someone you've barely taught?'

'Let me continue. I have my reasons, brat.'

So? Doesn't affect me. Wait. Two hundred years? Just how old can mages be? Gin wondered, sparking a new curiosity. Though he didn't want to hear the Alder's monologue, something prevented him from leaving either.

'I was trained under Maria's predecessor, the previous colonel of squadron W,' Alder said, taking Gin's silence as an excuse to tell his story. 'I was desperate to fight in the war that's been going for more than a thousand years now.'

Thousand years, huh? Really does put the manush's peace into perspective, Gin thought.

'Yes, I remember how it was back then.' Alder continued. 'I was rash and rarely wanted to do as my mentor asked when I first started. Just like you now. Did you know we had sparred a total of one-thousand-five-hundred-and-ninety-two times? I have lost all but two of them. Even the two I didn't was down to her needing to leave mid-fight.'

'Sounds like she had a strong ability,' Gin commented. 'Almost makes me want to meet her. Almost.'

'She's no longer around, so that's impossible anyway.'

A silence followed. Gin glanced at Alder to see what could be on his mind. Though his armour hid any emotion, Alder's sigh showed that he was in deep thought.

'One more lesson,' Alder said at last.

'What?' Gin responded, sitting up to face Alder eye to eye.

'One more lesson, in one week, and then I'll give you the liberty to decide if you want to quit training under me. Also, the equipment I've made for blade boxing should be done by then. If you don't like them, I can remove the changes. My Xernim is helping me.'

'Xernim? The colonel told me you're a Xernim user but I never got around to asking what that was.'

'You don't know?'

'Nope.'

Alder extended his arm. Branches grew out of his armour before they degraded just as quickly. They moved, forming hooks and needles. Gin analysed the shapes. They were too intricate to be premade like the blades. Then it hit him.

'Your armour's alive, isn't it?' Gin asked.

'It feeds off me and in return it provides me offence and defence,' Alder confirmed.

'Hold on. You're telling me a parasite is working on my INS?'

'I trust it more than I trust you.'

'Oh. Great. Thanks for the support,' Gin replied in a sarcastic manner. 'You still haven't told me *what* they're doing to my INS.'

'Again, I'm asking you to wait,' Alder replied with a firmness that put Gin off.

Another silence allowed Gin to process his thoughts. The lack of information from Alder still annoyed him but his initial eagerness to find out about blade boxing remained, albeit dwindling due to the time wasted.

Gin's desire to find out what made a mage a mage and not a manush also floated around in his sea of unanswered questions. Although he made significant progress in the past, he was stumped for the time being. This might be the thing he needed to boost his research.

'Fine,' Gin said with a wry smile. 'This better be worth it.'

'It won't.'

'Is that it for today then?'

'Yes. You are dismissed. I'll join you for battalion training a little late today.'

Gin got up from the floor, not saying a word more to Alder. As he left the room, he saw the colonel standing outside. Gin gave her a nod of respect before heading to his room. Once again, he needed a change of clothes.

When he arrived, Gin noticed that his room's door was left ajar. Knowing who did it, Gin slammed the door wide open. As he expected, Joan sat on his bed, preparing some medication.

'Oh, it's you,' Gin murmured, pretending he had no idea it was her that snuck in.

'I've been at your side until you've recovered and this the reaction I get?' Joan retorted.

'Sorry. I'm a bit peeved today. Anyway, you were meant to stop when I fully recovered.'

'That *was* the plan.'

'Then why are you back?'

'A high ranked mage from squadron A itself decided to transfer to our squadron.'

Gin didn't know the importance of the different squadrons but, based on the alphabetical ordering, he assumed that squadron A were the big shots of the Eurasian army. Yet another thing about the mages Gin had to find out.

'That still doesn't explain anything,' Gin criticised.

'Well, apparently this guy said he wanted to be your medic specifically,' Joan explained.

'Eh?'

'I know, right? Maria found it fishy too and told the man that you already had a medic.'

'An obvious lie.'

'Yep. But to make it into the truth, she told me to be your medic for real until we sort things out. By the way, your clothes have been dripping this whole time,' Joan pointed out, handing Gin a new set of clothes.

Gin looked down to see a small puddle forming below him. He took the clothes and put them on straight away. Taking a seat at his desk, Gin continued the conversation.

'Do you know who this person is?'

'Nope. Do you?' Joan questioned.

'I don't think so,' Gin said, stroking his beard. 'Unle– Oh no. Joan, do you know where he might be?'

'Um, I'm not sure. Probably looking for you.'

'I have a bad feeling about this. Got to go.'

'Wait. Where are you go–'

Before Joan could finish her question, Gin had already dashed for it, forgetting to close the door behind him. He rushed back to the marshy room. But before he could he noticed that a small crowd formed outside the room, blocking the entrance.

As Gin forced his way through the sea of mages, a hand grabbed hold of his shoulder. He swivelled, turning to see Michal indicating that he should follow him. Gin complied, taking a detour around the room and into a corridor on the side.

'There's a gap in the wall,' Michal whispered, pointing to the spot.

Michal went into a crawl, entering the hole with Gin following. Light seeped through openings between the branches inside the wall. The branches themselves stuck out of the passageway, cutting Gin whenever he got careless.

'Stop,' Michal instructed.

'Where are we?' Gin asked.

'The East side of the marsh-room. The Rezah is growing slowly in this spot, so we can use this passageway to have a peek.'

'How did you even–'

'A few of us found out about it and watched some of your lessons with Alder in our spare time. You're pretty agile, aren't you?'

'Shouldn't you be more focused on creating item seven?'

'Aha. That one's taking a while. It keeps collapsing under the weight.'

'Excuses,' Gin joked.

Gin shuffled to the side of Michal, who placed his foam-laden fingers on the wall. The wood eroded away, making places for them to spy from. Two men stood face to face in the centre of the room. One of them was Alder while the other was a lanky man with pale yellow skin. His white hair was long enough to cover his eyes but a clip held them back.

'Why does he have to be here?' Gin grumbled.

'Do you know him?' Michal questioned.

'He's called Wo. Let's just say I've known him from the moment I was born.'

'Oh, the MBP bred you two in the same batch?'

'Not quite but never mind that. From the looks of things, I think they're going to fight.'

Alder unsheathed his serrated blade. With the eyes of spectators watching him, Alder made the first move. He took a few steps forward, assessing his opponent. Then with a burst of pace, he leapt from his spot, twisting his body to put him in a position to strike while making sure he could dodge any sudden counter.

However, before he could swing his sword, the weapon in his hand began rotting away, as if it was being consumed by some invisible force. Alder threw it away, more by instinct than by choice, as the blade disappeared, leaving no trace of its existence.

Wary of Wo, Alder backtracked a couple of steps, gaining distance once more. He reached to a pocket in his armour and placed his right hand in it for a few seconds. Wo looked on, raising an eyebrow when Alder's hand emerged empty-handed. Alder raised his arm but Wo remained motionless and instead put on a grin.

An orb went flying towards Wo at an alarming speed. A direct hit would most definitely pierce an enemy and Wo did not have time to dodge it. However, Alder's eyes widened when the orb began to disintegrate just as it reached Wo.

Wo's grin turned into a smirk. He just stood there with his hands in his trouser pockets as if nothing happened. Wo began laughing.

'What's so funny?' asked Alder.

'You are way too similar to Gin, not gonna lie,' Wo responded, their conversation just about audible to Gin and Michal. 'Well, Gin asked me to test a weapon design. He must have told you about the INS, right? Anyway, he asked me to test something out and it works exactly like what you did now.'

Wo picked a metallic cuboid out of his pocket. An INS. He pushed his finger through one of the holes and the cuboid began to change shape. On one side, the cuboid began to elongate and narrow, leaving a circular hollow chamber in the end. On the other side, the INS began to curve downwards leaving three holes, where Wo had his fingers inserted in.

'What is that?' Alder asked.

'Gin called it a "gun". If I press my finger in the second hole and aim at this tree...'

A large banging sound echoed around the room. The once healthy tree now had a small hole running through its trunk. Sap oozed out of the gap, like blood out of a wound, showcasing the damage inflicted.

'Did you manage to see that?' Wo inquired.

'A small pellet came out of the INS, right?' Alder replied.

'Good eye. Probably not as powerful as your version but good enough to leave a mark.'

'Then how did you not get hurt from my shot?'

'I don't want to reveal my secrets in front of soooooo many people,' Wo said, smirking at the crowd.

The mages took the hint. They dissipated, some slower than others, gossiping amongst themselves. They enjoyed the fight and the talk of an overpowered mage in their squadron gave them an exciting prospect.

'Shall we get going too?' Gin asked Michal.

'I want to find out what he was bred to do,' Michal rejected.

'I can tell you later myself.'

'Where's the fun in that?'

'Alright,' Gin sighed.

They turned their attention back to the people in the room. Alder checked the entrances for any remaining people that decided to stick around.

'So?' Alder prompted.

'Hmm. Yeah, I should tell you, since you will be my in-charge soon. I'm a utility category mage, type: medic,' Wo explained.

'But medics —'

'But medics can't do that, right? Well, I am a sort of special medic. Although you can't see it, I am surrounded by a special type of microorganism. Much like your Xernim, I was bred to be born with it. It eats away at objects, both living and dead, at quite a quick pace. Your bullet was too slow to harm me. I can't do healing like some other medics but I do specialise in being an anti-poison slash Xernim slash virus type medic, so I do have my niche. It also allows me to be one of the few medics who can fight. Want a demonstration?'

Before Alder could say anything, Wo had already walked to the Eastern wall. He pointed his palm towards the wall. A fuzzy yellow mist formed around his hands. The mist then exploded, flying towards the wall, eating away at it and revealing the pair that hid behind it.

'Oh, hi Gigi!' Wo greeted.

'Gigi?' Alder and Michal said at the same time.

'This is exactly why I wanted to leave earlier,' Gin complained as water trickled around his thigh. 'Wo, please. Could you not?'

'Could I not what?' Wo replied, his grin as big as ever.

'Not make my social life hell like you always have,' Gin specified, helping Michal up from the floor.

'I don't know. When someone's as easy to tease as you, my answer's no. My. Dear. Gigi.'

'Ugh. You make me want to puke every time you do that.'

'I see you two are good friends,' Alder said.

'We're not,' Gin scowled.

'Awwww. How could you break my heart like this, Gigi,' Wo fake-cried, grabbing Gin around the shoulders and threatening to hit him with kisses.

Gin glanced back. He could tell Michal wanted to laugh to his heart's content but remained silent for the time being. However, when Alder burst out in laughter, the room chorused with the other mages joining in at Gin's expense.

'Is this what you've been doing all this time I was running around, looking for you?'

The noise died down as the men looked towards the entrance of the room. There they found Joan walking towards them. She directed a scowl right at Gin who averted his eyes.

'I think I'll go now,' Michal said, scared by Joan's expression and not wanting to be drawn in by what was going to happen. 'I need to make some stuff as you asked.'

'Traitor,' Gin griped.

'Hey, Gigi,' Wo whispered. 'A woman looking for you with an annoyed look on her face? You sure work fast.'

'It's not what you think,' Gin defended himself. 'She's just my medic.'

'Ooooh. I understand. But glad you picked yourself a bit. I made the correct decision sending you here. Hopefully you can find a sense of purpose and reason by being here. Better than the hollow shell you were before.'

'Do I need a purpose and reason to be in squadron W?' Gin gave an unimpressed look while hiding his surprise by the sudden father-like words coming out of Wo's mouth. 'Plus, since when was I a hollow –'

'What are you two talking about in secret?' Joan interrupted.

Wo let go of Gin, giving him a mischievous smile as he did so. He went up to Joan, grabbed her by the hand and gave it a small peck. Joan snatched it away just as suddenly, grossed out by the stranger's action.

'Very unladylike,' Wo remarked. 'I see why you like her, Gigi.'

'Um, Gin, who is this man?' Joan asked, cradling her hand, bemused by what is going on.

'My name is Wontiferus Poxim. Pleasure to meet you,' Wo replied in Gin's stead, bowing as he did so.

'Just call him Wo Pim,' Gin suggested.

'Seriously? This is the guy everyone's talking about?' Joan said in shock.

'The one and only. Did you miss the show I put on? I can do it again if you like,' Wo smirked as he began inspecting Joan. 'And you're the one that took my role from me, aren't you?'

Joan looked at Gin. From her expression, Gin translated the look as "This guy's definitely crazy".

He agreed and shrugged to show it. They didn't know where to go from their mutual impression of Wo and the silence made the situation even more awkward.

'Ahem,' Alder said, breaking the deadlock. 'Maria wanted to speak with you by the end of the day, Wontiferus.'

'Did she now?' Wo said, stopping his inspection. 'Well, it can't be helped. Lead the way, battalion leader guy.'

Wo walked beside Alder out of the room. But before he left, he signalled to Gin, giving him an "OK" sign followed by a thumbs-up.

'How do you know this guy again?' Joan asked.

'Don't ask. It's a long story,' Gin responded.

7

The Next Phase

'Yanus. Oi, Yanus. Ugh. Esper! Wake up!'

Esper opened one eye then went back to sleep upon seeing his disgruntled colleague. He felt tired. He yearned for that five minutes more in bed but a strong slap to the face made Esper jump out of his bed, crashing to the floor in his confusion. He looked up to see Jack's face more scrunched up than before.

'Yo,' Esper greeted.

'Don't "Yo" me,' Jack barked. 'We've been preparing the next phase of our mission for ages and you can't even get up on the day we've set?'

'Yeah, yeah. Is food ready?'

'Esper!'

'Relax for a moment. All I gotta do is arrive at your medic facility before that Lahel guy.'

'Oh, you actually remember his name. Looks like me hammering information into your skull finally paid off,' Jack said, helping Esper up. 'Anyway, I need to be at the clinic now. It's insane how early Tom Babacla has to work.'

'Ba-bye,' Esper waved.

'You *will* be there,' Jack reinforced, donning the vest made of vines that the deceased medic used to wear. 'Our mission depends on you getting off your ass for once. Make you get all the right documentation. Oh, and also my name is?'

'Ja- Tom.'

'Yes. It's Tom Babacla. Don't you forget it. I am no longer Jack when I'm outside, so don't blow my cover by being stupid.'

'Yeah, yeah. You can leave now.'

When Jack left for 'work', Esper headed down to the kitchen. He opened up a bag of rations, laying down red numius fruits that contained blue polka-dots. Beside them, he chopped up meat into thin slices and, with the help of a nearby torch, grilled them till they turned medium-rare. Using diced numius fruits, he garnished the food for a succulent brunch packed full of nutrients. When it came to food, Esper turned into a different person, especially when he could whip up a meal as good as this.

With a spring in his step, Esper skipped out of his home, almost forgetting to lock it, and headed towards the medic facility. The route he took led him past a district created for the utility familiar type mages. The people there carried, or even got carried in some cases, the various animals raised up with them, from birds to rideable canines called the Lupim.

A Tinoo flew past Esper, circling around him before landing on his shoulder. A simple electric shock would have ended its life, but Esper decided against it, stopping in his tracks to stare at the bird's white-feathered breast and red plumes on its head and tail feathers. It clucked a few times, showing off a piece of rolled up paper stuck to the underside of its beak. Esper pulled it out, inspecting the object without unravelling it.

'My, my. What a mischievous bird you are!' a pale, black-haired woman called out. She grabbed onto Esper's shoulder, allowing the tinoo to hop onto her hand.

'You should take better care of your familiar,' Esper scolded, hiding the scroll in his palm.

'Ah, my sincerest apologies. My partner here really loves people, you see,' the stranger apologised, caressing the bird's chin. 'Would you like me to do anything to make it up to you?'

'As a matter of fact, I do. Basically, I had the most amazing breakfast but now I'm running out of rations, so if you can give me some of yours, that'd be great.'

The woman squinted at Esper. She didn't expect him to answer her rhetorical question. She looked at the tinoo that shook its body in some form of dance.

'I agree,' she nodded.

'Oh, really?! Thanks!' Esper exclaimed.

'I wasn't talking to you,' the woman muttered before raising her voice. 'What I meant to say is that I believe I'm taking too much of your time already. I'm sure you have someplace you needed to go.'

'Oooooh, yeah,' Esper realised. 'Thanks for reminding me. I'll take the food some other time.'

'No problem,' the woman said. Then her voice dropped into a whisper. 'Make sure you give the letter to Tom Babacla.'

'Huh? Um, ok.'

The woman soon blended into the crowd with her tinoo, leaving Esper with the scroll he failed to hide from her. He wanted to open and read the contents but his illiteracy prevented that from happening. Instead, he pocketed it and continued his journey to the facility Jack worked in.

Once at a building that stuck out in a cubed shape, detached from other buildings, Esper knocked on the Earthen door a couple of times. A bulky man slid the door open. He stared at Esper for a moment, assessing the newcomer.

'Papers,' he demanded.

Esper's stomach turned inside-out.

'Aw, man. I completely forgot to bring them,' Esper admitted. 'Um, just call Tom. He knows that I was going to come.'

The man looked at Esper with a suspicious gaze then closed the door again. Esper did an air punch, due to remembering to use Jack's alias, and waited for the door to open again. This time Jack opened the door, glaring at his partner before putting on a bright fake smile.

'Ah, Yanus Temply! I was expecting you. Do come in,' he greeted.

Esper complied, giving the doorkeeper a nod as he walked past him. He followed Jack into a round waiting room. Sat on stone sofas, a few people glanced at the medic and his next patient. One of them, Esper realised, was the target.

The brown-skinned man called Lahel Bints fidgeted in his seat, nervousness emanating from every limb. He didn't look that special either. He had less muscle than the doorman and no notable traits on the rest of his body. Not that Esper cared since he got to do something for once.

'Right this way,' Jack guided, leading him to the end of a narrow corridor where his office was. Once he closed the door behind him, his grin turned into an immediate frown. 'Are you an idiot?!'

'Woah. Where'd that come from? What happened to the smiley man?' Esper said, surprised by the warranted change in mood from his compatriot.

'How did you forget your papers?!'

'It was an honest mistake.'

'Tsk. Just shut up. I don't have time for this. We got at most fifteen minutes to prepare before the other patients start to wonder what's taking so long. I need you to use your "ghosting" and wait for my signal. Understood?'

'You gotta chill, man. We got this.'

'Then go to the corner of the room and stay hidden.'

'Alright. Easy job, easy mission,' Esper said with Jack rolling his eyes at the comment.

Esper went to the edge of the room, closed his eyes and concentrated. He could sense the electrical impulses surrounding the room. With a bit more focus, he began manipulating the ones around him, redirecting them towards Jack. For reasons he couldn't explain, it masked his presence and made the main focus, in this case Jack, the centre of attention. He related it to an absence of the moment when something catches the corner of one's eye but the logistics of it all was too complicated for Esper to care about.

'Done with your "ghosting"?' Jack asked.

'Mm,' Esper replied.

'Here goes nothing. Lahel Bints!' Jack called out, putting on a cheesy smile again.

Moments later, the door slid open. Lahel entered the room and closed the door behind him. He shook Jack's hand, sweat transferring over, unnerving him.

'Please, Mr Bints, sit down,' Jack suggested.

'Ah, thank you. Tom was it?' Lahel asked, taking the seat.

'Tom Babacla, yes,' Jack confirmed, hiding his true identity. 'Shall we begin our check-up?'

'Ok,' Lahel nodded.

'I have your profile here,' Jack said, picking up a pile of papers and reading from it. 'Age: One hundred and fifty-two. Mhm. Next is height; eight feet two inches, exactly my height, funnily enough. Finally, your magi classification is Bestial Juggernaut. I see. You were also transferred to the Egypt division last year, right?'

'Yes.'

'Ha! To be honest you don't look like a juggernaut, let alone an A ranked one at that. Are you sure the data is correct?'

The comment sparked something inside the fan. From the fidgeting wreck, he sat up straight, looked Jack in the eyes with steely determination and uttered,

'I have fought in countless battles. I will be chosen to be the village leader's guide soon. I think my abilities shouldn't be in doubt or would you like a demonstration?'

'Be my guest,' Jack replied.

Lahel walked towards the wall where the exit door lay. He retracted his right arm before letting it fly into the wall at full throttle. A heavy sound echoed from where Lahel had punched the wall. He freed his arm and, in its place, a metre-long hole gaped open, the sound of dust crumbling from it.

'Very impressive,' the Jack remarked, 'Looks like I was wrong.'

'There's a reason why I got chosen to be the village leader's escort.'

'Really? That's amazing! And you received no injuries from that wall punch?'

'No. I have high regeneration so something like that won't hurt me'

'The two attributes do complement each other quite well, as expected from a Juggernaut. Now I am going to do some body checks if you please.'

Lahel took off his shirt while Jack inspected his torso first, then his arms and face before finally moving towards the back. With Lahel's back turned and unaware of his surroundings, Jack beckoned Esper to make his move.

Esper placed his hand on his target's back. He felt the electricity flowing through his palms then, with one final push, he sent the wave through Lahel's back. His body drooped, swaying on the chair, trying to keep balance.

'Are you ok, Mr Bints?' Jack asked.

'I don't know,' he responded, each word sounding like gibberish as his lips trembled.

'I'll check one more time then. I think punching the wall was a bad idea after all.'

'Ok.'

Lahel dropped to the floor, his body writhing in spasms. Foam began spewing out of his mouth. His eyes twitched in random movements. He clutched his heart as if pinpointing where the problem resided.

Esper guessed the shock stopped his heart like it almost always does.

'That was easy,' Esper celebrated. 'Told you we got this.'

'We're lucky he wasn't on his guard. With the A ranked bodyguard outside the door to the clinic and the fact that Tom was a medic, he didn't have anything to fear. If your ghosting got uncovered, it would have been a different story.'

Esper looked at the twitching body and stretched his arm towards it. He felt the electricity around his hands, ready to send another shock, just to make sure he finished the job.

'Esper! We don't have time for that now.'

'Aww. C'mon, man. I've been holed up for ages and finally got to do something. Let me have fun for once.'

'No,' Jack denied. 'Just take the body out of here. There's a back entrance where you can leave it in the storage room on the far right for the time being. I'll get to stealing his identity later. For now, I got more patients to tend to.'

'I'm surprised you can do this sort of work, man.'

'Tom was only a D rank mage. Most can do his work with little training.'

'Hmm.'

'Just go already. We're taking too much time,' Jack said, looking at the clock on the wall.

'Yes, boss-man,' Esper saluted.

Esper dragged the body through the stone corridor lit with torches. He arrived at the room and hoisted the body into it, dusting his hands off once done. He closed the storage room's door then headed for the exit, taking a deep breath of the fresh air outside as he did so.

'Did you give Tom the scroll?' someone asked.

Esper turned to see the same woman he bumped into earlier that day. Her tinoo perched on her shoulders, staring into Esper's eyes with killing intent. However, Esper didn't notice it and tilted his head in bemusement.

'Did you bring food?' Esper asked.

'What?' the woman provoked. 'The scroll I gave you. Did you give it to Tom Babacla?'

'What scroll? Oh, the one that was stuck in your bird's beak,' Esper realised before averting his gaze. 'I don't know what you're talking about.'

'Tsk. He was right. You really are an idiot.'

'Hey. What about the food you said you'd bring me?'

The woman ignored Esper's question and went around the building, towards the entrance and knocked on the door. The doorkeeper looked at documents she gave before allowing her to enter. Esper took no heed to her actions, although upset by the lack of food.

Esper's stomach grumbled. Taking the invitation to leave, he headed towards his home, thinking of the leftovers from brunch. A bright smile shone on his face because, for once, he had accomplished something as a low ranked mage. He deserved an early dinner.

8

Preparations for War

The diversity of the mages amazed Gin. From the rough skins of the fire elementals to the mages with tubular holes embedded within their flesh, every single person made Gin want to reach out and touch them, his curiosity overwhelming him. However, his self-control restrained him, binding him to his spot.

Gin estimated about two-thousand mages either sat or stood up in the packed hall, waiting on the colonel to take centre stage. Their chatter filled the room, each question along the lines of why she called them in the first place. Gin wondered the same question himself.

Then the noise died down. All eyes watched the colonel making her way to the front of the room. She eyed the remaining talkers, forcing the last of the chatter to dissipate. Her commanding aura radiated to the extent that you could feel a chill down your spine.

'I have gathered everyone here to make a special announcement,' the colonel boomed, making sure even those at the back could hear her. 'After decades of inactivity, the MBP has finally given us the chance to go to war!'

The room erupted. The colonel smiled. *Are the mages just fight junkies?* Gin thought, wondering how risking your life for something as trivial as war could be celebrated.

'For too long we have been looked down upon,' the colonel continued after letting the cheering die down, 'We are seen as the worst Squadron in the whole of Eurasia, only accepting the 'rejects' of the MBP. They wouldn't even give us a chance – how impudent! But now, we are given an opportunity to show our worth. If we win flawlessly, we are sure to be promoted and get much larger rations, more bases and a stronger force.'

'How did you do it?' a mage called out, the room bouncing with excitement.

'It is true that we have been only given the worst jobs for the past few hundred years; Harvesting crops, surveillance works in essentially our own backyard, taking in the low ranked mages that no one else would,' the colonel listed. 'Nothing that you can consider promotion-worthy. But we have a new asset that has changed all this. I would like to call upon our newest recruit, Wontiferus Poxim.'

All eyes set on the lanky figure that walked between the people. He strode in a swagger that oozed confidence. He didn't need an introduction. Most people already knew that he transferred from squadron A and mutterings amongst the crowd filled in those who didn't. Everyone wondered how such a weak looking figure could have come from Squadron A, but they still kept their distance out of the unconscious fear they had of him.

Wo stood beside the colonel, back straight, and searched around the room. His face lit up when he found his target, directing a grin straight at Gin.

'Yo! Gigi! Come join me!' Wo shouted, waving at Gin.

Gin looked away, adopting the uninterested look. However, his fellow battalion members stood nearby, smiling at their infamous ally. They chanted 'Gigi' over and over again, pushing him towards the front as they did so. The name spread and soon the whole room called Gin out.

'Gigi, set up the map like we discussed the other day,' Wo told Gin.

'Did you really have to call me Gigi in front of everyone?' Gin whispered to Wo.

Ignoring Gin's comment, Wo turned to the crowd, 'Thanks to Gigi, we get to see something, unlike anything we have witnessed in our lifetime. Take it away, Gigi.'

Gin grabbed an INS from his belt and activated the mechanism. The silver cuboid grew two rods, one on each side, which bent downwards. Gin placed the INS on the floor, with the rods acting as a stand, and pushed his finger into the second hole of the INS. A bright beam of light emerged from one end and shone on the wall opposite. Everyone stared in amazement. Right before them was the map of the world, with detailed labels of the cities and three large labels for the continents: Eurasia, Afro-Australia and The Americas.

Gin's skin crawled as the sudden silence unnerved him. He stood up and saw expectant gazes fixated on him. He wondered if he did anything wrong but dismissed the idea when Wo smirked at him. *What did he do this time?* Gin thought.

'As you can see, Gigi here has been bred to manipulate these objects for our use,' Wo explained.

Bred? Gin noticed.

'Because of that, we get to see the whole world in front of you, shown as a convenient map. Gigi, play the slides,' Wo continued. 'We are here, just outside the city of Israel in our little town of Jerusalem. Due to the sudden inactivity of The Americas, the Afro-Australian Alliance are increasing their pressure on us Eurasians. As a result, we are forced to move most of our squadrons to the bases in France and China. This leaves us short on forces elsewhere.

From reliable sources, we are now told the AAA is planning on sending a little scouting squad from Egypt. They're not really seen as a threat so the MBP is happy to let them go for the time being. However, along with my ties with Squadron A, I have managed to land the privilege of letting us take on the AAA's small army.'

At Wo's signals, Gin went through several pictures, including tactics, formations and zoomed-in maps of the place of battle. Most battles between the Eurasia and Africa were fought over the sea, but this skirmish was on land. A small strip of land connected the two continents, from the city of Jordon to the city of Egypt. Being relatively close to the strip, Gin could see why Squadron W became the ideal force to be dispatched for the mission.

'This was a plan we have planned a while ago,' Wo explained. 'In fact, we've already sent two of our squadron members beforehand. They will aim to assassinate one of the commanding officers. If they succeed, then we buy us several months while the AAA sort themselves out. If not, we best be prepared for departure soon.

'Oh, one last thing,' Wo added. 'There is a catch for our mission. We can't use any A ranked mages or above,' Wo proclaimed. 'As you may know, Squadron W is in a rough spot. The MBP is happy to let us be. In all honesty, it is a miracle they gave us this mission in the first place. We aren't given any meaningful missions that can alter our rank. Therefore, to test whether you're worthy to be used in the future, this limit is in place. I hope you don't fail our expectations. That's all for your briefing. Thank you for listening.'

With that, Wo bowed in front of the audience and made his way to the exit. Along the way, he patted Gin's shoulder and gave him an encouraging wink, though Gin didn't know what for. Wo's scheming nature always annoyed Gin and this instant wasn't any different.

'The whole of Eurasia sees us as the rejects of the MBP,' the colonel took over. 'The government doesn't see the AAA's invasion as a threat and so want to test us. They don't want the 'strong' winning the fight for us and want to see what these 'rejects' can accomplish by themselves. This is our only chance to prove ourselves. I don't want us to just pass this test of theirs. I want us to commit an act of perfection!'

The room exploded into a deafening cry by the rallies of their leader. The Colonel set the stakes high and the mages took them with outstretched arms. A sense of belief filled the room, each mage brimming with anticipation. *Was the societal pressure really that bad?* Gin thought. Despite the speeches from the colonel and Wo, he still wasn't convinced.

'I'll probably ask Alder later,' Gin muttered as everyone made their way out.

While the mages chattered throughout the corridors, excited by the mission, Gin went back to his room to work on his INS. For the first time using the projector, it went smoothly. However, Gin still went through all the slides to make sure it worked, to get rid of any possibility of beginner's luck.

'Hey,' Joan said, tapping Gin on the shoulder.

'Do you need anything?' Gin sighed, focused on his slides.

'It's time for your check-up.'

'I told you already, I'm fine. There's no need to do this after my heart was recreated.'

'Dealing with you is really frustrating, you know that? At least stand up and face when speaking to me,' Joan scowled, tugging at Gin's ear. 'It's rude just sitting there toying about on your, erm, whatever it is.'

Gin got up in reluctance, swatting Joan's hand away. He reset the projector back to its cuboid shape and slotted it on his belt before meeting Joan eye to eye.

'First of all, it's called an INS– Integrated Nanobot System – I'm sure I've told you already,' Gin clarified. 'Secondly, I don't need you looking after me.'

'Sheesh. Why must you be so hard to deal with? You do realise I am your medic?'

'Only to avoid Wo being my medic. You don't actually have to do any work.'

'I don't like it either but Maria assigned me personally.'

'So, it's the colonel? Just ask her to give you another task while you pretend to be at my side.'

'I did.'

'And?'

'The answer was still no.'

'Go figures.'

Gin sat back into his chair and took out the INS that Wo used against Alder. He twisted one end of the INS, detaching a segment from the end. Gin flicked a switch that resided on the inside of the smaller piece and then pulled on the edges. It extended, showing off a screen in the centre that turned on in a flash of light. After placing his fingers on the screen, Gin went to work.

'Shall I do the check–up?' Joan asked, using it as a reason to continue watching without being an awkward bystander. 'Might as well while I'm here.'

'Gah,' Gin moaned, slipping up in his work. 'Mind being quiet for a bit? Busy concentrating.'

'Oh, look at me,' Joan replied with sarcasm. 'I get special treatment but I'm going to act ungrateful.'

'Ugh. It's not like that, Joan.'

'Haha. I know. Just teasing you.'

'Just get on with it!' Gin snapped.

'Sure thing!' Joan obeyed in a mocking tone.

Gin took off his shirt for Joan to examine and went back to his INS. His body hair baffled Joan as always. Most mages opted out of having body hair, apart from the ones that have fur with defensive qualities. Even for those that do have hair without use, they grew it out like a coat of fur, rather than the thin strands that protruded out of Gin. He even had a beard. Who grows facial hair anyway?

Joan pierced Gin's skin around the right shoulder with her nails, entering his veins. It acted as a blood test. Her nails reacted to the different compounds in the blood. She took out the nail and checked. The pink hue meant that nothing was out of the ordinary, though the way the nanobots felt unnerved Joan somewhat.

'What are you doing anyway?' Joan asked.

Gin paused for a moment, wondering if he should ignore Joan or not.

'Trying to increase my gun INS' power,' Gin said, deciding to tell her in the end. 'It felt too weak when Wo used it against Alder.'

'I see. Right arm, please,' Joan ordered.

Gin shifted the INS towards his left side and stretched out his right arm for Joan. However, his speed remained the same despite the change of hand, his ambidextrous nature proving useful.

'Wow. Alder really likes cutting you up, huh?' Joan commented while inspecting the scars on Gin's arms.

'Don't care what he does,' Gin responded.

'Did something happen between you two?' Joan asked while adding gel to the scars from her nails.

'I'm just a bit annoyed at how he's using my INS,' Gin replied, wincing at the stinging the gel caused.

'What's he done? Did he break it? I know you hold your INS with a sense of pride.'

'He...well, I don't really know but he's using his Xernim.'

'Why's that a problem? Left arm,' Joan instructed, moving to Gin's left side.

As Gin switched arms again, he thought about Joan's question before giving a meek reply. 'Guess it's because it's a Xernim.'

'Wow. I thought you weren't like the high-ranked mages.'

'Eh? What did I do?'

'Are you one of those that think Xernim users are cowards that can't use their own strength?'

'I don't see why I should think that way. To be honest, I find his Xernim incredible. If I could, I would love to find out how he manages to control it.'

'Good.'

'You've lost me. Anyway, now that I think about it a bit more, it's probably because I don't like the idea of a parasite working its way through my devices.'

'Gin, squadron W is based on the lack of prejudice we hold on one another. I'm sure Alder wants the best for you. Give him a chance. Just don't make any rash decisions when you see him, ok?'

'Fine. I'm done with my programming, by the way,' Gin announced.

'Programming?' Joan murmured. 'Um, well I'm done with my check-up as well.'

As Gin put on his shirt, he went into deep thought about what Joan said. Maybe she was right. Gin didn't check what Alder was doing in the first place and made unnecessary assumptions in the process. With a new determination, Gin set his sights on his next lesson with Alder.

'Um, Joan,' Gin called, realising that she had already made her way out of his room.

'Yes?' she replied, turning back.

'It's not that you're a bad medic or anything. Talking with you is quite enjoyable, to be honest. Just please don't visit me every day at least. I'm quite busy, you see.'

'Did you just compliment me, Gin? Didn't expect that from you.'

'Well, you are the only one of the few that calls me by my real name.'

Smiles grew on both of their faces as Joan left.
Between the training with Alder and the
embarrassment caused by Wo, Gin hadn't had much
time to smile himself. He found it satisfying and
smiled some more.

9

Xernim Gauntlets

Gin took his time preparing for the last lesson with Alder. He checked each INS one by one, making sure they functioned as intended. Though tedious in nature, Gin managed to work on two INS at the same time, one with his left and the other on his right. Satisfied with the maintenance, Gin slotted them into his belt and headed out.

When he arrived at the marsh room, Gin found Alder meditating in the centre. Knowing how aggravated Alder became when his meditation got interrupted, Gin joined him. He focused on his breathing, calmed his senses and went into a train of thought, imagining possible scenarios of what the lesson may entail and how he would respond.

'Oi, brat.'

Gin opened one eye to see Alder holding a pair of wooden gauntlets. They each had two rectangular holes embedded in them. On the right-handed gauntlet, the INS Alder borrowed from Gin slotted inside of it.

'What is that?' Gin asked as he stood up.

'Gauntlets,' Alder answered. 'Put them on.'

'I can see that. What? Is this what took you a month and a half to make? I know there's a catch.'

Alder remained silent, the gauntlets creeping closer to Gin, begging him to wear them.

'You really are a shitty mentor,' Gin murmured, adamant in his refusal until he knew what he was getting into.

'Shi–'

'I'm sorry. I shouldn't have said that,' Gin apologised, interrupting Alder before he could say a word. He could almost feel the gentle caress of his mother, warning him not to swear. He would tell her, "It was a slip of the tongue," and she would reply "I know" with a kiss on the forehead.

'Not sure why you're apologising. I wanted to ask what it meant,' Alder inquired.

'Eh?' Gin responded.

Now that he thought about it, Gin had never heard a mage use vulgar language, no matter how angry they got. *Were mages not taught words like that?* he wondered. *Is this what happens when the MBP runs everything?*

'Guess it's old English,' Gin theorised out loud. 'Just don't use it. No one will know what it means.'

'Right,' Alder replied, unsure what to make of what Gin said. 'I suppose it's unfair to expect you to act rashly like the impatient brat you are.'

'Glad the insults keep coming, even if this *could* be our last lesson. So? What are they made of?'

'These are the daughters of my Xernim armour.'

'Are they alive?'

Alder paused for a moment before answering. 'Yes,' he said. 'They will make you their host. But in exchange, they will listen to you and protect you when you're unconscious.'

'Listen? How does that work? It's just a parasitic plant, right?'

'I don't know myself but, whenever I have a thought, the Xernim responds like so.' Alder shifted the gauntlets to one arm then stared at his free arm. Branches from the Xernim grew, interlocking with each other, creating a broad base that narrowed until a sharp tip formed. 'Magic maybe?'

'Magic doesn't exist, Alder. It's a folly of man to blame what we don't understand on magic. Normally I wouldn't do something so reckless without knowing the consequences, but...' Gin lied to both Alder and himself, convincing his mind it was due to what Joan told him the other day. Along with his fascination with how the Xernims worked, he decided to take the risk. 'I'll accept them.'

'Are you sure?'

'Why are you trying to make me doubt myself now? Give them to me.'

'Ha! Arrogant and impatient as always, brat. Though that recklessness is a cause for concern...'

Ignoring the comment, Gin took the right-handed gauntlet and put it on, the wood smooth and cold. All of a sudden, something sharp pierced his arm as if it was latching onto him. Gin writhed in pain. Several more needle-like wood punctured his flesh, draining Gin of his energy, making him weak to the point he struggled to stand up.

'Looks like it likes you,' Alder commented.

'What?' Gin responded, the word distorted by his agony.

'Being liked isn't normal for you, is it?'

'Just tell me how long this goes on.'

'I'd say give it ten minutes. It's "setting the roots" into your veins. How many roots do you feel?'

In between irregular breaths, Gin counted how many spikes pierced his flesh. 'Twelve?'

'That's more than I expected. You should be done within the next minute or two then.'

Gin clutched his arm. He gasped for air. His heart raced. Then, as the seconds rolled on, the pain subsided.

'Is it over yet?' Gin gritted his teeth, fearing it would hurt again upon speech.

'Has the pain stopped?'

'I think so.'

'Then it's settled in quickly. Let's move onto the next test. Brat, I want you to clench your right fist.'

Gin got up, a mixture of water and sweat dripping from his clothes. He closed his fist as instructed, waiting for the gauntlets to react in some way. However, nothing happened.

'Am I doing something wrong?' Gin asked.

'No, it's not meant to do anything right now. Now for the real test. Imagine the Xernim entering and activating your INS.'

'I don't understand. What would that accomplish?'

'Just do it,' Alder snapped

Though confused, Gin carried out the order. As soon as he pictured the motion, the gauntlets began to change. Thin branches grew and entered the first hole of the INS. They weaved their way, opening the hatch to the chamber below, pressing the button at the bottom. The mechanism activated, creating a blade without delay.

'How?' Gin gawked, dumbfounded by what he had just witnessed.

'I told you. I don't know how it works. All I know is how to use it,' Alder said before pointing to the other slots. 'You use a shield too, right? I've left slots for you to put them in.'

'This is amazing. Are you sure there are no major repercussions to this?'

'Apart from the constant need to feed it, there shouldn't be,' Alder assured, looking up for a moment before turning back to Gin. 'People may look down on you though.'

'Because of the Xernim?'

'Because of the Xernim. We're not exactly looked favourably on, no matter how strong we get. Relying on a foreign entity is seen as a weakness. We can't fight by ourselves, so we fight with a parasite. I apologise for not telling you earlier.'

'So? Does it look like I'm the type to care about such things?'

'Haha, true. If it's one thing I learnt about you, it's that you're not one for social norms. Anyway, put on the other gauntlet and then we can start Blade Boxing.'

Through gritted teeth, Gin braced himself as the left-handed gauntlet burrowed its way through and into Gin's veins. The process lasted longer but less extreme than its right-handed counterpart. Gin could manage it. He took methodical breaths, reducing the burden on his body caused by panic.

'Come with me,' Alder instructed.

Alder walked up to the nearest tree. He focused on the bladeless arm, allowing branches to form into a bladed spike, shorter than Gin's sword. He took up a stance, left foot in front of his right which Alder placed at a forty-five-degree angle. Alder then held his arms up, left in front of the right, covering the head. Despite the position, every joint in his body had a loose aura to it, like rubber ready to attack then bounce back.

Alder sent a jab with his left arm, retracting it the immediate moment he did so, leaving a clean, narrow horizontal mark where his blade pierced the tree. The depth of Alder's strike showed as sap oozed out of the cut.

'Listen here, brat,' Alder snapped. 'For ease of communication, that strike is called a "jab". A right-handed version is called a "cross". I'll be teaching you other techniques like uppercuts and such, but for now, practice on getting the jab and cross perfected. Equip another blade on your left gauntlet and we can begin.'

'Yes, sir!' Gin exclaimed.

Gin took his spare sword INS from his belt and slotted it into the left gauntlet. Like the first time he used the Xernim, Gin concentrated, forming a mental picture of the plant growing into the first chamber, activating the mechanism. The process took a minute, much to Gin's annoyance. *Why was this slower than the first time?* he wondered.

'This takes too long,' Gin complained. 'I'll be too vulnerable if I need this long to activate my INS.'

'That's expected,' Alder consoled. 'Once you get used to it, you'll be able to just say one word in your mind and the Xernim will react straight away. Just takes patience which I know you lack.'

'Hmph. Fine. Anyway, you just want me to go for a left-handed punch on a tree, right?'

'A jab, but yes. Make sure to copy my body position.'

Gin took a deep breath as he walked up to the nearest tree, taking up the stance Alder showed him. Gin sent out a jab, piercing it with ease but, when he tried to take the blade out of the bark, his shoulder jerked as his arm remained stuck inside the tree.

'It's harder than it looks,' Alder commented, hiding an obvious smirk under his mask.

'Ack! How do I free myself?' Gin asked, humbled by his failure.

'Think of the Xernim rotting away from your INS or however they go back into their mini form. I don't really understand how your weapons work.'

'Most don't. I get what you're saying though.'

Gin thought of the Xernim degrading away from the first chamber. Just like that, the branches surrounding the chamber rotted away into nothingness, deactivating the INS and freeing Gin from the tree's hold.

'Amazing,' Gin muttered before turning back to Alder.

'Let's end for today. I don't want to put too much pressure on the Xernims. They're getting used to you as much as you are getting used to them.'

'I see. Guess you're right. I do feel a bit tired,' Gin agreed. 'By the way, what did I do wrong with my attack?'

'What did you do right?' Alder retorted. 'Your right foot wasn't at a forty-five-degree angle, your hands were too low when you sent out the punch and, though your initial hit on the tree was clean enough, you too much time to retreat, leaving you stuck.'

'Anything else?' Gin asked, rolling his eyes - not aimed at Alder but at his own complacency.

'Lots. But it's still early days. If you remain under my guidance, all of this can be rectified. So? Do you still intend to make this lesson your last?'

'Heh. This was your aim all along, wasn't it? Whatever. I've come this far. Guess I'll continue our sessions.'

'A good decision, brat. To celebrate the birth of a new blade-boxer, how about I treat you to some of my rations?'

'Sure, why not?'

After unequipping the INS, Gin and Alder headed down to the lowest levels on the Rezah tree. The entered the largest room on the floor: the cafeteria. A few hundred mages sat down on the sandy floors, partly due to the fact squadron W had no furniture in the room. Some ate with their tinoos, lupims and other familiars, while others stayed with their fellow battalion members. Though the atmosphere had a relaxed air to it, Gin could see a divide between the low, middle and (few) high ranked. Whether the mages consciously did this or not, Gin didn't know, but he found the prejudice mages had for one another disturbing.

Walking further into the room, Gin noticed the long queue on one end of the room. A clerk with multiple rolls of fat on her stood behind a booth, checking wooden permits from the mages. She walked into the area behind the booth, bringing out either a bag of supplies or a pre-prepared lunchbox. With each valid permit, the clerk peeled off a thin layer of her skin and rubbed it against the wood. The skin dissolved, leaving a mark to indicate that the mage had received the rations.

'There are some of our battalion members,' Alder pointed out.

'You're right,' Gin acknowledged as he held his hands to his teammates, though no one noticed him at first.

'I'll go get the rations. We'll meet up where the others are.'

'Alright,' Gin said, handing over his permit to Alder.

As Gin walked closer, Michal spotted him first and got up, beckoning him over. Gin greeted him and the other teammates with a smile but only Michal returned it. The rest averted their eyes, attempting a glimpse of Gin's arms every so often. Not only that, Gin noticed mages from the other battalions did the same.

'What's up with everyone?' Gin whispered to Michal.

'Aha,' Michal replied with a weak laugh. 'It's your arms.'

'Yeah, they're Xernims. What of it? Doesn't Alder use them too? Why isn't he getting dodgy looks?'

'You do know what people think of them, right? Alder was bred to use them. You didn't, meaning you chose to have them. Some mages might think you're crazy.'

'Alder warned about the same thing. So, what if I am? Does it matter? Should I ostracise you guys for being low-ranked like everyone else does?' Gin said, giving a piercing glare to his fellow battalion members who gave him a meek smile in return. 'I took the decision to take them on and I stand by it.'

'Ha,' Michal sighed. 'To be honest, I don't mind myself but I'm not sure about the others. I'll go talk to them, so come join us.'

'I was planning on doing so anyway.'

Gin sat cross-legged with the others. He took the opportunity to show off his new-found abilities, demonstrating the growth and degradation of the Xernim. Though he received the cold shoulder at first, with the help of Michal, the situation cooled down soon.

'Oh, I'm done with the armour you asked for,' Michal remembered.

'Really?' Gin responded in surprise. 'That's brilliant! Send them to my room.'

'What's this about armour?' an all too familiar yet annoying voice asked.

'What do you want, Wo?' Gin replied.

'Can't a friend go and eat with you, Gigi?'

'Ugh. Not with that smug face you carry all the time.'

Wo took that as an invitation to join Gin. He opened up one of the lunchboxes, showing chopped fruit, slices of meat and a cup holding water mixed with tree sap.

'You ate already?' Wo asked, wolfing down the meat.

'I didn't see him bring any,' Michal said.

'No, I haven't. Alder is getting mine,' Gin explained.

'Y'know,' Wo said, gulping down his mouthful. 'I'm surprised. Didn't expect you to accept the food so quickly.'

Gin squinted at Wo. 'What do you mean by that?'

'Oho,' Wo sniggered. 'You didn't know what you're eating? The meat is made from human flesh.'

'Ahaha,' Gin burst out in laughter. 'Of all your pranks, this has got to be the most farfetched, Wo.'

Gin continued to chuckle to himself but that died down when Wo continued to smirk, followed by strange looks of his fellow battalion members.

'What's so funny?' Michal wondered.

'You're kidding me, right?' Gin said, unwilling to believe what Wo said.

'Oi, brat,' Alder called out. 'You're in luck. I managed to persuade the clerk to give a little extra mage–meat. You don't get this opportunity too often.'

Gin's jaw dropped. He could feel his lunch trying to go up his throat but managed to keep it down. He still couldn't believe his ears. However, Alder confirmed the truth.

10

Escape

Lahel stood outside the city of Egypt for what seemed to be ages. He shielded his eyes from the dust, that scattered in the air, caused by a combination of the wind and the ventilation from the potholes above the city. Though he didn't know what to expect, Lahel did know who to expect.

It wasn't until half an hour of waiting did Lahel spot a group of people trudging along the cracked, rocky surface. They huddled around a man who waddled rather than walked due to the excess skin that rolled over itself. As he came closer to Lahel, the man held his hand up to the entourage and made the remainder of the journey by himself.

Lahel bowed, raising his head when the man told him to.

'Welcome, Village Leader,' Lahel greeted.

'No need more formalities,' the man said.

'Forgive me, Mr Ching.'

'Just Larry is fine.'

'Oh, but you are a man of high status. I cannot possibly call you by your first name, sir.'

'You have earned the right to be my guide for today. You must have accomplished many feats to be given this task. For that, you have my respect.'

Lahel bowed once more. 'Your words flatter me, sir.'

'No problem. I'm actually quite relieved you're here. Have you heard about the utility medic type mage that died the other day?'

'I am aware.'

'Well, between you and me, I believe there's an insider, so I can't trust any of my escorts, you understand?'

'Yes, sir. I will do everything in my power to make sure I can fulfil my role to the best of my ability.'

'And I'm sure you will, Mr, er...' the village leader stuttered, racking his brain for a name.

'Lahel Bints,' Lahel prompted.

'Ah, yes. Mr Bints. Anyway, please guide us to the barracks.'

Lahel knocked on the floor three times before the ground gave way, revealing a set of stairs. He led the village leader down them, followed closely by the group of people that accompanied him. The sound of their multiple footsteps echoed all the way to the city, causing a small crowd to gather at the bottom of the staircase.

A woman pushed past Lahel, ushering the people away, using hardened spikes made up of her skin as a deterrent. She then raised her hand, beckoning everyone to continue. *Did they all have such tedious jobs?* Lahel wondered, looking back at the people that escorted the village leader.

Though the barracks were only a few hundred metres away, it felt like a chore to walk the distance as Lahel slowed down to match the leader's waddling speed. *How was he a high ranked mage with such low mobility?* Lahel questioned. Not sure as to why, Lahel decided to keep up the slow pace until he knew of the answer.

Upon arrival, Lahel showed a letter to the guard posted outside the barracks. He flicked through the letter and further documentation before nodding, turning to open a door completely made of stone and several metres tall. Despite the weight, the guard made opening the door look effortless, using just one hand to pull on the doorknob while using the other to shake hands with the VIPs.

Gusts of air hit Lahel as the spacious hallway bustled with animals and soldiers alike. The walls arched into a criss-cross at the top, allowing gaps for water to roll down, dripping into buckets for consumption.

Lahel also admired the tapestries and craftsmanship of the building, noting how the homes couldn't compare to the barracks. However, the village leader looked unimpressed, as if he'd seen better. Lahel couldn't help but feel a tinge of jealousy, understanding that the leader witnessed even greater works of architecture, but he hid his emotions well by handling more paperwork at the reception of the barracks. Picking up a metallic but rusty key, he handed it over to Mr Ching, who held it tightly in the palm of his hands.

'Shall we continue with the tour?' Lahel asked, turning to the village leader and his impatient entourage.

'Let's make the tour short. My time is precious, Mable,' Mr Ching ordered.

'Uh, it's Lahel,' Lahel attempted to correct.

'What?'

'Nothing.'

The village leader made a hand gesture, causing half of the group that accompanied him to disperse. The others joined Lahel and the leader on the tour of the barracks. Most of them came with an air of boredom, sighing or yawning as they went along. It didn't faze

Lahel, however, as his job was just to guide the village leader. He had no responsibility for the others.

During the tour, Lahel showed off several rooms, ranging from the stables, where the mages kept animals such as Lupims, to the storage rooms containing jugs of food and resources. Along each stage of the tour, one or two members broke off from the entourage, leaving half a dozen bodyguards at the end.

'The final stop is the bedrooms,' Lahel explained.

'Ah, ok. Then I'd like my privacy,' Larry Ching requested.

'We can't allow that,' a beefy bodyguard rejected, edging closer to the leader and turning to Lahel. 'We must go wherever he goes.'

'Even to the bedroom?' the leader scoffed without Lahel's input. 'Your rooms are nearby, so go get some rest. We'll have a busy day tomorrow.'

'Yes, sir.'

'I'll be accompanied by Rachel too, so no need to fret.'

'Lahel...' Lahel murmured.

'Fine. We'll rush over if anything happens,' the guard asserted.

'As expected of my subordinates,' the village leader praised.

After leaving the bodyguards behind, Lahel and the village leader made their way down a long corridor. They reached a door unique to the building. Instead of the automatic knocking system that riddled the barracks, this door required a lock which had to be opened by a key. Having received the key earlier, the village leader opened the door to a pitch-black room, breathing a sigh of exasperation.

'Not bad, Neal,' he lied. 'Spacious and clean enough.'

'You can see what's inside? You must have an amazing night vision, but I'm glad the room's to your liking, leader,' Lahel replied.

'I'd like to rest now,' the leader yawned. 'I've travelled several kilometres and am very tired.'

'Then I hope you rest well.'

The door closed. The leader turned around. A hand reached out to him, sending a shocking sensation through his body. His legs gave way. His eyes rolled. He couldn't see straight. He saw two people. Was he hallucinating? No, he knew someone else stood beside Lahel. He panicked. He opened his mouth. He aimed at random. He fired pressurised water from the gaping hole. He heard cries of pain – words he couldn't quite catch. He felt another shocking sensation. His mind went blank. His heartbeat stopped.

'You Idiot!'

'Calm down, man. I was just toying with him. No fun killing him straight away.'

'What is wrong with you?!'

'Chill, Jack. I killed him now and that's all we needed.'

'He's made so much noise just before he died, and you want me to 'chill'?'

'We're far away from anyone. No one is gonna hear.'

'You underestimate of some of those bestials, Esper.'

The pair heard the sound of footsteps. They had no time to hide the lifeless body of the village leader. The steps grew louder. The voices that accompanied them confirmed the destination: their leader's bedroom.

Jack cursed his luck.

'We can take them on, Jack,' Esper hesitated, clutching his arm. The pain from the pressurised beam of water that hit him caused him to wince.

'There are three thousand people in the building. Even if we manage to beat his bodyguards, we will not survive everyone else,' Jack replied.

'So, what? It's easy stuff.'

'We are not going to win!'

The pursuers grew ever closer. Jack had no time to talk with an idiot like Esper, who lived only for excitement. He steeled his resolve. With the mission complete, he decided to make sure both of them didn't need to die. He lowered his heartbeat and body temperature, matching the thirty degrees in the room, and entered into stealth. Esper's eyes widened as he realised his partner's intent.

'Hey, Jack.'

Jack didn't reply to his partner's call. Instead, he moved to the other side of the room, where the standing right beside the door. The sound of footsteps stopped. The voices turned into whispers. Time froze to the point that even a drop of sweat would refuse to fall.

Esper started to panic. He had no plan and he definitely didn't want to die. In a last ditched effort, he tried calling out again, eyes fixated on the location where he last saw his partner.

'Jack! Jack! Hey! Man, you gotta be kidding me.
Without me, you wouldn't be able to do anything.
This mission wouldn't have succeeded without me!
Stop staying silent! If you leave me here, I will make
sure you die with me! Jack, are you listening?!'

Jack heard everything. He made his mind up. He
couldn't save his partner, not with people right
outside the room.

The door burst open. A group of ten entered, all well-
built. In a one on one, Esper would struggle to win,
let alone against this many.

The guards had a look at the floor, where the village
leader laid, then at Esper who stayed static, petrified
by his bleak future. A white man with curly brown
hair, the same one that tried to stop the village leader
from leaving the bodyguards in the first place,
stepped forward.

'It seems like the leader was electrocuted,' the man
analysed. 'The guy over there must be a mage that
can use electricity. Kabal. Ren. Pin down the suspect.'

Two men, who looked exactly like one another, with
their albino skin, black eyes and crew-cut hair,
rushed at Esper. They floored him with ease,
strapping Esper's arms behind his back and mashed
his head against the floor.

In desperation, Esper sent out a wave of electricity
through the men holding him down. However, they
didn't even flinch, as if it had no effect on them. With
how helpless he felt combined with the hatred he
radiated towards the man who abandoned him,
something snapped in Esper's mind. He began
laughing a madman's laugh, mumbling gibberish in
between his fits.

'What do we do now, boss?' asked one of the men, still pinning Esper down.

'Poor guy's gone mad. Did he try doing anything to you, Kabal?' the boss asked

'He did try to electrocute me,' Kabal replied.

'Ren?'

'Same here,' added the other.

'Luckily I brought some Electricity resistant types with me,' the lead bodyguard lauded himself. 'But that confirms it. He must be the culprit. Kala, what's the status?'

A woman looked up. While Kabal and Ren pinned Esper down, she inspected the body. From her frowning face, everyone in the room knew the outcome. They looked down, mourning the loss of their leader. His death dealt a major blow to the upcoming battle.

Esper's laughter died down. However, he didn't shut up. He shouted at the guards who ignored him, all except the boss of the group.

'What did you say?' he asked Esper, crouching down to meet him face to face.

'You're all idiots!' Esper screamed.

'Sintal, why are you speaking with him? He's obviously crazy,' said Kala, referring to the leader of their group.

'Hush. I think he knows something,' Sintal replied before turning back to Esper, 'Why is that?'

'Did you really think I could kill him?!' Esper mocked, a grin on his face.

'All the evidence is there. I don't see who else it could. No, wait.'

Sintal's eyes darted around the room, looking for any more evidence. Failing to do so, he gritted his teeth,

'Boss?'

'Think about it. The leader was always with that guide. He was also the one who went with him to his room. I didn't see the guide leave though. On the other hand, I've never seen this guy before in the database. He couldn't have done this alone. Prayan, light a torch in this room,' Sintal ordered.

Jack darted for it, leaving the manic laughter of Esper behind him in his silent steps. Why was he such a fool? Did he really think he could save him? He bit his camouflaged lip to bring back his rationality. With all that time he lost, he knew the people in the building would be notified of his existence soon. Jack needed to come up with a plan.

With over two-thousand rooms, combining to stretch several kilometres long and wide, and with him being in the centre of the barracks, Jack couldn't escape in one go without losing his camouflage through fatigue. With the whole Egyptian army after him, a single breath or beat of the heart could alert the guards of his presence. His body demanded oxygen but, with the lowered heart rate and breaths per minute, he couldn't afford to last long distances.

Luckily, Jack knew the barracks' layout inside out, having to do so to play his role as a guide. Out of all the rooms in the building, he deemed one room as safe to hide in: the King's Room; a room found in every city of Africa, dedicated for the chance arrival of the King of AAA himself. No one dared enter the room out of fear for being punished by the smallest of reasons rather than anything else, making it the ideal place to take shelter.

Jack glided his way past those on patrol, listening in to some of the conversations. As he predicted, no one knew of the village leader's death from what Jack overheard, to avoid any panic to occur, but word of his disappearance circulated around the mages. However, knowledge of him being a stealth bestial type, or even his real name, hadn't been discovered yet. On high alert, the soldiers searched not for Jack Darius, but Lahel Bints, the man whose identity Jack had stolen. He could use that to his advantage.

Sticking to the dark corridors, Jack meandered towards the King's room. Where torches perched on the walls, Jack kept to the shadows, making sure his own shadow overlapped with them. Though his stealth allowed him to be unseen, a stray ray of light would reveal his location through the shadow it created.

At last, Jack reached an alley without a torch in sight. He placed his hand on the walls, rubbings against it as he walked down the path, catching weeds and insects that made him want to recoil in disgust. Though the dim lighting made the search difficult, he felt a line that ran vertical. He found the entrance to the hidden passageway.

Jack opened the sliding door, causing several plants to get knocked off the edges. He stared into the passageway he uncovered but he couldn't see anything. The black abyss waiting in front of him beckoned him to go forward, which he accepted without hesitation.

Having closed the entrance behind him, Jack dropped his stealth and breathed a deep breath. His body ached from the lack of oxygen in his body and he lied down, heart beating at a frantic pace. Although he could keep hold of his breathing and heartbeat for much longer, the symptoms that came after such a feat took a toll on his body. He remembered attempting it once before but fell unconscious for several days after that; a mistake to avoid this time.

Jack's breather let his mind to wander. He couldn't concentrate. He remembered the smiles of Maria as she handed him squadron W's first real mission in decades. He thought of how he prepared, planned and executed every single step, assuring the success of the assassination. He slammed his fist against the wall at why, despite how perfect his methods might be, he couldn't account for the chaotic nature of Esper which ultimately led to their demise.

'I miss squadron W. Maria, Humin, Tobi, Quintero, Rial, Obliin, Raphael, Tenage...' The list continued as Jack mumbled all their names to himself, reminiscing on how they accepted him into the squadron despite being an E ranked mage. '...Kyle, Kieran, Alder.'

The final name snapped Jack back into reality, noticing the surroundings for the first time since he entered. He couldn't see anything nor could he hear anything. Just black silence. At first, the silence soothed him, indicating that no pursuer caught onto his location but, as time went on, the quiet corridor soon became a curse.

Jack started to hear the meticulous thumping of his heart followed by the pumping of blood through his veins. His lungs made an almighty racket, his bones creaked under minimal pressure and a buzzing sound in his ears all unnerved Jack. How long had stayed floating between the planes of consciousness and unconsciousness? A minute? An hour? A day? Jack couldn't think straight. He had to get out.

Jack made his way through the passageway, slapping the walls at irregular intervals to keep his sanity. He tried to forget about each factor that went wrong but all he could think of was the series of events that led to his predicament. Maybe Jack should have planned things out more. He should have predicted the possibility of something going wrong. He should have figured out more escape routes. Yet, why didn't he? Did something deep down inside him tell him that Esper would do as he was told without a hitch? Jack cursed his ineptitude. He deserved to be a low ranked mage – a failure of the Eurasian MBP.

Caught in his train of thought, Jack crashed into a wall opposite him. He stammered backwards, getting a sense of the world around him once again. He shook his head and pushed the wall. After some effort, the door began to push forward. Rays of light graced Jack, bringing a sense of joy to him. He clambered up some stairs to the source of that light. He opened up another door above him and turning the rays into bursts of light, blinding Jack in that very moment. Rubbing the initial daze away, Jack regained his vision and climbed his way out of the darkness.

A lavish room awaited him, with floors and walls made of marble shiny enough to see your reflection in them, all carved to perfection. A king-sized bed with the softest mattress Jack had ever seen seduced him. He stumbled towards it, falling headfirst into the covers, allowing a wave of exhaustion to overcome him, making him fall into a deep sleep.

****

Jack opened his eyes. A gentle illumination welcomed him, unlike the burning sensation he felt earlier on. As he laid on the bed, he took a moment before realising the source of the light. A huge shaft above the bed let the stars and moon to shine into the King's Room, mesmerising Jack.

'Nighttime already?' he noted. 'What happened to the pursuers?'

A rumbling stomach prompted Jack to look for food instead of answers. He got up, searching the room for anything to munch on. As luck would have it, Jack found some fruits placed above on a sink on one end of the room. He removed the moulded half, chewing on the fresh side.

With his hunger sated, he made looking for water his next task. However, before he did so, A tinoo fluttered into the room via the shaft. It nestled beside the eating Jack, cooing in delight. Jack caressed the bird's feathers, enjoying the company. For once, a living being he could trust!

'You're Syndra's tinoo, aren't you?' Jack asked, getting an affirmative squawk in response. 'I see. Any chance you see water? I need to regain my energy if I want to get out of this place.'

The bird nodded, raising its wings towards a stone bowl he had never seen before. Attached to the wall, the bowl stood on a pillar with no apparent purpose. Not only that, on top of the bowl, a weird metallic tube, that arched downwards, stuck out with knobs attached to either side.

'That thing? Really? Huh, might as well try it out.'

Jack moved towards the bowl, turning his head around the contraption, figuring out whether how on Earth it produced water. He tapped on the tube then the knobs, waiting for something to happen, but just a single drop of water fell instead.

'That it?' Jack said, turning to the bird.

Even though the tinoo couldn't speak, Jack knew
what its face tried to convey. *Are you kidding me?* he
heard loud and clear. It then flew towards the tube,
placing its claw on one of the knobs and turning it. A
stream of water gushed from the tube, falling into
the bowl and through a hole in the bottom.

'Wow. The AAA's king sure is spoilt. We'd have to
walk more than a kilometre to get out water and he
gets his just like that! Where did you learn about this
thingy anyway?' Jack said for a lack of a word to
describe the bowl, tube and knob mechanism.

A lack of response from his animal companion
prompted Jack to gulp down the water, gasping in
relief after each handful. He splashed some more
water over his face, closing the knob when finished.
With that done, he slapped himself awake, realising
the gravity of the situation he was in.

'Thanks for the help. Tell Syndra that I'll leave
tonight. If I'm not out within three days, assume I'm
dead. Leave ASAP if that happens. She's in as much
danger as I am.'

The bird cawed in agreement, flying off through the
shaft again, away to its master. Though brief in the
time he spent with the tinoo, Jack gained new hope
through it. He lost his partner but not his life. Now
he had to make sure he didn't lose that either.

Drying his face off with his arm, Jack looked for
misplaced objects and furniture. From his knowledge,
two more hidden passageways connected with the
King's Room. Jack couldn't use the one he came out
of, lest he feared people waited outside the entrance.

A box caught Jack's eyes. Like the bowl earlier on, he
had never seen such a thing. A black stiff material,
that made an echo when flicked, surrounded a glass
plane, which slotted parallel to the walls. Jack peered

into the glass but all he saw was greyish darkness – not quite pitch black as he could see his reflection.

On top of the box rested a stick with buttons attached to it, each with a symbol he couldn't recognise. Did that open up a secret passageway? Only one way to find out. A big red button on the stick drew Jack's attention in particular. He pondered whether to press it or not, settling on his initial gut feeling but a thumping in his head told him otherwise. Perhaps his mental fatigue still plagued him. How long was he out for again? He clutched his head, shaking off any remaining drowsiness.

To calm his nerves, Jack imagined the praise he would get from colonel for his success to the point he could feel her gentle touch on his head, making his body lighter. However, in his daydreaming, his knees buckled causing him to fall forwards. Unable to react in time, Jack failed to cushion the impact. His chest collided with the side of the box, winding him in the process. His eyes looked up towards the glass in befuddlement, gazing into the reflection, head throbbing in pain.

He saw spiky hair.

'Found you.'

11

The Mentality of the Mages

Gin created a mental picture while looking at his gauntlets. A small branch grew out of the Xernim gauntlets. It wrapped its way around the INS, entering the first chamber before hovering just above the button at the bottom. So far, so good.

Blades, Gin said in his mind. The branch continued growing, pressing the button. The mechanism activated and the blade formed itself in an instant. The silver shininess of the blade contrasted heavily with the darkness of the gauntlets' wood. Despite the contrast, it had its own beauty that Gin couldn't help but admire.

Once more Gin said the word "blades" in his mind and the branch degraded back to its original position, just above the button. The INS mechanism deactivated, causing the blade to disappear into thin air. Having decided that the experiment succeeded, Gin grew more branches that wrapped around and entered the INS.

'Whoa, that's pretty cool.'

'I'm not sure. It's putting a large burden on him. I might need to make our appointments daily from now on.'

Gin turned his head. He found Joan and Wo looking (and speaking behind his back), both with keen gazes at what he was doing. As usual, Gin never invited them but that didn't stop them from coming, especially when the colonel, for whatever reason, gave them a spare key to his room each.

'Why are you two even here?' Gin asked.

'When you decided to host a Xernim, I decided to have more frequent appointments,' Joan responded.

'Same here, Gigi,' Wo added.

'You're not even his medic!' Joan exclaimed

'But I am his very, very, VERY good childhood friend.'

'Don't listen to him, Joan. He's been torturing me ever since I was born,' Gin said.

'You can't really call those things "torture",' Wo replied.

'Oh, really? Are you saying that almost letting me drown in a lake and telling my friends and relatives that I was "learning to swim" not torture?'

'Nah,' Wo shrugged. 'That was an educational experience. You managed to swim in the end, so it was worth it.'

'What about that time when you left me on top of the roof of the town hall for a whole day?' Gin continued.

'It was to allow you to experience nature in all its beauty. The night sky is a wonderful sight, Gigi.'

'And the nickname "Gigi" that annoys me to this very day?'

'Hehe. Gets you every time.'

'Ugh. Why are you like this? Just leave already.'

'Oh, come on. Don't be so mad. No need for me to go, right Joan?' Wo said turning to Joan who just gave him a look of disgust in response.

'You are a horrible person, Wo,' Joan said. 'I'm with Gin here. You should leave. I need to do his checkups anyway,' she said.

'Not you too,' Wo whined, giving them both puppy eyes.

'Leave!' Joan and Gin snapped in unison.

'Alright. Alright. I'm outta here.'

With Wo closing the door behind him, Joan began preparing for the examination. She picked up the relevant medicines, pouring a few onto her fingers and absorbed them into the nails, ready for use. She pierced Gin's arm, extracting a blood sample while injecting the medicine into his veins.

'Huh. From the samples I got, everything is normal apart from your protein levels which are lower than average. Are you eating your rations?' Joan asked, piercing her nails through Gin's skin and injecting the vaccines.

'Everything apart from the meat,' Gin responded.

'What? Why?'

'It comes from mages. Goes against my morals.'

'Not this again,' Joan sighed. 'So? Those mages shed their skin for everyone to eat. It's a very good source of protein and other essentials.'

'I guess I'm the only one who sees a problem with eating human flesh.'

'It's what they're bred to do! Their whole life's purpose is to feed the rest of us. They don't even die in the process and are willing to do it as well. Keeping humanity alive is a noble cause so, of course, there's no problem with eating mage meat.'

'But still –'

'But nothing! Don't you understand how dangerous it is to be deficient in any substance, especially after you took on a Xernim? I'm making you eat it whether you like it or not. This is for your sake, Gin.'

'Can't, Joan. I need to meet Alder soon, so I got no time,' Gin explained, giving an innocent tilt of the head. 'I also gave all my meat rations to Wo.'

'Then I'll just have to give you some of my own,' Joan replied with a mischievous grin. 'Oh, and I'm making sure you can't escape.'

Gin felt a thin spike lodge into his lower back. His body froze up, refusing to move. His eyes shifted towards Joan who grabbed hold of Gin, positioning him onto his chair so that he couldn't fall. With a final pat on the shoulders, she left Gin alone to wait for her return.

Gin tried to see if he could move anything or if Joan had paralyzed him completely. Working from the ground up, he found out that his toes, fingers and eyes moved with ease but the rest of his body didn't budge. Gin couldn't do anything but wait and be at the mercy of Joan. The thought made him shudder (mentally rather than physically as his body wouldn't allow movement).

Then an epiphany struck Gin. Though a bit of a stretch, he knew he could make it work.

Gin took a deep breath and concentrated. He thought about the Xernim creating another branch. As he imagined, a branch sprouted out of the Xernim, wriggling its way around the side of Gin's body and reaching the back. It worked its way up before snagging against an object sticking out of his back. Gin thought of the branch now wrapping around the object. Just touching that spike brought intense pain.

One. Two. Three, he counted to himself, pulling the spike out on three. Gin bit his tongue, avoiding an outburst by fighting pain with more pain. The spike came out at last and, with a single thought, the branch degraded, rotten bits of wood falling to the floor.

A few stretches later, Gin moved to his heart's content. He inspected the blood-tipped spike which, to Gin's amusement, turned out to be one of Joan's nails. *Was she always able to use her nails like that or did she come up with it just to subdue me?* Gin wondered. If it turned out to be the latter, she was more persistent than he thought, much to Gin's annoyance.

Before Joan came back, Gin concluded that he should go see Alder. They weren't meant to see each other for another hour but Gin wasn't going to stay in his room and be forced to be a cannibal. *Since when did it become morally acceptable to eat the meat of your own species?* Gin questioned. However, if Joan didn't find it strange, the other mages wouldn't either and might try to make him eat it too, so Gin decided to keep that question to himself for the time being.

Along the way, he saw a group of mages being guided by a skinny woman riding a behemoth of a lupim, a canine covered in brown and black fur with its tongue sticking out, panting for air. *A utility familiar type,* Gin classed, wondering how the ranking system worked for those with animal compatriots.

With the squadron getting busier, ever since the announcement of their first battle, Gin found it refreshing to see the hustle and bustle within the corridors, compared to the emptiness of before. It reminded Gin of the marketplaces of his (now ruined) village, a time of ignorance and tranquillity.

Categorising all the mages he saw along the way, when Gin arrived at the usual training room, he found Alder speaking with a ginger man with rough dark skin and a beefy build that glistened under the torchlight. *Another fire elemental?* Gin guessed.

'Ah! Brat, we were just talking about you,' Alder called out.

'You were?' Gin queried.

'You're a bit early but I planned on introducing you two,' Alder said.

'I'm Brim Stones. Nice to meet you,' the man greeted, extending a hand.

'Likewise. My name is Gin Julius Gale,' he replied, shaking Brim's hand. 'So, what's with the sudden introduction?'

'I was going to explain to you when we were meant to meet up but I'll tell you now. Brim, mind letting us talk for a moment?' Alder requested.

'Sure,' Brim replied, stepping aside.

'Essentially, I am going to retire,' Alder said.

'You can retire?' Gin questioned.

'Yes. The MBP has contacted me asking me to be used to pass on my genetics to the next generation. I've rejected them in the past but I've now grown too old for them to accept my refusal. My two-hundredth birthday is next month.'

'Two-hundredth?!'

'Yes. Is something wrong with that age?'

Yes, for a manush whose average lifespan is ninety, Gin thought.

'No, you just look younger than that,' Gin lied.

'Haha. Thanks for the compliment, brat. But as I am about to retire, I will need someone to take over the battalion.'

'And so, you brought Brim over to be the next battalion leader?'

'No. He's transferred to take over another battalion. As for my battalion, I've decided that duty will be placed on you.'

'Thought so.'

'Not surprised, brat?'

Gin kept his surprise to himself. He would have lied if he said he didn't feel that. After all, what person in their right mind would give a position of power to an inexperienced nobody who came out of nowhere after a few months of meeting them? The decision felt complacent, poorly thought out and just plain reckless. Then again with how unprofessional everything seemed to be, from the initiation test to the lax nature of the colonel's battle announcement, he didn't even know what to expect anymore.

'It was kind of obvious,' Gin decided to play along in the end. 'When you took me out of training sessions with the others and only allowed me to observe and memorise the formations, despite me being one of the better combatants, I knew something was off. Along with the changes going on in the squadron due to the upcoming battle, it fell into place.'

'That astute observation of yours will take you far.'

'Oh, a compliment. Don't get those too often,' Gin snarked, glad Alder fell for it.

'But that attitude will not,' Alder corrected himself.

'You two have quite the relationship,' Brim noted, unable to help eavesdrop on the conversation. 'What do you even want me to do?'

'I'm presuming you're taking over the training that I normally have with Alder?' Gin replied.

'He's correct,' Alder acknowledged. 'I wanted you to train him, Brim. Oh, Brim's a fire elemental that specialises in flame boxing which is very similar to blade boxing, which is why I brought him to Squadron W, brat. The only difference is that you do piercing damage while he does damage over time.'

'Makes sense,' Gin agreed.

'Wait. What rank and type are you?' Brim asked.

'Let's say I'm on the level of most rank Fs,' Gin answered, assuming his knowledge on the mages' ranking system was correct. 'I'd prefer not to say my typing.'

'Don't worry Brim. The brat can't fight by himself so he uses those metal things and now the Xernim. He's stronger than his rank suggests,' Alder added.

'Are you sure about this, Alder?' Brim responded, disbelief in his voice. Gin could tell why and so did Alder.

'Yes. For today, just watch Gin. I need to speak with Maria about handing over leadership. It's exercise session three, so you know what to do, brat,' Alder ordered, his words hinting at another task which Gin caught upon.

'Understood,' Gin obeyed.

'Then I'll let you two be,' Alder said, leaving the room.

'I don't understand why he always has a soft spot for low ranks like you,' Brim muttered to himself, loud enough for Gin to hear.

'Neither do I,' Gin replied. 'That still doesn't stop me from trying to improve under him.'

'Improve? You? You couldn't achieve a high rank in the MBP when you were still a child with unlimited potential. What hope do you have as an adult that hasn't achieved anything except being a burden to Eurasia?'

'Let's just do as Alder ordered. I'll do my normal training session while you watch me, okay?'

Brim didn't respond, instead giving Gin a scornful glare before walking towards the edge of the marsh room. Gin smirked in response, fire lighting up inside of him with a resolve to show off his worth to the man who looked down on him.

Gin walked up to the nearest tree, keeping an arms-length distance between him and the plant. He took up the stance drilled into him since the day he took the Xernim on, concentrating on the positioning of his arms and feet.

Blades. Shields.

Branches hovering above all four of Gin's INS activated the mechanism, creating a shield and blade on each arm. He took a step to the side, then sent out a jab followed by a cross, repeating the manoeuvre in multiples of twos until he felt no friction between the tree and his blade.

'Damn,' Gin sighed, 'not clean enough.'

He wanted to create a thin line, in the shape of the cross-section of his blade, not the hole that could fit a fist in it. At least his punches didn't get stuck like when he first started off, but he still needed to improve his technique. *I go again,* Gin stoked himself up.

Gin continued honing his technique for the next hour, taking a break every ten minutes and using up several trees in the process, until Brim had enough. He walked up to Gin, tapping him on his shoulder.

'You need something?' Gin asked, putting down his arms and shaking off the sweat on his forehead.

'Why do you do this?' Brim replied.

'Do what?'

'All of this training.'

'Is there something wrong with my training?'

'No one does it. This is the first time I've seen a squadron where everyone trains.'

The world was in a war, right? Surely the mages would want to improve themselves to increase their battle proficiency, Gin thought, perplexed by the notion Brim suggested.

'If the other squadrons don't train, what do you do?' Gin asked.

'Eat, sleep and wait for orders to go to war,' Brim said, no hint of dishonesty in his tone.

'I see. Well, we train to improve our abilities,' Gin explained, sitting down on the watery floor, using the marsh to cool off.

'You can do that?'

'What do you mean? Of course. Did you think that's impossible?'

'The adult body can't develop anymore and only deteriorates afterwards. We are all trained and developed during puberty. Those who couldn't keep up died in the process and those who could were ranked based on their skill. What's the point of training more if your body can't develop further?'

'I see why you think the way you do,' Gin looked down, getting into a train of thought.

From the way Brim phrased it, the MPB sounded like they brainwashed the children, built them up and trained them from birth stopping at adulthood. *The mages sure are an interesting bunch,* Gin thought to himself, formulating theories on how their society came to be. *Is this why they eat the meat of other mages?*

'However, it's not true what they say in the MBP,' Gin continued, 'because you can improve yourself even as an adult. Yeah, sure you don't have that growth or energy you did when you're younger but you can get valuable experience. They reside in your subconsciousness and help you when you need it. But you need to make those experiences happen in order to use them. Sometimes what we're taught by society could be wrong.'

'I don't believe you,' Brim gave an immediate reply.

'Thought as much. You've spent eighty years in the MBP being told otherwise. How about we spar and see if that'll help you trust me.'

'Spar?'

'Just pretend I'm an enemy.'

'I'm not sure why I have to.'

'That's the whole point. I want to expel your doubts.'

Reluctant, Brim agreed and they both distanced themselves by ten metres. Gin activated his blades again while Brim coated his arms with a greasy fluid he excreted from his skin that made him shine under the light of the torches. With a flick of his fingers, his arms went into a yellow-orange blaze.

'Ready?' Gin asked.

'Ready,' Brim confirmed.

Brim made the first move, charging at Gin before sending a low punch aimed at Gin's stomach. Gin sidestepped the punch and sent a jab of his own but Brim pushed the arm to the side with his forearm. Gin jumped back into his stance and looked for an opening.

Brim hurled a flurry at punches at frightening speed. There was no time to think. Gin dodged everything to perfection through instinct alone. However, Gin couldn't counter. Brim's body position didn't allow for it while deflecting any punches Gin managed to throw out.

Gin backed off, regaining his composure. His face and body began to hurt. *Why?* He had been dodging every attack. Then it dawned on him what Alder meant by Brim having damage over time. As Gin watched another one of Brim's punches brush past him, he felt the flames burn into his skin. He had to end this quickly or he would lose.

Gin sent a right hook in a desperate attempt but Brim deflected the attack, using it as an opening, smashing Gin in the ribs and sending him to the ground. Gin looked unconscious with his back on the ground. That's that. It cemented Brim's thoughts that training proved useless.

'See? There's a reason why the low-ranked are low-ranked,' Brim mocked in triumph.

'Nice fight,' Gin complimented, picking himself up and into a squatting position. 'Didn't realise how you worked at first but I got a good grasp now. Ready for another round?'

'What? Another?'

'I got stamina for days. Also, your punch didn't deal too much damage. I got Michal's stone vest to absorb most of the impact,' Gin explained, pointing towards a hole in his shirt caused by Brim's flames, revealing the armour.

'You're just asking to lose again.'

'That was never my intention. Ready?'

'Yeah.'

'So am I.'

Gin hurled mud at Brim. Brim's reflexes made him deflect the mud and try to get back into his stance but it was too late. Gin already had a blade at Brim's throat. Brim raised his arms above his head. It was Gin's victory in an instant.

'That was a disgusting move you played!' Brim exclaimed.

'I don't have honour. I got into this squadron by hiding in a shell for a few minutes. Using a distraction is nothing for me. Victory is what counts,' Gin replied, lowering his blade. 'That makes us even, no?'

'I guess it does,' Brim chuckled. 'I still don't get your point from earlier, though. Why did we need to spar?'

'During that fight, I realised that you always deflect attacks rather than dodge. So, I took you by surprise, sent some mud from the floor and as you deflect it, created an opening. I can't beat you in a drawn-out match but this faster approach got me a swift victory.'

'You figured that out just through training?' Brim wondered, slumping against a tree, his mind opening up to Gin.

'Not quite. Through training, I have learnt how to block, how to attack and how to dodge. But coming up with a tactic to beat you was done during the fight itself. But thanks to that spar, I've learnt another way mages could fight, with its strengths and weaknesses. You have my gratitude.'

Gin saw Brim's puzzled look. He sighed, realising that changing a person's belief took much more effort than a simple spar. In the end, he decided to rephrase things.

'Look. The point is that if I never took the steps and never took any action, I would never have learnt how to deal with potential problems until it is too late. What if I face another flame boxer on the battlefield? Now, because of our spar, I have found out that style of fighting's strength and weaknesses, so I'm better prepared for next time. Understand now?'

'Kind of. Still don't believe you though.'

'Fair enough,' Gin shrugged. 'Hopefully, I can change that eventually.'

'We'll see. To be honest, you're very profound, Gin. It's different from what I've heard of you.'

'Let me guess. I've been depicted as an arrogant, impatient brat by Alder, right?'

Brim burst out in laughter. It was an infectious laugh that led to Gin joining in too. They had a mutual understanding and both looked forward to working with one another. However, a shout across the room cut their moment short.

'Gin!'

'Who's that?' Brim whispered to Gin, nodding towards a woman by the doorway.

'Just a crazy stalker of mine,' Gin replied.

'I go through all this trouble preparing your food and, when I come back to your room, you're not even there!'

'See? She's even going to my room without permission,' Gin said.

'I heard that!' Joan shouted as she stormed towards them.

Steam seeped out of some meat, covered by seasonings and fruit, all inside a box Joan carried. The brownness of the roasted meat combined with the juice, dripping from the sliced fruits, made Gin salivate but the thought of that meat coming from the flesh of mages also made him want to vomit. Despite the fact his body was telling him to eat, Gin decided to follow his morality.

'Ah! Sorry, Joan. I have to go. No time to eat!' Gin excused himself.

'Gin!' Joan scolded.

Gin made a dash for the exit. If he stayed, Joan would have made him eat it. He turned around waving goodbye at Brim and Joan. Brim waved back while Joan just gave an unimpressed expression. *Doesn't matter*, Gin thought. *No way am going to be forced to be a cannibal.*

But as Gin reached the door, he bumped into an unimpressed Alder, cutting his intentions short. Next to him stood the colonel while Wo watched from behind both of them, grinning the grin Gin hated the most.

'Sorry, Alder. Can you let me through?' Gin asked.

'We heard that you don't eat your meat rations, child,' the colonel said. 'As the next battalion leader, we can't have you malnourished.'

'I have my reasons,' Gin reasoned.

'Well, hurry up. I need to go through some admin work with you if that's alright.'

Alder took control, grabbing Gin by the arm and pinning him to the ground. With his hands locked into place and his legs held down by Alder's knees, Gin had no chance of getting out.

'Your warped morality isn't a good enough reason, brat. Your health comes first,' Alder said.

'Wo! Help me out here!' Gin shouted in desperation.

Wo didn't say anything. He didn't do anything. He just stood there, grinning his face off, enjoying the spectacle. Of course!

'Brim! Help me!' Gin called out.

Joan explained the situation to Brim. He thought about it for a moment before agreeing to help. Joan already had prepared the wooden cutlery, as if she knew the outcome and, without mercy, the pair made their way to force feed Gin.

'No! Don't do this, Brim. I thought we've established a beautiful friendship!'

'You are severely lacking in protein, Gin. If you're not allergic and it's just a problem of morality, then it should be fine,' Brim said. 'Not sure why the MBP would tell you it wasn't right to eat the meat. They haven't told the rest of us. You sure you're not in the wrong?'

Him being wrong? It was true that the mages involved do it voluntarily and they were treated well. It was also true that the mages who provide the meat were bred for this exact purpose. They don't even need to be slaughtered! But eating mage meat was still wrong, right? Cannibalism was still wrong, right? It didn't matter in the end, though.

As Joan force fed Gin what she had prepared, one thought came to Gin's mind: mage meat tasted like veal.

12

Successor

After another sparring session, Gin made his way to the desert room. He rubbed lotion, courtesy of a peeved Joan, on his burn marks and let the medicine soak into his skin, creating a soothing sensation like a cool wind blowing over your body after a hot summer's day. Gin savoured the moment, especially after witnessing the disgruntled look of his sparring partner.

'What's the score again?' Gin taunted.

'Three of those matches didn't count. You cheated,' Brim scowled.

'Funny way of saying five-three to me.'

'You're lucky I ran out of fuel.'

'Stalling you out was another strategy of mine.'

'Just because you have a freakishly large amount of stamina, doesn't mean you managed to beat me, especially since you still needed to use those underhanded tactics of yours.'

'Can't you admit that I outplayed you?' Gin suggested, grabbing his partner's shoulders and giving an all-infuriating smirk.

'No,' Brim denied.

Gin shook his head in disapproval as the pair walked past the battalion training room, stopping as something caught his eye. Per usual, Alder stood in front of everyone, giving out orders. However, this time the focus wasn't on him but on low-lying tinoos that glided over the sand, going around in circles, flying at the same speed as each other, making sure no two birds collided. As soon as a mage whistled, the formation changed into a Reuleaux triangle, a triangle with rounded vertices. The battalion responded, shuffling into a pincer formation with the melee combatants in front of the medium-ranged mages.

A higher pitched whistle echoed across the room. The tinoos reversed the directions of their flight, but a rogue bird didn't understand the command, crashing into the others, feathers scattering in the air.

'Why so slow?!' Alder barked, overlooking the mishap. 'Move it!'

The battalion switched positions, with the melees behind the mid-ranged, making sure the procedure went as smooth as possible. They huffed and puffed, tired from the new exercise which tested them both mentally and physically.

'Huh. They're better than I expected,' Brim acknowledged.

'They could still be better,' Gin pointed out. 'They can beat low C ranked mages and probably could handle B ranks in the future with a few more alterations to their training.'

'What, really? Most of these mages are ranked E or below. I don't see how B ranked mages would lose to some three tiers lower than them.'

'Didn't you lose to me, somebody on the level of an F rank?' Gin smirked again.

'Shut up,' Brim scowled again.

'Heh. No need to be so salty. Care for a rematch?' Gin asked with a mischievous smile.

'Later. I need to replenish my oil reserves,' Brim replied, returning the smile as he parted ways while Gin remained to watch the training.

'Alright. Take care.'

Gin turned his attention back to the training. At first, he didn't understand the use of the tinoos but, as the training went on, he noticed how the birds' movements correlated with the battalion's formation. With each unique flight pattern, he linked them to the corresponding formation until he could predict how everyone would react at a moment's notice. *What a convoluted way to give out hidden orders*, Gin thought.

'That's it, everyone. Well done!' Alder praised. 'Relax now, I got something to announce.'

Most of the leaner mages flopped to the floor, exhaustion getting the better of them, while some mages placed all their weight on their legs, kneeling due to their roundness. They shuffled into a semicircle with Alder standing in the centre.

'We've done formation training,' Alder continued. 'I talked about battle tactics. I've assessed your best positions and will continue to improve you. I've been doing that for the past year or so anyway.'

Alder held out a finger. He concentrated, allowing a branch to grow out, creating a long stick. Breaking it off, he planted the stick into the sand, drawing lines and writing the words "Formations", "Tactics" and "General Training".

'However, as you all know, I'll be leaving the squadron in a few months. In that time, I plan on getting everyone up to scratch on what you were never taught by the MBP due to your low-ranked status. But that means I need to appoint someone to take over in my absence. Originally, I had planned on

Jack Darius to succeed me, but that looks more unlikely by the day. Although he has bought us time – several months in fact – I cannot wait for him.'

Alder took a deep, long breath, then sat down on the sand, cross-legged. He placed his arms on his bent knees and puffed out his chest, giving him an air of authority and humbleness, a combination that didn't mix together except on this occasion.

'Therefore, I will pin my aspirations on Gin Gale instead. He's improved leaps and bounds over the past few months with me and he doesn't look down on any of you. He's even beaten me a couple times too, so his strength is real. I'm sure he'll be a worthy replacement. Any objections?'

Not even a single squeak from the mages.

'Good. Then go greet and show your respect to Gin when you see him next time, ok?'

'Um, he's right over there,' a bestial type pointed to a grinning Gin leaning against the entrance.

'The brat's here?' Alder swivelled on his spot, jumped up and strolled over to Gin, his expression hidden under his mask. 'How long have you been there?'

'I got interested in the training so I watched. Nothing wrong with that. And what's up with you calling me brat when I'm here but my real name when I'm not?' Gin sneered.

'Aha. Got me there. Good timing though. I wanted to talk to you in private,' Alder admitted, turning back to the battalion. 'Everyone's dismissed. Like I said, go show your respect to your future battalion leader.'

The mages nodded, getting up from their seats. As they exited, they either bowed to Gin or patted him on his shoulder, leaving stray hair, water, what seemed to be mucus and other excess material from the mages' various traits.

'I am never cleaning this shirt again,' Gin murmured as the last of the mages left the room.

'What?' Alder queried.

'So much research material for my notes. Can't let that go to waste, right?'

'I see,' Alder processed, unsure to be weirded out or accept that Gin acted like this from time to time. 'I've noticed you've taken Michal out of training, not that he participated in the first place. He's working with you on something, right?'

'Oh, that's what you wanted to find out,' Gin repeated, taking a stroll over the desert room with Alder. 'When he's not doing anything productive, I guess I thought "might as well think of something for him to do". He's been a great help, so I don't regret it.'

'You're talking about that armour chest plate you've hidden under your shirt?'

'Ah, you've noticed, huh? Well, yeah. If I'm going to be the next battalion leader, I want to do things my way. Michal's and a few other stone elementals are part of my plan.'

'Are you planning on getting armour for everyone?' Alder asked, stopping in his tracks.

'Hm? Yep. Got a problem with that?' Gin stopped as well, looking over his shoulders.

'No. But the others might. Though they are low-ranked, they probably don't want to be even more belittled for relying on such things.'

'What a stupid reason!'

'I know,' Alder sighed, stopping for a moment before leaning in and whispered, 'Do you know how many people accepted my proposal to take on the Xernim?'

'No,' Gin replied, eyebrow raised.

'Just you.'

'And how many did you offer them to?'

'All of my battalion and many more.'

'Wow. The Xernims are awesome. No obvious side effects and I haven't dropped my blades once unlike when I just wielded a sword and shield, so I can concentrate on actual skill rather than a mismatch of strength. How could they reject you like that?'

'It's not their fault,' Alder retreated back to his original position. 'It's just how everyone was brought up in the MBP. They wouldn't want something so passive. I mean, I thought the same until I witnessed how effective defence was, saving me time and time and time again because of it.'

Alder's Xernims began to decompose, starting at his feet and head then working towards his hip. The rotten bark of the parasite fell, heaping into a brown sludge on the floor. The decay stopped until Alder stood naked, bar the Xernim remaining on his pelvis, like shorts that ran halfway along his thigh.

Gin's eyes widened. He didn't know how to describe it. He didn't know what to say.

A stub took the place of Alder's right arm. However, that didn't compare to the left which drooped under its own weight, muscles ebbing in plain sight beneath missing skin, consumed by maggots that no longer existed. Acid marks seared into the flesh, revealing half-eaten bone supplemented by miniature Xernims holding everything together.

Holes riddled Alder's body with thin vines coming out of them, connecting to the Xernim on his hip. Chemical burns patterned Alder's torso except for the ashen marks that surrounded his chest and neck. The membrane around his heart pulsated with each beat, almost falling off like a tattered zombie. Compared to the rest of his body, the forked electricity on his legs looked normal.

'Az ou can shee, I an in a ery itiful sake,' Alder attempted at speech.

Confused at first, Gin realised why Alder spoke this way. His jaw was completely dislocated, hanging on thin strands of tissue, unable to move on its own. *What did Alder go through to get to this point?* Gin wondered.

'I an eek, sho I ee-aye on aye er-in, rat,' Alder continued, his jaw swaying from side to side.

'What are you saying? You're incredible!' Gin responded, somehow understanding the gibberish Alder said and complimenting him in return. 'Weak? As if! You gave up your ideals in order to survive. How can I mock you for that? And to think this is what the Xernims are capable of. Wonder how I can use this for myself!'

'Heh.'

Alder's Xernim branched out from his hip and the vines on his chest. They spread out, first to his face, wrapping around the broken jaw, creating a delicate veil over his mouth. More branches pierced the bone, making cracking noises as they did so.

'I'm glad,' Alder said, the Xernim moving his disjointed jaw for him. 'I doubt anybody else would react as excited as you. Disgust, pity and scorn come to mind.'

'Maybe everyone would actually listen if you did show them this side of you,' Gin suggested.

'Who knows? They're too afraid of wearing a piece of cloth lest others think negatively of them. Would seeing their leader half-broken change that?'

'Haha. Probably not. I *do* have some ideas for them to see an immediate impact.'

'Is that so? I don't regret choosing you as my successor then.'

'In my opinion, I think the transfer's too quick,' Gin confessed, watching the Xernim now growing around Alder's stub, forming the beginnings of a new arm. 'I've been in the squadron for half a year, I don't really have a purpose or objective being here, I've pretty much done nothing the entire time and yet I still get chosen.'

'Some people have the quality and mentality that can't be taught. I believe you are one of them. As for a purpose, why not do it for the sake of the squadron? I know it sounds simple, but at least it'll give you some motivation.'

'Motivation, huh?' Gin pondered, unconvinced by the random praise.

'Just think about it,' Alder concluded, concentrating on the wooden hand that began to grow. 'Or Do you want me to rescind the decision to make you the next leader?'

'Nope,' Gin gave a quick and honest reply.

'Good. I'm still here for three or four months, so I'll make sure to have you ready by then.'

'Fine by me. Oh, that reminds me, who is this Jack Darius? You said he was meant to be the leader before me.'

'Jack? He was part of an assassination mission. He succeeded, buying us a lot of time, but there's a suspicion that he's been captured. He's squadron W's poster boy; a low-ranked mage that somehow developed the abilities of a mid-ranked one in his adult years. Very bright too; always planning things out in advance.'

'I see,' Gin said, contemplating on the information he had been given. 'Sounds like someone I'd like to meet. Shame he's probably dead.'

'I have a feeling he's not executed yet.'

'Really? I wonder what happened to him then.'

'Me too,' Alder agreed, testing out his new arm.

13

Prisoner

The ship swayed from side to side, the waves crashed into the wooden hull of the vessel and the rain pattered on top of the deck. The wind roared the boat forwards while the sun's light failed to pierce the storm clouds, let alone the ship, leaving the captives below in complete darkness.

Having woken up a while ago, Jack fumbled around in the murkiness. Straw covered the floor beneath him and a low-lying ceiling stood above, preventing him from standing up without banging his head against the metal. As he reached out, he noticed the several cold bars that surrounded him with gaps too small to escape through.

With the constant churning in his stomach causing him to curse his seasickness, Jack knew he resided in a ship. *Why did I have to have such a ridiculous condition? More importantly, just where am I being taken?* Jack thought, attempting to keep sane. The growls and brays of animals that filled the room didn't give any hints, nor did the moans, screams and manic laughter of the other human beings. But they at least provided a sanctuary for his mental health.

Jack decided to investigate further, checking out the dimensions of the cage he squatted in. He felt something wet trickle beneath him, recoiling in an instant to the back of the cage as, combined with the putrid smell that emanated from that spot, he was sure it wasn't anything sanitary.

'Ugh. Another one? Damned Eurasian scum,' a voice said from above.

Jack heard the footsteps from behind him. It grew louder and louder until it stopped right beside his cage. He saw the silhouette of a person feeling the floor thanks to the thin ray of light that opened up from the entrance of the upper deck. However, that still didn't help jack understand the situation as a faint splashing sound followed by a slurp confused him even more.

'Yep. Another one's gone. Oi! Come help carry him out,' the same voice called.

Another pair of footsteps made its way beside Jack's cage. Jack listened in as the screeching of metal being dragged along the boards echoed across the room. The animals howled in response. Jack covered his ears instead. *Did someone die?*

Jack's attention turned back to the liquid he touched earlier on. He made out an image in the reflection, watching as the puddle morphed into a dark man with scars across his face, caused by multiple scratch marks. His silky black hair laid in tatters. They fell off as the seconds ticked by along with flakes of skin. The cut mouth moved, whispering reminders of what Jack once was.

'No. That isn't me. I'm stronger now. Not this low...ranked...mage. No. No. No! GO AWAY!' Jack screamed. The animals joined in his agony.

'Oh, shut up, will ya?' A voice bellowed from above.

Jack's body felt heavy. His mind went blank. He curled himself up into a ball. He drowned out the chaotic sound of the animals, unwilling to think about what was in store for him.

As the day or night (Jack couldn't tell) went on, his eyes adjusted to the darkness, though less than perfect. He still couldn't trust his vision as, half the time, what he thought he saw was just his mind playing tricks on him. The mages looked like animals and the animals looked like mages but that didn't matter. With everyone covered in excrement and slaves to the masters of the ship, you couldn't distinguish anyone even if you tried.

Occasionally, these very masters would grace the prisoners with their presence recognisable by the greenish glow of their eyes, like fireflies dancing in the night as they bobbed up and down in their strange walk. Their presence changed the prisoners' attitude, Jack included, making them act like frogs, anticipating these visitors for it meant only one thing: food.

The food wasn't anything to be excited about. It came in small bowls, with some sort of gruel slopped inside in a liquid mess. It tasted horrible too but, as the only source of nourishment, Jack forced it down with his bare hands. In his weakened state, and without utensils, the gruel dripped to the floor whenever Jack ate. The stains never got cleaned nor did the bowl.

This routine continued for weeks. At some point, Jack couldn't hear the howls and moans coming from all the other human prisoners anymore. Either he drowned them out or the prisoners all died. Either way, the shouts of 'another one gone' followed by the screeching of cages moving mingled with the other sounds. How many were there at the beginning? How many will remain? All Jack knew, and what mattered in the end, was that he lived.

****

A loud clanging against the bars of the cages jolted Jack up. The animals chorused in response, while the other prisoners groaned. The source of the clanging came from several pairs of glowing eyes. Jack counted at least a dozen, more than double the usual amount. They separated into several sections of the floor, hitting the bars of the cages, making sure they woke everyone up.

'Fifty-two animals, twenty-seven humans,' Jack heard from one of the glowing eyes.

'Not bad of a turnout this time,' said another.

'Is he here?'

'The ones the boss wanted alive?'

'One of them, yes.'

'Which one?'

'The chameleon.'

'That weakling? Oh, well. Just bring him out for transfer.'

Jack pretended he heard nothing as one of the guards stared into his cage. A jangling of keys, followed by the creaking of the cage opening, led to the eyes edging closer to him. A smell Jack hadn't smelt for ages filled the cage and into his nostrils; a fresh, delightful scent of tree bark and leaves. It reminded him of Eurasia.

'You're coming with me,' the guard ordered, cutting Jack's reminiscing short. 'Everyone else, make sure he doesn't escape.'

Jack felt warm mucus being slathered onto his arms, supported by slender arms that slithered their way in loops around his hands, fortifying the hold. His feeble attempt to move free led to the grip getting tighter.

An arm grabbed the nape of Jack's neck. It pulled him out of the cage where another person gripped onto his arms, leading him towards a staircase. He tripped several times along the way. His legs didn't want to cooperate, like a baby learning how to take its first steps all over again. *Three guards just for me?* Jack noted.

Somebody tutted in disgust. By the tightening grip of his hold, Jack could tell that the guard also resented his useless state. It took one more tumble to the floor before the guard roared angrily. He swept Jack off the floor and hurled him over his shoulders, the other arms letting go. Too weak to tense his stomach, Jack vomited upon collision with the guard's hefty shoulders.

'Oh, you got to be kidding me!' complained the guard. 'Eurasians are the worst. I should have killed him while he was still in the cage.'

'You can't do that,' replied another walking beside him. 'The boss wanted them alive. We'd be used for one of the boss' experiments if we brought nothing.'

'Ugh. I hate it when you're right. Get the door for me.'

The second guard took a few quick steps up the stairs and pushed against a wooden hatch. A stream of light burst through, blinding Jack momentarily. His head writhed in pain and his eyes burned along with his body, the sun's gaze searing through him.

Once his eyes adjusted the light, Jack surveyed his surroundings. Movements impaired and vision limited, Jack saw what laid in front of him: a vast landless ocean, sparkling in the sunlight with water clear as air as fishes swam amongst the coral in the seabed, catching the waves the boat produced. *What a complete contrast to the murky waters of Eurasia!* Jack admired.

As Jack moved, courtesy of the guard, the ship's top deck came into view. It felt out of place. The filthiness of the ship ruined the image Jack had a few moments ago. Smears of red, black and yellow, along with the stench of the ship, battled with the perfume-like and mesmerising nature of the ocean.

'Oh! That him?!' a man squealed in delight, though Jack couldn't see him yet.

'Yes, boss.'

'Put him down. I want to inspect him. You can go get the others afterwards.'

The guard hurled Jack onto the deck of the ship. He felt something soft squelch beneath his head, grimacing at the thought of what mixed with his hair. With legs weak and arms heavy, in his current state, Jack just wanted to bathe in the sunlight, so he closed his eyes and gave into his desires.

'You're not dying on me, are you?'

Jack opened his eyes again to find a little boy, no older than forty by Jack's judgement, looming over him. The boy had pale white skin, dark-blonde shoulder-length hair and freckles on his face.

'Oi! Can you speak?' the boy asked.

Jack didn't feel the need to reply to a child. He had lost interest anyway, so he closed his eyes once more. A slap rectified that attitude. The child looked angry this time but still failed to be intimidating in any shape or form. In fact, Jack thought the boy looked quite cute with his plump cheeks that puffed out. Did Jack ever look like that before? Jack smiled at the thought. Oh, how a hundred years changed the way you look!

'Not one to talk, are you? Were you like at birth or did you lose it along the way? Are you a bestial stealth type or a simple shapeshifter type? Oooo, so many wonderful things to find out! Alfred, carry him!'

'Yes, sire,' a man in a black and white suit said, picking Jack up.

Jack found the attire strange. Alfred's grey hair and wrinkled face didn't give any detail away, whether his mage classification or any hidden abilities. Instead, he wrapped Jack over his shoulder just like the guard did.

'Alfred. Has my 4DS charged yet?' the boy asked.

'Yes. The PS8 is also ready,' Alfred confirmed.

'Finally! Do you know how fucking long the journey is? I need my FFVC and AC9, otherwise the trip goes to sh-'

'Please watch your language, sire. It'll undermine your progress. However, I do concur that it was quite the trek getting here.'

'All worth it now that I got several more beauties like this one!' the boy said, tapping on Jack.

'Indeed, sire.'

'Turn him around. I want to sit on his lap!'

'Certainly.'

As Alfred flipped Jack into a sitting position on his shoulder like a ragdoll, Jack wondered what they were talking about, particularly about the words he had never heard about. He found the interactions between the two strange too. Surely there was no way that child was the grown man's superior, right? However, the respect the man gave the child and the way the child ordered him, suggested that was the case. The fact that Alfred bent down, allowing the boy to clamber onto him and on Jack's lap, cemented the idea.

'Let's go already!' the boy exclaimed, tugging on Jack's stained trousers.

Jack heard the gushing of water. The boat began to sink, along with the water level, to reveal an orange-yellow wall extending to as far as the eyes could see. It protected the continents from getting flooded, while acted as a defence at the same time. Jack knew they existed in Eurasia, but did the other continents have them too? If not, just where on Earth was he?

The ship tilted forwards, moving along using the flow of the water, into the wall. The sun's brilliance disappeared and replaced with bright lights, not from torches but instead a glowing thin strand of metal that lined the underside of glass containers, illuminating a stream the ship rode on and pathways either side.

The new experiences didn't stop as someone handed the boy a metallic box. He opened it and pressed a button with a strange symbol engraved on it, a 'U' with an 'I' in the middle. The next moment, some images popped out from the inside of the box. The images seemed to move in accordance with the child's button pressing. The images took the appearance of a man in a white hooded jacket, killing others. *Why was it doing that?* Jack didn't understand. *Was this a new type of mage?* Maybe, but Jack couldn't help but be mesmerised by the fancy footwork of the miniature murderer killing other miniature people.

The trance Broke when the ship ground to a halt. An anchor dropped into the stream creating an almighty splash that echoed inside the cave-like continuous thunderclaps.

The noise prompted Alfred to move, carrying both Jack and the boy in the process. They went down a plank that extended down to the pathway beside the stream where pads with numbered buttons on stuck on the wall.

The child closed the box, handing it to Alfred, jumped down from Jack's lap, and pressed them in a certain order. A hidden door slid open, leading to an area where the walls, floor and ceilings were made of stainless steel. Compared to Squadron W's Rezah and the stone homes Jack used to live in, it all felt unnatural.

Some guards carried cages containing animals and humans. *These were the people I lived with the past few weeks,* Jack thought. They looked filthy but it made Jack conscious of his own appearance. He was no better. His clothes were ragged, covered in blood, vomit and pus while his limbs looked like twigs.

'Hurry up, Alfred!' the boy commanded.

'Yes, sire,' the suited man obeyed.

The child climbed onto Jack's lap again and the trio headed down the metallic hallway, layered with more glass lights but of several colours, this time, placed over doors. However, with no signs on them, Jack couldn't tell what they were for.

In the end, they went through a door with a green light above it. Jack saw a lot of people, all dressed in white coats, busy writing something down on paper. There were also several large glass cylinders, people floating inside of them in a vegetative state. Some had a crumpled look on their faces, writhing in pain, while others watched on with blank expressions.

They all had masks on, allowing them to breathe within the liquid.

Jack realised what was the earlier discussion was about. A cold sweat ran down his brow. He squirmed and wriggled, trying to get free, but Alfred's grip was too tight and the mucous on his arms difficult to break through. He didn't want to be an experiment. He didn't want to go become a lifeless body at the mercy of these people.

'Place him in container LZ-one after preparations,' the child ordered.

The boy jumped off, signalled to a few of the white-coated men who prepared a few injections. They stabbed Jack with the needles, injecting some sort of serum into Jack's veins. His will to escape dropped and his body collapsed, somehow in a weaker state than before. He couldn't move at all, allowing the strange coated people to change his clothes into thin garments. If he looked pathetic before, he was a complete joke now.

Alfred took Jack to one of the cylinders. After opening the glass door, he placed Jack inside with a mask, connected to a hollow tube, attached to his face. Air funnelled through the tube, forcing Jack to take it in. It smelt fresh but Jack could tell something else was mixed within it, his consciousness seeping away with every breath.

Alfred closed the door before activating a switch on the side. A greenish liquid began to flow into the cylinder, surrounding Jack who shuddered upon contact, helpless to stop his fate. The garments began to absorb the liquid, making it bulge. As more of the liquid began to flow into the cylinder, Jack floated with the help of his new clothes, bobbing up and down like the others. He couldn't even force himself to turn around, unable to avert his gaze from the little boy in front of him, donning the same uniform as everyone else.

'Welcome to my Mage Breeding Programme a.k.a the MBP! I am Bastion East and I will be your supervisor. Please enjoy your stay because this will be your new home,' the boy greeted, grinning at Jack with enthusiastic eyes. He seemed to have an important role despite looking so young. *Just what was he?* Jack thought.

'Now where shall we start?' Bastion continued. 'You're a special one. According to my sources, you can camouflage *and* change your appearances to an extent. Amazing capabilities you have there, but here's the catch! You're only an E ranked mage. How is that possible? My ranking system is highly accurate. You shouldn't be able to do what you do, so what gives? Do you have a mutation that only occurs during adulthood? Or maybe there's a fault with the system? What makes you tick? Oh, there are so many questions to ask and so many answers to find out!'

Bastion couldn't hold his excitement as he jumped up and down in delight. He mumbled some numbers off the tip of his tongue before nodding to himself.

'Oh, I know! Let's fix that speech disability you have. Elivia! Come!' Bastion called. His loudness got on the nerves of the others in the room but no one dared to scold the boy.

'Yes sir?' a skinny woman with long dark hair answered, holding a clipboard and pen.

'Carry experiment fifty-seven on this one.'

'Certainly.'

The woman called Elivia jotted something down, glancing up sometimes to make sure she got it down properly.

'Um, sir?' Elivia murmured.

'Yo, what's up boo?'

'Don't these containers take too much space? I mean, we could easily stack the subjects into square arrays instead and allow room for more devices.'

'Does it look like I give a damn about room?'

'Excuse me?'

'Does. It. Look. Like. I. Give. A. Damn? Stupid woman.'

Elivia looked scared and scurried away. She didn't want to be a victim of her boss' whims. Bastion, on the other hand, didn't care who's involved. As long as his curiosity is sated, the people he used didn't matter. That was his philosophy. That and the desire to entertain himself.

'I saw this design in a movie once and it was cool as hell. Look at how the people float. Isn't it funny? I ain't gonna jack to it,' Bastion exclaimed, unaware that no one was listening to him. 'Oh, that reminds me, is the Blu-ray ready, Alfred?'

'Yes,' the suited man answered, coming into Jack's sight and standing beside Bastion. 'Which movie would you like to watch today?'

'I'm in the mood for the eleventh transformers movie.'

'I shall prepare it straight away, sire.'

'Brilliant! A good movie and a new toy to experiment on. What more can a guy ask for?'

Movie? Blu-ray? What are these words? Jack wondered, closing his eyes and accepting his fate.

14

Battalion Training

The colonel's office was at the very top of the Rezah tree. Due to the limited space at the summit, hers was the only room on that level, like a loft, making navigation to her room easy. The journey to get there, however, was another matter, needing someone to climb over a hundred sets of stairs, starting at the bottom of the tree, leaving most exhausted by the end. Was it worth it? Gin let out a deep breath, out of annoyance at how time-consuming the walk was rather than tiredness, got himself composed and knocked on the door to find out.

'Come in,' the colonel responded.

Gin opened the door and entered the room, surveying the place as he did so. For someone said to be the leader of a squadron, the room wasn't in the best conditions. The walls were thin and covered in untrimmed branches. The floor was covered in dust with some dark marks as if burnt by something. The ceiling wasn't really a ceiling either; just a mesh of the tree's branches that seemed to converge to create a makeshift roof. Even then, it had several holes that allowed rain could easily drip through.

'The tree's still growing, child. In a few years, this floor will have much more room and another floor will be created above this one,' the colonel explained, almost reading Gin's mind as she wrote on documents with her quill and ink.

'I see,' Gin murmured.

'Of course, we must hollow the floor out, cut down the inside of the trees and so on to make it habitable but we've got a lot of time on our hands, don't we?'

Gin didn't comment. Instead, he looked at the ceiling once more. The more he stared, the more he felt like the branches were indeed moving, trying to cover the gaps by themselves. If it takes a few years to create a whole new floor, just how long did it take to grow the whole tree out?

'The MBP sure is amazing,' the colonel continued. 'They had this idea centuries ago and now all the Eurasian squadrons use the Rezah as their place of residence and work. It's only in the past two hundred years that their plan has come to fruition. You are definitely too young to know this, child, but we used to live under metal and wood roofs called 'houses'. Even now, the MBP uses its metal fortress in Russia to raise the next generation. But you're not here for this monologue, are you? Tell me what brings you to my office.'

'Thank you, Colonel,' Gin began, having enjoyed the short story. 'I actually have two requests.'

'Oh? You become a battalion leader just last week when Alder left and now you're already demanding so much, child. You're not getting too greedy, are you?'

'Apologies. But if you could hear me–'

'Ha! I was just joking, child,' the colonel jested, putting down her equipment and looking Gin eye to eye, her gaze as stern as ever. 'No need to be so formal. No need for this colonel nonsense,' Maria said with Gin laughing a meek laugh in response.

'I get the feeling of Deja Vu, colonel. I don't feel right calling you by name, colonel. I came from a place where you can't really drop these honorifics, *colonel*.'

'That's fine with me. Shall we hear out these requests instead, *child*?'

Gin took out the INS, the silver-coloured cuboid used as a projector, from his belt. He activated it to show some handwritten documents, projecting them onto the colonel's desk. She looked through them and realised what they were.

'These are the documents I had sent out to all battalion leaders, right?' she questioned.

'Yes,' Gin confirmed, flicking through the slides. 'For my first request, I just wanted to go through a few things and give my opinions, if that's alright. If you need my INS, feel free to take it.'

'I know the documents off by heart. No need to show me.'

'So, is it true that we're now expected to face five-thousand?'

'Indeed. It seems that our assassination plan has somewhat backfired. Without a leader, they decided to opt for raw man-power rather than proper leadership. All information in the document is reliable, by the way.'

'Do we know the type of mages we're going to face? Didn't see the specifics in the documents.'

'We were forced to withdraw most of our intel before we could find out. We'll need them for scouting when the time to leave has come, so we can't risk them all in enemy territory. We just have to estimate at the moment. There are multiple places the AAA will dispatch their army to many locations, with The Path being one of them, so how the Egyptian barracks will separate is unknown, even if their numbers are not.'

'While that makes sense, I still don't get why it is taking so long. Their plan to attack through The Path was decided a months ago and they're still not ready?

Surely, they could have attacked us while we were unprepared.'

'You make it seem like travel is quick, child,' the colonel doubted, leaning a bit closer in her chair. 'Not everyone has rideable familiars! To call for reinforcements, after the death of their leader, would take several months at the minimum due to the slow pace of walking. This assassination has bought us a lot of time, though it did bring its downsides admittedly.'

Familiars? Who said anything about familiars? It became apparent to Gin that transport, such as the hover-cars he drove as a young teen, weren't used by mages. *It was probably because of the fall of the age of science,* Gin thought. He took those pieces of knowledge of the past world like that into account and kept them to himself. The problem was that he didn't know what he shouldn't know most of the time and made assumptions too eagerly. *Still so much to learn about the mages.*

'The intricacies of war sure are difficult to wrap your head around,' Gin commented, scratching his head.

'That's why I was bred to do this and you were not,' the colonel smirked.

Gin ignored the remark. 'Anyway, back to the topic at hand. If they don't have an experienced leader, they're pretty much all brawn now and will most likely try to brute force their way through our lines. We have less than two thousand combatants. With our numbers, we wouldn't stand a chance if we fought them head on.'

'So, what are you proposing, child?'

'We're fighting on our home turf, basically. I would like to use that to our advantage. If the maps are correct, the plan should work, I think. I put everything on my projector. Go ahead and look through it. The relevant slides are at the end.'

Gin handed the INS over to the colonel. She fumbled a bit with the technology but, after some guidance, she got the hang of it by the end. She flicked through Gin's slides and, although Gin's handwriting was on the brink of illegibility, she got a grasp on what he wanted to do.

'You want to use our non-combatants, child?'

'Yes. I've gone through everyone's profiles and realised that most of our non-combatants are just people who haven't found a role in the squadron because of their lack of individual ability. But I think I can make use of them. Its success might bring our numbers up another five-hundred. If you could send the names on the final slide to either my or Brim's battalion, that'd be great.'

'Ha!'

'Something the matter, Colonel?'

'No. It's just that you only just received the mantle of battalion leader from Alder a few days ago and you've already shown this much composure. Guess he was right to pass it down to you. This plan of yours could work, maybe not. I did have something in mind but I will have to make some amendments to your plan before it could be considered. As for the F ranked mages, that will be possible.'

Gin smiled meekly and bowed down in gratitude. Although he showed humility to the colonel, he couldn't help but feel ecstatic from the small win, even if her response was a bit ambiguous. He was thrust into this alien world that he never knew existed until the attack on his village, but he was determined to conquer it. It's what his father would have wanted and what his mother would have watched with affection. Despite being a manush adult, Gin still had that child-like ambition.

'What was the other request?' the colonel asked.

'Oh, right,' Gin said, standing upright again. 'I need a lot of mouldable stone and wood and people who can create things using them.'

'I can grant that request since we have a lot in reserve. What do you need them for?'

'You'll see. I've actually got quite a lot planned.'

'If that's the case, then I'll enjoy finding out what you will do. Is that all for today?'

'Yes, ma'am.'

'Then you are dismissed.'

Gin bowed once more and Maria watched as he left the room. She enjoyed watching his progress from behind the scenes. She felt like she was his guardian and wanted to nudge him in the right direction but Gin had been doing that by himself, without any help. Even when Alder was leaving and Gin didn't come to see him off, it turned out that instead of sulking (like all adolescents would have upon losing a role model), he was busy drawing up plans for both the squadron and his battalion.

Despite the fact the rise in his responsibilities seemed to be growing too fast, Gin seemed to make rational decisions, acting calm and responsibly as if he was an experienced man. Maybe Gin wasn't in puberty and actually was an adult like he tries to tell her. But an adult at thirty-three? That's impossible! Maria couldn't convince herself and continued her opinion of Gin being an immature child.

With his requests over and done with, Gin headed outside the Rezah tree, dreading the climb back down to the lowest floor, where he had gathered his battalion together for special training. Though the rooms used for training were very realistic, they could never compare to the feeling of nature's wind blowing across your face, cooling those enveloped by the warm air at the expense of sand getting in fur and eyes.

With a few members yet to come, Gin decided to start. He ordered everyone to get into a standard block formation. With only a hundred at his disposal, he didn't have much flexibility in what formations he could create. The ten by ten block would have to do for now. Gin stood at the front and got everyone's attention. Their faces were filled with doubt and confusion, as they looked towards their new battalion leader. Gin felt the same. Not long ago, he stood by the others as equals, but now he was an unproven leader.

'As you know, Alder has retired and he has made me his replacement,' Gin began, taking a firm approach. 'I can see from a few of you that you either disapprove or are uncertain of the decision, even resulting in some becoming tardy or unwilling to turn up to my training. My aim is to change your minds and to gain your trust. I will say one thing, however, and that is that my methods will be different from what you've experienced in the past. Everyone understand?'

Gin saw a few nods and heard a few mumbled yeses. He wasn't sure what tone he should have spoken in. Should he have been harsh? Should he have been lax? Or maybe a more forceful approach would have been best. Instead, he opted for what felt more natural.

'I'm presuming this is the first time you've ever been brought outside for training, right?' Gin continued followed by more disgruntled words of agreement. 'Well, I brought everyone here for some sparring training. After each spar, I would like you to go over to the man over there.'

Gin pointed to Michal, who stood outside of the formation, right next to surface roots from the tree.

The battalion began to talk amongst themselves. The main topic of interest was 'sparring'. Gin sighed a breath of annoyance. It seemed that, even within Squadron W, sparring was an uncommon practice. *Why did Alder only spar with me and not with the others in his battalion?* Gin thought, beginning to think that he should expel any confusion.

'It seems that no one wants to spar. I'll be honest with you here. I find it weird that training, sparring and any other form of improving one's battle prowess, apart from when you are raised in the MBP, is not practised at all. Are we not in times of war? If so, shouldn't we strive to be the best, even during adulthood?

Of course, the MBP has told us that we can't improve once we hit adulthood. But with my relatively unorthodox methods, we will dispel that notion and reach new heights! But that's not what you want as an answer, I'm sure. To explain why I want to spar is one thing, but to show its effects is another.

If we looked at the overall stats of everyone, I would lose to each of you. But I really want to show you why I support my methods. Therefore, I will fight everyone in a one v one. Sound impossible? Well, let's see. First on the list is Emily Blunt. Would you step forward.'

A chubby woman stepped up. She had holes in the palm of her pale-skinned hands and the sags of skin seemed to wobble with every step. She found it hard to walk, but Gin waited with patience for her to get to a large square-shaped open space he had set up as the arena, using his blades to carve the outlines. The rest of the battalion gathered around while Gin and Emily faced each other.

'Oh, before we begin, Michal could you bring gauntlet type beta for Emily to wear?' Gin asked.

Michal nodded, hopping over the tree root, rummaging through stone equipment he hid behind, out of sight from the battalion. He picked out a gauntlet with a convex cone attached to the centre, a hole at the very tip, and joints held together by an array of flexible vines.

'This one?' Michal asked.

'Yep!' Gin confirmed.

'Um, sir. You want me to use that?' Emily questioned, followed by a few sniggers from the crowd, prompting her to add, 'I don't want to.'

'Heh. Then why not stop me as you are now. Demonstrate the power of an E rank water elemental. Don't worry, I won't dodge.'

Blades. Shields. Gin activated his INS and charged at Emily. In response, she held out her hand and fired a weak stream of water that couldn't even reach Gin until he got into range, taking the full force of the attack. However, the water didn't even leave a dent in Gin's shirt let alone the armour he held beneath it. It was an easy victory as Gin held his blade's tip against Emily's neck, startling her into falling onto the floor.

'The holes on your hand are too loose, too large and not suited to damage others. You expect to fight with that level of ability?' Gin criticised.

'I know!' Emily shrieked. 'This is why I'm low-ranked! Are you happy that you beat an E rank with your high-ranked abilities?'

The other members of the battalion looked away in self-pity. *Why do they think I'm high-ranked?* Gin took a deep breath and decided to dispel the notion.

'Take away my weapons and shields, take away my Xernims, take away my armour and what am I afterwards? A person who's weaker than anyone else on Earth. Yet all of you blame your weakness when you could just as easily improve by setting aside your conditioned pride like I, not to mention the very leader you loyally followed before me, have.'

'Tsk.'

'I know I'm sounding harsh, but how about you wear the armour and see the difference for yourself? I'm not forcing you to keep it if you don't like it?'

'Fine,' Emily pouted.

With the help of Gin, she rolled her way back onto her feet and trudged her way to Michal who handed her the gauntlet. She slotted the gauntlets over her hands, surprised by how snug they felt, especially the cone that fitted over the cusps on her hand without causing pain.

'Go for a test run,' Gin suggested, the rest of the battalion watching on with eager gazes.

Emily nodded, holding her arm up straight, aiming right at Gin who stood outside her range. She aimed and fired, taken aback by how streamlined the water became, tripling in its initial range and power. Gin blocked the attack with his shield, smiling at the success.

'This...' Emily muttered.

'What? Don't like it? We can take it o-'

'No!'

'Oops. Sorry, I got too presumptuous there,' Gin said, not showing how smug he was, causing Emily to cover her mouth in embarrassment.

'Shall we get on with the next step and spar then?'

'Yes, please.'

Though only a handful of mages looked as impressed, Gin had grabbed the attention of everyone. *Perfect.* He stood on one edge while Emily stood in the centre of the circle. With blades, shields and armour at the ready, there was one more thing to say.

'The rules are simple. Your aim is to knock me out or even kill me. I, on the other hand, have to be in a position to assure my victory. You can't go out of the makeshift arena as well. Understand?' Gin explained, with Emily nodding in agreement. 'Pay attention everyone! Let's begin.'

Gin beckoned Emily to make the first move. He saw that she was nervous. It was probably her first time fighting someone with her new capabilities so it was only natural. She was also an E ranked water elemental, so he didn't expect her to have much confidence. But despite all that, she raised her hands at aimed straight at Gin who just grinned in return. He knew what she wanted to do. He was just a melee ranged Xernim user, after all.

Gin used his shields to immediate effect as Emily fired a jet of water right at him. He deflected the water out of harm's way, recoiling a bit by the impact. If it had hit him directly, he wouldn't even be sure whether his chest plate would have protected him.

Gin then made his move, rushing at Emily. She panicked and aimed both her arms at him, firing two piercing streams. Gin ran in a circle around her, avoiding the water in the process. His speed outpaced her aim and she couldn't keep up. Gin watched her as he ran. Her sags of flesh seemed to deplete and when they looked to be gone altogether, he shifted his weight to his feet, changing directions and ran straight at her.

Emily thought this was her chance and tried to send a large blast of water at him but it came to nothing. Nothing came out of her hands. She had used all her water reserves. Before she knew it, Gin had a blade at her neck.

'As you can see, I win that,' Gin remarked. 'Now here's the part where I tell you where you can improve in the future.'

Gin lowered his blade at his speechless opponent. Her gauntlets fell as the stone armour no longer fit on her shrivelled arms, causing a cloud of dust to rise up from the ground upon impact.

'I want everyone to listen up. It will help you in your future battles as well as give you ideas on your own battle techniques,' Gin continued. 'Emily here is obviously a water elemental. When facing her, you can see that the bloated skin she had the beginning deflated during our spar. I figured this out ages ago but those sags of skin are probably her water supply, right? Once that ran out, I went for the finishing move with success. I didn't rush things. If I did, I was sure to get hurt.'

'There's probably some work that could be done on the gauntlets,' Michal admitted after watching the fight, contemplating on what could be improved. 'They shouldn't slide off at the end like that.'

'True,' Gin agreed, turning back to Emily. 'Now, my advice to you is that you need to be more conservative in your water usage. Use it when you're sure to do damage or if you aim to move them to a certain location. You just continued your assault while I just ran in circles. There was a lot of wastage. If in battle, you run out of water, you will become useless and a hindrance to us. Do I make myself clear?'

She took everything into account and nodded once more at Gin without saying a single word. It seemed that Gin got a loyal follower in his ideology already. *One down, roughly a hundred to go*, Gin thought.

'Now, the rest of you will probably still have doubts and thought that I fixed that battle. So, as I said, I will take the rest of you on. Emily, go to Michal and he will suit you up. Next up is Ritordo.'

Gin went through the same process again. Equip armour on his next opponent, fight, win, and give advice at the end. With each fight, he gained another person who looked up to him. They were going to get stronger as a result and Gin enjoyed engineering that.

By the Fiftieth spar, Gin's large pool of stamina began to show signs of reaching its limit. His movements were slower. His reactions weren't as sharp as before. He started getting hit and as he won his sixtieth match, he was covered in cuts, bruises and burns. But he soldiered on. The adrenaline that flowed through him carried him through the pain. His desire to make his battalion accept him allowed Gin to speak and give advice with a smile.

With just less than twenty to go, his battalion stopped him from continuing, his legs shaking from exhaustion, his stance no longer existed. The battalion didn't want him to overexert himself, telling him to rest instead. Gin accepted with glee and collapsed to the ground. He wondered what he was going to do for the next training session.

****

Gin woke up to the sight of Joan. He was propped up on her lap, in a room he had never seen before. It was circular instead of the standard rectangular shape. Apart from that, and a few containers with fluids on the shelf, that Gin presumed was for medicinal purposes, the interior was similar to Gin's own room. He looked up once more to see that Joan had a needle in hand and was concentrating. Gin felt a sharp pain as the needle, which turned out to be a detached nail, went through his face.

'Don't move. Don't talk,' Joan ordered, 'or you'll make me mess up.'

Gin followed her instructions. He was too tired to do anything anyway. The feeling of lying on a person's lap felt nostalgic. The last time he did it was when he was a child on his mother's lap. It was nice, apart from the pain of Joan's stitches.

'Ok. All done,' she said.

Gin remained where he was. His eyes were closed and body relaxed. He didn't hear Joan and completely missed her look of annoyance. She waited a few more moments before giving up and bashed him in the head with her fist.

'Ow! What was that for?' Gin exclaimed, getting up immediately.

'Everything,' Joan frowned.

'Everything?'

'*Everything.*'

'Yeah...repeating the word doesn't help me understand, Joan.'

'You're just an idiot, Gin.'

'Because I got injured again?'

'No! It's because you decide to get injured –'

'That's what I just said.'

'Let me finish for goodness sake! You go and decide to do something that will obviously get yourself hurt *and* you never tell me! I'm your medic. You need me! Do. You. Understand. Now?' Joan shouted, tapping Gin's forehead for each word on her final sentence.

'But –'

'Don't give me the 'but I got Wo, I don't need you' nonsense. He does absolutely nothing. He wants you to suffer for the sake of his amusement.'

Gin wanted to say something in defence, but the more he recalled his memories of Wo, the more he remembered of all the teasing, bullying and pranks he pulled on him. Even when he was being forced fed mage meat, Wo stood there and enjoyed the scene. Gin realised that he couldn't defend Wo.

'Look, Gin. What I was trying to get across to you, is that I want you to tell me what you plan to do. I know how stubborn you are. I know how much you strive for self-improvement. I know how annoying it must feel for you to be a low-ranked mage. Why else would you decide to get a Xernim? But I just want to be there when you overdo it.'

Gin remained silent, processing what Joan had just said. *When did she get so accepting?* He wondered, half-believing that this was a strange dream of his.

However, the pain he felt throughout his body said otherwise.

'Yeah, I don't approve of half the things you do,' Joan resumed, taking her own words into account and adding to them. 'I also have this feeling you just don't want me telling you not to do this or that. So, I won't. I will just be your support and when you get hurt, I will treat you on the spot, so you don't have to come to be bleeding like this time. Or any time for that matter. I have been doing so for the last few months anyway.'

'How did I get here, wherever I am?' Gin asked, trying to take the subject.

'You're in my room. Some people from your battalion brought you here. I guess your self-abuse paid off this time. They seemed worried, wondering when you would be available for sparring again.'

Gin breathed a sigh of relief. That confirmed their trust in him. They also wanted to spar again so they at least accepted his new method of training. The only thing Gin forgot to do was ask Michal how the armour was doing. He could do that later. For now, he wanted to rest. The training session took a greater toll than he had anticipated. The high he felt during the session crashed down into the draining low now. But before giving in to his body's desire, he wanted to ascertain one more thing.

'Do you really mean it when you said you won't tell me what to do?' Gin asked.

'Mmm. Probably not. I'll show my frustration here and there, but I couldn't stop you even if I wanted to. Alder's gone too so I can't use him like last time. Remember to eat your meat rations!'

'Yes. Yes. I guess that's as good a deal as I'll get with you. Mind if I sleep now?' Gin asked as he rolled onto the ground and off of Joan's lap.

'Sure. Make sure you recover properly. I'll just go rest in your room.'

'Do you need my –'

'I have keys to your room,' Joan interrupted, standing up and leaving the room.

'Of course, you do,' Gin remarked before going to sleep.

15

Making the Useless Useful

Gin pointed the gun at the tree. He made sure to steady his hands, aiming for the perfect shot. He wrapped his fingers around the ins and into the chambers. *This time I'm going to hit the mark,* he told himself. He then pressed the button inside the second chamber. Bang! The sound echoed around the room. Gin looked at the tree once more, only to feel dejected as it remained unscathed. The same couldn't be said about the wall next to them.

'Wow! How bad can you get?!' exclaimed an amused Wo.

'For fu–'

'Language, Gigi.'

'For Fudge sake then,' Gin rolled his eyes. 'Happy? Anyway, I can aim all I like, but the moment I pull the trigger, the gun goes all over the place. The recoil hits too hard.'

'Or maybe you just suck.'

Wo took the gun INS off Gin and aimed at the tree. He acted like he wasn't even trying as he activated the mechanism. The shot was perfect as the bullet hit the target right in the centre, piercing the tree.

'Screw you, Wo.'

'Get good.'

'Ugh. You never cease to annoy me,' Gin said as he went to another tree and began making another target with his blades.

'It's fun getting on your nerves,' Wo shrugged back. 'Anyway, you should stick to blade boxing. The gun's not for you.'

'But I need to improve my arsenal. Can't rely on my blades all the time.'

'Doesn't seem to be working for you though.'

'Looks like I need to calibrate it so that it's less powerful. But then It's no longer useful as a long-range weapon like I want it to.'

Wo waited a few moments for the nanobots to return back the INS, filling up the chamber and ready for use again. He twirled the gun around his finger, showing off his hand-eye coordination in an attempt to peeve Gin further, stopping when he went into deep thought.

'How did your ancestors manage to make one?' Wo wondered.

'They had disposable bullets. The nanobots dissipate as soon as they leave the chamber, in order to return back to the INS to be reused. Since the bullet doesn't hold its form for long, it weakens the bullet's power as it flies. I can't really recreate what my forefathers used entirely.'

Gin flopped to the ground, opening up another INS, making sure the marsh water didn't enter the system even though the device was waterproof. *Better safe than sorry,* Gin thought as he mumbled words Wo didn't understand, but his face showed frustration.

'Like father, like son,' Wo muttered.

'Did you say something?' Gin looked up, putting the cap of the INS on his lap and separating the other parts.

'No, I just wondered what happened to the fire mode you used to have on your old sword?' Wo asked instead, deciding to be helpful for once.

'Ran out of oil. I haven't been back home in ages to pick up more.'

'So? Just ask one of the fire elementals to give you some of theirs. It's not like they run out permanently.'

Gin stopped, staring at Wo in surprise. It never occurred that there was an alternative right in front of him. Of course, he needed the right type of oil but, with the amount of fire elemental type mages in the squadron, it shouldn't be too difficult. The revelation put Gin's mind into overdrive. He had a sudden realisation that it didn't have to stop at fire elementals. He could use several different mages to advance his research; to widen his capabilities; to make him stronger.

'Not a bad idea, Wo. Guess you can be useful every once in a while,' Gin's face lit up in a moment of genius.

'"Every once in a while"?' Wo replied, charging Gin, catching him off guard before he put him in a headlock. 'Go on. Tell me how great I am!'

'Ow! You're just a coward who needs his bacteria to fight,' Gin retorted.

'Says the xernim user!'

The pair collapsed to the floor and began laughing. Despite the trouble he causes, Wo was a good friend in Gin's opinion. Maybe it wasn't so surprising considering how close Wo was with Gin's father too. *Like father like son,* Gin mused to himself. The thought of his father made him want to go back to his village someday. But that train of thought got derailed when he saw the time on the pendulum clock.

'Ah, I need to go,' Gin admitted.

'What for?'

'My battalion needs me. Had something special in mind for some new members.'

'You're a popular man at last, Gigi! Your father would be so proud,' Wo said with a fake tear in his eye and a forced sniff.

'Again. Screw you, Wo.'

'I'll just stay here while we wait for the nanobots to go back in the INS,' Wo said with a mischievous grin.

'Alright,' Gin replied, rolling his eyes and picking his equipment apart from the gun, heading down to the ground floor of the Rezah.

Outside, the wind blew sand into a wild frenzy, making vision near impossible. Protecting his eyes, he squinted into the distance, making out a recognisable scaly person, though he couldn't be a hundred percent sure. Gin waved, but the man didn't respond, either because he had his back turned or the sand blotted his sight too.

'Brim! That you?' Gin called.

'Ah! Gin! There you are,' he responded, turning around and waving back with a confused look on this face.

Gin lifted his shirt over his head as a sort of veil, using the stone plate underneath for protecting his body. He then made his way to his sparring partner who didn't seem to feel the sand rapping against his arms, or at least didn't show it, while a thin layer of oil covered his eyes, acting as a barrier and allowing him to see at the same time.

'What's wrong, Brim?' Gin asked, noticing how ridiculous he looked.

'I got several questions,' Brim replied.

'Yeah. I had a feeling it was going to be something along those lines. What're the issues?'

'Uuuuuh. Why here? This weather's horrible!'

'Exactly. We need to adapt to all sort of situations, no? Yeah, it's bad but do we call off the battle with the AAA mid-fight if a sandstorm blows just like that?'

'Still, these are horrible conditions.'

'Who's winning twenty-seven twenty-four in our spars?'

Brim pursed his lips. He looked into the distance then back at Gin when he was unable to think of a comeback.

'What about the new members,' Brim said at last, trying to find a chink in Gin's logic as a retort.

'What about them?'

'They're F ranks. They barely even deserve that rank. Do you know how hard that is? They're the worst of the worst and you want them in my battalion too?'

'They have their uses.'

'They're useful? Really? You didn't skip on eating your meat rations again, right?'

'I get the feeling it's the prejudice you gained from the MBP that's telling you this. Remember, we are a battalion. Not a group of individuals. And no, I don't miss out on my meat rations. Joan makes sure I have them.'

'I really don't think you can blame the MBP this time. Have you seen the abilities of these pe-'

'Look out!'

The pair looked up. Hurtling towards was a massive ball of fire. They jumped out of the way, dodging the attack, but blobs of oil ended up splattered across the ground. The blobs continued to burn even after crashing into the ground. Luckily, neither of them got hurt. Gin looked over his shoulders to see Brim in utter disbelief. *Another easy believer in the regime,* Gin thought.

'What was that?!' Brim exclaimed.

'*That*, my friend,' Gin started, a smirk forming underneath his veil, 'Is the power of the mages you called "useless" a while ago.'

'No way! A fireball of that size? That's got to be a rank S fire elemental at least!'

'I'll show you once the weather eases up. Let's get to safety first. Even I didn't expect this range.'

After an hour or so, when the sandstorm disappeared without warning, Gin pointed to a certain location. Brim squinted. Roughly one kilometre away was four mages, with one being significantly larger than the others. They had smiles across their faces and were congratulating each other. Were they the ones that caused the fireball? No, that can't be right. What low ranked fire elemental had a range like that?

'The big one's the fire elemental that threw the fireball, right?' Brim asked, still reluctant to believe the truth.

'Well, you're half right. Let's go over to them.'

As Gin and Brim got closer, the group of people noticed them. They were brimming with excitement and began running towards their leader. All except the big one, that is. He trudged along, unable to keep up. His size and notably large hands weighed him down, limiting his movements.

'Leader! Leader! Did you see that?' a woman with rough skin exclaimed while jumping up and down on the spot.

'Yes. You almost hit us as well,' Gin responded.

'Oh, er...sorry,' a timid, bald man with slimy skin that glistened under the sun, said.

'Yeah. Our bad. We didn't expect to go that far,' a different slimy-skinned mage said.

'You see,' Gin commented, turning to Brim, 'all four of these mages, including the big guy, are F ranks yet they managed to produce such a powerful fireball. In a battlefield, they would be a great asset.'

'But they're F ranks!'

Everyone looked unimpressed at Brim. He saw what they just did. He had seen Gin's other methods working. He knew the MBP wasn't always right (Gin's victory over him in the spar was still fresh in Brim's memory). Yet, Brim still didn't trust Gin when he said the F ranks could be useful.

'Look,' Gin said at last. 'One of the slimy skinned can produce oil but can't light it up. The other one can do both but doesn't have fire-resistant skin. He'd burn up if he lit his hands up. The rough-skinned woman can light a fire without burning herself up but doesn't have the flammable sweat the other fire mages have to make one. Finally, the big guy with large hands over there, that's slowly making his way to us, he's fire resistant and has incredible strength but is extremely slow. All of them are F ranks!'

'I still don't get it,' Brim responded, causing Gin to sigh in disbelief with the others mimicking him.

'Alone, they aren't useful to us but, as a group, they are a strength to our battalion. In short, the men pour oil into the big guy's hands, the woman lights it up and then the big guy flings it at the enemy. Larger sized and larger ranged fireballs than any individual could manage,' Gin explained, the group nodding in agreement.

'Uh huh,' Brim said trying to process the idea. 'That's actually amazing. Guess when the MBP taught us that the low-ranked were trash, we took it to heart.'

'That's what I've been trying to tell you! Just like that, we gained three-hundred or so more soldiers in our squadron. But anyway, good work you guys. Keep up with the practice.'

'Yes sir!' the group shouted in unison, moving further away from the Rezah to see if they could launch projectiles even further.

Brim contemplated for a moment. Gin began to tear through his views, conditioned into him by the MBP, bit by bit. Although most of his factual knowledge still held true, the subjective ideologies were in question. He could see why Alder spoke so highly of Gin. Maybe it was for the best.

'Hey, Gin.'

'What's wrong, Brim?'

'Mind if my battalion joins yours in training? I get the feeling we could learn a lot from yours.'

'Finally given up on your prejudice? Sure. The more the merrier. In return, you need to give me some oil every now and then.'

'What for?'

'I want to improve my blade boxing. I need some flammable material to do so though.'

'I don't understand what you're planning but ok. I'll prepare a batch soon.'

Suddenly, Gin heard someone calling for them. Brim heard it too, and they both turned to see a lean woman riding a massive Lupim, bounding towards them. The canine had brown fur, with streaks of black. Its teeth were razor sharp, its muzzle rough and claws snuggled within the paws of the beast.

'Who are you?' Gin questioned.

'No time for that,' the woman replied. 'There will be an emergency meeting in three hours. All battalion leaders need to attend.'

'Calm down,' Brim ordered. 'What's going on?'

'The AAA have started making their move.'

16

Colosseum

It's cold, a tired Jack thought as his head rested against a solid surface in an unfamiliar location. He sat up, surveying his surroundings. Stone walls surrounded him in a circle with stair-like seats on top of them and doors embedded within while a roof loomed over all. The placed looked symmetrical apart from one area containing a tunnel, presumably for an entrance or exit, and a lavish throne in front of Jack, ordained with jewellery and feathers of some sort.

A bright light smothered Jack, blinding him for a moment. When he regained his vision, he saw someone sat on the throne, the same little boy he met on the boat, hand resting on a smug face, surrounded by people in white coats and holding boxes that lit up and showed a floating image.

'Welcome to the Colosseum!' the boy remarked. 'Or at least my own knock-off version. Can't exactly use the original nowadays. Yikes. That was a dark time in history.'

'Huh?' Jack said, bewildered.

'See. This is why I hate being old while being in a child's body. Either they don't get my awesome references or they ignore me for looking like a ten-year-old, or it might be forty ever since the lifespans of man increased. Isn't that right, Alfred?'

'Yes, sire. Your references are on point,' the suited man that always accompanied the boy replied.

'Thank you! Good to see someone appreciating my brilliance. Yo, Jackie boi. Come here.'

Jack stood up and began walking to the boy, the spotlight following him with every step. He remained confused, unsure why he was following the boy's orders. The chill from the ground ran through his bare feet. *Was it winter already?* Jack's breath didn't make steam nor did his body shiver, so the ground's temperature felt unnatural. He looked up at the boy who leaned over the edge of the wall and stared back.

'Jackie, Jackie, Jackie. I think this nickname suits you,' the boy mused. 'Have I already told you I'm Bastion East? Maybe. I don't know. Anyway, can you talk now?'

'Uh, where am –'

'Good. Experiment seventy-nine was a success. Take note boys and girls.'

The white-coated people fingered the floating images, causing more images to come up. They had the occasional glance up to look at Jack before turning back to their devices. When they finished, they whispered into the ears of Bastion, getting a nod out of him in return.

'Now, Jackie boi. Have you checked out your new weapons?' Bastian asked.

'Weapons?'

'Are all Eurasian mages this stupid? Look at your hands.'

Jack peered at the palms of his hands, wondering what was different, but saw nothing out of the ordinary. However, when he turned them over, he couldn't see his nails. Instead, the pink flesh of the underside stuck out like a sore thumb.

'Did you pull them out?' Jack asked.

'Wow. You suggest something so macabre and still act so calm like 'tis but a scratch. How awful was your childhood?' Bastion said. Someone leaned in, whispering in his ear, giving him information he didn't know. 'Oh. You're one of the low-ranked mages. Ah, then it's kinda my fault. Whoops.'

'What?'

'Fear not! For I am a generous God. Your nails are still there. Check your shadow.'

With the spotlight still over him, Jack looked down at the floor, noticing the long, thin, black spikes that stuck out of the shadow his hand created. He wiggled his fingers and the spikes followed even though you couldn't see any spikes from Jack's hand. He then attempted closing his fingers into a fist but pricks, five in total, forced him to retract the motion, speckles of blood seeping out.

'Like your new weapons? Or should I say your new nails? Thought you could use the manicure, especially after how much you wanted to improve yourself,' Bastion explained.

'Um, sir. Should we tell him why we knew about it?' A woman whispered, the same one Jack remembered seeing before being bundled into the container. *Elivia, right?*

'Goddammit, woman! Who gave you permission to speak?' Bastion snapped, causing the others, bar the one called Alfred, to cower into their devices.

'Sorry, s-'

'Zip it. Forgive me for my rude-as-fuck minion, Jackie boi. I just wanted the best for you. That's all.'

Was this not the enemy? Was I actually not taken by the AAA? What was going on?! Jack stood there gobsmacked. He didn't know what to do. Confusion, gratitude, a hint of fear and several more emotions meshed together into whatever he felt at that very moment, silencing him in his bemusement.

'I thought I cured your voice. Why so quiet? Maybe I should tell you the truth. Y'see, Jackie boi. I know all about you.'

'What?!' Jack exclaimed, snapping out of his confused state of mind. 'How?'

'Your friend spilt everything from your name to how you hated yourself since you couldn't do an assassination. Enough chit chat from my end though. How about you speak to him yourself. Everyone! Take notes of the fight!'

Fight?

A door slid open on the far side of the Colosseum, causing Jack to turn around, wary of the sudden turn of events. Another beam of light shone on the opening, illuminating the darkness and revealing an all too familiar face, surrounded by puffs of smoke, making his entry as flashy as possible.

'No way,' Jack murmured.

'Hue. Now, this is where the fun begins,' Bastion announced. 'Jackie boi, say hello to your fellow Eurasian. Oh, and he's also a snitch. Thought I'd mention that.'

'Esper...'

Esper looked paler than before, his cheekbones showing, with his eyes being those of a madman, the same ones witnessed back in Egypt. His usual spiky hair slanted forwards, as if it aimed right at Jack, ready to be fired.

'You,' Esper snarled.

'Esper. I'm glad you're alright,' Jack said with a smile, relieved that he knew someone at least.

'You left me for dead!'

Jack realised the situation he was in and the cause. Esper was the one who didn't listen to the plan. Esper was the one who screwed up the assassination. Esper was the one who betrayed his partner and revealed the rendezvous point within the King's Room. Yet, Jack couldn't act out against his fellow Eurasian. He didn't want to. Surrounded by the AAA, Esper was the only one Jack could trust now. He needed to get on his good side.

'I tried to save you. I waited in –'

'Shut up. Shut up. Shut up!'

'Where's the ditzy Esper who didn't care about the world? Can't we talk it out like we used to? What have the Africans done to you?'

'I said Shut. Up.'

'When I meant fight, I didn't mean bickering between lovers,' Bastion spoke up, catching Esper and Jack's bewildered attention. 'Um, you do realise where you are? Oh, come on. Don't you know what a colosseum is used for? I demand a fight to the death. To sweeten the deal, I'll free the winner. How's that sound?'

'Fine by me,' Esper grunted.

'No, Esper wait,' Jack pleaded. But he couldn't get through to him.

Esper charged at Jack. His hair stood up, crackling as he got closer. He stretched out his hand and aimed at the exposed flesh on Jack's arms. Jack dodged the attack but a line of electricity arced through the centimetre gap between the two. Jack yelped in pain. His right arm became a ball of fuzz, jerking every few seconds.

'Please stop this, Esper. They're our enemies. Why do we have to listen to the African's orders?' Jack questioned, rolling away from another of Esper's swipes.

'Oi, Jackie. Stop being a whiny bitch and fight him mano a mano. I know you can go invisible and I've given you tools to land a KO. Here, let me help you.'

Bastion took out a mask and placed them over his face with the other mages following suit. With a flick of his fingers, the spotlights faded away, the artificial lighting dimmed down and the place went dark, reducing everyone but the masked mages' vision.

Jack skipped backwards, avoiding another attack and restoring his control over his spasming arm. He went into stealth, using the darkness to cover his own shadows.

'What are you doing?!' Esper screamed.

'Hey, I never said I couldn't interfere with the deathmatch,' Bastion teased.

'This is perfect,' Jack mumbled to himself before calling out to Esper. 'Let's calm down for a moment. We can both get out of this if we work together.'

'Really?' Esper responded, his voice quivering but, to Jack's relief, less angry in tone.

'Jackie boi, stop being a dick and ruining my fun or do you intend to make me use every cuss word in the English dictionary? Oh wait, no one taught you them.'

'That is correct, shire,' Alfred responded, the mask giving him a slight lisp.

'I don't want to fight him!' Jack yelled. 'Esper! Please team up with me.'

'Jack...'

'Haaaaaaah,' Bastion sighed. Flicking his fingers once more, the room lit up, exposing Jack's location, via his shadow, a few metres away from Esper's distraught face. 'Tell you what, either somebody dies or both of you get killed by my men. How's that sound instead?'

'Esper, please don't listen to him,' Jack pleaded again.

The Colosseum went quiet.

'Aha. Hahaha. AHAHAHAHAHAHAAAAAAAFuck you, Jack. I'm the one going to survive, *man*.'

Esper charged at Jack, taking him by surprise and hurling him to the floor. Esper readied his hand, filling it with a static charge, predicting where Jack's chest was for the killing blow. Jack stared at his crazed ex-partner, resenting his inability to get through to him. But if gaining strength meant betraying Eurasia, he didn't want it. He'd rather Esper have it instead.

Jack closed his eyes and removed his stealth, becoming an easier target. He waited for his demise. What was it going to be? An electric shock, stopping his heart from beating? A stranglehold, taking away his breath? Or maybe a simple slice of the throat, if Esper was capable of course. Maybe this was for the best. Jack never amounted to anything, always being weak, always relying on others. No...

Crack.

'Bravo, bravo,' Bastion applauded with the others clapping along with him. 'Alfred, please take care of the dead body.'

'Yes, sire.'

With that, most of the white-coated mages left while Alfred jumped down from the top of the walls down into the arena, walking to where Jack and Esper's body resided. He picked up the carcass of the loser, flinging it over his shoulder and nodding back at Bastion.

'Hey. Wake up,' Alfred nudged the victor.

'Huh?'

'What an attack at the end. I knew you had it in you. Great finale.'

Jack opened an eye, his chest feeling lighter than before. He looked around in a daze, unsure what had happened. Attack? What attack? A sticky liquid fell on his shoeless feet. He looked down at his hands. His nails no longer were invisible, absorbing the red substance like a leech and returning to their original state. He then looked at the marks on Esper, all five holes in his neck letting blood seep out of them.

'Did I do that?' Jack quivered.

'Yes,' Bastion confirmed.

'I see.'

'I'm sorry. I know you two were close,' Elivia tried to console, only to get piercing glares from her boss. But just as he opened his mouth to scold her, a faint chuckling drew their attention back to the arena.

'What's so funny?' Bastion asked.

'Me close to that imbecile? Ha! I don't give a damn about him. He ruined everything. He betrayed me. He tried to kill me and I'm meant to still be friends with this idiot? Don't make me laugh. He deserved to die!'

'Woah. He finally broke!' Bastion exclaimed. 'Love this guy. He's hilarious. Hey, Jackie boi.'

'What?!' Jack growled, baring his teeth and into an instinctive animalistic position, his arms outstretched, ready to attack at a moment's notice.

'I like you a lot. You're a great experiment. As a reward, how about I get you promoted and show you the truth?'

17

Meeting Amongst Battalion Leaders

With the time of the meeting upon them, Gin picked up Brim and the pair made their way to the allocated room. An ominous silence surrounded them in the initial stages of their journey, both knowing that their peaceful lifestyle, relative to the other squadrons, was about to end.

'You're awfully silent,' Brim said, breaking the deadlock at last.

'Hm? I was busy thinking,' Gin replied.

'You do that a lot, don't you? What's on your mind this time.'

'About other combinations like the human fireball catapult like if I have some water elementals instead of fire elementals. They would then form an anti-fireball team. Add some earth elementals and we could use stones as projectiles too! I can't wait to see how they will do in the battle, Brim.'

'I can see why Alder thought of you as a brat. You're way too enthusiastic for an adult.'

'Brim. I don't expect this of you.'

'Haha. I jest. Anyway, if we succeed and get promoted, we could have other types of mages joining us.'

'Eh? There are other types of mages?' Gin asked in confusion, causing Brim to raise an eyebrow in suspicion.

'Have you been living under a rock or something?'

'I didn't learn about other mages when I was growing up. Squadron W is also the only squadron I've been in. My only experiences of mages are the ones in this squadron,' Gin responded, choosing his words wisely.

'I see,' Brim replied, accepting the twisted truth. 'Well anyway, some types of mages are high ranked by default. You won't see an acid elemental, or at least a living one, that is ranked D or below for example. Low ranked versions would probably have died to their own acid eating away at them.'

'Wow. That just makes me want to get promoted even more. Imagine marching on the battlefield, with no vision of the enemy, and a random blob of acid falls on top of you.'

'Errr. Alright then,' Brim said, not knowing how to respond.

'Hey. Don't give me that. You've got to be a little crazy to make progress. It's something someone always told me.'

'If you say so. Oh, we're here.'

Gin paused outside the door. His last comment sent him into deep thought, making him remember of a past he thought he locked away years ago.

'Are you afraid?' Brim broke Gin's trance.

'Afraid of what?' Gin perked up.

'I know squadron W hasn't been in any battles in their history. This being your maiden is probably a big deal. I know it was for me when I first went onto the battlefield.'

'If I was so afraid of death and killing, I wouldn't have accepted being battalion leader in the first place!' Gin paused before adding a, 'Yeah. That part of me is long gone.'

Unconvinced by what Gin said, Brim gave him a consoling smile. He understood the feeling well. Gin was still human, just like everyone else. With that hint of hesitation shown, Brim opened the door for Gin, allowing him to enter first. Inside the room was a large round table, surrounded by about twenty chairs and only one of them was being used.

The occupant was a man covered in so much fur that you couldn't see any skin. He wore just a pair of shorts, long enough to reach his knees. It reminded Gin of his fight with Varunel. Like Varunel, he was covered in fur. However, the man in front of him did not have horns, nor did he have an elongated snout, so he had his unique distinctions. Instead, his nose was short and closer to Gin's in shape. *Wait. Have I seen this person before?* Gin wondered. *Oh, I remember.*

'Hi!' Gin greeted with an outstretched arm. 'I believed we met once before when your colleague bumped into me. My name is Gin Gale. What's yours?'

The man didn't move at all. He just shifted his eyes towards Gin, grunted in an unfriendly manner. Gin couldn't help but feel offended, expecting an insult like a comment about his rank, but then he smiled through his hair and met the handshake.

'It's Rob. Nice to meet you.'

'Not going to lie, but I thought you were going to show hostility. I do remember your comments several months ago. Glad I'm proven wrong,' Gin said.

'Yes, I apologise for how I acted back then. I didn't expect such progress in such a short time.'

'Apology accepted.'

'And you must be Brim Stones. You transferred from another squadron, right? Gratz on your role as battalion leader.'

'Thank you,' Brim acknowledged with a bow before turning back to Gin, whispering, 'Do you two know each other?'

Gin did an unnoticeable shake of his head. *Looks like you can't judge someone on first impressions*, Gin thought.

The door to the room swung right open, not a moment before Gin and Brim sat down. Five people entered, three of whom Gin recognised. He knew Michal, the woman that rode on the lupim, whose name Gin found out later to be Emsee, and the colonel. The other two were new. Brim seemed to know them though, greeting them with open arms.

One of them had the same rough, dark skin as Brim. His hair was black and braided. The other looked like a manush. She had pale white skin, average proportions, neither looking too weak nor too strong, with no defining feature that hinted at an ability. Instead, she had a tinoo resting on her shoulders, playing with her black hair. *A fire elemental and a utility familiar type respectively*, Gin assumed.

Everyone sat down apart from Emsee, who handed out some documents containing detailed descriptions about the proposed plan. The first few pages had hand-drawn maps of the supposed battlefield. The later ones were about the battle strategy. Everyone took a few minutes to skim through it before the colonel called for everyone's attention.

'Is everyone ready?' she asked. Brim raised his hands in response.

'Aren't there more battalion leaders? Shouldn't we wait for them?'

'You've probably haven't read that far into the plan, have you? Basically, we've split into two main groups. I just had a meeting with that second group, which explains my lateness. The six of you will have a different role in the battle, so your briefing will be different from the other group.'

'Ah. I see,' Brim understood.

'Maria,' Emsee whispered. 'I don't think everyone knows each other.'

'Oh, right. An introduction is called for then. The fire elemental on your right is Brim. He's transferred from Squadron L. Other transfers from squadron L are Jake, another fire elemental, and Syndra, the utility familiar type,' the colonel introduced, gesturing towards Brim and the other two mages that he was friendly with. 'The hairy sasquatch bestial is Rob and the child with the Xernims on his arms is called Gin. The stone elemental is Michal. Of course, you should know my second-in-command, Emsee, and myself. Just call me Maria.'

Second-in-command? Gin realised, shocked by the statement considering he never noticed her before.

'Both Emsee and Syndra have come from their mission in Africa,' the colonel continued.

Ah.

With the introductions done, everyone nodded to one another, acknowledging their positions. However, Jake and Syndra looked at Gin with doubt in their eyes. Was it the Xernims, the rank he gave himself, or his height (Gin didn't take anything out of the potential reason)? Not that Gin was too bothered by the looks, half-expecting them in the first place.

'Any other questions? No? Let's begin then. I'll hand it over to Emsee,' the colonel prompted, sitting down into her seat.

'Our scouts set out to complete an assassination in Egypt and then retreated once that was complete. Out of our men, five remain in the city while four got captured and their whereabouts are unknown,' Emsee reported. 'However, our intel says that the AAA will send a force of roughly five-thousand. We expect to have four-thousand by the time we depart. Since we're splitting into two groups, the combined strength of your battalions is closer to two-thousand-five-hundred.'

'Surely, that's not nearly enough!' Jake complained. 'That's a suicide mission. Not to mention seventy percent of this squadron are rank D or below. We wouldn't stand a chance anyway. The best course of action is to have everyone on defence, not separate into two groups.'

'I understand what you're trying to say, Jake. I'm sure everyone has the same concerns. However, our aim is not to beat the enemy in a battle of strength. Rather, we will win by outwitting them. I'll tell you how later on. But first, we will split your group into three small teams: utility, artillery and defence,' The colonel ordered.

'Maria and I can't join this battle. She is SS rank while, even though I am E rank myself, my lupim is S rank. The MBP said my lupim isn't allowed, so I'm pretty much useless. The rest of you meet the requirement of being B rank and below.

The utility team is composed of Michal and Syndra, with Syndra being the overall in-charge of the team. Your role is to provide backup for the other two teams. Syndra, with the other utility familiar types, will send and receive information. I'm sure everyone has memorised the signals by now. Michal, on the other hand, has recently been creating armour for Gin's battalion. He will be on maintenance duty. Any questions?'

'No ma'am!' Syndra and Michal said in unison.

'Good. Now for the artillery team. That would be run by Brim and Jake, with Brim in charge of that team. Your job is simple. Bombard the enemy with your fireballs and such. Whittle them down. Give our defence team protection with your water-balls. You guys are the support.'

'Looks like we're working together again,' Jake commented.

'Looking forward to it,' Brim replied.

'The final team is Gin and Rob. As the offence team, you are the backbone of this operation. You cannot let the enemy pass through you. With the armour and the training going on, this should be manageable. Just hold your ground and we will have a good chance of victory. And the one leading this team will be-'

Emsee turned to the colonel. They whispered something to one another. A mutual nod later and Maria faced the others once more.

'Yup. The one leading the defence team will be Gin.'

'What?!' Jake exclaimed, jumping out of his seat and slamming on the table.

'Is there a problem, Jake?'

'*That* man can't be leader. He definitely can't be in charge! He's a low ranked, weak, inexperienced, Xernim user. Putting him in charge of the most important part of the army just confirms the loss!'

'Me a weak Xernim user?' Gin retorted. 'Care for a duel if that's the case?'

'With pleasure.'

'Enough! Stop. Both of you,' the colonel ordered. 'My choice was based on several things. First of all, Gin is your senior in this squadron, Jake. He's been here for almost a year while you transferred only two weeks ago.'

The colonel's piercing glare sat both of them down. She stayed silent for a few more seconds before continuing her explanation.

'Secondly, he is a pupil of Alder. I trust his recommendations more than I trust you. According to Alder's and my observations, Gin is great at adapting to a situation. Gin wins duels in which he would lose head on. His methods are unorthodox but it gets the job done. He's constantly coming up with ideas. The armour Michal makes, the F ranks that can now be used in the battle, increasing our fighting force by five-hundred, all add to his repertoire. He holds no prejudice to the other members, which is what our squadron is based upon. His battalion holds huge respect for him. Even our battle plan came from an unpolished idea Gin came to my office to speak about.

Compared to that, you reckon he isn't leadership worthy? How about we have a vote. See if the others have the same opinion. All in favour of Rob being in charge instead, raise your hands. Now all in favour of Gin, raise your hands.'

With a vote of six to two, Gin won. Brim, Maria, Michal and Emsee put their hands up straight away, with Rob following soon after. Even Gin, who wasn't sure whether he was worthy of the role or not, put his hand up, without hesitation, after hearing the colonel's opinion of him. The only vote against Gin came from the newcomers.

'I thought the same thing at the start but I believe he'll be better in the role too,' Rob admitted, taking away his credentials as the alternative.

'Tch,' Jake tutted.

'Don't disrespect your superiors like that. That includes Gin,' the colonel snapped, with Jake looking away in response. 'Now that's settled, let's discuss the plan. Please go to page two.'

Everyone turned the pages to find a map labelled 'The Path'. The path began at Eilat, in Israel, and ended at Suez, a town in the city of Egypt. It was the strip of land that connected Eurasia to Africa. Either side of the path was the sea and in-between the land and the sea were walls, all supposedly several kilometres tall. In fact, the entire coastlines were surrounded by the same wall.

Gin found it odd. In books of the past, he saw maps of the exact same area. The land that connected the two continents was more than five-hundred kilometres in width. The map in front of him showed that the path was only thirty kilometres wide instead. The area, that was once land, was now water. *What happened in the past to cause that?* Gin wondered.

'All your battalions will hold the defence in Eilat,' the colonel continued. 'It's a four-hundred-kilometre trek from our home in Jerusalem. The AAA's barracks, in Cairo, is more than five-hundred kilometres from Eilat. Along with the fact that their army is larger, it should take them two months to reach us. On the other hand, it should take us a month and a half to reach Eilat. We will depart in ten days, so be prepared by then.'

'What's the plan once we get there?' Syndra asked for the first time that meeting.

'Defend,' the colonel responded. 'Unfortunately, we don't have information on what type of mages you are facing. Just don't let them through and the other group will do their job. However, if you can't stand your ground, then it's all over. Winning is one thing, but not losing is another. That's why being outnumbered isn't as much of an issue.'

'Then what happens?' Brim asked.

'The other group will do what I assigned them to do. They're leaving tomorrow morning so that they could be prepared on time.'

'You're avoiding telling us what the other group is going to do, aren't you?' Rob pointed out.

'Indeed,' the colonel confirmed. 'It's actually a request from someone. Not knowing what they're doing won't hinder you, so it's irrelevant information anyway. For now, finish any last-minute training, get your battalions prepared and we will rendezvous outside the tree in about ten days. Does everyone understand? Good. You're all dismissed apart from Gin.'

As everyone but him got up, Gin could feel the scorn coming from Jake but Brim patted his sparring partner on the shoulder. It was a supportive don't-worry-everything-will-be-fine sort of hold. Gin thought it wasn't needed, but it was good to know someone trusted him.

'Do you have a goal, child?' the colonel started, making sure everyone had left.

'What do you mean?' Gin responded.

'Do you have a plan, an ambition, something you want to achieve in your life?'

Gin placed his hand on his beard and thought for a moment but the colonel interrupted him.

'The fact you need to think about it says a lot,' she said. 'I'll be honest here. I'm disappointed in you.'

'Why are you saying this all of a sudden?' Gin asked.

'You were, supposedly, an unranked thirty-year-old man that looked like he was a hundred and thirty. You had no distinct abilities and used pieces of metal that I have never heard of as your way of fighting. You got trounced in the initiation test but got through via a technicality. You should have died, but somehow lived without a heart. You would have thought someone like that was someone to look out for, but no. Your actions are predictable, your attitude is suboptimal and your personality is so uninteresting and bland that I couldn't help but feel disappointed.'

'Is that a problem?'

'You're just proving my point. You lack a direction and have such a carefree approach to life that it's infuriating to most. Who sparks a fight with your fellow battalion leader like you did? Do you want us to fall from within? Do you not care about the consequences of your actions?'

'Ah. I understand now. You're right,' Gin sighed, contemplating his next choice of words. 'To be honest, I used to have a goal but that was no longer possible, or rather there's no point in achieving it now. Too much has happened. I just don't really care at this point.'

'So, you're lost and aimless.'

'I wouldn't say that.'

'Child, do you know why I think your training with Alder was complete and utter shambles?' the colonel's eyes began to narrow.

'Alder said I was improving though,' Gin said in defence.

'In terms of skill. However, as a character, you're still as bland as ever. You lack a spark. That's what I want to develop. You could tell why I was sceptical when Alder said he wanted to appoint you as his replacement. Do you know his reason as well?'

Gin thought for a bit before saying, 'Because I had potential?'

'No. Although he had said that at one point, the real reason was different. It's actually nonsensical now that I think about it. He wanted to appoint you as the next leader of his battalion because you accepted the Xernim.'

'Wow. That really is bull-' Gin said, stopping himself from swearing.

'I guess it's not his fault. We were in the same squadron at one point and he was always bullied for being a Xernim user. They're sort of a hated bunch. The MBP conditioned everyone to believe that the successful are those who are strong by themselves. Those who rely on parasites to be their strength are considered weak by most, even if they are stronger in a one v one.'

'So, what does that have to do with me?'

'You treated him differently. You didn't see him as a Xernim user, but as a mentor to be respected. You *accepted* to use Xernims by your own accord. Even though you were arrogant and rash with him, he valued you highly. He sat you out of training so that you could observe everyone else. He was preparing you for the role.'

Gin could tell the colonel looked unimpressed. She paced a couple of times before taking a seat, sitting down in a manner that turned the conversation into a casual discussion rather than the lecture prior.

'I, on the other hand, didn't like the appointment. In fact, I was about to demote you as the war was coming ever closer. But then you came to me. You had ideas. You presented them to me in my office. You do have potential though. But you need guidance. Use your brain a little, set a goal for yourself and you'll go far. Not only that, Joan has been enjoying her time with you as well.'

'She has?' Gin said in a surprised tone.

'Yes, child. She was actually my medic before you, but she decided to become yours.'

'She used to be yours? And she voluntarily decided to become mine? This is news to me. Thought she hated babysitting me.'

'She didn't have to do anything when she was with me. I never got injured or did anything stupid. You, on the other hand, are rash and got hurt regularly. Although she isn't the type to say it, she enjoys helping you heal. It keeps her busy. She also found a passion for cooking. I'm presuming that was because of you too?'

'Possibly,' Gin responded, thinking back to the mage-meat meals Joan made for him.

'I'm sidetracking a bit. Essentially, the point of this talk is that you need to figure out why you do what you do, but I admit your luck is incredible. If you didn't apply to this squadron, you would never have gotten a chance to join. If you didn't face Varunel, you would never have piqued my interest. If you never had contacts with Wontiferus, we would probably never have gotten this mission. If you never met Alder, you would never have been a battalion leader. If I wasn't the way I am, I might not have been so lenient with your ideas. While the other leaders needed to be B rank and battle experience, you just happened to be in the right place at the right time, doing the right things. Am I making any sense to you?'

'Yes.' Gin gave an immediate reply out of fear that she would say something about his hesitation again.

'I'll re-iterate again,' she said anyway. 'Your luck is incredible. It's like a supernatural power, beyond our control, is governing your fate. However, whatever the reason for your rise in power was, you have my full support. Grow and take everyone else with you.'

'Was this the point of keeping me behind to give me this pep talk?' Gin asked, buoyed by the encouragement.

'Ha! No, child. I actually wanted to speak to you about something else, but I sort of spoke my mind to you.'

'A lot of people tell me how they feel without meaning to. Don't know why though. Anyway, what did you want to talk about?'

'I believe that one of you should know what the other group doing. Having no one know might lead to doubt, and a loss in morality when things get rough.'

'Oh, right. Your plan is nothing like the one I proposed,' Gin noticed. 'Was something wrong?'

'Your plan was terrible. I could point out a score or so flaws in it. The others didn't need to know though, so I put credit for this plan upon you.'

Her serious tone made Gin realise that she wasn't lying about finding his plan terrible.

'Heh. I see. What are they going to do then?'

'Remember the abnormality you pointed out?'

'In the documents I gave you?'

'Yes.'

'Oh, we're actually going to use them?' Gin perked up.

'That's the only good part of your plan I used. Now, let me show you how,' the colonel grinned, opening up a hidden document she kept in her trousers.

18

Departure

Gin didn't know how to react to the pile of boxes on his bed. Each and every one of them had the same, mage-meat-filled, premade meal. On top of it all was a letter, written by Joan with handwriting so horrendous that Gin ruffled his face, trying to figure out the message. Even then, the legible words were written as they were pronounced, rather than their correct spelling.

The letter contained instructions and warnings, ranging from how to eat the food to, in her own words, "Dont you dare get badly hert or Ill kill you insted". *So much for her enjoying being my medic,* Gin thought, reminiscing on what the colonel said the other day. As he read further, he concluded that the rest of the letter was just as bad. Granted, Gin wasn't perfect in his own prose, but at least he was miles above this atrocity. It reminded Gin of how Joan left in a not-so-peaceful-manner.

'They need to practise or we'll be outclassed,' he said at the time.

'We need them healthy. I.E. not in the pathetic state you leave them in after each session,' she snapped back, in front of the entire battalion.

'They won't be efficient if they ease up on the training.'

'They won't be efficient if they get injured pointlessly.'

'There's a point in practice!'

'There's a point in resting, too!'

There was no chance of winning against her, so Gin conceded. He didn't believe he was wrong. Just that Joan put out valid arguments. There's a difference in his mind. But, with that scene put into the back of his mind, Gin focused on the task ahead. He equipped his Xernims with blades and shields, loaded his belt with the INS and put on the stone chest plate Michal made for him.

'You in there Gigi?' Wo called.

'Yeah. Co–'

Wo barged in without neither letting Gin finish his sentence nor putting on his armour. He carried two small capsules in his hands, throwing both to Gin. They had a 'do not use unless emergency' label on them.

'What are these?' Gin asked, catching both of the capsules and inspecting them.

'The last of your nanobot-boosters,' Wo replied in a solemn tone.

'Thought so. Are they really what's left?'

'We didn't bring that many when we left the village. You had to use two when you were in a coma as well. We didn't even bring the machine that makes them with us. If something similar happens again, you'll only be able to recover once. Get another fatal injury after that and you probably won't live.'

'All the more reason for us to go back to my village, no?'

'I'll ask the colonel to allow a side mission once your battle is done.'

'Does she know?'

'That you're a manush? No,' Wo rejected the notion, sitting on the bed before continuing, 'That's our little secret. Not sure how everyone would react if they found out. Can't have that now, can we?'

'I would have expected you to joke about telling everyone.'

Wo pursed his lips, staring at Gin with the kind of intent that spoke more than any words could.

'You're awfully serious today, huh.' Gin noted.

'I'm worried about you,' Wo replied straight away. 'I won't be around for this mission, so I got to make sure everything's alright.'

'Woah. Did not expect you to say you actually care for me. Where's the aloof Wontiferus Poxim who mocks me that I know and don't love?'

'Gin.'

'Sorry.' Gin composed himself after enjoying the rare brief moment of power over Wo. 'Why the sudden concern?'

'Will you be ok?' Wo's response once again instant.

'Oh, that's what you're getting at.'

'After what happened all those years ago, I'm not sure how you'll act this time.'

'I told you already. I'm fine now. The fact that I'm letting you speak with me proves it.'

'You're right.'

The room went silent again. Gin looked down, fiddling with his Xernim, double-checking that the INS had no room to slip out. He ignored the sympathetic gaze of what he considered his uncle turned best friend, unsure whether he wanted to talk more about their past or not.

'Liz would be rolling in her grave if I ever caused you serious harm,' Wo mumbled.

'Instead, you send her son to war?' Gin taunted.

'Better than letting you be the fat-ass you were,' Wo joked back.

'There we go!'

Gin leapt from his bed and grappled Wo by the waist, knocking him down, before latching onto his head into a headlock. His target's face turned red but in return, a smile, one that ran from ear to ear, brightened the mood for both of them.

'Haha looks like you've learnt some new tricks,' Wo wheezed, patting Gin's arms in surrender.

'Your age must be getting to you,' Gin smirked, letting go of his hold.

'I let you have that.'

'Sure, whatever. By the way, where's the colonel? Haven't seen her yet and I need to do final checks on the battalion before we leave.'

'She went and took some of the A ranks and above towards Squadron M's base. She said she needed to get something.'

'Huh? I wanted to ask her about something.'

'Save it for after you've won. You should be going anyway, Gigi. I took too much of your time.'

'That's true,' Gin said, getting up and back to his desk to tidy things up. 'It was nice to have a decent conversation with you for once!'

'Hey, I'm not that bad!'

'Sure, you aren't,' Gin replied, his voice riddled with a smug sarcasm.

'Anyway, Good luck, Gin. Win one for Eurasia, even if this is a low-level clash.'

'Thanks.'

Gin placed the nano-boosters in an INS-sized container and fitted that on his belt. With that done, he was ready. After a final goodbye to Wo, Gin headed out towards the ground floor where his battalion waited for him.

The walk along the way was relatively quiet. With half of the squadron already gone and the rest were waiting outside, except a certain group of mages that remained. Their skin looked layered, like several rolls of fat, and flaky, as if to fall off any moment. There was nothing to suggest any offensive capabilities nor any defensive ones on these mages, so Gin carried on as they continued a small briefing with the colonel's second-in-command, whose name Gin had forgotten.

It turned out those mages weren't the only firsts for Gin. Several wooden carts and caravans, lined up and filled with food, water and material, stood proud outside the Rezah. Each was assigned a lupim; smaller that Emsee's, (*Oh, that's her name,* Gin realised), but were packed with more muscle to carry the carts.

Maybe mages thought using animals don't count, Gin thought as he wondered why the prideful mages used the Lupim without hesitation. But Gin concluded that the way the mages used technology made it seem like anything made in the last three-thousand years didn't exist. It would have been a different story had he showed them the cars from his village. The mages probably would have rejected them straight away. *Probably.*

A squawk drew Gin's attention to the sky. Tinoos flew overhead, going around in circles. All of them had red plumes, and eyes that that lit up under the dark before the dawn. Their formation signalled that everyone was to stay put with only a matter of time before they change their flight pattern.

'Gin!' someone called out.

'Hm?' Gin looked towards the origin of the sound.

'Looks like you're all ready to go now' Brim rushed towards him as he finished talking with members from his battalion.

'Yeah,' Gin agreed, double checking his equipment. 'How long left until we leave?'

'Still a couple more days. Most of the combatants are out though,' Brim said, indicating to the battalions standing in a half-hearted square formation. 'We're just getting our supplies loaded now. Want to help out?'

'Maybe later. My battalion is probably waiting for me.'

'Suit yourself. Your battalion is next to the caravans anyway. Might as well accompany me.'

Gin nodded. After letting Brim have a few final words with his battalion, the pair headed towards the caravans. The usual items, like jugs of water, fruit, meat and tents, were loaded into them. However, what caught Gin's eyes were the same, flaky-skinned mages boarding them as well. Alongside them was another new type of mage Gin had never seen before, each covered by shrubbery on their fronts and back, like a walking, talking bush.

'Who are they?' Gin asked.

'Those guys? Oh, they're our food,' brim replied.

'What?!'

'Don't tell me you haven't seen the utility farmer types before?'

Gin stood still for a moment, taken aback by the revelations.

'They're the farmers?' he tried to say in a calm manner but still failed to hide his shock.

'Why are you so surprised? What did you expect?'

'People with a plot of land and tools,' Gin said, causing Brim to raise an eyebrow.

'I don't even want to know where you get these ideas. But no. The flabby ones provide us with the meat, and the ones with the bushes grow fruits on their body.'

The thought, that even the fruits were tainted by the mages, made Gin's stomach churn in rejection to the "vegetarian" meal he ate for breakfast. Did that count as cannibalism? He already tried to boycott the meat, but now he didn't know if the fruit and vegetables were safe to eat either. Both the meat and plants tasted amazing and he was assured they were good for his health too. There wasn't a reason not to eat them. *Why did it still feel so wrong?* Gin wondered.

'Alright. This is where we part ways,' Brim said. 'You're free to come and help out after you're done.'

'Sure,' Gin replied, trying to forget what he just witnessed.

'Oh! Forgot to give you this.'

Brim handed Gin over several cuboid-shaped stone containers. Gin opened one and smelt the distinct aroma of a fire elemental's sweat. He drowned himself in the stench, taking away the thoughts of his newfound dietary issues, anticipating how he could incorporate the mage-oil into his blade boxing.

'Thanks! Can't wait to use them,' Gin said.

'Still, don't know what you plan on doing with them,' Brim responded.

'Oh, they're so I can continue my winning streak and lead against you to fifty forty-two.'

'It's forty-seven forty-five'

'I'm still winning,' Gin's scoff showed its effectiveness as Brim grimaced under the truth.

The distant calls for Gin made him look up to the sight of a few battalion members beckon their leader. He returned a faint smile before turning back to a salty Brim.

'Heh. Looks like everyone wants to speak to me today.'

'It's fine. Go meet them. I'll continue loading the cargo.'

'Sorry I couldn't help.'

'No problem,' Brim waved before making his way to his duties. 'Take care!'

With their temporary parting, Gin headed towards his battalion. Once they all noticed him, Gin's battalion went into a block formation within seconds, granting a satisfying feeling at how disciplined they became, proving that the training paid off. It also allowed an easy method of counting attendance. The maths was simple, counting the rows multiplied by the columns, or at least it was for Gin. Joan's letter made him question whether the mages got any proper education in basic subjects like English and Mathematics. The mages didn't care though, wearing their new armour with pride. They looked stronger. They *felt* stronger. Their arrangements within the formation only sought to complement each other, with the mid-ranged (long-ranged mages were part of the artillery team) in the rear and the beefy, melee-only, mages as front-liners and the agile, vulnerable mages acted as support in the middle.

'Um. Leader, sir?'

Gin hadn't realised that he got lost in admiration of his own efforts. When he snapped out of it, he saw the new stone elemental. As he examined him, Gin realised that the mage's stone exoskeleton acted like a mask. You couldn't see his face, or any body part for that matter, apart from his hazel-brown eyes.

'Do I know you?' Gin queried.

'Oh. No. I don't think so. Actually, yes. I bumped into you once. I'm Sam.'

The voice was muffled through the mask. It was still audible though but had a rough sound. It still didn't help Gin remember who this person was, but he decided that he'd play along.

'And you're here because?' Gin asked.

'Right. I was told to be your handyman. I help carry your stuff,' Sam said.

'Um. I don't have anything for you to carry. Did someone say I needed help?'

'No. I was in Rob's battalion. I watched you. I liked you. I asked for a transfer. I didn't know what I can do. I thought I could help carry stuff.'

Gin felt irked somewhat. He didn't know why. Was it his style of speaking or the stalker-like personality Sam seemed to have? Or maybe it was the fact that it felt like talking to a golem rather than most of the mages he encountered so far.

'Does leader not need me?' he asked, with a little sadness in the muffled voice.

'It's fine. The more I command, the stronger my battalion becomes. I'll find out your abilities later. How about you act as my messenger and help carry out my orders?'

'Mm. Ok!' Sam said, excitement in his body language rather than the voice. 'Oh. Why is leader here? Why aren't you in the caravan? Other leaders are sitting in the caravans. The Lupims will pull them. Rest of us will walk.'

'Are they?'

'Yes.'

Gin thought about it for a moment. He didn't like the idea of walking for hundreds of kilometres, but he also wanted to gain the respect of his battalion even further. *So that's why Brim left his battalion to go to the caravans,* he realised.

'I'm not lazy like him. I think will walk alongside my battalion,' Gin announced.

'Really?!'

'Yeah...I guess.'

'Leader is amazing! I like you more now.'

'Thanks,' Gin replied, turning a little red from the praise. 'As my newly appointed messenger, mind relaying that to the other battalion members? They probably will try to make room for me.'

'Mm. Will do!' Sam accepted, scurrying off to tell the others.

Gin went around talking to everyone in his battalion. As D, E and F ranks, they were just as inexperienced in war as Gin was. Their nervousness showed, but as the day went on, talking with their leader calmed them down. It was the least he could do.

The chatter went on into the nights, as the mages camped outside the rezah as practice. Gin struggled setting up his tent. As a battalion leader, he was given one while the others had to sleep outside. It collapsed three times before he asked for help. How was he supposed to know that you were meant to stake down the corners first or where to put the wooden poles? His battalion laughed at his helplessness. It just meant that he was just like them; weak by himself, but his reliance on others made him strong.

They discussed tactics the following day. It was different from the usual training sessions (Gin had to, otherwise he risked facing Joan's wrath). It got mixed opinions, from the downright bored, to those who stuck to him like a snail–like Sam who stuck right beside him, in whatever he did, watching with eager gazes through the confining mask.

Suddenly everyone went quiet and their eyes were focused onto the skies. The tinoos above them screeched a deafening sound. They dived down, before soaring back to their original heights. Two more tinoos joined the original three as they changed their formation from the circle to a V–shaped arrowhead. Gin knew what that meant.

'Alright!' Gin ordered. 'Everyone into formation!'

It was time to go.

19

Dunes, Duties and Dreams

'Three, two, one. Heave!'

The bestial juggernaut types tugged on the vine rope attached to the cart, preventing the churning sand from swallowing it like anything else caught within its spiral of death. The whirlpool of quicksand grew and grew, forming a depression in the centre where all the sand converged. Where it led to, the mages could only guess.

'Good job everyone,' Rob praised his battalion.

'Can't believe how strong you guys are. Pulled that cart out effortlessly,' Gin added.

'That's our job,' Rob replied, giving Gin a gentle punch on the shoulder.

'This is our chance. Support team help out,' Brim ordered.

'Wait. Help out with what?' Gin questioned.

A sudden stench filled the area. The mages carried pots of their waste, chucking the excrements into the sand whirlpool. The faeces circulated the sand, crushed with each rotation and grounded into a stinky pulp before getting lost inside the vortex.

'Why on earth did we chuck our literal shit into there?!' Gin exclaimed.

'Shit?' Rob got confused.

'Really? Not even that word?' Gin sighed, pinching the bridge of his nose. 'Ok, dung then?'

'Oh!'

Michal watched the whole ordeal from the side-lines, chuckling at Gin's occasional moment of stupidity and his constant need to have things explained to him. How did he not know the excrements helped the desert's fertility? Sure, the sand above couldn't even allow a brush to bloom, but down below was an oasis of nourishment for those plants capable of reaching it. Wasn't it obvious the sand whirlpools helped deliver the manure down to the depths? *But Gin's a bit special in the head, isn't he?* Michal argued with himself.

'What should we do?' one of the stone elemental type mages under Michal's command asked him, tugging on his shirt to grab his attention.

Caught off guard, Michal panicked. 'Um, Er. Er. What we could do is...' he looked around, seeing if he could get any inspiration.

Unable to find any, he glanced at Gin who nodded after whatever explanation Rob gave him. Gin did his signature hand on chin motion, going into a moment of thought. He then looked up and around and, after noticing the pickle Michal was in (or at least Michal thought he noticed), he turned to Rob again.

'From the sounds of things, you guys need some way to make getting the last bits out of the pots. Not to mention the pots are a bit inefficient in keeping our wastes being so small,' Gin said out loud.

Michal smiled, understanding the (probably) intentional hint. 'Let's go make tools to help with the process.'

'Order understood!' the mage responded, rushing back to the battalion.

With the whole squadron put to work, the tinoo formation in the sky changed to that of a line that slanted, indicating that the leaders needed to gather at their caravan for a meeting, though there was no rush based on the tinoos' speed. However, knowing that he wasn't of much help when it came to creating tools, Michal headed towards the meeting point, arriving first.

Having found time for himself, Michal unhooked one of the stones attached to his limbs. He caressed the slab, letting his sweat to change outer stone into a malleable material but still allowing the core to remain solid. He tweaked one end, elongating the side in five places, before snapping the finger-shaped objects off. His sweat then turned foamy, eating away at the insides of the fingers, leaving a hollow gap that his finger could slide into, only for the acidity to eat through the whole thing, creating a tube rather than anything he could use.

'Ack!' Michal cried out in frustration.

'Will you shut up?!' a disgruntled and sleepy Jake clamoured back.

'Oh, Sorry.'

Jake went back to sleep while a startled Michal placed his failed creation under a piece of cloth. How long was he there for? Ignoring the man, Michal went into a thoughtless daze until the others arrived. It wasn't until the sun set, as well as all the duties getting completed, did the other leaders join the pair. All except for the other support group's leader.

'Where's Syndra?' Michal asked.

'She needed to scout something,' Rob responded, his voice as gruff as ever, though still sounding friendly at the same time.

'Oh. Why do we need to have the meeting then?'

'Huh. What's happening?' Jake wondered too, rubbing his eyes awake.

'There are more sandpools further in our path,' Gin explained. 'They're fine to navigate for most of us, but for some of the wagons and particularly the less mobile mages, it's too dangerous for them.'

'And so, Jake's and my battalion, as well as half of Syndra's, will take a different route to avoid them. It'll set our group back by two days from the main group,' Rob picked up.

'We can't predict these natural events, unfortunately,' Brim admitted. 'Anyway, we decided to leave by tomorrow. We'll rest up for today since we're still ahead of schedule.'

'Ok,' Michal agreed.

Jake didn't respond, going straight back to sleep with Rob and Brim following suit. Gin, however, placed a hand on Michal's shoulder.

'You did well,' he whispered. 'The tools helped us immensely. They couldn't have done it without your orders.'

'That's because you helped me out.'

'What are you talking about? I haven't spoken to you at all today,' Gin said with a smile, emphasising the last sentence while keeping his voice down. 'This was all of your own making.'

'So, I was useful?'

'Very. Anyway, I'm going to sleep outside.'

'Again? We do have the tents and the caravans for leaders, y'know.'

'Heh. Promised the battalion I would. Not that I mind either. Some of the bestial types are super fluffy and a great pillow! Wonder what the fur is made of,' Gin mumbled in the last sentence.

'Ah, ok,' Michal replied while thinking, *He really is a strange one.*

As Gin left, Michal went back to his project, but he could already predict the glares Jake would give if he made any noise. He couldn't sleep himself. His heart thumped with a sense of accomplishment, his chest puffed out more than usual and he had a grin that he couldn't contain. So, to calm down, Michal let out a sigh but that only caused Brim and Rob to stir and moan. Knowing he was becoming an annoyance, he stepped out to get some fresh air.

A cold wind blew over the cinders of the campfires but a clear sky allowed the stars and a full moon to illuminate the desert in a bluish hue. The animals and mages slept like the haxors after a good hunt. Deservedly so after five days and fifty kilometres travel under the squadron's belt.

It didn't feel like a battle that decided the squadron's fate was imminent but Michal enjoyed that. No tension. No unrest. No worries. Just the camaraderie between fellow mages fighting under the same banner of Eurasia. And Michal was part of it! Oh, how that thought put a spring in his step, prancing on the sand as if no one was watching. Or at least he thought that was the case.

'Are you ok?'

Michal froze mid-air. He landed an awkward leg on the sand that shifted below him, causing him to lose the little balance he had and tumble head-first into the cool embrace of the desert. He picked himself up, using the stone attached to his arms as leverage, turning to see Syndra giving him a scrunched-up look in disgust.

'You're a battalion leader how exactly?' she questioned.

'Squadron W needed me,' Michal replied, brushing off the sand and giving Syndra the same gleeful grin.

'I see. Doesn't explain anything, but I see.'

'Oh. Oh. But it's different. I'm –' Michal clasped his mouth, realising he spoke louder than he should have after seeing a few mages roll over in their sleep. He crawled up to Syndra, speaking in a whisper this time. 'I'm following my dream, you see.'

Syndra sighed, keeping a watch on the moonlit skies, but decided to entertain Michal. 'What dream?'

'I was born a low-ranked stone elemental mage. I'm not very strong nor am I smart or fast. I can only manipulate one type of stone, have really low range, so I need to attach the stones to my limbs like now, and have to constantly replenish my resources. Never would I have expected to become of use to someone let alone to a whole squadron or even be a leader of a battalion.'

Syndra paused before giving a dry, 'right.'

'Sorry, I can't contain my excitement. Just smelling the sweet, musky, smelly, er. Um. Smell of the desert. Anyway, that lifts me up. It feels so much better than being holed up in a tree all my life I can't even sleep as a consequence though which is annoying.'

'Mhm.'

'Say, Syndra?' Michal caught her attention, twiddling his thumbs when he did so as he wondered whether to ask his question or not.

'Yes?'

'Do you have a dream too?'

A chill blew over the sand, chaining a sound orchestra with the sand particles rubbing against each other followed by animals scurrying after being uncovered. This let the miniature predators the opportunity to snatch their unlucky, even smaller prey, the crunching resonating in the area, prompting birds to squawk in response. But despite the noise, all Michal heard was the silence of Syndra who stared at the sky as if he wasn't even there.

'Sorry,' Michal apologised. 'That was a –'

'If I did have a dream,' Syndra interrupted, a thin smile running across her face. 'It'd be one I share with Nasir.'

'Nasir?'

She held out her arm and, out of nowhere, a tinoo swooped on top of it before climbing onto her shoulder. The pair nuzzled their noses, or beak in the bird's case, Syndra's smile growing with each rub. Once done, she lowered the tinoo down to peck away at stray beetles and joining the chorus of sound.

'I just want to survive,' Syndra continued, watching over the tinoo, a sense of adoration for the bird in her body language. 'If I'm with Nasir, then I don't care what I do or where I go or who I help out.'

'That's a good dream! That's why we need to help out and end this war as soon as possible. It'd be bad if we watch from the sidelines all our lives. Then you guys can live in peace.'

'You do realise we could have just lived in the rezah without being sent to battle?'

Michal flopped to the floor, watching the tinoo hunt. 'But what if we end the war with our own strength? Wouldn't that make the peace more satisfying? I think that belief is what the whole squadron is running on.'

'Pfft. *Our* strength? What do you mean by that? We're the *low-ranking support group*. We all rely on the offence and artillery group to do their job. Without them, we're just sitting tinoos. Tsk,' Syndra tutted.

'That's why I've been trying to correct. What if the support group can contribute offensively too? Then we won't be a hindrance.'

Michal paused then jumped up the next moment, startling both Syndra and himself.

'Ah, don't tell anyone though. I'm not finished my project yet,' he added in a whisper.

'Not that I care.'

'Aww. Don't be like that.'

'I hate unrealistically optimistic people like you. Do you not fear the threat of death, both from nature and the enemy?'

'I know. But if I was pessimistic, then I would have died alone in the desert instead of applying to squadron W all those years ago. So, this optimism is what's keeping me going, you see,' Michal admitted, lying on his back and watching the stars above.

'Ugh. I'm going to bed.'

Syndra called on Nasir who fluttered onto her shoulder and the pair made their way to their tent. Michal, on the other hand, felt a rush of fatigue. Was it the cool air, the low after his high, or the conversation with Syndra as he let his feelings be known? Whatever the reason, he closed his eyes and went into a deep sleep out in the open desert.

20

Resources

Even with his resistance to the heat, Brim could feel the sun's gaze bringing sweat to his brows. At its zenith, moving became a chore and constant hydration was a must. At least with over two-thirds of the journey over and done with, the squadron could relax and catch their breath.

The squadron's growth astounded Brim. In all honesty, he thought they needed much more time but they held their own, soldiering on through the searing temperatures. Even their puffed-out chests, strides that turned into waddles, and the obvious fatigue amongst the mages made for a determined air to them.

'Mr Stones. Message.'

Brim looked down at the petite armoured man (or woman? Brim settled with man in the end). The same one that followed Gin during the journey, acting as his messenger, though Brim could tell he had ulterior motives by the way they slept together out in the open like a single entity. Or when Gin carried the midget to the caravan due to an "injury" even though it turned out to be nothing serious. Or how Gin would give him some not-so-secret slices of food in order to appear like he finished his meat. Wait. How close were these two? Didn't they meet just before everyone departed? Brim shook his head in disbelief.

'Um, sir?'

'Ah, sorry. I spaced out for a bit,' Brim admitted. 'Sam, was it? What message did Gin send you for?'

'Harvest. It's ready,' Sam responded, his sentences still short and unfinished.

'Already? That was faster than I was anticipating. Are we stopping now?'

'No. He not want harvest. You help.'

'Is he still squeamish about harvesting? How can someone be so pathetic and be reliable at the same time?' Brim commented as he scratched his head at this enigma. 'Oh, well. I needed to talk to him anyway. There's a fledgeling rezah a kilometre west from here. Tell everyone to head there and get the relevant utility types for extraction.'

'Will do!'

The tinoos' formation soon changed, calling everyone to head west as Brim instructed. Then, as they got closer and beyond a mountainous sand dune, the rezah came into sight. Although a fraction of the size of the squadron's home, the tree still stood tall and mighty, perfect for taking materials from.

A few caravans pushed on, overtaking Brim's battalion and parking themselves outside the trunk of the tree. A couple of mages hopped out followed by their familiars: the moles. Around ten of the brown-furred rodents bounded out. They were so small that each one could fit inside the palms of a person's hands if not for the claws that protruded out of their four-fingered paws. They were almost as large as the animal's bodies.

The rodents, after being given the order by their masters, burrowed their way underneath the tree. Their claws arced in such a manner that digging was made easy, each swipe more of a scoop that flung the sand out of their way than a dig. Either way, it took only a few seconds to go out of sight, leaving a trail of dirt and sand behind them.

In the meantime, the others brought out jugs, one side thinner and flatter than the other, from the caravans and placed them beside the tree trunk with the flat side facing the tree. The two familiar types then lathered a sweet-smelling substance on the bark right above the jugs. It didn't take long for the moles to dig their way out of the exact spot the substance was placed. They held onto the tree using their claws as they lapped up the substance. Behind them were the holes they made from which flowed a stream of water that trickled into the jugs.

Nodding in approval, Brim headed towards the other caravans where the utility farmer type mages rested. From a few of them, he could hear the huffing and wheezing, most likely from the mages ready for harvest. He opened the veil to one caravan to see a pair of mages, one covered in bushes and fruits growing on him while the other's rolls of skin were about to peel off the person's main body underneath the light clothing she wore. They both stared at Brim, unsure how to react to the arrival of the battalion leader.

'Need some assistance?' Brim asked.

'Battalion leader!' the bushy one exclaimed, putting down the specialised feed he ate. 'Oh, no we can't possibly trouble you.'

The thick-skinned one attempted to respond in a similar manner but her heavy breathing and visible pain prevented her from uttering a single word. Despite the inability to speak, the woman managed to lift a flabby arm, some skin falling in the process, to stop Brim who sighed in response.

'Just because I'm a leader, doesn't mean you can't rely on me,' Brim scolded. 'The farmer types were the only mages I always had the utmost respect for, even the low-ranked ones. You guys provide the sustenance for the whole battalion. It's the least I can do.'

Brim climbed into the caravan and inspected the meaty mage. He could almost roll the brown flesh off her pink skin if it wasn't already doing so under its own weight. But the most disturbing part was the pus and areas of swelling that occurred on her main body, most common in the low-ranked. However, that didn't faze Brim.

'I think she needs help,' Brim commented. 'Pass me a cup.'

'Yes, sir,' the man obeyed, handing over a stone cup.

'What's your name?' Brim asked.

The woman couldn't respond, so the man stepped in. 'Jaina. I'm Basil.'

'I see. Nice to meet you both.'

Brim covered just his fingertips with his sweat, making sure he didn't use too much nor too little. With a flick of his thumb against his palm, he created the spark that allowed the oil to combust, creating a small yellowish flame. He then hovered the cup over the flame, heating the bottom until the time was right, knowing when through years of practice rather than precise measurements.

'Alright, I'll begin now,' Brim instructed.

After lifting the woman's clothes, he pressed the cup on the area of swelling. A deep breath from Jaina comforted Brim. He knew the technique was working, relaxing his patient's muscles and helped relieve some of the mental stress that being a farmer type came with by default. In the meantime, the man called Basil offered one of his fruits, but Brim shook his head and refused the offer.

'The others need it more,' Brim argued.

'Ok,' Basil agreed, going back to picking his fruit.

The process of Jaina peeling the meat off and Brim cupping the swelling continued. Though he couldn't prevent any bleeding, the treatment proved helpful. The moans of pain lessened until all the excess meat came off, leaving an embarrassed and skinny, reduced Jaina to pick up the food.

'T-thank you,' Jaina showed her gratitude.

'No problem,' Brim replied with a smile. 'Oh, I helped with the swelling but I suggest you go have a medic help with the bleeding, though they're only minor wounds.'

'O-oh, Ok.'

Jaina gave a meek smile, only to open a wound on his mouth. She covered the cut, dropping all of her produce by mistake. Brim chuckled at her clumsiness and helped sort things out before offering to assist Basil too. However, he had to retract his statement when Gin's messenger arrived at the caravan's entrance.

'Mr. Stones.'

'Oh, it's you again,' Brim said, looking down at Sam.

'This way,' he said, tugging on his vest, impatient as he said his brief farewell to the farmers.

Sam guided Brim around the battalion members. Fatigue replaced the earlier determination, creating a union of both sighs of relief and groans of pain. Though Brim wanted to scoff at how embarrassing the mages made themselves look, seeing even Gin sweating his face off and gulping multiple handfuls of water changed his mind, especially when he knew he had the luxury of using the caravans.

'Go speak,' Sam instructed, before scurrying off to his battalion.

'Alright,' Brim responded, turning to Gin and raising his voice so that he heard him. 'Quite the gluttonous one, aren't you?'

Gin turned around to the sight of a smiling Brim. He decided to drink another handful of water, letting out an exasperated gasp from his quenched thirst. Wiping the drops off, he returned the smile, choking a bit as he did so.

'Where did that come from?' Gin asked, clasping his hand over his mouth to stop the coughing.

'Three meals a day and several drink-breaks like now. Not sure what's going on in your body, but it's a bit much in my opinion. You sure you're not a really low ranked water elemental?'

Gin paused for a moment before answering. 'Is that why people are looking at me with estranged faces? Well, it's not my fault my body isn't as efficient as the rest of you. I don't know about you but travelling two-hundred kilometres in twenty days isn't that high on my things-I'm-good-at list.'

'I'm glad it isn't,' Brim commented, causing Gin to raise an eyebrow.

'Not sure what you're trying to say.'

'In the MBP, we went through gruelling exercises to build up stamina, strength and speed. Most of us couldn't keep up. The rate of mages reaching adulthood is roughly ten percent, so the majority of those that come out are mostly high ranked mages. The F ranks are basically those that have failed everything but survived the ordeal. They were immediately cast away and unused, despite survival being a major achievement in itself. War didn't need weaklings after all.'

Brim frowned, reminiscing his past experiences. The friends he grew up that no longer lived. The pain he endured. Those he had to kill with his own hands and those he scorned for being worse than him. All for what? His own survival?

'What does that have to do with me?' Gin asked, noticing the unease in Brim.

'I'm assuming your muscles are aching, your stamina is dwindling and your will to carry on has been dropping since the first day,' Brim snapped back, regretting the immediacy of his response the next moment.

'Mm. yeah. You've assumed correctly,' Gin admitted, rubbing the back of his hand and forcing a weary laugh.

'Such simple-minded honesty. Not sure if you've noticed, but the others feel the same. They're probably more tired than you are, even if they don't want to admit it. But they're grateful that you've allowed time to rest.'

'They are?' Gin looked back at his battalion and noticed the signs that confirmed Brim's observation. 'Wow. Here I thought I was the only one struggling. Guess they were all putting up a very convincing poker face.'

'So are you. They probably just want to impress their leader.'

'Heh. I don't know about that. Being a role model is tough. But if what you said is true, it's good to hear how they feel. But let's keep the fact that the real reason for having rest breaks a secret.'

'Of course. Can't let them think their fearless leader is *completely weak and useless*, now can we?'

'That's rich coming from you, Brim. I'm not the one who's idling around in the caravans.'

Brim began a light jog, did a couple jumping Jacks before returning, giving Gin a pat on the back.

'See? I do my fair bit of exercise too,' he joked. 'I've walked this sort of travel before. It's not that hard. Not sure why you're struggling this much.'

'I'm sorry. What's the score between us?' Gin retorted cupping his hand around his ear.

'Didn't I win the last five matches in a row?'

'Ah, but the score?' Gin pointed out.

'You're afraid that I'm catching up now,' Brim deflected the question with ease.

'If you say so. Want to have a rematch if we get back in one piece? Settle things once and for all.'

'For sure.'

'Heh. That's the spirit,' Gin stretched his arms to show his exhaustion for once but stopped in an instant to point at Brim. 'Oh, just to remind you, it's seventy-nine seventy-seven to me.'

'Yeah, yeah,' Brim rolled his eyes at that remark. He frowned some more before turning back to Gin.

'Hm? Something wrong?'

'Everyone's still going to be tired even after the break, aren't they?'

'If their stamina and recovery rate are like mine, then yeah.'

'How long do you think it will take for you to be in peak form?'

Gin stood there thinking for a moment, hand on ching before responding with a, 'I reckon a day or two.'

'Hmm. I think we can make it work then.'

'Make what work?'

Someone interrupted their conversation, asking for the jug Gin drank from. The pair complied, taking their leave to a location more private, arriving several hundred metres away from the battalions at the cost of losing the cool shade of the rezah.

'Anyway,' Brim continued. 'We're just over a hundred kilometres from our destination and we have roughly two weeks to trek it before the enemy is expected to arrive. We'd want a day to be prepared on the battlefield, so if we travel sixty kilometres within the four or five days, then we can rest for two days before making one final push.'

'Eh. Why sixty in particular?' Gin queried.

'There's a forest at that point,' Brim explained, drawing a small illustration in the sand with his feet.

'A forest in this desert?'

'Yeah,' Brim confirmed, adding a large circle and two horizontal lines to his drawing. 'There's a massive oasis a few kilometres off of our path. I'm sure the change of scenery will amaze you. I do have a request though.'

'Yes?'

'I want to stock up on some water at the oasis.'

'Don't we have enough water?'

'I'm a bit worried about our water elementals,' Brim said, looking back at the squadron when he did so. He observed for a few seconds before turning back to Gin, adding, 'They're sweating like crazy in this heat and using up their own water reserves at this rate. Once they run out in battle, water elementals are useless. So why not have jugs of water as extra ammunition? Also, there's an area where the stone elementals can mine some materials.'

'That's actually brilliant. But why aren't you collecting the water from the rezah like we're doing now?'

'That would either take too long at the rate the water is pouring out now, or we might kill the tree if we take too much too quickly.'

'Huh. Didn't realise you guys took such care to preserve wildlife. Our ancestors would have done the complete opposite,' Gin commented out loud. 'Can the oasis take the stress of us taking its water?'

'Yes. It's massive. I'll take you one day, but you guys need your rest first.'

'That's a shame. I guess it means we're splitting up further. Who do you need?'

'I'll take all of the artillery group as well as half of the remaining caravans. I'll also take a few of the more able utility familiar types so we can message you. We can take the diminished rest period without a problem. I'll leave those who can't with you. If you continue on the planned journey, there's a path that bisects the forest. We'll rendezvous there.'

Brim pointed to the horizontal lines he drew earlier. As he said before, it split the outlines of the forest. Though he didn't know why it did that (nor did he particularly care), he let nature do its thing and used the opportunity to its full effect.

'Do you need Michal's battalion?' Gin asked first.

'Do you need them?' Brim asked back.

'Not really.'

'Ok. I'll bring them along as well. It will make the mining process faster.'

'So that leaves me with just my battalion and a few others to travel to the rendezvous point. The slower group will join a day later at their rate. I'll get someone to send a message to them, to notify them of the change of plans.'

'Yup. Oh, that reminds me. I've been meaning to ask you this, but you didn't put Jake in with Rob's group for ulterior motives, did you?'

'I don't know what you're talking about,' Gin replied, failing to hide his smirk.

Brim sighed. 'You guys really need to reconcile. Not everyone can lose their prejudice as I did. Even for me, it took some time.'

'I'm just flexing my power as leader somewhat,' Gin gave a half-hearted chuckle to his remark.

'Don't abuse that.'

'Heh. Don't worry. I know my role.'

Brim looked back at the squadron. He never expected to even think of giving rest breaks, let alone getting more resources due to others' inefficiencies and splitting up a whole army because of slowness. *When did I become so soft?* he wondered. But the mages' contagious smiles spread to him as he turned back to Gin.

'Shall we get back? I think we've discussed everything we needed to,' Brim said.

'Sure. Thanks for helping with the harvest by the way,' Gin replied.

'I'm not done though.'

'Wait. You're not?' Gin stopped in his tracks.

'No. You called for me before everyone finished. You're not coming?'

'I'd rather not find out where my food comes from. Some of them are also naked, aren't they? I don't want– never mind. I just don't want to help.'

'Oh, come on. There's nothing to be afraid of. You know already and this is a good experience for you,' Brim smirked, grabbing Gin around the shoulder and bringing closer to the caravans, albeit a bit forceful. 'This is for your own good.'

'I'm sure it is,' Gin grumbled, conceding at last.

What is wrong with him? Brim thought. But he didn't care. He knew he was in good company.

21

The Forest

To eat or not to eat, that was Gin's question as he stared down at the pre-made lunch, hating himself for salivating at it. It was a mish-mash of fruit, mage meat and (what seemed to be) rice. On the one hand, it was very well made and the procedures to get the food seemed humane enough. On the other hand, it made Gin question his moralities with every mouthful. If only he had his mother's cooking. He'd have had no problems with that.

In the end, he compromised his beliefs once more. With his right hand, he ate his food; with his left, he picked up a pen and paper and placed them on his lap. He began the start of another notes page. He wanted to do a short sketch of the journey, mapping out the key areas. In terms of his notes, this was the most productive he had been in a while. There was so much he had learned in this short journey that he was overflowing with ideas. He just had to put them down on paper.

'Um, leader. Can I come in?' Gin heard Sam's voice from outside the caravan.

'Yes,' Gin answered, finishing his mouthful and tidying up first.

Sam struggled to climb onto the moving vehicle due to his lack of height and strength but Gin helped him on without too much difficulty. Even then, the sound of loud breathing could be heard from underneath the mask, making Gin wonder how this person managed to travel so long despite his stamina.

'Did you have a message for me?' Gin asked.

'Mm,' Sam confirmed, still panting with every breath. 'Rob nearly here. Half a day behind.'

'Half a day?' Gin put his hand on his beard, stroking it as he calculated some numbers before concluding, 'Isn't that too short? Shouldn't they be at least a day behind?'

'I don't know. Their message said half.'

'Ok, fine.'

Gin headed out of the caravan but stood frozen the moment he stepped outside. He didn't realise at what point the sand turned into soil or when the horizon turned from a hazy blue to a luscious green. He also didn't expect the family of (what the textbooks from his village called) foxes that greeted his battalion before scampering back into the forest. The trees were much shorter than a rezah, their roots emerged out of the ground, and their trunks were smooth making for interesting terrain. The sight took his breath away.

Further down the forestry, an unnatural dirt path that spanned a few hundred metres in width and several kilometres in length divided the forest in half. However, it allowed the battalion to set up camp in convenience and, so, they headed towards the clearing. Brim was right. Gin couldn't help but be mesmerised by the scenery; One that he never expected to see in his lifetime.

'Sir?' Sam poked at the living statue.

'Alright. Let's set up camp and get prepared for the slower group's arrival,' Gin instructed, snapping back to his senses before taking a short jog through a sudden burst of energy that overcame him.

Upon closer inspection, he noticed that the ground differed from the one the trees grew in. The silt the clearing was made up of made for poor quality compared to the heavier, more nutritious (Gin could tell from experience) soil on either side of the opening. Finding the cause of such an environment, especially how all of this managed to grow in the desert despite the odds, intrigued Gin. However, he decided to track back, hopping into the caravan to pick up a piece of paper, a quill pen and began taking notes. He also jotted down the procedures for setting camp (something he failed to do before for lack of time). From the way the mages used the farmer types' excess shrubbery as firewood to the careful positioning of everyone's resting spot as to avoid damage to the surroundings, Gin enjoyed learning about the intricacies of the mages' culture. He made light work of filling up several pages' worth of notes as a result.

However, as Gin looked on, he noticed how small the numbers that accompanied him were. Of course, as promised, Brim took pretty much everyone while Rob's battalion was yet to come. However, it unnerved him when he had to consider that they were the first and only line of defence against a supposed five-thousand. On the plus side, with fewer numbers to supervise, it allowed Gin to examine the area without needing to keep an eye on more than he could handle.

A few of the animals poked their heads out to see the aliens that had just invaded their territory. They all ran when Gin tried to get close, so he had to make do with the colourful snail that forced its way along the ground only to get picked up without being able to resist.

'We don't have this species back home,' Gin commented out loud.

He then put the mullusc down again in order to draw a rough sketch, drawing the attention of the family of foxes again. The more strokes Gin made, the more the foxes got curious. It got to the point that one of them, the smaller of the bunch, mustered the courage to approach Gin, tilting its head in expectation.

'Want to be my model?' Gin asked, smiling to the youngling.

It lowered one of its pointy ears and began prancing on the spot. Gin chuckled and began drawing the pup. *Four paws, each with four toes. Ears as large as its head,* Gin thought, annotating his notes with deliberation and precision. Though the final article didn't look too impressive, he held the picture towards the animal, getting a yip of excitement in response.

'Leader not tired?'

Gin jumped up, startled by the voice, causing the fox to also scamper towards its family. Cursing his luck, he composed himself again. He was so enthralled by the new scenery that he didn't notice Sam walk up to him. The mask that continued to hide any expression and the muffled voice didn't help either.

'Ah. Sorry,' he apologised.

'No. I was just being absent-minded. What's up?' Gin asked.

'Rob's group here now.'

'What?! Already?' Gin looked up and noticed the setting sun and the prepared campsite. *How long was I occupied for?* he thought to himself before saying, 'Never mind.'

'Jake wants to see you too.'

'Ugh.'

'Um. I see how you act. Does leader not like Jake?'

'No,' Gin flinched at how blunt and swift he responded that question.

With reluctance in his stride, Gin left his research and carried out the formalities of greeting the oncoming battalion, only to grow concerned as he saw their fatigue. Instead of walking, the mages were closer to dragging themselves across the ground. *Guess they're still human beings,* Gin thought, concluding that the resting period was a much-needed activity.

Despite the state of the battalion, Jake, the sole fit mage from what Gin could see, leapt out with a scowl. His expression got more and more crumpled the closer he got. Gin smirked, aggravating Jake's anger, before preparing for what was about to ensue. Everyone else stopped in their tracks and spectated from afar.

'What do you think you're doing?' Jake howled.

'Greeting you of course!' Gin replied, putting on a fake smile. 'Your group has finally caught up. Enjoy your two-day rest.'

'Rest? Rest?! We don't have time for rest!'

'By my calculations, we have plenty of time.'

'Are you kidding me?' Jake narrowed his eyes, ready for the confrontation.

'No, I'm dead serious. Everyone's tired and we need to recover.'

'Ahaha. Do you think we're tired? Shows how pathetic you are as a leader. *We* are not as weak as you and your fools. We *can* and *will* carry on, isn't that right?' Jake asked, turning to his battalion. Gin could see the tiredness in their faces, but they nodded all the same.

Was it out of fear or tiredness and unwillingness to complain? Gin wondered. Either way, he didn't want to drag out this fiasco any more than he wanted to.

'As the in-charge of the artillery group, Brim was the one who suggested doing this,' Gin explained, playing his trump card, causing Jake to scrunch his face in anger. 'I simply listened and agreed.'

'Aha. Nice joke,' Jake said, forcing the laugh.

'Joke?'

'Do you know how long I've known Brim for?' Jake paused, seeing how Gin would react only to get a puzzled look in reply. 'He would never do this! Since when did he side with low-ranks like you and your whims?'

A few murmurs circulated around the crowd as well Rob's battalion grinding to stop. However, Gin didn't pay attention to them. All his focus was on the man in front of him. He noticed Jake's rough skin beginning to glisten under the setting sun and continued the conversation with caution.

'Brim has learnt a lot in his brief time with Squadron W,' Gin said, lifting his arms as if he was about to hold a heavy object. 'He enjoys our sparring too when he thought he wouldn't.'

'Ha!' Jake scoffed. 'The same ones where all your victories are through dirty tricks and dishonourable tactics? You're weak, have no skill nor any quality of a good leader. Rob should have been leader and you know it.'

'Honour means nothing if you're dead,' Gin retorted, raising his arms higher. 'As for Rob being the leader instead of me, *all the leaders but you disagree*, or did the meeting not help get that through to you?'

'Tch.'

Shields.

Jake ignited his arms but Gin was prepared, blocking the immediate punch aimed at this head with his shield, putting Jake off balance in the process, then took the opportunity to sucker punch Jake in the gut.

Now winded, Gin sent the final blow, sweeping Jake's leg, knocking him over, pinning him down by the scruff of his neck.

'Who was the weak, no-skilled one again?' Gin remarked, as he let a shocked and disgraced Jake go, both the mage and the crowd now in complete silence.

'Jake, you idiot!' A familiar gruff voice said in the distance.

Gin looked up to see a seething Rob leaping in bounds with his long legs towards him. However, Gin could tell the anger was directed at Jake instead of him and gave a welcoming smirk, showing no remorse in his actions.

Jake used the distraction to lift himself and head towards the caravans. But as he did so, Rob stopped beside him. Jake looked up, unsure what to expect, only to get an almighty wallop to the back of his head, sending him crashing back into the dirt. No words were said but the message was clear enough and the sudden wind that blew on Rob's long body hair made for a convincing picturesque moment.

Rob then headed towards Gin, leaving Jake to drag himself towards his destination. Everyone resumed their duties straight away, looking away from the scene, acting as if it never happened.

'I'm sorry about that,' Rob said to Gin, sighing afterwards which sounded more like a frustrated growl.

'No problem,' Gin consoled, leading him back to the campsite.

'I heard what happened. It's not your fault.'

'I know.'

'Still. Did he tell you about our situation?'

Gin paused, thinking if he missed anything before responding. 'No.'

'He really did come to pick a fight with you,' Rob commented, slapping his forehead. 'Basically, one of our storage caravans got eaten by one of the sandpools because of him. Then when we heard about your change of plans, we sped up in order to catch up to the main group.'

'I see. Most of the resources are with Brim and his lot though. I'm not sure we have enough food to help your battalion out these two days if what you said is true.'

'That's why I wanted to suggest going on a hunting expedition to get some.'

Gin pondered for a moment. He knew the mages advocated preserving nature and they ate flesh and fruit from their own evolved kind. *Was hunting animals allowed or was Rob referring to a different task altogether?* Gin asked himself.

'You sure?' Gin questioned Rob, deciding to play it safe in the end and pretend he knew what he was doing.

'I know we normally shouldn't but, in times like these, it's safe to hunt some of the wildlife for our

243

own health. We shouldn't go overboard though. We can't harm the environment after all, so let's make a small group of ten or so for the expedition,' Rob explained, relieving Gin of his misunderstanding.

'Then shall I prepare a group?'

'Yes, but let's leave it till tomorrow. Most of us are tired and we got enough supplies to last till then anyway.'

'Unlike what Jake says,' Gin remarked, enjoying the irony.

'Don't be too harsh on him,' Rob replied, stopping for a bit before adding, 'he doesn't know any better.'

'Alright, fine. I'll think about it,' Gin's said, his words coming out flat. He didn't want to dwell on the topic any further and decided to change the subject. 'Shall we help prepare our tents?'

'Yes,' Rob took up on the offer as the pair resumed their short trek towards the campsite.

22

Predator

For the first time in a month, Gin felt revitalised. His muscles no longer ached, nor did he suffer from mental fatigue. Granted, his nanobots helped with the former and the eighteen-hour nap with the latter, but that didn't stop him from brimming with energy.

He stepped out from his tent, took a deep breath of the earthy musk from the forest, then surveyed the troops. Despite the sun already past its zenith, most of the mages slept, ignoring the tempered heat and the insects that buzzed around their bodies. It prompted Gin to sniff his own body, regretting his actions as he gagged on the stench of the weeks-long worth of unwashed skin.

'Maybe I should have joined Brim to the oasis,' he murmured to himself.

'Oh, you're up already?' Rob's sudden gruff voice came from behind. 'When will you be ready for hunting?'

'Me? Am I needed?' Gin turned around, meeting Rob with a confused expression.

'Yes. I'll tell you why later.'

'Ok, I guess?' Gin paused for a moment, contemplating what to say next. 'Well, everyone's tired apart from a handful of us, so it makes sense.'

'That's the spirit!'

Gin thought he saw Rob smile. He couldn't be quite sure as he based the action on the way the long strands of hair that covered Rob's face moved.

However, just to make sure, Gin returned the notion as he gave a warm smile back.

'We'll wait another hour or so and pick the participants from those capable,' Rob suggested.

'Fine by me,' Gin accepted before going back to his tent. 'I'll prepare my equipment.'

From the corner, beside his makeshift bed, Gin picked up the stone chest plate. He tapped on several areas, a task Michal would have done. But without him, Gin did it himself, listening in to the sound the knocks made and sighing a breath of relief when he heard no echo.

'No inside deterioration,' he mumbled to himself, stopping before adding a, 'or at least I think so. Damn. Should have practised the technique more.'

Satisfied with his analysis for the most part, he took off his shirt, put the armour on, then placed the shirt over it, concealing the stone underneath. The final pieces, both for the legs, slotted over the shins with ease, making Gin want to thank Michal for all his precision and hard work, even if the armour chaffed him at first. But, after a few minutes, the feeling disappeared and, after some final checks to the INS, he was set to go.

Gin found Rob waiting outside the Eastern side of the forest, along with half a dozen of his battalion members, all of them mid-ranked juggernauts, as well as the familiar face (or rather helmet with two eye sockets) of Sam. Though the mages still looked fatigued, they stood proud as if to say it was nothing. *That's the higher ranked mages for you,* Gin assumed.

Even from his distance, Gin could tell the team were drawing up plans, using sticks to draw shapes into the ground. It wasn't until he got closer that he saw a nonagon, marked by dots on the vertices and a squiggle in the centre.

'What is that meant to be?' Gin asked, startling the whole group with his presence apart from Rob who remained steadfast with his stick.

'I thought you'd take more time to get ready,' Rob thought out loud before making a replica diagram in the dirt and turning back to Gin. 'We're discussing the formation plans. And you're pivotal to the plan.'

'Yes. Yes. Leader is needed,' Sam nodded in agreement, as did the other mages. 'Look. This one you.'

Sam pointed to one of the dots that didn't align with the other vertices. Instead, it concaved and was closest with the squiggle. It was only then Gin realised the dots represented the hunting team.

'But what's the squiggle for?' he asked.

'That's the unsuspecting animal in question,' Rob mused, his grins more visible that his smiles. 'I've scouted a few of the creatures, so I know they're out there.'

'Which ones?'

'The deer.'

Gin raised an eyebrow. All he saw were foxes and other small wildlife. *There were deer too?* he exclaimed within, but kept his cool in front of the others, looking at the diagrams and nodding in confirmation.

'Wait!' someone called out. 'Where are you going?'

A few of the mages groaned as the shout roused them up. Upon seeing Jake causing the commotion, they went back to sleep, enjoying the comfort of the dirt.

Gin scoffed at the reaction of the mages towards the supposed battalion leader.

'Why wasn't I informed of this?' Jake scowled, most of his visible anger directed at Gin.

However, before Gin could say anything, Rob stepped up to Jake instead. 'This was my idea. You know the situation regarding our reserves, or did you forget it was because of your lapse in judgement that we lost them in the first place?'

Jake gritted his teeth but didn't turn away from everyone's gaze.

'Yes. And I apologise for how I acted,' he said, his words without complete sincerity but still had that hint of remorse at the same time. 'I need to step up, so I'll play my part in this activity too.'

'You sure?' Gin questioned, testing where the man stood on his beliefs and pride. 'You *did* sleep the most out of the ten of us despite saying how hardy you were.'

'Tch.'

'We don't have a fire elemental,' one of the bestial types mentioned.

'Yes. Fire useful,' Sam added when no one spoke the next moment.

'True,' Rob confirmed. 'What do you say, Gin?'

Gin shrugged, letting Rob take control of the situation. The hunting expedition wasn't his plan after all. That and his heart was bouncing in anticipation of all the potential research material he was about to meet. The faster he got into the forest the better, even if that meant allowing Jake to tag along despite his rudeness earlier on.

'No objections then,' Rob confirmed. 'I'll redraw the plans. Gin will still be the pivotal member.'

Again, Gin questioned what he was meant to do, but kept quiet and watched Rob change the shapes to include Jake, turning them into decagons, followed by an explanation on who represented what. The details of the plan remained a mystery, but Gin assumed it was a reactive rather than proactive strategy and so no real strategies could be formed at this point in time.

'I already notified the battalions they should expect us to arrive around after sunset. Maybe even earlier,' Rob explained, rubbing out the markings in the dirt. 'We're all ready now, so let's go.'

Rob led the way as the group followed in a straight line behind him. At first, the pathing made the formation easy. However, as the shrubbery and trees became denser, keeping in shape grew difficult and the group diverted somewhat while moving in the same direction. Though it meant travel became smoother, the task of creating a path through the jungle proved tedious.

Gin learned that all too quickly and, after getting hit by one too many branches to the face, he activated his blades and started hacking them down. They tumbled to the ground, causing hidden bugs to scatter upon impact. If hunting wasn't the key objective, he would have easily become immersed with the wildlife. That didn't stop him taking mental notes of the animals he saw along the way for his physical notes back in camp though.

'Hold your ground,' Rob ordered, holding up his hand.

He then signalled to come closer before switching to a "keep the noise down" hand motions. Everyone complied, tiptoeing towards the leader of the group, making sure not to step on stray branches.

By the time Gin got close enough, he noticed why Rob called everyone to a halt. Around fifty metres ahead of the group was a brown-haired, quadrupedal animal, with horns on top of its head, facing away from the mages, unsuspecting of their presence. *Was that a deer?* Gin wondered, basing his assumptions on the descriptions in books he read back in his village, though he couldn't be sure. It had its head lowered, grazing on the shoots on the forest bed while looking up every so often. But, for some reason Gin couldn't pinpoint, the animal only looked in one particular direction when it did so.

'What are we waiting for?' Jake asked, careful not to make too much noise.

'Wait and see. It's hunting,' Rob answered with confidence.

Hunting? Gin picked up on the word. He grew confused but didn't question the phrasing. Instead, he made sure to observe the creature's actions without fail for future reference. It was then that the Deer pricked its head and remained still, staring in the same direction as before where a group of plump birds came into view, pecking at insects on the ground along their journey. The next few moments remained silent, bar the splatters of crunched up insects, as the birds stepped closer towards the deer in their search for food.

Gin's confusion turned into shock and disbelief as the deer charged at one of the unsuspecting creatures, impaling the bird right through the stomach. The rest scattered in frantic chaos, leaving their dead brethren to the mercy of the predator which used a nearby tree to unhook its prey, letting it drop to the ground. The animal then revealed a set of fangs as it dug into the innards of the feathered creature.

So much for the books saying they're herbivores, Gin thought.

'Great. Let's use this as a distraction and into position,' Rob instructed, letting the group crawl away before turning back to Gin. 'You stay here until I get behind the animal. Then walk slowly towards it.'

'Again, why me?' Gin asked, impatient at the lack of detail he was given.

'I didn't want to offend you earlier, but you stink,' Rob answered, chuckling to himself for a couple seconds. 'I find it hilarious how you low ranks can't control your own body odour without a constant need to wash.'

'Heh. Thought it was for some stupid reason and I was right.'

'The deer knows you're here too.'

Gin looked back at the deer and noticed one of the ears, the one furthest away from him, was lopsided while the other remained straight. It also twitched its nose every so often and took slow steps to angle itself to have better vision on Gin's position, though it didn't seem to see him just yet.

'Alright,' Gin understood.

With a nod, Rob made his way around the forest, keeping at least twenty metres between him and the animal. The other mages were also in position, ready to cut off any escape routes which the deer hadn't noticed yet, keeping its senses aimed at Gin instead.

When Rob got into position, Gin made his move, tiptoeing forwards while stepping on twigs to alert the animal, but not hard enough for it to become wary of the hidden mages.

The deer straightened both ears as it saw Gin at last. It analysed the foreigner, attempting to evaluate how much of a threat he posed. It turned back to its dinner but, the moment Gin activated his blades, it changed its mind, tracking back only to fall into Rob's grasp. It flailed around, but Rob kept hold of its neck and body with all his might, strangling the creature until it stopped trying to escape.

'Gin! Finish it off!' Rob shouted.

Gin walked up to the unconscious beast. He poised his blade and aimed at the throat. He nodded at Rob who nodded back and released his hold on the neck. Gin went for the strike, but the animal sprang back to life, kicking Rob right in the stomach. The blade still hit its target, puncturing the arteries, blood draining out of the wound. Despite all that, the deer managed to break free of Rob's hold and bounded away from both of them, blood splattering with each leap.

Sam stood of the way of the escape path but the animal didn't stop, sending the mage flying into a tree as well as catching branches with its horns. The other mages rushed over to him, checking for any wounds.

'Leader, Sam's unconscious,' one of them shouted.

'Are you alright? Gin asked.

'I'm fine now but we should get Sam checked out,' Rob replied, wheezing for a moment before adding, 'Sorry. I lost my grip at the last moment.'

'No problem. But I think I dealt enough damage for the game to not get very far.'

'True. We have the trail of blood to guide us.' Rob took a breather, psyching himself up back to shape, leaping back to his feet when he was ready. 'I'll take Sam back to camp. The rest of you secure that deer and come back.'

'Do we have enough?'

'I would have liked to get some of those birds. Just the deer wouldn't be enough.'

'I can do it!' Jake exclaimed, overhearing the conversation.

'You're awfully enthusiastic,' Rob questioned while Jake stood there for a moment, mulling over his words, giving enough time to interrupt his thoughts. 'That's fine by me. But only if Gin can accompany you.'

'Why me?' Gin wondered out loud.

'That's fine,' Jake pursed his lips before anyone could answer. 'Makes things a lot easier.'

'Then that's settled. I'll take Sam back; my battalion members will deal with the deer and the two of you will catch some poultry. Is. That. Clear?' Rob reiterated, stressing the last sentence towards Jake.

'Yes, sir,' Jake obeyed.

'Yep,' Gin added.

Rob ran over to Sam and told the other mages the same orders, leaving Gin and Jake by themselves. The chirping of nearby insects made the loudest noise as the pair watched the others head separate directions and out of sight.

'Rob, Brim, half the battalions. I don't get why everyone cosies up to you,' Jake said at last with no one able to hear them.

'Finally got the courage to trash talk me now that we're alone, huh?' Gin remarked, meeting Jake eye to eye with a gritty determination.

'Of course. You got no honour, no skill –'

'You told me that yesterday,' Gin interrupted.

'– and worst of all, you have no direction. You expect me to follow such an aimless leader?'

'You're starting to sound like the colonel.'

Jake leaned in closer, once again thinking of his next words through his gritted teeth. 'And she would be right. I'll be honest here, I find you way too suspicious. You're not one us, are you? You act too calm and act too differently.'

'Heh,' Gin smirked but was taken aback by the comments on the inside. *Did Jake figure out I'm a manush?* he wondered while saying, 'You obviously don't believe your own lies the moment you accepted being alone with me.'

Jake stared some more, retreating when he couldn't think of a reply and looking at the light streaming through the trees. 'The sun's already set. We should get this job over and done with.'

'For once, I agree with you.'

'After you,' Jake prompted, gesturing for Gin to take the lead.

'Alright,' Gin accepted, picking up his guard as he moved forward towards the corpse of the long-dead bird still attached to the trunk of the tree, kneeling when he reached it. 'Shed some light on this area.'

Although disgruntled by receiving an order from Gin, Jake obeyed, lighting the oil on his dark skin and hovering it away from any vegetation while still illuminating the remains. The first thing Gin noticed was that the heart was the only organ missing from the carcass. *So, the deer ate that first. Was it by chance or deliberate?* he examined.

'So?' Jake said, ruining the train of thought.

'There are some trails where a few of the birds headed off to,' Gin pointed out.

'Then let's go.'

Gin stood up, despite wanting to observe the remains more, and followed the trail of squashed leaves and footprints on the dirt, going deeper into the forest. As luck would have it, the journey didn't take long as the pair found three birds huddled together, still shaking from the ordeal they faced some time ago.

Jake stepped on a twig, alerting the creatures of his presence. Two of them darted further into the forest, leaving one to remain and peck on the ground.

'Tch. Why always my fault?' Gin heard Jake mutter to himself as he ran after the birds.

'No! Wait!' Gin called back but it was too late.

His suspicions growing ever greater, Gin decided not to follow, focusing on the remaining bird instead. He found it ironic how both their compatriots had deserted them, even beginning to sympathise with the creature. Yet, he wanted the task over and done with, not caring what Jake went off to.

Wary that his smell might alert the animal, Gin opted for a long-range attack, unhinging the gun INS from his belt and activating the mechanism. He focused on his training back in squadron W, remembering the feeling of a near-perfect shot as he aimed the contraption at his target through a thicket of trees. Then, with a press of a finger, he fired the bullet, hurtling towards the unsuspecting being, hitting it right on the breast.

Ping!

'Huh?' Gin said, confused by the noise as a yellowish liquid began trickling out the creature's body. 'Do the bullets make a noise like that at max range?'

The bird fell nonetheless, immobile and most likely dead. Gin stepped with caution, recalling what happened with the deer when assuming something was dead, sneaking up to the game and salivating at the thought of having meat that didn't compromise his beliefs. Though the darkness that fell upon the forest meant he couldn't, or rather shouldn't, wait for Jake to return.

Gin felt something rake across his chest, ripping his shirt to shreds and scratching the stone armour.

Blades. Shields.

Gin took a defensive stance, his eyes shifting from side to side, searching for where the attack came from.

Am I just imagining things? he wondered, trying to remain calm and methodical.

Gin looked down at his shirt and noticed five distinct lines. But that move proved naïve as another five-pronged attack slashed Gin's back. Again, the armour protecting him.

Someone's there.

Gin swivelled on the spot, finding not a single animal in sight let alone an attacker.

Where did it come from? Left? Right? Definitely not up or down!

Another slash, this time high enough to brush against Gin's neck, scratched the armour once again. Gin twisted but found nothing in his efforts. His breathing became heavier. His artificial heart's beating became quicker. His mind became more archaic.

Who? What? Why? Where? No. Idiot! Think! He's attacking from behind. Defend that area!

Gin slammed himself against the nearest tree, protecting the nape of his neck with the cover along with his defensive stance. The blades and shields covered his face and armour protected his body. With his newfound defence, he began thinking of a strategy.

I can't keep defending. I need to-

The mental thought got cut short when another slash went for the chest, hitting the armour once again. Gin went for the counterattack, sending his blades in front of him. However, he hit thin air, regretting his actions when something sliced across his forehead, just missing his eyes.

Gin snapped back into his defensive stance.

There was nothing there. No, this pain is an illusion. This throbbing is an illusion. No one is there. There can't be.

Yet, the blood that trickled over his brow confirmed the opposite.

Sudden needle-like objects pierced his upper arm but before Gin could react, they retracted just as quickly as they entered. He bit his tongue to contain his urge to scream in agony.

Do I call for help? No. There might be more enemies. Bear the pain. Think, Gin, think. Faster. Harder. Smarter. Get out of this situation. Slow time. Create a thousand thoughts a second. Create a hundred plans a second. Think!

The needles bored into the other arm, deeper than the previous attack. Gin's will to hold up his arms wavered. Both begged him to rest them with every ebb.

Think. Think. Think. The more I think, the less the pain takes over. I need to keep my arms up. The moment they fall, I die. So, think you idiot! But what? My goals? My ambitions? My direction? Why the fuck is Alder and the colonel's words coming to me? No. This is good. This is just what I need!

Gin's right arm became the main target, receiving strike after strike, but they still didn't drop, locked into place in order to cover his face.

Why am I fighting? Why did I join the squadron? Family? No. They're all dead. Father? Dead. Mother? Dead. Jacob? Dead. Friends? My whole village is dead! Wo? Screw him. Do I really not have a reason to fight? It's always been like this. Alone. Dark. Tiresome. Do I just let myself be killed? Would anyone care? Wait. What about the mages? What about my battalion? Yes! That's it! Who will warn them of this threat? Who will lead them into battle? Who will tell them reinforcements will turn the tide of battle? Why am I so blind? Why didn't I see this? Wait. See? See. See!

A plan formed in Gin's mind. He waited for the next attack before moving, his senses dulling and time moving so slowly that he ran on instinct while his mind wandered again.

There's too much to do. I have to go back to my battalion. I have to know more about the world, about the mages and about their lives.

The nails dug into his right arm once again, sparking Gin's plot. He reached to his belt using his left and chucked a cylinder into the air at that moment between attacks.

I have to make my parents proud. I have to make everyone proud.

Through hope rather than expectation, the invisible enemy sliced through the capsule-like it was paper, spilling its liquid contents.

Heh. Simply put, I have to live.

Gin thrust his arm, betting everything in this one strike at the expense of exposing his face to another swipe.

Flames.

His Blades ignited the liquid. The flaming oil splashed onto the ground. Luckily, the trees weren't fireproof like the Rezah. Instead, the fire spread and spread and spread until it turned into a raging inferno, eating up anything in its path. Why did he do that? What did he expect? Did he think that the fire would ward off the enemy? Maybe. Gin had lost all rationality at that point. But the attacks stopped.

Gin felt dizzy from the blood loss. His legs and arms gave way as he collapsed backwards, crashing against the tree. The fire edged ever closer to him, but he couldn't move away. His body didn't allow him.

'This idiot,' someone murmured. 'I'm not getting caught up with this.'

Gin looked up. He thought he heard something. One eye was blinded by blood; the other just saw a hazy blur. But, for one moment, he thought he saw something. A silhouette of some sort running away from the fire. Was he imagining things? He couldn't tell what was real or not. *A mage?* he thought. *Is it possible for mages to go invisible?*

When the silhouette disappeared, Gin unequipped his right shield with his functioning arm and held it above him, pressing the second chamber. The shield expanded into a dome, surrounding him in the process.

Then, with his last ounce of strength, he unhooked an INS from his belt. He stabbed it into his bleeding arms and injected its contents into his veins. He wanted to use another nano-booster, but he couldn't muster the ability to do so.

Gin could hear the crackle of the fire around him as he began to lose consciousness. If his battalion saw what he had done, they would probably look down on him. It was just like his fight with Varunel. He couldn't beat his opponent so he cowered and hid in a dome shell. It was the only thing he could do. He also started the beginning of the destruction of the forest. Was this the actions of a Eurasian soldier? Where was the honour? Where was the skill? Again, Jake's words entered his mind. *But there was no honour or skill in survival*, Gin thought. Surely, his battalion would understand their leader's actions. *Right?*

23

Whispers from the Unknown

Jake found something wet sprinkle against one cheek and something else squelch against the other. His felt cold, devoid of the natural heat fire elementals possess. His mind scattered in a million directions, unable to process what had happened, but the sudden snapping of branches brought him back into rationality.

'Well, that was easy.'

Huh? A woman? Jake thought. He didn't recognise the voice but the ominous nature of it sent a shiver down his spine and a ringing in his head. His eyes remained shut, out of both curiosity and fear, then his ears pricked up when he heard a different set of footsteps following close by.

'Is that all of them?' a male voice asked, again unrecognisable to Jake.

'Let's see,' the woman paused. 'One. Two. Three. Four. Five. And the others?'

'Burnt in the fire.'

'Brilliant. Just dispose of *that* by the others.'

Others?

Something thudded against a nearby tree, rolling against the sloping bark, making a bumpety noise every odd interval. The sound turned into squelching that grew closer and closer until silky softness caressed the tip of Jake's nose. It tickled his nostrils, causing him to almost sneeze, but he held his urges, shifting his head against the mud to avoid further contact with the round object. However, the object rolled once more, smacking his nose with something pointy and rubbery.

Jake opened a single eye bit by bit, adjusting to the darkness, turning the hazy silhouette into something recognisable. The silky softness became hair and the pointy rubber became a nose. As Jake looked further, he noticed a single hole before he realised that the person was missing an eye while the other stared into the void, bereft of life. A trickling on his chest alerted Jake to look down, his brain processing the image as slow as possible, unwilling to understand what he was witnessing. Still, his eyes wandered until he saw nothing more but a puddle underneath the head. Then it dawned on him.

Jake flinched backwards, scraping his scalp against the roots, letting out a soft yelp. On the spot, he bit his tongue before he made more noise. His heartbeat raced and he closed his eyes, trying in vain to get the image of the severed head out of his mind.

'What was that?'

Shoeless footsteps grew closer, squelching on the mud as they did so, stopping right beside the back of Jake's head. He held his breath, unsure whether the mystery person was friend or foe, hoping the person would go away.

'By the way, is it wise to have the guy behind you listening to our conversation?' the man questioned, his breath tickling Jake's ear.

He knows?!

'Who? Oh! He's not dead yet?' the woman exclaimed.

'Hmm...'

The presence of the man became so apparent that Jake could feel the heat emanating from the body. He wanted to breathe. He wanted to shake in fear. He wanted to just dash for an exit. Yet, he remained still like the corpse the assailants thought he was, controlling his instincts through gritted teeth and bleeding tongue.

'Guess not,' the man confirmed.

'I could finish him off in one go if he *does* try anything,' the woman assured.

'If you say so. Though I've recently taken a carefree approach to life, I'm still a perfectionist at heart. Don't want anything to go wrong because of him.'

'Ha! Don't you worry.'

'The ex-colleague of mine didn't take these sorts of things into account either and screwed us both over because of it.'

An awkward silence fell upon the two. Jake just laid there, too scared to move. Too many questions circled his mind. *Who was this man? Who was the woman? Where did he come from?*

'My job's done anyway,' the man said, breaking the silence. 'The boss doesn't like it if I'm gone too long.'

Boss?

'Too bad. You don't get to see when I succeed,' the woman joked.

'*If* you succeed,' the man warned, before his footsteps weakened, the echoes growing fainter and fainter from the forest.

'If you say so,' the woman continued. 'Hey, Gin. Help a childhood friend out here and finish this trash off. I know you've hated him for a while now, so think of it as a present from me for helping us out this past year.'

Gin? Ha! I knew it. I was right all along. He really was a AAA spy. I need to tell everyone. Then Brim could praise me for protecting everyone. I need to escape.

A new pair of footsteps, this time heavier than the others, walked up to Jake's location. But, before he could react, a deep sharp blade pierced his right leg, causing it to twitch and squirm under the pain. He wanted to scream but he knew his situation didn't allow for it. However, that didn't stop Gin from continuing the assault, as the left leg became the new target with the blade penetrating the thigh, leaving it dead and unresponsive.

'Please finish him off. It looks pitiful and I can tell Rob's on his way. We need to dispose of the other bodies too,' the woman ordered as Jake began to lose consciousness. 'Although, for a manush, you sure know how to get a job done, Gin,'

Eh? What? Manush? So that explains everything. Brim...Rob...anyone...please save m-

But a third and metallic thrust through Jake's abdomen sent a shock that cut off all remaining thoughts.

24

That Which Divides All

Jake found something wet sprinkle against one cheek and something else squelch against the other. He felt cold, devoid of the natural heat fire elementals possess. His mind scattered in a million directions, unable to process what had happened, but the sudden snapping of branches brought him back into rationality.

'He's alive! I hear heart!'

A familiar voice, Jake thought. He recognised the muffled voice, calming his nerves and welcoming him. However, he kept his eyes shut, still fearful of what happened the night before, *(or was it a dream?* he questioned himself), then his ears pricked up when he heard a different set of footsteps following close by.

'Is he all that's left, Sam?' the gruff voice asked, bringing immense relief to Jake's conscious.

'I think so,' Sam replied. 'Five bodies. No heartbeat. Just Jake alive. Where're others?'

'I wonder if that inferno got to the rest.'

Bodies? Jake wondered, a sense of déjà vu enveloping him.

'Um, sir? Are you ok? You not waking?' Sam's voice encouraging Jake to open his eyes in what seemed like forever. He opened the right before opening the left when he saw a group of ally mages surrounding the area.

Propped up against a tree, Jake watched juggernauts search the forestry while Sam and Rob towered over him as they witnessed a utility medic type tend to the wound on his abdomen. *Eh? Wounds?* Jake realised.

'So, it wasn't a dream after all,' Jake mustered the strength to talk, half-expecting a sudden rush of pain but instead received numbing pulsations.

'Dream?' Sam picked up on.

'Let the man rest,' Rob instructed, getting a nod of understanding out of Sam.

'I'm fine. Really, I am,' Jake assured.

Rob gave him a worried look before saying, 'That's the medic's anaesthetic talking. You *are not* in the condition to say anything.'

'No!' Jake protested, raising himself up with his arms, only to cry out in agony as a wound opened up on his left leg.

'Leader! Please refrain from frolicking too much,' the medic snapped. 'Ugh. I have to stitch it again.'

The medic dislocated one of her fingers and twisted it, allowing a white serum to seep out of the joint. With her other hand, she pinched the substance, elongating it until it hardened in a matter of moments, turning into a thin strand. Then, with the fingernail of her needle-like pinkie, she intertwined the thread around a hook at the tip and began weaving the nail in and out of Jake's leg, closing the wound in the process.

'I'll leave you two to it then,' Rob said, turning around to head back to his battalion members. 'Come, Sam. We need to carry on with the investigation.'

'Wait!' Jake called, lowering his voice after realising how loud he was. 'What investigation?'

Rob glanced back before shifting his head to indicate that Sam should go ahead.

'Should I leave too?' the medic asked, biting on the thread to break it off from the finished stitches.

'No. I'll need your opinion on something in a moment,' Rob answered, getting a nod from the medic then turning back to Jake. 'Did you cause the fire?'

'Huh? What fire?' Jake said, confused by the sudden information.

'So, you really don't know,' Rob said, staring into the tree-covered sky, lost in thought.

'I'm really confused. Can someone fill me in on what is going on?'

Rob snapped out of daydream but his expression turned into pensive thought. *Does he not trust me?* Jake wondered, afraid of learning the events that led up to this point. Was he branded as a traitor? No. That couldn't be. Unless...

'Alright,' Rob muttered, kneeling down to meet Jake face to face. 'After the hunting session, I took Sam back to camp to get treated, thinking the rest of you will join us shortly. However, an hour passed and no one came. Not even those after the deer.'

'Oh,' Jake's eyes widened.

'And then it happened. A fire began burning the forest. I don't know how it started but with you the only fire elemental...' Rob paused, staring at Jake for a moment and biting on the hair that dangled in front of his hairy face. 'Roxanne, check his hands.'

The medic took Jake's palms and inspected the crevices. The piercing touch of her nails made him flinch. Yet, he couldn't move out of fear of being suspected.

Fortunately, with a shake of her head, the medic spoke up, 'His hands are clean. No sign of usage within the last few days.'

'I see,' Rob mumbled.

They really don't trust me, huh, Jake thought, disappointed by the notion.

'Am I needed further?' the medic asked, putting her broken finger back into place, stopping the secretion.

'No. That is all. Thanks for the help, Roxanne. Go see if there are any other survivors and treat them,' Rob ordered.

'As you wish.'

Rob watched the medic leave the immediate vicinity, making sure no one else was in hearing distance as well, before leaning closer to Jake.

'Do you have any idea where the other bodies are?' Rob whispered, his face close enough to touch if Jake turned his head.

'What bodies?' Jake asked.

'Out of the ten that went on the hunting expedition, we have only found seven of them. You, me, Sam and four bodies - all of which are most likely dead and unrecoverable. That leaves three we haven't found yet.'

'Wait. Of those missing, is it one woman and two men?'

'Yes. One of them being –'

'Gin.'

Rob's eyes narrowed. 'How do you know?'

Jake stopped speaking. He wasn't sure what to say. Did he just out the truth of what happened just a few hours ago? Did he even believe what he witnessed? But the information Rob told him lined up and, along with the wounds on his legs, it was too coincidental to be just his imagination.

'Jake?'

'Sorry,' Jake paused once more, his thoughts running wild. 'I'm not sure myself, but I believe those three aren't dead.'

'They aren't?!' Rob exclaimed, causing Jake to flinch at the booming into his ears.

'Yes,' Jake admitted, stopping again to regain his composure. 'Hold on. How long has passed?'

'Since I took Sam back to the camp? It's an hour or so past sunrise now.'

'I see. Then it really was last night. Can we move elsewhere? I don't feel comfortable with everybody still close by.'

Rob looked around and nodded in confirmation. 'Can you walk?'

Jake focused on his legs. He could move one just fine, but the other didn't cooperate, only twitching at the simplest commands. With a groan of frustration, he looked back at Rob and shook his head. He knew he wouldn't be able to in his condition.

'Grab hold of me,' Rob understood, hoisting Jake over his shoulder.

The pair limped further into the forest, away from the other mages. They made no sound bar the flicks of low-lying branches. It wasn't until the voices of the search party disappeared did Rob let Jake down onto the nearest tree.

'So, what did you want to tell me privately?' Rob asked.

'Let me check one more thing,' Jake asserted, wiping a few blood stains from his leg. 'One of the missing bodies went barefoot, right?'

'Dmitri? Yes. He never wore footwear.'

'Ha! I think it's all too much of a coincidence now.'

Another pause followed before Rob prompted, 'Can you stop beating around the bush, please?'

'I want you to trust me on this. Gin and the others. They're traitors. They betrayed the battalion, squadron W, no, all of Eurasia.'

'Hang on a minute,' Rob stopped Jake, his eyes widening in shock, making his thought process obvious to understand. 'Traitors? That's impossible! I've spoken with him and those around him. They adore him. He's a good guy himself. I've seen his progress just like everyone else.'

Jake gave Rob a solemn expression, receiving a startled response in reply. A simple nod from both of them indicated how they wanted to proceed with the conversation.

'I think it's obvious now. He planned this from the start,' Jake speculated.

'From the start? How far back does that go?' Rob queried.

'I don't know. At least just before we left the rezah. From the way he got us to split up, first with our battalions during the sandpools, then with sending

Brim and the others to the oasis. He whittled us down; made us weaker.'

Rob clasped his face, hiding his obviously confused expression. 'Weren't all of those events just pure coincidence?'

'He might have known what was to happen. He might have just used the events to his own advantage, with a backup plan at hand.'

'This is beyond believability. Where's your proof?'

'Still don't trust me, huh?' Jake sighed, once again doing his reoccurring pause. 'Last night, I woke up, face on the floor. I was surrounded by bodies as well.'

'Yes, that's how we found you this morning.'

'You didn't see the others?'

'No. It was just you lot.'

'Well, I heard three people. Two men and a woman. It was obvious they killed everybody else. It was them who started the fire.'

'No wonder you were found so far away from the inferno. It was a distraction all along.'

'Now you're thinking like me!' Jake announced, receiving a sharp pain in his stomach as punishment for his sudden energy. 'What happened to the fire anyway?'

'Luckily it rained, otherwise we would have still been dealing with it.'

'Thankfully. As for what I witnessed, the woman sounded like the leader of the three while the other man – Dmitri you called him, right? – seemed to have picked off our people.'

'What did they look like? What were the wounds of those they killed like? Dmitri was in my battalion, so I know how he fights.'

'I don't know. I was too scared to open my eyes. All I saw was a severed head.'

'Yes, that does sound like something he'd do,' Rob admitted. He then howled in annoyance and punched the tree behind him, causing the bark to snap off. 'How did I not realise earlier?!'

'Rob it's ok. I trust you and they were clever about it. It's not your fault.'

'Thanks,' Rob said, going into a train of thought afterwards. 'Though it does make me wonder if the AAA has more backup. How many were on their side? What type of mage were they?'

'I didn't hear anything to help answer that.'

'That's frustrating.'

Rob's eyes wandered down to the three linear wound marks that had clotted and begun healing already.

'Now that I think about it,' Rob analysed. 'Those cuts. They're–'

'Gin stabbed me. These are the marks of his blades,' Jake interrupted.

'No doubt. None of the other mages have the ability nor the skill to be able to make such clean slits. How did you even survive?'

'Through luck. He thought I was dead already and just did not-so-deep stabs. I lost consciousness right after. They left me to rot with the others. I don't know what we should do now.'

'Of all the times for Brim's battalion to need another day...'

'What?'

'Oh no.'

'Hu-'

Rob lifted Jake up, catching him by surprise, and rung him around his back.

The very next second, they darted through the forest, heading towards where the search party were. Jake wanted to speak up but the speed told him all he needed to know. The urgency required pure silence and he abided, keeping quiet while his heart thumped and wounds throbbed. Then, as the chatter of the others echoed through the forest, he heard the deepest sigh of relief in his entire life from Rob.

'Rob?'

'Everyone's still here,' Rob mumbled.

'Oh, I understand now. We can't leave anyone alone now,' Jake concluded, glad to see Rob worried about the others.

'Yes,' Rob confirmed as he stood up straight, puffing out his chest. 'Everyone! We're leaving now.'

The mages turned towards their leader, baffled by the sudden command. Yet, his assertive voice made them obey, having them clean up the mess they made and leaving the forest in its natural condition first.

'Leader? What's wrong? You found Gin?' the petite Sam questioned Rob.

'Worse,' Rob replied. 'Hurry up everyone! This is urgent! Throw the bodies to the nearby mage-eater nest and head back to camp as soon as possible. No detours, even if you find something.'

Jake didn't hear their reply as he lurched backwards from the sudden acceleration from Rob. They headed towards the other mages, bursting through the clearing in one, single bound, shocking all and grabbing their attention.

'What happened to Jake?' one of them asked, leading to murmurs amongst the crowd, the wounds drawing eyes.

'We need to leave. It's too dangerous here,' Rob warned, his eyes stern enough to pierce the hardest of hearts while avoiding the mage's question altogether.

'Leave? You haven't told us what happened!' another protested.

'There's a high chance of an AAA army in this forest. We have to leave as soon as possible,' Rob added, leading to more discussion, all of which were of disbelief.

'Shouldn't we wait for the others?' a mage different from the other two suggested.

'Yeah, Brim, Michal and Syndra are on their way,' added a second.

'What about Gin?' a third chimed.

'Yes! We should find Gin too,' a few agreed. 'He'll be able to help.'

The noise in the camp grew so loud that birds flew away from the branches. But that didn't grab Jake's notice. Instead, the chatter and concern peeved him off. Every other sentence contained the word "Gin". Gin this. Gin that. How could they all be so blind to the truth? However, when Jake turned to see what Rob had planned, he could see the visible frustration of a man who couldn't control the mob.

'Let me down,' Jake whispered.

'What? Why?' Rob responded.

'Trust me.'

'Are you sure?'

'Yes.'

Rob obeyed, lowering Jake onto the ground to sit. But he insisted on standing up, using all of his strength to do so, his legs still numb from the anaesthetic. He waited to see if the crowd would die down though it never happened.

Jake took a deep breath.

'Silence!' he bellowed, grinding everyone's words to a halt. He might have ruptured something, but he didn't care, using everyone's, even Rob's, shocked looks as fuel for his determination. 'Don't you see that your own weak, low-ranked lives are at risk? The enemies are just beyond the clearing, waiting to attack us. Rob is trying to protect us all and you still stand there, gawking and asking questions and not seeing the urgency of the situation! And Gin? He betrayed us all! Us splitting up. Us being distracted by the fire. Us getting caught out and slaughtered one by one. My wounds, our battalions, Eurasia's squadron W — Gin orchestrated the downfall of each and every one of them from the very beginning! So please! Listen to Rob and leave this place!'

'Gin betrayed us?' the sound of Sam came from the clearing.

The silence that followed unnerved Jake. It was only at that moment that he noticed the confused and disbelieving glares of his peers. *Did I say anything wrong?* he wondered, starting to shake under the pressure exerted on him. Then he realised the lot of them waited on his answer to the question.

'Yes,' Jake confirmed, making sure to ooze confidence in his reply. 'Their negligence failed to kill me off, but the hunting party was definitely assaulted. And Gin was there. The blade marks on my legs prove it.'

The camp remained silent. Some still disbelieved while others began to shift, packing up the tents and caravans. Though slow, their movements lifted an immeasurable weight off Jake's chest, and he could see the gratitude from Rob.

'But I know Gin,' Sam argued over the silence. 'We talk lots. He wouldn't do this.'

Of those that stayed firm in their beliefs, they nodded after some thinking over and started trying to convince the others to stop. It pained Jake to see such a sight. *Just how much has Gin brainwashed the poor folk?* he asked himself, gritting his teeth. He wanted to protect everyone. Just like Brim would have had he been here. However, he couldn't find the words to do so.

'Unless,' he muttered.

'Did you want to say something?' Rob asked, drawing the gazes back to Jake.

'I am not mistaking this. I heard it in front of the assailants. The reason Gin betrayed us all. It's not that he's not working with the AAA,' Jake spoke up, taking his time to think of his next words. 'Well, he is, but it's something more. Something worse. He's not even one of us. He's not even a mage.'

The chorus of "huh?", "What?" and general puzzled groans filled the air. Jake knew he couldn't go back but something felt off. His mind began doubting itself. Did he even believe what he heard? His conscience told him to shake the whole news off, aiming for a different method instead. Anything but telling the full truth. However, a firm hand on his shoulder made him look up at a reassuring smile from Rob. Their mutual trust spurred Jake on to turn back to the crowd.

'Yes. I am certain! The reason he's so weak. The reason he betrayed us. The reason we need to leave-'

'You can't mean...' Sam realised.

Jake took one more deep breath.

'It's because he's a manush.'

25

A Leader's Decision

With the caravans filled to the brim with water, stone and other commodities, Brim held onto the reins to the lupim carrying the lot. He patted the furry beast, receiving warm nuzzles in return before it barked at the other canines, ordering the pack around. The other dogs howled back, turning into whimpers when their leader roared in response.

'Oho, he has taken quite the liking to you,' the utility familiar type remarked, controlling the lupim with ease with a ruffle of its back.

'I can tell by the happy panting, Lewis,' Brim replied, addressing the driver by name.

'No, no. Not just that,' Lewis said, chuckling for a moment.

'Oh?' Brim raised an eyebrow.

'Tigger told the other lupims that he's claimed you and for them to not try anything.'

The dog looked away at her master's comment, sparking a fit of laughter from Brim. He stroked the fur once more, getting the affectionate pants once again. *Or was it contempt?* he wondered when he noticed the jealous stares of the others.

'We can't be having that. The only thing I belong to is Eurasia. Can't be hogging me all the time,' Brim gave Tigger a teasing scold. 'As punishment, I'll leave you now.'

Hearing that statement, the dog yelped. Then she began whining and nudging brim's shoulders, begging him to stay.

'Haha! Don't worry, I'll come back. I'm only toying with you. I just need to check some things first,' Brim said and, though reluctant at first, the pooch allowed her secondary owner to do his duties.

He began a light jog, heading towards the caravans the other leaders resided in. He wanted to visit his own one but, through the small cracks in between the wooden planks of the caravan, he noticed Michal hard at work on his miniature project. It made Brim stop and grin. He knew the stone gauntlets were meant to be a "secret" —the number of times he found the poor fellow rushing to hide them under his blanket proved that —so he left the man be and headed to the other caravan.

This time he heard clapping to a certain rhythm; four slow ones followed by two sets of three fast ones. As he got closer, he saw Syndra's tinoo spinning in circles to the beat of her clapping. *Looks like they haven't noticed me,* Brim concluded.

He backed up, cleared his throat, and said out loud, 'Ah, sorry I can't help you out. I need to go see Syndra really quick for an important discussion!'

The clapping stopped and the bird flew out of the caravan the next moment.

Brim decided to wait a minute before knocking on the wood. A long pause followed, prompting him to knock again. The longer the silence went on, the more that laughter began to well up inside, but he held it in to avoid letting Syndra know that he knew what she was doing.

'Syndra?' Brim called.

'Yes? Come in,' Syndra's voice beckoned from within.

'Yo! How is everything?' Brim said, climbing inside the moving caravan.

'Brim Stones, I am certain you didn't come for small talk.'

Her pursed lips and piercing stare would have reformed anyone, but Brim remained unnerved. Maybe if he didn't witness the unexpected side a few moments prior, he would have felt the same but, after seeing what couldn't be unseen, he smirked instead.

'What's so funny?' Syndra pouted.

'Nothing. You're just as serious as always.'

'It's my job. Miscommunication and misinformation for stupid reasons can lead to death. I thought you knew that too.'

'Anyway,' Brim's smirk turned into a warm smile as he diverted the awkward atmosphere. 'You're right. I wanted to find our status at the moment.'

'If that's the case, we didn't need to drag it out as much as we did.'

You just wanted more time with your tinoo, Brim presumed while saying, 'Let's not then.'

'I've sent Nasir to scout ahead. We're a few kilometres away from the campsite. Last time we messaged them, we confirmed the group that split from us had re-joined Gin's battalion. At this slow rate, it'd take us several hours to reach them but we've notified them about our delay beforehand, so they'll know.'

'Several hours? Longer than I expected. But I guess we can't help it with all the resources we need to take care of.'

'Or you could tell our battalion to stop messing around,' Syndra's eyes began to narrow.

'Hmm?'

'Instead of helping out and speeding the travel up, they decide it's a good idea to play games! Shouldn't you be supervising them? Get them into the right mentality? I know we can't rely on Michal, but I thought you at least had some tact.'

'I'll go check on them then,' Brim conceded, getting off his seat. 'But you really ought to lighten up a bit. I know war is nothing to joke about but being serious and stoic all the time will only demoralise everyone. I think you'll learn a thing or two from Gin, Michal, Rob and the other mages here in squadron W if you give them a chance.'

'I don't have time to relax,' Syndra snapped.

'You having dancing lessons with your tinoo says otherwise,' Brim chuckled, seeing her shocked expression just as he jumped off the caravan.

He decided to search for his battalion. However, before he could start looking, a plated ball skidded in front of him. He inspected the object, realising what it was in a matter of seconds, then picked it up, poking the shell a couple times to lure the creature out of hiding. When that didn't work, Brim secreted some of his oil. He watched as the ball unfurled, the plates slotting underneath the fur, revealing a mole that had its forked tongue sticking out, tasting the liquid formed in front of it.

'Oh, sir!' someone called, racing towards his leader.

'What is it?' Brim responded, stroking the mole's fur as he did so.

The person stopped in front of Brim. He opened his mouth, closing it straight away afterwards without uttering a word. Instead, silence filled the next few moments as they walked side by side at the pace of the vehicles.

'Did you want to say something?' Brim pressured, noticing how the person – one he recognised was from his battalion – kept glancing at the feeding animal.

The man stayed silent for a bit longer before asking, 'Can I have the mole back?'

Brim smirked, leaning closer his teammate while holding the mole higher than before in one hand and pointing with the other. 'That is a nice scaly skin you got there. It's a shame that you seem to be a fire elemental instead of a utility familiar. Maybe I'm mistaken and the MBP has cooked up something different.'

'Um,' the person whimpered, unable to respond. He looked back, prompting Brim to follow his line of sight. Beyond them both was a large portion of the artillery group, watching the pair with eager eyes. But when they noticed the gaze of their leader, they diverted their attention as if they knew nothing.

'You guys are doing something suspicious,' Brim commented.

'We're doing a training exercise to help improve our range on our throws while not using our fireballs and it's something other people can do, not just us fire elementals, and it helps us –'

'I'm gonna stop you right there before you run out of breath, but I understand.'

'Sorry. I got carried away,' the man admitted, scratching his bald scalp. 'But we need the mole, please. Its owner allowed us. As did the animal itself. I'm telling the truth, sir.'

'Is that so?' Brim questioned, watching the animal's reaction. The mole looked back, licked the palm once more for the final droplets of sweat before curling back into the plate-covered ball Brim found it in, rolling a few times to indicate that it wanted something done. 'Alright then. But only if you let me participate in this "training exercise" of yours.'

Brim watched with glee as the man in front of him turned his head to his group and back in quick, dizzying succession. His comrades remained uninterested, but their nervousness seeped through.

'You're not going to lead me?' Brim asked in a mischievous tone, putting the mage on the spot.

'Oh, yes,' the man stopped again before adding, 'Right this way.'

He led Brim towards the group of people, who could no longer pretend they weren't part of the "training" anymore, giving meek nods of acknowledgement to their superior to show it. Their eyes focused on the mole, waiting for it to get retrieved.

'Wait right here,' the guide instructed.

Brim listened, watching the man's rigid walk towards his teammates. He couldn't quite hear what he said, but he could recognise the teasing going on with all the light-hearted punches and headlocks on the unfortunate victim. It wasn't until the group let him go, nodding in approval to the man's request, did he turn back with a forced smile.

'They said yes,' he said.

'I know,' Brim replied, a wide grin on his face. 'So, what do we do?'

'Um...'

'Hey, Alfar! Hurry up so we can play!' his friends yelled at him.

'"Play"?' Brim questioned, realising he never asked for a name.

'No, sir. This is purely training,' Alfar tried to divert. 'But we basically split ourselves into two teams. Their team is a few hundred metres ahead of us. You'll join our team, sir.'

Alfar pointed towards a group further ahead, all watching the conversation at hand, or rather Brim speculated they were watching the animal still rolled up into a ball on his palm. As he examined further, he saw five more people separate from the other team's group and, when he looked back on the team on his side, he noticed five people were detached from his team.

'The aim is to get the ball to our team's catchers. We got five of them as you can see. The other team has five on our side too,' Alfar explained. 'If you catch the enemy team's throw, you get three points. If you prevent the catchers from getting the ball, you get one point but if your team's catchers get the ball, you win ten points. First to one-fifty wins. Also, you must keep a minimum distance of three-hundred between teams.'

'I see. So, what you're saying is the best way to win is to get to the catchers? In that case...'

Brim pulled back his arm, dislocating his shoulder and repositioning the joint, increasing the length of the limb. He focused on his technique, utilising all the muscle in the one area of his body to its utmost potential. Then, with a lightning quick slingshot, he let the mole loose. The creature flew through the cloud-filled sky, over Brim's team, over the desert, over the enemy team, over the catchers and, at last, landing on the area behind everyone. Those on the other stood static for several seconds before the catchers burst back to life, using their distance advantage to snatch the mole off the ground.

'Well, that was an easy ten points,' Brim self-praised, slotting his arm back into its natural position.

'Woah.'

'Hmm? Did I do something wrong.'

'N-no,' Alfar stuttered. 'You just covered seven-hundred like it was nothing.'

'Well, I got lucky with the wind in my favour and all. Though the mole is heavier than I expected. On a good day, my fireballs can reach eight-hundred. Think that was my record during the battle of Lisbon,' Brim explained before he realised that both Alfar and the other teammates looked at him with gobsmacked expressions. 'What?'

'You are amazing!' Alfar exclaimed out, the other people soon joining in to listen to the conversation. 'I don't think any of us could throw as far so we just left made sure to cover the front.'

'Oh, tell us about the battle of Lisbon!' another blurted out, getting muffled agreement from the others.

'Yes, it sounds like an awesome story,' a third added.

'I think I'd rather get back to the game haha,' Brim jested. 'But to keep it short, the enemy was surprised by our range and we managed to sink TA's ships. They haven't bothered us since!'

'Wow!' the crowd admired in unison.

'Well, I'm sure you guys will accomplish similar feats. For now, can I ask what stops you from holding the catchers down? Or how about having people defending the backside to prevent the enemy team from getting behind us? I think we can improve on this "training" of yours,' Brim said with a comforting smile.

'Look! We can see the campsite!' someone called out.

Everyone looked up in unison, spotting the thin strands of grey coming out of the forest in front of them, meshing with the gloomy sky. An excited cheer roared through the area at the sight, with fist-bumps and the odd fireball coursing through the air.

'You guys really want to see the offence group that badly, don't ya?' Brim commented.

He put on a calm demeanour, but still felt like something was off. *Thought we were too far to see the remains of campfires. Though I guess we travelled further than Syndra expected. But that's still a lot of smoke lines anyway,* he questioned before shaking his head and putting it down to multiple fireplaces.

'I'll just have to scold them for wastefulness,' he noted to himself, turning back to the upbeat battalion. 'Shall we get started on the game changes then?'

'Yessir!'

With his guidance, Brim's battalion ironed out the flaws while adding more complexity to the game until it actually turned into training-programme worthy. As each point played out, they worked on improving tactics, rules. Different modes were added, increasing or decreasing the rewards, adding an element of risk such as the "No one's allowed to move" condition giving bonus points if catchers caught the mole (who was having the time of its life).

Not only were the participants enjoying themselves, the other people marvelled at the spectacle. Some joined in, testing out their strength and capabilities despite knowing they have never used projectiles in their life. Even the animals got curious. A few of the moles rolled into balls of their own. The tinoos cawed up above at each throw. The lupims began howling in joy. One lupim howled, then two, then five, then ten lupims. Too many of them in fact...

Hang on a minute, Brim realised, his eyes widening at what he saw further into the distance. Beyond the forest, the strands of smoke had turned into a multitude of plumes that no campfire could have created.

'Everyone!' he bellowed, disrupting the peaceful atmosphere in an instant. 'Get to your stations. Formation nineteen. Artillery group help the lupims out in travel and move to the campsite ASAP. We don't have much time! The others are in danger!'

Brim's orders were brief but clear.

The next moment, he darted through the sand with a few others following close behind. He could hear the sound of the wheels from the caravans turning faster while more distant at the same time. His lungs burned, but he continued his sprint, making sure not to slow down lest he arrived too late. Then before he knew it, he saw the beginning of the clearing he was all too familiar with and used the goal in sight as the final fuel to burst into vision of the campsite.

However, all that remained was a mere fraction of who should have been there.

'What is going on?!'

But no one answered. Those that were present formed small groups, not wanting to talk with each other, or rather, completely avoiding their own allies. And yet, the spontaneous shivering of everyone told Brim that they heard him loud and clear.

'Tsk,' he tutted before singling out someone who didn't belong to any group. 'You over there! I know you can hear me. Tell me what is going on.'

The woman shook even more, using her hair to cover her face. The crowd also shuffled away, isolating the person, much to Brim's annoyance. He decided to take it upon himself, storming to the poor soul. He made sure to maintain eye contact until she couldn't look away.

'I won't repeat myself,' he snapped. 'Tell me what in Eurasia is going on.'

The woman gawked at the battalion leader, her lips quivering. Words didn't come out.

'Well? No response? Lives are on the line here,' his voice became more assertive with each passing word.

'Rob and Gin and others. They're not here.'

'What?! Where did they go?'

'Jake,' the woman whimpered, stopping right after saying the name.

'What about him?'

'He knows.'

'And you don't?' Brim interrogated but the silence that followed answered his question. 'Where is he then?'

As if everyone heard the conversation, the offence group moved, leaving a direct line of sight for the woman to point her finger through, revealing Jake's location. He sat against a tree, holding his stomach while a medic tended to him. Despite the gravity of the situation, he looked smug, only aggravating Brim's furious mood further.

Brim tore through the dirt underneath with every step. Those in his way didn't hesitate to move without needing to be told. His rampage sent the message that even the medic understood, moving out of the way when he got close. Yet, Jake remained the only one oblivious.

'Jake.'

'Oh. Brim, you're here at last! I did it! I saved everyone,' Jake exclaimed with a stupid enthusiasm.

Brim took a deep breath. He knew Jake for far too long and understood how stupid the man could be at times. A simple scolding or forgiveness would never work on him or else the situation spiralled down beyond salvation.

'How did you save everyone?' Brim started.

'I found out the truth! I had a feeling all along but now I'm certain. Gin's a traitor and he betrayed us all.'

'Is that so?' Brim said in a calm and methodical manner, inviting Jake to tell the lie he believed.

'Yes! A few of us, Gin and Rob included, went for hunting on the eastern side of the forest. We made a plan in the dirt and everything. Then we managed to secure a deer. Someone got injured but needed more food so we split up. I don't remember much after that but I was surrounded by at least five people from the AAA. Gin was one of them! I fought killed off half of them but they were still too much so they took me down. Then Gin stabbed me as you can see,' Brim could tell Jake exaggerated as he showed off the scars on his legs and abdomen, 'But I was able to escape with the help of Rob. Gin caused the forest fire but luckily Rob and rain helped quench the disaster. It also turned out he's a manush too!'

'A manush, huh?'

'I did a good job right? I saved the squadron. I figured it out by myself. I mean, I kind of knew he was suspicious since the first time we met but I kept to myself so that you don't get hurt yourself. That's why I-'

Brim didn't concentrate on what Jake spouted afterwards. He went into deep thought, picking apart what was truth and what was fabricated. However, certain questions reoccurred more often than he would have liked. *Him being a manush? It's so ridiculous that Jake couldn't make it up. But still...*

'What is going on? Where is everyone?' someone yelled.

Snapped back to reality, Brim found Jake still talking followed by the panting of an exhausted Michal. The rest turned the corner one by one, speeding up as soon as they saw the aftermath, all as perplexed as another by the situation.

'Brim! I am so confused,' Michal caught up with the leader, still catching his breath. 'Do you know what's happening?'

'Kind of,' Brim answered, turning back to Jake. 'And where is Rob now?'

'What? Oh, he went ahead,' Jake explained. 'He's taken most of the offence group to safety. He should be only a few hours' worth of walking in front of us. It's too dangerous to stay here and yet most of Gin's battalion and other equally stupid people still remain.'

'Which explains why you're here,' Brim mumbled. 'Ok, Michal go and get a tinoo to scout ahead and look for Rob. Then get someone to go to the eastern side of the forest. Look for where the plants got crushed. There should be some drawings nearby. After that, you speak with the others and talk with them and find out what they think. Got it?'

'Still clueless but understood,' Michal obeyed, jogging to the familiar users.

'Brim,' Jake hesitated before asking, 'Do you not trust me?'

Brim took another deep breath, responding, 'Are you certain Gin caused all this?'

'Hundred percent.'

'Did you see him?'

'Huh?'

'Did. You. See. His. Face?' Brim spelt out each word.

'No. Not exactly.'

Brim's eyes narrowed.

'Thought he attacked you. How could you not see his face?'

'I had to play dead –'

'After dealing with half of the assailants, right? So damaged you had to collapse and pretend they got you, right?'

'Um,' Jake's eyes began to dart from side to side, avoiding eye contact. 'Yes.'

'Then you must have heard his voice, right?'

'No.'

'No sight. No sound. Then how did you know it was Gin? Did you just happen to brush against the bristles of his facial hair?'

'T–they said his name.'

'They? The enemy? The traitors?' Brim's anger finally got through to Jake. He trembled in his seat, unsure what to do next. 'Well? Nothing? Jake, we can't make baseless assumptions just because you trust *the enemy's words* more than your trust your own allies!'

'But these stab wounds,' Jake got quieter with each word.

'You think the AAA's MBP wouldn't be able to breed metal elementals? That it's an exclusive breed just for us Eurasians?'

'Um.'

'Brim!' Michal called out again, still breathless by all the running around he did.

'Yes?'

'Spoke with the other mages. They said they don't trust Rob. They want to find Gin instead but are too scared to speak up. And what's this about him being a manush? Aren't they extinct?' Michal reported.

'Want to find Gin? Are they crazy?' Jake scoffed. 'Don't trust Rob? He's looking in the best interest of ever–'

'Jake! Shut it,' Brim scolded. 'If anything, he's the prime suspect from your story.'

'What?'

'What about the drawings?' Brim asked, ignoring Jake's state of shock.

'There is none.'

'None?!' Jake exclaimed. 'Then Gin must have rubbed them out before we went hunting.'

Brim grabbed hold of Jake's vest, slamming him against the tree and lifting him at shoulder height. Pus oozed out of his wounds upon impact but no one paid attention to that. Instead, eyes were focused on the heated moment between the two leaders. Even Michal's mouth opened agape.

'How can you be so sure it was Gin? Did you see him do it? How do you know Rob or the others that joined your hunting didn't do it instead? Why are you so fixated on him being the culprit?!' Brim roared.

'B-but he's a manush,' Jake gave a half-hearted, ill-informed, weak-minded argument.

'And what if he is?!' Brim fumed, his teeth gnashing together to make a frightening sound. 'If anything, that would him so weak, so stupid and so powerless that he shouldn't be able to do anything against us. So, how has he managed to betray us while being a manush as you say he is? Or is that more lies of the enemy that you just happened to believe?'

'But Rob would never –'

'Leader! Leader!' a messenger hollered, holding a piece of paper in his hands.

'What?' Brim bellowed, his anger carrying over to the next recipient of his wrath.

'Um, the tinoo came back. Rob and the offence group are nowhere in sight.'

'You were saying?' Brim turned back to Jake.

'But Gin –'

'Jake, stop. It's Gin this, Gin that with you. You are so far up your own ego that you have lost all ability to think logically. Not once did you inform us of your circumstances nor did we receive a tinoo's message from Rob himself. Now he's missing and you continue to push your outlandish theories upon *me*? On all of us? You have single-handedly put all of squadron W in jeopardy and *still* have the audacity to say you're in the right? You refuse to stop for a moment and assess your claims which I have dismantled one by one right in front of you. And yet you still blindly believe your own delusions? And what if Gin really is a manush? How does that change anything? Is he not Eurasian? Does that mean he's not on our side? Well?!'

Jake's responded with quaking lips and a gawking mouth. He didn't say anything but a few forced "ah"s and "um"s. Brim wanted to punch the child back into adulthood but decided against it. Instead, he calmed himself, not wanting to bring morale further down. That was one thing he couldn't afford to do.

He looked Jake right in the eye and said in the most relaxed and authoritative manner, 'So, until you learn to stop being such a judgemental moron, I use my position as leader of the artillery group to hereby strip you of your role as battalion leader. You're dismissed.'

Jake stopped resisting. He slid down the trunk, deflated and in shock. The man clutched his wounds once more, disbelieving that he was wrong, but everything pointed towards the case. But his hopelessness didn't concern Brim.

'Everyone! We've got a lead on the true perpetrator. Gin is not the prime suspect. I repeat. Gin is not the prime suspect. Regroup and reorganise yourselves while we wait for the caravans to join us,' he demanded the silent few. He could tell from sighs of relief that he lifted a great burden on their chests with his statement. The quiet chattering afterwards felt like a cheer instead. 'Hey, Michal.'

'Yes?'

'Grab a few volunteers. We're going to the heart of the forest fire. If not Gin, I believe we'll find some clues there. As for the rest of you,' Brim turned to those still in doubt, and his arriving battalion, with a fire in his eyes that rooted every soul in the area in their spot. 'You *will* hear rumours about Gin being a manush. Now, I will give you an ultimatum on the matter. You leave right now and disappear from the face of the planet because of your prejudice, just like those who went with Rob, or you stay and we can think rationally about the whole situation. The choice is yours. Do I make myself clear?'

No one moved a step. Fear prevented them from doing so. All they could do was nod in agreement to choose the latter option. After all, death awaited those who left.

'Good. Let's go find Gin now,' Brim said rather than ordered, taking one last deep breath. 'Today has been a long day.'

26

Gin's Resolve

'Is it over?' the boy asked as he fidgeted restlessly, waiting for an answer. His palms were sweaty, but he crossed his fingers, holding his breath as his father studied him with an inscrutable expression.

'Yeah. You're cured. You also don't need to wear glasses now as a bonus,' the doctor concluded.

'Really?!'

'Yep. Read the chart across the room. What does it say?' the doctor gestured to the chart hanging on the wall six meters away.

The boy squinted at the chart, half-expecting the words to blur out like before but, to his delight, he could see them as clearly as if they were right in front of him. 'Um. Q. U. I. G. J. L. T. S. B. T. N-'

'Alright, you can stop. You weren't able to get past the fifth letter before.'

The doctor nodded and cut the enthusiastic rambling child off before he could get carried away, though the young boy still perked up in delight.

'Wow! Thank you, father!'

'Now you can go outside and play with your friends.'

The boy's father opened the door and waved outside, as if impatient to shoo him out of the room. However, the boy didn't seem to notice, his thoughts preoccupied with something else.

'Can I go see Jacob first?' he asked.

'Sorry. He's not ready yet,' the doctor denied.

'Was something wrong with our operations?' the boy gulped as he began to fidget again.

His father gave a welcoming smile and placed a hand on his shoulder. 'Not for you. Your nanobots can and will recreate themselves, just like your ordinary cells. It's just that some minor problems have appeared for Jacob, which is why you can't see him at the moment.'

'Aww,' the boy complained. 'I haven't seen him for a year now. When will he be healed?'

'Soon,' his father assured him with a now strained smile.

'You said that last time.'

'Don't probe into the matter.'

'But I want to go see him now.'

'Go outside and play.'

'But father!'

The doctor had lost his smile and his expression grew stern. 'Look. I understand you want to see your brother. I understand you're a smart kid that's interested in my work. I understand your concerns, but can't you act like a normal kid for once?'

'Mmm. Ok,' the boy said as his shoulders slumped.

'Thank you.' His father turned away, sighing in relief.

The boy glanced at him for a second, and then obediently slid out of the room. Act like a normal kid? Yeah. He could do that. He's a normal boy now. No more illnesses. No more weaknesses. No more collapsing suddenly. His friends would accept the new him.

If only that was what happened. For the boy came back a few hours later, bawling his eyes out.

'Father! Please turn me back to normal!' he pleaded as he ran into his father's office.

Concerned by the sudden outburst, his father picked his son who hid in the cover of his dad's lab coat, sobbing into his shirt.

'What happened?' the father asked as he began stroking his hair to comfort him.

'I saved her and then I got hurt and then I'm not hurt anymore but it was too quick and now everyone thinks I'm a monster,' the boy clamoured, all in one breath.

'I don't know what's going on, but you're definitely not a mo-'

'Look!' the boy interrupted, shoving his hand into his father's face.

He inspected it but saw nothing unusual. There were a few scratch marks, but surely that was normal for boisterous kids of his age.

'I don't see anything strange,' the doctor admitted.

'Exactly! I want to go back to normal!' his son pleaded, sobbing again.

'Woah. Woah. Woah. Slow down. Take a deep breath and tell me what happened.'

'James and John said I didn't need glasses because I wasn't human anymore. I told them I was still human. I thought they believed me. But I was wrong.'

The father wanted to speak up but decided against it. Though he was distressed by what had happened, he knew simple name-calling wasn't something that would get his son upset. There had to be something else, so he let him continue.

'They never believed me! They said monsters don't protect anyone, so they threw rocks at Samantha, but I blocked all of it. I protected her and I thought I proved them wrong, but I didn't. My hand was bleeding but now my wound is gone. I healed too quickly. I really am a monster. Even the adults are looking at me funny.'

'So that's the reason,' the father hugged his son tighter, letting the tears form marks on his clothes. 'Look, son, the sudden burst of inhuman power would scare most children and raise the eyebrow of most adults. I hoped to explain all the changes that happened to your body during the operation, but it's too soon. You'll understand with time. You're not a monster or freak. That's only the regenerative properties of the-'

'Change me back! I hate this! I don't care if I'm ill again! Please, father!' the boy exclaimed, his eyes now red from the crying.

The father sighed. He wanted to reassure his son. He could easily prove that his son was human, both technically and physically, but against a child who was in no mood to change his mind, there wasn't anything that would work.

Why must children be so illogical?

In the end, he considered the boy's request but, realistically, trying to reverse the procedure would bring more harm than good. Maybe he could turn down the effectiveness, but for now, he had to stop any more tears from falling out.

'I'll see what I can do,' the doctor said at last. 'In the meantime, do you want to see my latest invention, the Integrated Nanobot System? INS for short.'

'Huh? Really?! You never show me your work!' the boy sniffled. 'Yes. Yes. Yes!'

At least he stopped crying.

****

Gin felt something pecking his arm. It was more of a tickle, but its consistency roused Gin up. He opened his eyes, reliving the all too familiar feeling of looking upwards after regaining consciousness. On this instance, he saw a cloudy sky, neither too dark nor too bright which told him that the sun already rose. Either that or it was about to set (he lost track of his bearings).

'Ugh. It's been a while since I dreamt like that. Why was I always such a whiny brat?' he regretted.

As he sat up, he groaned as his body hurt with each movement, like pins pricking his pierced limbs. Then shock overcame his pain, soon followed by a sinking feeling of guilt when he witnessed how ash, decay, and burnt plants replaced the lush green of the forestry the day before. Though he did feel relieved that he could still see trees in the distance, the cataclysm caused by his selfish desire for survival still left a sour taste in his mouth.

'Mother, father, Jacob...I'm sorry. It's all my fault again.'

Gin wanted to go back to sleep and forget his troubles but the pecking persisted, this time on his thigh, prompting him to look down instead, finding a bird no larger than the width of his leg. The black feathers of the creature combined with the elongated neck and the odd teeth protruding out of the beak of its round head made one thought come to his mind: *This isn't a tinoo.*

The bird tilted its head, staring at Gin. It squawked, revealing the rest of its impressive array of teeth in the process. It then tried jumping onto Gin's legs but, due to the difference in size, it proved to be a difficult task. But, no matter how many times it fell over, it got back up and jumped again, albeit failing like normal.

'Heh. Tenacious one, aren't you? Need some help?' Gin asked, wondering if the bird understood words.

It stopped flailing around, fluttering its wings and squawking in delight upon the offer. It was weak, feeble and out of place, though for some reason Gin found solace with his newfound companion. He extended his arm for the bird to hop onto. However, as he did so, he noticed that the Xernim gauntlets covered his whole arm. Then a simple check confirmed that t he same happened to the other arm.

'Huh? When did they do this? Swear it was meant to be just elbow height,' Gin wondered, turning back to the bird on his palm. 'Oh well.'

He let the animal down on his thigh. It scurried up and down before stopping at where scratch marks tore through his trousers, revealing lined scabs. The bird twisted its head in a three-sixty, mesmerised by the shape and colour. *What a strange creature*, Gin concluded.

The bird went back to its natural position. It took one more look at thc scabs. Water started seeping from the bird's mouth, its head edging closer until the tip of its beak touched the wound. Gin wanted to shoo the creature away, knowing full well what the animal planned to do, but curiosity got the better of him and he watched its next movement with anticipation instead.

In an instant, the beak opened and closed, snipping the wound open. Using the long, spindly tongue hidden inside its mouth, the bird lapped up the oozing blood. Despite the rough texture of the licks, to Gin's surprise, he didn't recognise anything he would call pain. To him, the best description of the feeling was a muscle-relieving massage, so he let the animal be, enjoying the strange moment.

After having its full, the bird looked at its benefactor with eager and grateful eyes. It walked up against his leg, nuzzling him once it reached the stomach. Did offering blood warrant such affection? Maybe. Probably not. However, Gin found the actions amusing, stroking his companion back in appreciation. He wanted to pet some more but several caws cut their time short.

All of a sudden, the bird looked up. Gin didn't realise why until he saw a flock of birds, all similar in shape to the chick, yet he couldn't quite figure out their size due to how high the others were flying. Regardless, the animal on his lap recognised them. It looked back once more and gave one last squawk. Then, using Gin's legs as a launchpad, it flapped its tiny wings, lifting off in an awkward fashion.

'The world sure is a weird place,' Gin commented, watching the creature catch up to the family overhead. 'Heh. It seems like my self-deprecation flew away with the fella too. Alright.'

Through the aches, Gin hoisted himself up, using the half-burnt tree trunk behind him as leverage. He inspected the surroundings further, finding two of his INS on the floor; the green of the shield and the silver of the nanobooster. Not far from both, he spotted a burnt, broken container cut into five pieces. The liquid that was once inside no longer remained; a testimony that the fire started from that exact spot.

Taking the nanobooster, he tried injecting the serum into his arm, only to remember how the Xernim had grown again. *Where do I put it now?* he asked himself.

Guess via the chest would be the most effective method. He did just that, first taking off his torn shirt and chipped armour, and caressing the scars he received from his first day in squadron W. The veins bulged somewhat out of his skin, allowing for an easy target for the serum to enter the bloodstream through.

'Hey! Guys! We were right, he's here!' someone shouted from behind.

'Where?'

'I see him!'

'Hurry! He looks like he's about to collapse!'

Out of the voices, Gin only recognised Michal's. He didn't shout nor did the voice in any way feel desperate like the others. No, it sounded like he carried an "I knew it" vibe rather than anything else.

'Search the area for anything suspicious. I'll take him back to camp,' Michal ordered. He walked up to Gin, his boots squelching on the wet ash beneath with each step. 'Hey.'

'Ah. Michal. How are you?' Gin asked, his words coming out more feeble than he wanted to.

'Don't worry about me,' Michal said as he put Gin over his shoulders. 'You're hurt.'

'Heh. Since when did you get so capable? Ordering the others like a natural leader and taking control right now.'

'A lot has happened in the past few days.'

'Tell me about it.'

The pair walked towards camp, silent and recollecting the events prior. Their quietness bothered Gin more than he thought it would. It wasn't until they reached the first set of trees that he spoke up.

'Did something happen while I was unconscious?'

'Gin, can I ask you something first?' Michal asked instead, hesitant in his speech.

'Ok, sure. Go ahead.'

'Are you,' Michal paused before finishing. 'Are you a manush?'

Oh. How did they figure that out? Gin thought. He didn't know how to answer. Should he respond at all or divert the question?

'Your silence probably means Jake wasn't lying then.'

'What? Oh. I'm sorry. Wo warned against this. You guys probably think I'm worse than the worst now. I'm sorry. I should never have taken up my role of battalion leader. It was inevitable my secret would come out. I'm sorry. I always make a mess of everything. I should have just given my job to someone else. Someone who can lead better or come up with better training. I'm sor-'

'Gin!' Michal interrupted, taking a deep breath to calm his nerves before continuing. 'Don't worry. I've thought it over a lot myself. And honestly, I don't care. What about you though? Are you ok? Because you're acting weird. What do you mean someone who can lead better? *Nobody* could lead our battalion like you do. We only managed to get so far because of you.'

Gin's heart shook. Once again, he was left speechless but for a different reason. Like something lifting his nerves, doubt and self-deprecation.

'It's like Brim said, "And what if Gin really is a manush? How does that change anything? Is he not Eurasian? Does that mean he's not on our side?"' Michal quoted, letting out a sigh when he finished. 'What happened to you Gin? Are you really gonna let a single loss and a little secret make you believe we won't care about you anymore? What you said better be a joke because I *will* tell Brim and Joan and they *will* beat you to the next continent if they see you acting like this.'

'Please don't,' Gin begged, unable to hide the encroaching smile.

'Good. Then we never talked about this,' Michal pouted.

'They're the two people I can't get worried, heh.'

'Look, everyone here who stayed is here for you, so cheer up, ok?'

'Huh? What do you mean "stayed"? Don't tell me...'

But before Gin could get an answer, they both emerged from the forest and into the campsite. It was just as he feared. Worried and disbelieving eyes fixated on him, a feeling he thought he rid off in the distant past. He heard their comments, each containing his name, "mage", "manush", or a combination of the above. However, what worried him the most wasn't the reactions of those present but those that weren't. The scolding Michal gave to sort him out almost became null.

'Don't mind them,' Michal assured, realising his words weren't enough.

But from the crowd, one person made his way towards the pair, the only one that was close enough and on equal terms with Gin. From what he could guess from the looks of things, Brim appeared the most distraught by the revelations.

Gin wanted to go back to how it was before anyone knew anything about him. He wanted to find a way to make amends. He wanted to deny everything. But he had no faith in his lying capabilities, especially after spilling the truth to Michal. Not after last time.

As Brim got closer, Gin had made his mind up. He no longer found any point in hiding his identity. If he did, then what would happen if he had a bigger army? How was he going to manage deserters in the thousands rather than the hundreds? Better to tell the truth now than suffer later.

'Is it true?' Brim asked, his expression as stern as ever. 'Are you a manush?'

'What if I'm a manush?' Gin retorted. 'It just means I've always have been and always will be weaker than you mages. I'm worse than F ranks for crying out loud! I got no special powers, no innate evolutionary advantage. It means I have to rely on my wits rather than my strength. It's how I survived up to now and I will continue to survive because of it. I just want to travel the world with you guys. What are you going to do about it?'

'Gin,' Michal murmured.

'Ha! That's just like you, Gin,' Brim responded with a smile. 'That decides it. You heard him, everyone! Let's continue to follow you.'

'Eh? That's how you react?' Gin said, with a puzzled look across his face, watching the doubtful gazes turn into warm grins.

'Were you expecting me to hate you all of a sudden?' Brim smirked.

'Um,' Gin didn't know how to respond, still in a confused shock. 'Maybe.'

'Gin. Look,' Brim asserted himself. 'You made me overlook my initial prejudice of the low ranked. I think I can overlook you being a manush. It doesn't change much about you, does it? If you denied everything and I found out the truth, that would have been a different story. But you blatantly revealed yourself to everyone without fear. As I said, that's just typical you. Everyone here feels the same way. I've made sure to convince the doubters to stay anyway.'

'I agree,' Michal added, putting on a wry smile. 'Brim's death-stare was too much for everyone.'

'I suppose it was,' Brim chuckled back.

'Wow,' Gin gaped, taken aback by how well everyone was taking it. 'But I still don't think the offence group feel the same way, Brim. They left because of me, right? I'm sure that's why we're so depleted. Wouldn't it be better if you took charge?'

'Don't be an idiot, Gin. Ask me again after you've taken the opinion of what's left of your battalion,' Brim said, pointing to where his battalion was resting. 'I'll talk to the doubters in the artillery group, while Michal will talk to the utility group. We'll also talk to Syndra's battalion. They're still bringing the caravans. You sort out your side of this mess.'

'Alright,' Gin conceded, not in a position to argue. 'Michal, you can go. I can walk by myself.'

'Alright,' he obeyed, letting go of him. 'I'll try my best to persuade everyone to listen to you again. Then we'll fill you in on everything we found out.'

'Thanks.'

'No problem.'

Gin hobbled his way to what remained of his battalion. Their faces showed too much brokenness. They didn't even notice his arrival. That didn't surprise him in the least. Rather, his shock came from the fact that Jake sat with them. He looked just as depressed – remorseful in fact.

'Guys, he's here,' Jake pointed out, the first to notice.

The battalion looked up at their battered leader in unison. Their faces lit up in an instant, a wide smile filling each of them. They sprung up and rushed Gin, enveloping him with such affection that tears began to well up.

I'm such an idiot, he thought to himself within the chaos. He looked back to find that Jake stayed behind and looked away from the rest. *Seriously, what the hell happened?* But that didn't take away the sheer joy he felt, surrounded by those that looked up to him.

Though technically, they're looking down on me, Gin mused, conscious of his relative height all of a sudden. He made his mind up again, smiling to his peers. He steeled himself for the worst but no longer cared. He couldn't doubt himself. Not anymore. He was going to see this battle through and lead them to victory. He was going to gain back the trust of the deserters. He was going to fulfil the promises he made when he got attacked. That was Gin's resolve.

27

Investigation

Gin concentrated on his arm, picturing the image of the Xernim returning to the default position. It complied, though instead of decaying like usual, it peeled off his arm like the skin of a Bandra fruit. Regardless of the parasite's methods to reveal the sliced-up limbs, he found the underside of the Xernim the most interesting discovery as small, thin spikes riddled the peels, each secreting a liquid that solidified upon touch.

'Is it meant to do that?' Michal questioned, watching the whole spectacle.

'Not sure,' Gin admitted, applying medicinal lotion on his wounds.

When he finished, Gin thought about the Xernim going back to its usual position. However, it didn't listen, wrapping around his whole arm and planting the spikes into his flesh instead. For some reason, the multiple pin-like objects didn't hurt or leave any sensation his nerves could have picked up on for that matter.

'Hmm. I wonder if that's the case,' Gin mumbled to himself.

'What is? Did the Xernim not listen to you? Maybe I should check it out to see if there's anything wrong,' Michal offered, shuffling closer.

'No. Well, yes, it's not acting as my thoughts ask it to.'

'Oh?'

'But, and this is a big but, based on Joan's analysis when she does my check-ups and how Alder also describes his Xernim, it might be possible that it's not my thoughts that the Xernim listens to. Rather, it's what I truly think if that makes sense.'

'No. You've lost me. Not your thoughts but your true thoughts? Maybe the Xernim really has affected you. Let me take a look,' Michal outreached his hand.

'Let's see if there's a better way of saying it,' Gin rejected Michal's offer, pushing his hand away. 'My verbal words could be lies, the thoughts I tell to myself could be lies. However, under no circumstance would my body be able to deceive the Xernim.'

'Gin, now you're speaking gibberish,' Michal's hand still hovered.

'Still don't get it?' Gin asked, pausing for a moment to think of an analogy before saying, 'Let me put it this way. I can tell an enemy I'm not scared. I can lie to myself and say mentally that I'm not scared. But if my body still trembles, I am obviously shaken, even if I've disciplined myself not to. So, maybe the Xernim picks up on the truth and is trying to protect me? What if the fact it's covering my whole arm – what if those spikes and that strange liquid are actually good for me and my body knows it but I don't? It might explain why it's not going back to normal.'

'I don't think that's it.'

'Yeah, maybe. Just random speculations.'

'You're definitely suffering from exhaustion. You need to be checked out. Extend your arm towards me,' Michal became a little too assertive, causing Gin to raise an eyebrow in suspicion.

'You're awfully interested in my gauntlets all of a sudden. Is there a reason for that?'

'Oh, not really. Just looking out for your wellbeing,' Michal gave an alternative truth, his hands sliding towards the blanket beside him.

'Right...'

'Sorry,' Michal apologised despite no provocation at all. 'I'll show you later. After the battle, ok?'

'So, you really were up to something, huh?'

'What? Oh, you heard nothing.'

'If you say so,' Gin smirked.

The next few moments consisted of a couple of tests. First of all, he tried growing the Xernim further. It listened, crawling over Gin's shoulder blades without a problem. Then, he tried to reverse the command and, as he expected, the branches decayed instead of peeling, returning to the (new, current) default position. *Maybe I really do want the Xernim to go so high,* he concluded.

'Y'know, I talked to my battalion and Brim talked to his,' Michal started.

'And what did they say?' Gin continued the conversation.

'They're fine with everything. Well, not fine with how a third of the battalion just went up and left, but they're fine with you. Some took more time to convince than others but still.'

'That's good to hear. What's left of my battalion are happy with me too. What about Syndra?'

'Oh, I tried talking to her.'

'And? I haven't spoken much with her at all – used Sam to relay messages for me - so I don't know what to expect.'

'She thought it was pathetic that you sent me instead of yourself to settle things.'

'Didn't she know I was injured and needed treatment?' Gin asked, stopping his tests for the time being.

'Not sure. I didn't tell her explicitly,' Michal's eyes began shifting.

'If that's the case, then I should get going and see her.'

But just as Gin prepared to leave the caravan, Michal called out to him. 'Gin,' he said, contemplating whether he should speak his mind.

'Yeah?'

'Syndra's a bit, how should I say it? No-nonsense? Excuses won't work on her.'

'Ah. So, she's *that* type of person. Don't worry, I know how to handle them,' Gin assured with confidence. 'Fight serious with serious, no?'

'Alright. Good luck. She's a bit scary, not gonna lie.'

'Heh. It's my fault that most have gone. I should at least make sure those who remained are on the same wavelength as the rest.'

Scanning the surroundings, Gin found the mages hard at work. Some prepared for departure, a few entered the forest to search the area, while others did their usual chores of harvesting, shifting of resources, and getting rid of waste. It was as if the last few days never happened but, deep down, he could tell everyone kept their nerves hidden, using duties as a mask for their anxiety. No one could hide the doom and gloom that overshadowed the squadron. No one except for Syndra that is. She stood at the end of the clearing, hands locked behind her back, watching the clearer skies with a steely determination. Though that didn't faze him as he walked towards her.

'What's our status at the moment?' Gin began, putting on a serious expression and joined her in staring ahead of them.

Syndra neither answered straight away nor turned her head to talk to him. Instead, she rolled her eyes in his general direction, assessing him somewhat, before speaking.

'I have sent Nasir, my tinoo, further ahead along with others. They're still scouting ahead for any of the deserters,' she reported.

'I see. And what of those that entered the forest? Have they found anything?' Gin asked another question, making sure to not break from his stoicism.

'We interrogated Jake beforehand who said he saw the deceased members in a set location. Some have gone to search the area but it seems that they're gone already.'

'Do we have a lead where the bodies might be?'

Syndra didn't reply. Instead, she pouted, leaving a small gap in between her lips. No sound came out but the way her chest deflated indicated that she was blowing through the hole. Her face then crumpled enough for Gin to notice it from the corner of his eyes but not enough to decipher the meaning of such a demeanour, especially coupled with the strange actions prior.

'There's a mage-eater nest nearby,' she announced, nonchalant as ever. 'They probably disposed of them there.'

Mage-eater? Gin questioned the unfamiliar terminology. But he kept that to himself out of his desire to not ruin the impression Syndra might be forming about him.

'We've also found the odd hair that belonged to no one in our squadron. I believe it's safe to say that they are the enemy in question.'

'Any details on the hair?' Gin noticed Syndra's pursed, frowning lips loosening a little. Whether that meant something, he couldn't be quite sure. Still, he decided to press further. 'Colour? Shape? Size?'

'The suspicious strands were all long and straight. A few brown, some black and a couple white. However, it is also possible that animals have left those unknowingly as well, so we need more time to separate what's what. Does that mean anything to you?'

'Other than the long brown ones that could possibly belong to Rob, no. It might be as you said and the others are red herrings. The assailants sure thought this attack through. I'll keep it in the back of my mind though. Anything else to report?'

'No. That is all. If my suspicions are correct, we will leave by nightfall and travel faster than normal to catch up for the time we lost here,' Syndra finished, her head unmoved throughout the whole conversation.

'Understood. Keep up the good work,' Gin gave a professional reply.

He glanced at the unmoving leader, gauging her emotions in that brief moment. Though on the outside she seemed the stern and scary type, as Michal put it in his own, blunt way, Gin could tell she hid another side to her. A side that someone wanted to show while still keep it hidden for the sake of others. A feeling he knew all too well.

'If there's nothing else to report, I'll make my way back to my battalion,' Gin said in an attempt to break the barrier.

'I believe you should wait for a moment,' Syndra interrupted before he could even turn around.

Heh, Gin scoffed to himself, while saying a composed, 'If I've been given all the information, I don't see the point in staying. If you wish to have idle chatter, then I'll have to decline as I don't see how productive that will prove.'

'I am of the same mindset,' she acknowledged the reasoning, turning her head to face Gin eye to eye for the first time. 'However, with Nasir and other scouts arriving at any moment, it will be counterproductive to fetch you so soon after you leave.'

'You make a fair point.'

'Yes. As opposed to the alternative of dealing with the joker that is Brim or the naïve optimism of Michal, you seem competent enough. At least you understand the gravity of the situation.'

'That I do. In fact, I wanted to tell the situation to you in person but the others insisted on me resting and, apparently, Michal even went to you in my stead without my asking,' Gin admitted, gesturing his hand to show off his innocence.

'Is that so? Then I may have misjudged you. Yes, Michal did come to me to vouch for you, but I assumed that was you being somewhat cowardly.'

'An understandable misconception. Though keeping such thoughts and feelings to yourself and not speaking with the person in question is unhealthy in the long run.'

'Hmm?' Syndra raised an eyebrow and glared at Gin like a person about to make a final, unchangeable decision.

'If one were to keep our true thoughts hidden, it'll only lead to situations like now with Jake where we suspect each other without proper basis and overlook the true threats. Miscommunication and misinformation, including the hiding of feelings, can lead to death.'

Syndra's right eye twitched at the last sentence as if it hit her hard at heart. Or at least that's how Gin saw the reaction. He also theorised the possibility of there being no hidden meaning by the spasm, but his gut told him to trust in the former conclusion.

'I see,' Syndra said after taking a minute or so to think things over. 'We've seen first-hand the issues with unwarranted doubt amongst others, so I'll take your advice into account.'

'Indeed.'

'Oh, Nasir is here!' Syndra changed the topic, staring at the distance once more. She had an expression that didn't seem like much to the unknowing but, compared to the solemn, moody and impassive look beforehand, it radiated some form of positivity.

It's as if she's...happy? Glad? Relieved? Gin couldn't quite put his finger on the emotion.

So, in order to understand why she felt the way she did, he watched her while keeping an eye at the distance. At first, he didn't notice anything, but soon a flock of birds came into vision, later becoming distinguishable as tinoos. *Heh. I see how it is*, Gin chuckled to himself, stopping the next moment to avoid ruining the impression of him he built in an instant. *That's some pretty good eyesight too.*

The tinoo landed in front of its master who pouted her lips and began blowing like before. The bird responded, spinning round and moving its wings like a ceremonial dance. Though silent, the pair understood one another somehow.

Gin heard a weird sound all of a sudden, like a high-pitched screech that disappeared as quickly as it appeared. Yet, the noise aligned with the breathing of Syndra along with the fact the tinoo responded as soon as the sound ended. *Wait. Is she whistling?!* Gin realised, taken aback once again by how amazing the mages were.

'It's just as I suspected,' Syndra said, her tone less dry than before. 'Nasir has found a group further ahead.'

'Group?' Gin questioned. 'Does that mean not everyone's together?'

'He didn't take note of individuals but it's definitely not the full amount. The others are still MIA. At least we won't be a gaping hole any more if we get them back. Let's get ready to depart and retrieve them.'

'What if it's a trap?'

'We can't afford to be as cautious,' Syndra assessed, biting her lower lip at her own judgement. 'We've wasted enough time already and need to prepare for the battle.'

'I agree. Our reinforcements will be sitting ducks if we're not there on time either.'

'We'll scout the area around them as we travel just to make sure there are no surprises. Would that suffice or shall we take a different approach?'

Gin thought for a moment before responding, 'Let's go with the former plan. We need all the help we can get.'

'I concur.'

Syndra whistled her silent whistle, telling a hidden message to her tinoo. The animal understood, grabbing a piece of paper it hid in its feathers, punching holes with its beak before flying off, relaying the message around the campsite.

'I'll admit that I get the feeling I'm not given the full plan of our battle strategy,' Syndra brought up, facing Gin with the no-nonsense look he grew accustomed to. 'I assume Maria has told you though. Is that correct?'

Gin analysed the woman, wondering why she asked, or whether he should tell her the truth.

'I understand why you don't want to say anything, Gin. There's an air of distrust no matter how hard we try to hide it. I'll leave it up to you if you want to discuss the matter with me or not.'

'No, it's alright,' Gin made a decision. 'If anything were to happen to me then we'll be clueless. I believe it's best if I were to tell someone else. Shall we head to the caravans? I'll talk there.'

'Sure,' Syndra agreed, the pair of them turning around. 'I'll go gather the other leaders too.'

'Sounds like a plan,' Gin gave a soft sigh as she walked away. His work was done for now.

28

The Deserters

Feeling ominous glares surrounding him, Gin opened a single eye. It took a few seconds to gain his vision but, when he saw the curious faces of Brim and Michal, he wanted to go back to his slumber. However, the gazes prevented him from doing so, provoking him to keep awake instead.

'Can you stop?' Gin requested.

'But this regeneration is amazing,' Brim replied, with Michal nodding in agreement.

'Is that what's so interesting?' Gin lied down flat, using the vacant space the demoted Jake left behind to his full advantage.

'Mhm,' Michal added, again getting too close to the gauntlets for Gin's liking. 'Even most A ranks don't regenerate this quickly.'

'Is that so?' Gin gave a thoughtless reply, yawning straight afterwards. 'Thank my father for that.'

'Huh?' Michal responded in surprise.

'Father? What's that?' Brim reiterated the confusion.

Gin sparked back up, giving the others a puzzled look who returned the favour as if he said something alien to them. *Are fathers not a thing for them? Are mothers a thing? Did mages even have parents?* He knew the basics of breeding within the MPB and yet, the lack of parents was such a strange notion that Gin formulated more questions than answers. *How do you even explain what they are?*

'Just someone I looked up to,' he came to the best explanation he could think of at that moment.

'Oh, I understand!' Michal concluded.

'You do?' Gin doubted.

'Yes! That means you're my father!' the excitement and sheer confidence radiated from Michal's voice.

'Oh, I look up to Gin too. He's my father as well, no?' Brim caught onto the drift of the conversation.

'Gin must be half the battalion's father then.'

'I think you're onto something, Michal.'

'No!' Gin interrupted the strange turn of events. He placed his hand over his face, filled with regret for bringing up the topic. 'Ugh. None of you get it! Like at all. Look, what I meant by father is that –'

A sudden gust of wind, followed by the caravan rocking from side to side, almost ready to collapse under its weight. The pressured didn't stop either as more blasts of air hit the wagon in bursts, forcing the leaders to hold onto the railings to keep stable.

'Don't tell me,' Brim muttered before yelling, 'Driver, stop this Instant!'

'What is going on?' Gin asked when the shaking stopped.

'Follow me.'

Brim jumped out of the caravan with Michal next. With Gin coming out last, he noticed the mages all looked up to the sky, and another gust of wind made him do the same. Up above were low-flying birds. They had long necks, fangs that protruded out of their beaks and sleek, black feathers all over their body. They were massive; twice the size of Gin, or four times if you measured from wing tip to wing tip. However, only one thing entered Gin's mind as they flew: *That chick grows into that?* he shuddered at the thought of an adult version wanting his blood.

'Guess the reports are true,' Michal said out loud.

'What's wrong?' Gin asked.

'The mage-eaters are heading in the same direction as us,' Brim analysed.

'Mage-eaters?' Gin queried, alarmed by the name given to them and remembering the nest Syndra talked about. 'Don't tell me they're going to attack us.'

'No,' Brim reassured. 'They're scavengers that prey on dead corpses. They have no interest in the living.'

'Oh, that's goo- Wait. Then that means-'

'A large number of people probably have died ahead, yeah.'

'Should we really be saying that out loud?' Michal whispered.

'Doesn't matter,' Syndra interrupted, arriving with her tinoo. 'Everyone knows what's happened the moment they saw the mage-eaters.'

'Hang on,' Gin said, realising something. 'What about the mages ahead? Are they safe?'

'They should come into sight at any moment,' Syndra explained. 'The mage-eaters aren't stopping there, so I believe they're fine. We've checked the surrounding area too and found no ambush-in-waiting.'

'Then the AAA have probably made contact with Rob's battalion,' Brim concluded.

'It would seem so. We can't find their bodies at the designated spot we planned on defending.'

'Either the mage-eaters already had their fill or the battalion were taken further than expected,' Brim analysed, stopping to think everything over a bit more before continuing. 'I'd say the latter because we would have found the African army along the way, even if by some miracle they got whittled down somewhat by the deserters. Isn't that right, Syndra?'

'Yes. The enemy is still too far away for them to arrive at the entrance to The Path.'

'Um,' Michal spoke up after listening to everyone. 'What if Rob killed his battalion and met up with the AAA afterwards?'

A solemn silence fell upon the leaders as they mulled over the possibility. The more they thought, the more the idea became realistic and aligned with the mysteries surrounding the missing members. However, they still couldn't be quite sure and it wasn't until another mage-eater flew overhead did Brim break the silence.

'Speculating will get us nowhere. We shouldn't waste time questioning the missing, so let's focus on those we know are retrievable. Michal, get your battalion to prepare some food. The group up ahead are probably resourceless and likely to be hungry. Syndra, get the scouts to push further ahead. See *where* the enemy's position is on The Path.'

'Will do!'

'Understood.'

'As for you Gin,' Brim said, watching Michal and Syndra head off to their battalions.

'Yes?'

'You go rest. I'll handle everything else.'

'Really?' Gin questioned, grabbing Brim's shoulder just as he was about to leave.

'You're still injured.'

'You complimented my regeneration earlier on and now you're telling me to sit back and do nothing? Like, come on. Need me to beat you again in a spar?'

'Gin,' Brim addressed in an assertive manner. 'Are you ok? You seem awfully angsty, considering your "naps" when you're actually wide awake and your sudden eagerness now that there's work to be done. You haven't even done your signature "heh" these past few days. Don't think I haven't noticed.'

Gin let go, taking a step back right after. He stretched his entire body, letting out an exasperated groan, culminating in a sigh that proved Brim was right.

'I guess I'm just being a bit self-conscious. The deserters left because of me-'

'Because of Rob's manipulation,' Brim corrected.

'-They still used my secret as a tool for said manipulation,' Gin continued, looking away into the distance, sorting out his thoughts. 'Maybe if I'm actively helping out then that might lower their doubts.'

Brim snorted, trying to contain his laughter, catching Gin by surprise. He then punched Gin on the shoulder and said with a smile, 'If that's the cause of your worries, then how about you draw up some plans for our formation?'

'Huh?'

'We all know those we get back won't nearly be enough to fill the original plan. We need to improvise a little. While the other leaders and I do the menial activities, you think of a way to arrange the offence group and we can get back to you. If anything, that'd give you time to sit down and relax while giving you an equally important job as the others.'

'Heh. You're right. I'll do that then.'

'There we go! Even managed to sneak in your "heh" there. Keep that attitude up. Sulking is the last thing you want to do.'

With that, Brim left to join his battalion, leaving Gin to head back to the caravan. He didn't hesitate to whip out paper and a quill pen. A flick of the wrist later, a drawing of the current numbers and potential formation laid in front of him. The artillery and utility remained intact but the way the offence group stayed barren, even with the potential returnees, proved a troublesome problem to solve. That didn't stop Gin though as he made more diagrams, using all the formation training he oversaw while Alder side-lined him as a reference.

'God dammit. Why did he have to be so right,' he joked at his own expense, realising how impatient he acted back then.

Then he realised an option he didn't think of before. The pen began flowing on the paper in the burst of inspiration, like waves crashing against a coast. By the end, the formation looked less lop-sided than before. However, the more Gin stared at his plan, the higher his unease piled on as if he was missing something. His gut told him that the AAA was up to something and he should take that into account. Yet, he couldn't quite pinpoint the issue.

'Ah!' a voice startled Gin. He looked up to see the eyehole-armoured Sam peeking in from outside. 'You're alive!'

But before a word could be said, he ran off. *Isn't it a bit early to meet them?* Gin thought, wondering if he got a little too carried away with the drawings and lost track of time. To make sure, he stepped out, checking the location of every one.

The majority stood much further ahead of the slow-moving caravans. The group was larger than before too, with the recognisable faces of the deserters adding to the squadron's numbers. At the forefront of the confrontation stood Brim and Syndra, talking with the others and explaining the situation to them, while Michal scurried around with food attached to his stone tablets, busy helping distribute them.

'Now where did Sam get off to?' Gin mumbled to himself, rummaging through the crowd. *Now that I think about it, Sam joined the deserters, right?* He could hear the chatters of those shocked by his presence and those still doubtful of his ability to lead. However, he didn't pay any heed to them, concentrating on his thoughts and beliefs. He couldn't doubt himself anymore. He couldn't afford to.

Somebody tugged on his shirt, pulling him back. Gin looked down to see the short-as-ever Sam holding a burnt piece of paper in his hand. He picked it up and recognised the outlines of the map he drew, the burn marks encroaching over The Path. His heart sank at the sight of his work in ruins.

'What's this?' Gin asked anyway.

'Rob wanted to burn,' Sam responded in his shortened sentences like usual. 'He told us to strip.'

'Eh?'

'Look,' Sam pointed ahead of them.

Lying in front was a field of chest plates and other pieces of stone armoury, all of which developed and crafted by Michal's battalion. They laid there like used scrap, ready to be demolished and recycled. The sight angered Gin along with the sheer disgust at how the mages must have been tormented and manipulated. But he didn't show it. He couldn't afford to in the battalion's moment of transition.

'He said it's your idea,' Sam continued. 'That it's bad. So, he told us to strip.'

'I see.'

'I told them stop. But some not listen. They went with Rob. Don't know what happened after.'

'The scouts say they're already gone,' Gin spoke with a heavy heart.

'Oh,' Sam said, realising what he meant by that.

'Ahem. Sorry for disturbing the mood, but are you done with your work already?' Brim interrupted the conversation, grabbing hold and giving a forced grin that told him "why are you out? Go back and rest."

'I did and actually wanted to discuss some things,' Gin replied, nodding to Sam to say that he was dismissed who obeyed the order.

'Is that so? Well, ok then,' Brim raised an eyebrow. 'Let's go somewhere quieter then.'

Brim turned back to a few people he talked to a few moments ago, telling them he needed to go. The mages nodded in agreement, allowing the leaders to leave for open space within the desert, away from the prying ears of the others.

'So, what have you come up with?' Brim asked.

'You're not going to fill me in first?'

'Aha. You're right.'

'Brim?' Gin took his turn to raise an eyebrow.

'Sorry. It's nothing. Anyway, you've heard that Rob took a quarter of the offence group, right?'

'Yes, Sam told me.'

'Good. Even though the numbers are much better than we first anticipated, we're still a bit thin, aren't we? Not to mention all the armour left lying around is buying them some time while we clear it all.'

'Can't we leave them and come back later?'

'And if we lose and get wiped out? The armour will only damage the environment if not dealt with. That'll affect not just us but all of Eurasia in the long run. I don't see the AAA cleaning up after us. Do you?'

Gin didn't say anything at first. He wasn't sure if he should be worried at the fragile, ludicrous nature or amazed by the intricate co-dependency of the mages' lifestyle. Not only did they care for the environment but they also took into consideration the worst-case scenarios.

Maybe this is why my ancestors became near extinct while they thrived, Gin theorised before saying, 'You're right. We can't risk that. If it's unavoidable then we'll have to give up on the other deserters for the time being.'

'Seems so. You're going to have to use that for the formation plans.'

'I think I already did.'

'Oh?'

Gin unfurled the piece of paper with his annotations that he brought along with him by mistake. He showed the plans to Brim who took a moment to assess it, nodding throughout the analysis. Then he looked up, handing back Gin's work.

'I kind of understand your drawings, but I can't understand the writing,' Brim admitted.

'I suppose I do have bad handwriting,' Gin took a moment to look things over. 'Basically, I wondered if it's possible if I could borrow mages from both the artillery and utility group to bolster the frontline.'

'Eh? Utility group? You know they can't fight. They don't have any training let alone ability. This isn't even me being prejudice like I used to be,' Brim said, his expression and voice full of scepticism.

'I know. But, especially with all the spare armour lying around, we could use them not for attacking purposes but as a distraction instead.'

'Oh!'

'Yes.'

Gin grew the Xernim out, creating a thin, long branch. He snapped the twig off and used it to draw dots into the sand to represent the mages. He took a few minutes to make sure he got the idea down as best as possible, using arrows to represent the change in personnel and where they would go to.

'If we have a bulkier frontline, the enemy might attack them,' Gin explained. 'Since they're armoured, the utility types will still be pretty tanky, not to mention fireproof even if they can't contribute offensively.'

'It'll mean those that can fight will have one less enemy hounding them,' Brim understood.

'Exactly.'

'I don't see much issue with that plan then. I'll send off my troops too. Like me, they can be used for both melee and ranged attacks so the transition isn't as extreme for them.'

'Perfect. How about the lupims? Or the other animals for that matter. Surely, they can be used for warfare too, no?'

Brim stopped himself for a second but couldn't contain his laughter that turned into a sigh that indicated regret.

'What's so funny?' Gin asked, worried by the reaction.

'There's a reason these are low-ranked familiars. They're too docile. If anything, they would befriend the enemy instead of attacking them. The moles let us throw them around for fun for crying out loud!' Brim responded, covering his face with his hand in both amusement and pity.

'I see. What a shame,' Gin sighed. 'Everything else ok though?'

'Yeah, I'll make sure to send some people your way as well as get Michal to make some arrangements on his side too. Let's head back to the others and tell them the plan, ok? We only got a few days to prepare when we get there, so everyone needs to be briefed.'

'Sure. We're really close to this battle, huh?' Gin realised, his tone getting quieter.

'Mhm,' Brim agreed, his voice also softening.

As the pair walked back to their battalions, Gin couldn't relieve himself of a sinking feeling in his chest. *My first battle... Wonder if we're ready.*

29

Calm Before the Storm

Jake's senses heightened. His heart wouldn't calm down. He looked in front of him where the sand sloped upwards. He then heard the sound of water crashing against the hundred–metre–tall walls surrounding the edges of the path either side of him. Above him flew the tinoos, flying in a figure eight that indicated that they could relax for the time being. And yet, Jake's body showed anything but relaxation. The Path, squadron W's appointed battlefield, laid in front of him after all.

'Are you sure he called for me?' he asked the messenger that stood beside him.

'Yes. Mr Stones asked for you specifically,' the messenger confirmed. 'He's with Ms Syndra.'

'Ah,' Jake said, his dread growing further. 'Ok. I'll be right there.'

Checking if he could do anything productive before meeting Brim (and failing to do so), Jake dragged himself across the appointed battlefield, towards the utility group. He used the other mages as cover, making his way from person to person, until he saw the man that called for him, talking with Gin.

Peering over someone's shoulder while pretending to be occupied, he interpreted the state of Brim. Was he happy? Was he angry? The warm smiles he gave indicated the gentle side that Jake admired remained. However, in all the years he knew his idol, that warmth and compassion could change in an instant. He experienced it first hand in the forest. So, in order to read the mood better, he searched for a way to get closer without looking either lazy or needy.

His dilemma drew him to Michal who carried a chest plate half his height. The way the low-ranged mage walked meant the armour weighed less than it looked. *Perfect timing*, Jake thought, revelling at the opportunity that laid in front of him.

'Michal!' he called out.

Michal peeped from underneath the chest plate. 'Yes?'

'That must be heavy,' Jake gestured, giving Michal a pat on the back and extending a hand. 'Let me help you with that.'

'Oh, I can handle this. I should be done carrying this one to the caravans quickly anyway. It really isn't that heavy.'

'All the more reason for me to help out. I'm sure that there's still a lot to be done, so I thought I'd make things easier. After all, the faster we're done, the faster we can prepare.'

Michal stopped walking, considering the offer before saying, 'Yeah, you're right. Thanks. Here you go.'

Jake held out his arms as he glanced back at Brim, not concentrating on the oncoming task at hand. He lurched forwards, buoyed by the sudden weight put on him. *Not heavy?!* Jake screeched on the inside but kept his composure on the outside to avoid drawing attention. *How is this not heavy?!*

'Are you ok?' Michal asked, realising his mistake.

'You just placed it in the wrong spot,' Jake directed the blame.

'Didn't realise positioning had an effect. Reckoned you'd be able to handle the weight regardless.'

'Are you mocking me?'

'Ah, no, not at all,' Michal bowed his head in apology.

'Then I can carry this just fine,' Jake hoisted the armour into a comfortable position but still shocked at how much it weighed him down. *How did someone so low ranked manage to do it so easily?*

'Ok, I'll leave you to it,' Michal doubted but didn't bother arguing.

With the minor hindrance out of the way, Jake made his way past Brim. Each step took several seconds as he carried the hefty stone. On the flip side, it gave an excuse to walk past the conversation without raising suspicion as well as providing cover to hide his face, so he didn't complain.

'Is that so?' Jake caught the first recognisable words of the conversation.

'Yes, Gin. They say the walls were envisioned by a man called DJT,' Brim answered back.

'DJT? What does that stand for? Was he a mage?'

'I don't know. It's just some rumour I heard from my travels.'

'I see. Well, the past still eludes us. Imagine meeting such innovative minds!'

'I know, right?'

He seems like he's in a good mood, Jake thought, unaware of his surroundings. He crashed into a passing lupim, almost dropping the armour save for the bulky body of the dog holding it up. That still didn't prevent the animal from yelping in pain, putting Jake under the scrutiny of the other mages.

'Oh, there he is!' Gin noticed.

'Jake!' Brim called out.

Jake twisted his neck to face him, his heart pounding in a mixture of fear and anticipation. 'Yes?'

'Come here,' Brim ordered.

Following the commands, Jake heaved the chest plate and placed it right beside the leaders. He calmed his nerves somewhat, waiting for the conversation to resume.

'Perfect timing,' Brim announced, the lack of harsh words calmed Jake down further.

'I'll head off to my battalion there. Meet me there,' Gin ran off, waving to the both of them.

'So, a rundown of what we planned,' Brim continued. 'We've started moving some of the other group members into the offence group, understood?'

'Yes,' Jake responded, adding a muted 'sir' at the end for good measure.

'Good. As you know, we lack personnel who can be of use in both long range and melee combat.'

'You're absolutely right.'

'And with the offence group lacking a leader ever since Rob went MIA, while still keeping its original size. Gin won't be enough. On the other hand, the artillery group is reducing in numbers and so doesn't really need a second leader.'

'Mhm.'

Brim stared at Jake for a moment, analysing the man's expressions. 'You get what I'm hinting at, right?'

'Eh?' Jake gave an instant, honest response.

'Look,' Brim sighed as he wiped his entire face. 'I'm asking you to be a Pseudo-commander to Gin; his second-in-command in Rob's stead. Despite your complete idiotic actions, you're still one of the most experienced in squadron W, and I can't take that away. Plus, if anything were to happen to Gin, I'd need someone to step in and I don't really have any other option. Now, do you understand?'

So, it's about Gin, Jake concluded, disappointed by the notion. He still didn't like the manush, but he knew he couldn't protest. He didn't have the proverbial high ground to do so. Not towards Brim at least.

'Jake?'

'I understand,' Jake replied, his voice deflated by his thoughts.

'The enemy will be here within the next twenty-four hours. We're getting into formation soon. There's a few thousand over the horizon, making their way towards us, with some reinforcements joining them a bit afterwards. We suspect fire elementals and juggernauts respectively. That's all we've scouted of the enemy.'

'Yessir. Understood sir,' Jake gave a flat acknowledgement.

'Then I wish you good luck.'

Grabbing the armour, which he still found way too heavy, Jake carried it over to the caravans. He pondered on his mixed emotions, the upcoming battle, the series of events that led up to rise to leadership, suspicions and eventual downfall. Even when placing the chest plate in the caravan, he didn't feel like any burden had been lifted.

He walked passed the makeshift formation, passed his (now former) battalion members, and towards the offence group that started to form into the blocks they drilled into their conscious; A stupid exercise squadron W did, considering the MBP should have provided all the training they needed. *That's the low-ranked for you*, he cursed. And yet, someone even worse than the lot, with no training from the MBP whatsoever, led them to what could be the beginning of their end.

Jake wanted to protest. He wanted to rebel. However, he couldn't. Not when everyone else put their faith in such a person like Gin. So, he gritted his teeth and locked away his pride. Brim gave him a task and he made sure he was going to fulfil it.

'Gin,' he addressed.

'Oh. You finally arrived. Beautiful day, isn't it?' Gin replied with a giant grin on his face.

'Yes, it is,' Jake went with the flow of the conversation.

'I love the way the tinoos fly in a set way too. You can easily distinguish our ones from the chaotic free-flying wild variants.'

'Uhuh.'

'And the shade the walls hit you just right. Heh. Earth really is a mesmerising place!'

What's wrong with this guy? No class. No urgency. No nothing. He hasn't changed one bit! Jake thought while saying, 'Yeah...I'm going to check on the others if that's alright with you?'

'Sure thing. Brim did say you'd be my temporary right-hand man, so I guess that's normal.'

Jake didn't waste a second further, taking his leave to inspect the others. At least their nerves showed as they should. *In a matter of hours, the land will become a bloodbath for crying out loud!* Jake screamed internally, still peeved by the brief conversation with Gin. How in Eurasia could anyone like someone as immature, aimless, and bland as him? The answer was beyond Jake.

To take his mind off the matter, Jake carried out his excuse. He looked at all the formations, making sure they aligned while scolding those out of place though, to his surprise, the original battalion didn't need the telling off. *Maybe the training did do some good after all,* he considered the possibility of him being wrong before denying the notion in an instant.

Without warning, the atmosphere got tenser. All eyes locked on a single tinoo that flew towards the offence group. It gave a piercing screech before flying back to the other tinoos, changing the formation to that of an ellipse. That meant only one thing.

'Enemies approaching!'

Michal tensed up. He rushed the final checks before running towards his own position in a block of mages next to Gin's. Nervousness welled inside him but he didn't show it. His experience told him to do so. However, he still could never get used to the feeling. Concentrating on the sandy slope in front provided the only distraction. He made out figures, spanning a couple thousand, the gentle slope of the land preventing him from seeing them earlier. He couldn't make out any distinguishing feature but, from the way they stopped several hundred metres away, he could guess they were the AAA's artillery group, while the glistening limbs under the setting sun confirmed their fire elemental typing.

'Concentrate!' Jake heard Gin's command. The silence of one caused his neighbour to fall quiet, eventually silencing everyone in a ripple-like effect.

Eh?

The sky became filled with an orangey-yellow colour. Thousands of fireballs arced across it, heading towards squadron W.

Squadron W's artillery group sent fireballs of their own, along with waterballs to counter the enemy's attack. However, for everyone they sent, the enemy returned fire tenfold.

Jake covered his face, protecting his vulnerable eyes from the fire as they crashed against his body. He could feel the heat on his limbs but the armour and skin combined protected him from any meaningful harm. The groans of his allies meant that they too felt the full barrage of the enemy's attack. However, all Jake could do was hold on for his own life, unable to protect his comrades.

But then the attacks let up. The fireballs had stopped for a brief moment, allowing Jake to survey the situation. The battlefield was now covered in blobs of flaming oil that died out within seconds, leaving thick smoke in their remains. The offence group, though battered, looked unharmed for the most part.

The enemy's limbs stopped glistening; stopped being alight. Squadron W's artillery group also stopped attacking, putting everyone in a stalemate. The pause felt out of place. Jake knew the squadron couldn't waste resources, but why did the AAA stop?

The pause turned into a minute. Then ten. Then twenty. Before long, the pause passed the half-hour mark, allowing the cloud-and-smoke-filled night sky to come into full view. The unease amongst the offence group reached an all-time high. Yet, the tinoos didn't give orders to take the initiative. Gin didn't give orders to take the initiative. What was everyone waiting for? Jake had enough, leaving his position to confront the man in charge.

'Gin!' he called out.

'Yes?' Gin answered, eyes on the land in front of him.

'Their reinforcements will be here any moment and the enemy must have run out of oil. Why aren't we attacking?'

Gin didn't answer straight away. He stared some more, watching the empty gap between the two armies.

'Gin! What is going on?' Jake demanded.

'Sure is dark, isn't it?' Gin gave a reply that didn't answer the question.

'Is that you're worried about?! Not that we could die at any moment but your fear of the night!'

'Their numbers are smaller than I expected. The fire's all gone out too, huh.'

'What is wrong with you?!'

The final words brought doubt amongst those around them. They didn't know what to do. On the one hand, Jake felt guilty for making their morale go down like this. On the other, at least they started to realise how much of a fake their so-called leader was.

'Hey, Jake?' Gin answered, his voice neither raised nor agitated.

'What?!' Jake bellowed back.

'Is it possible for mages to go invisible?'

'Huh? Are you really that stupid? We're in the middle of a war and you ask these sorts of things?'

'Is there or isn't there?'

'Really? You didn't know about stealth bestials but still–'

Gin didn't wait for Jake to finish the sentence. He stepped out of his position and walked forwards.

'Oi! Where are you going?' Jake called back to no avail.

Gin's activated blades began to glisten as if drenched in the same oil Brim used. Then the Xernim grew, arching around the third hole in his metal rectangle. The next moment the weapon got set on fire, lighting up the gloomy night. That's when Jake noticed the shadows produced.

Gin sent a hurtling jab into the nothingness. But it connected. What he pierced was still in doubt, but it definitely connected.

It was as if time had stopped.

Blood gushed onto his blades, like a river over a waterfall. It painted Gin's Xernims and armour red, causing Gin to give a smile directed above him as he drove the blade further into the wound he created. A body began to materialise around it, starting with the torso which soon formed into a fully visible human being.

'Oh, I'm sorry. Were you meant to be hidden?' Gin taunted, loud enough for everyone in the vicinity to hear.

The enemy didn't respond, already dead, either from the shock of being attacked or from the wound itself.

'No way,' Jake muttered, shocked by the course of events

Gin kicked his victim off the blade. The body collapsed to the ground, like a ragdoll. Then, without looking back, within sight of both ally and enemy, Gin bellowed a single command.

'They have stealth bestials! Look for the shadows and attack accordingly!'

A sense of vigour emanated from the squadron. It wasn't enough to dispel the nerves of the mages, but it was enough to give everyone a sense of belief.

Jake stood there, gobsmacked by how the leader they put faith in managed to do it. He didn't know how else to react. However, he did know that squadron W's maiden battle had well and truly begun.

30

Maiden Battle Part 1

What was that feeling? It wasn't quite excitement. It wasn't quite fear. No, that feeling of allies rushing past you, fireballs flying through the air, illuminating the battlefield; the feeling of catching the enemy off-guard and piercing their heart with blades. A feeling that had no description. Either way, Gin relished every moment of it.

Focus.

Each second slowed down. Shouting filled the battlefield. Orders flew across the air, telling everyone to attack in a certain pattern. Another stealth bestial found, another one dead. Even the armoured utility types played their part, wasting the enemy's element of surprise when they hit the hard stone. Gin would have found the scene wonderful if he could step back from the chaos.

Lead by example.

For every mage Gin killed, his confidence grew. His attacks became more fluid. His body danced on the desert stage. The yellow sand reddened in the onslaught. The crimson of blood splattered around him. He became a spectacle to his allies; a bladed demon to the enemy. But beyond the instructions be tinoos, Gin only fought his own battle, unwilling to get distracted by the happenings of his teammates.

His eyes darted every five seconds to look above, waiting for the –

Horizontal.

'Formation twenty-one. Spread out and conquer!' he bellowed out a command, followed by the echoes of his subordinates.

Faster next time.

Gin stabbed. One fell down.

Their bodies are frail.

He sliced. A head fell off.

Barely any muscle.

He jabbed multiple times. Shock sent the next one to the floor.

They lack armour.

With each passing fireball, more hidden mages were revealed. The enemy's only strength of stealth gone in an instant. But that didn't stop them attacking in their desperation.

With each passing fireball, more hidden mages were revealed. The enemy's only strength of stealth gone in an instant. But that didn't stop them attacking in their desperation.

Gin felt the scraping of nails on his chest but his chest plate protected him. It was as if the only place the enemy could aim for was his heart. A futile attempt that did nothing but reveal the mage's location. Another foe dispatched.

Not a moment's rest as another stealth bestial pierced Gin's shoulders. However, the Xernim prevented any damage this time. Now stuck, he used the opportunity, spinning around, dragging the invisible foe off its feet. His next strike materialised a man before an ally finished him off.

'Thanks. There's another one five metres ahead of you,' Gin ordered.

'Yes sir!' the mage obeyed, running and mowing down the target with her flaming arms.

Gin touched the marks the enemy left on his Xernim. *Was this why the Xernim grew?* he wondered. But that lapse in concentration proved reckless as the sands below him shifted, unbalancing him.

A fireball rushed towards him. He didn't have time to move. He raised his shield in reflex but somebody held down his arm, leaving him open to the projectile.

A hairy bestial stepped in, blocking the fireball, reducing it to mere sparks that still landed onto Gin. His armour stopped most of the damage but some sneaked inside, searing the flesh on the inside.

'Ack!' someone screeched in agony behind him.

Gin forgot his pain and swivelled around, knocking the saboteur off his feet before plunging his blade into the chest, leaving the enemy lifeless.

'Leader! Are you Ok?' the bestial asked, getting in front of him to cover.

'Get two more and cover for me,' Gin replied, grimacing as he did so as the pain returned.

He deactivated the blade on his right arm and put his arm behind his shoulder. In the heat of the battle, he knew he shouldn't stop for even a millisecond, but the burning oil prevented him from moving let alone fighting properly.

'Enemy three metres at thirty degrees. Two more at two-seven-five,' Gin instructed, making himself useful despite his inactivity.

The mages noticed as they deflected projectiles that came their way while shifting into a defensive formation to protect Gin. 'We see them!'

'Good.'

Gin didn't waste the time they bought, thinking of the Xernim moving around his body. It listened, slender branches wrapping around his torso, stopping at where the oil resided. The Xernim curved, wiping off the hot liquid. A sense of relief filled Gin as the pain stopped, albeit a bit of throbbing from the scorched areas.

'I'm fine now. Back to formation!' he commanded with his allies nodding and returning to their positions.

That brief pause made Gin realise how tired he was. Sweat dripped from his forehead, mixing with the blood. He noticed his panting. Compared to the one v ones he fought with his battalion, this was on a whole different level. This time his opponents didn't stop coming. For every one he slew, another two popped into view.

You idiot! Gin snapped back at himself, remembering and regretting at how his lapse of concentration almost led to his demise. *Concentrate!*

Gin steeled himself, degrading the grown branch and reactivating his blade. He let his subconscious take over, drowning out the fatigue but losing his long-term memory in the process. All he could remember were the constant slicing, dodging and split-second decisions that he needed to make. He harboured no feelings for his victims. He couldn't even remember their faces. They all fit into the same generic mould.

Morality played no role. Hesitation meant death. If he didn't do the killing, they would have killed him instead. The more he killed, the less that could kill his fellow Eurasians. He already lost too much to the AAA. He couldn't afford a repeat of the past where he was never there. Not this time. The enemies' lives paled in comparison to those that meant too much to him.

He killed and killed and killed.

'Leader!'

Gin twisted his body, swinging his blade for the next kill. His attack aimed for the neck.

'Ah,' he heard the same voice whimper.

Gin's arm froze. It stuck to stone armour, cutting a few centimetres deep into it. His eyes widened as he realised who he almost decapitated.

'Sorry, Sam,' Gin apologised, lowering his blade. He then turned to his block and bellowed, 'Formation three!'

An echo of "formation three" made its way around the battlefield as his battalion repeated the order, making sure everyone heard. They moved around Gin, displacing him from the front line and shuffling both him and the messenger towards the middle of the block. Away from the front lines and safe from a sneak attack from the back, they resided in the safest place to be in their situation. Gin looked forwards, turning his back to the messenger and prepared to defend him, just in case a stray fireball flew towards them.

'Did you want to report something?' Gin asked. But Sam didn't respond. He just shivered in his spot.

'Um,' Sam said a sole word.

'Now!' Gin's fury snapped the messenger into place.

'Y-Yes,' he replied, still tense from his near-death experience. 'The utility group spotted the group of juggernauts bestials approaching.'

'How many?'

'Three-hundred mages. All at least B ranked.'

'Still that many?' Gin confirmed, batting a fireball out of the way. 'How much longer till our reinforcements?'

'Um, about an hour,' Sam confirmed, reading a letter he held.

'Tsk.'

'Your orders, leader?'

'They're much stronger than us. We'll get decimated if we continue to be spread out like this. Execute group formation five.'

'Understood.'

Same ran off towards somewhere but a minute later, the tinoo formation turned into that of an inverted pentagon. The shouts of "formation five" soon led to the battalion shifting position once again, tracking back into a more defensive position. The several blocks meshed into a singular compact one, arcing in front of the artillery group. A sea of bodies laid in front of them. Beyond that, the enemy fire elementals looked on in horror as their surprise attack had been so easily dealt with.

But that changed when the enemy's artillery team split down the middle, allowing three-hundred tall, beefy mages to march their way towards the battlefield. This was the AAA's last attack. This was squadron W's last stand.

31

Maiden Battle Part 2

Brim wet the palm of his hands with his flammable sweat. He left his middle finger and thumb dry, rubbing them together in a quick motion. From the roughness, a spark flashed, lighting the oil ablaze. He looked around, checking that everyone else had done the same.

'Enemy juggernauts estimated five-hundred metres ahead of us!' He roared, making sure he was heard in the chaos. 'Ready?! Aim! Fire!'

The artillery group flung a flurry of fireballs over the battlefield. They arced through the air, mixing together to create larger projectiles before crashing into their desired location. Upon impact, Brim turned to his designated messenger.

'Damage report,' he ordered.

The messenger whistled, calling a tinoo to arrive. The animal cooed back. The man nodded in response.

'Eighty percent of the fireballs hit the enemy and,' the messenger said, stopping before he sighed.

'And?'

'Barely any damage to the opposition. The flames hit them, but the smaller fireballs died down too quickly. The larger ones that combined just left a scorch which the enemy juggernauts could shrug off. They seem to have a mild resistance to fire.'

'We're practically useless offensively against these juggernauts then,' Brim complained. 'How have the offence group faired?'

The messenger whistled once more, getting a chirp in reply from his tinoo. 'It seems we've dispatched over a thousand stealth bestials while we've suffered only a one percent casualty rate.'

Eh? They lose a thousand while we lose less than ten? Why is it so easy? Brim's thoughts left a sinking feeling in his gut. Something felt off. He knew squadron W improved in strides over the year, but this... *No. They probably were buying time for the juggernauts. They're the trump card. Focus.*

'How are our water reserves?' He asked instead, shaking his doubts away.

'Fifty percent of it has been used up.'

'Good enough. Tell them to focus fully on defence. Make sure the offence group suffer from as little enemy fire as possible. As for the fire elementals, have them switch to fueling the large artillery of the big-handed mages. If the larger projectiles are dealing minor damage, we need to go larger and be smarter with our resources.'

'Yessir!'

Brim took his leave to inspect his battalion. He watched the tactics change as the fire elementals began to pour oil into the massive, webbed hands of the mages Gin indoctrinated into the artillery group. They did their jobs, hurling S-tier fireballs across the battlefield. And yet, despite the relative success of their deeds, something still didn't sit right with Brim. The more he looked on, the more uneasy he felt. He even double-checked the tinoos above, but their formation remained unchanged.

Maybe I really am overthinking thi-

'Aaaaah!' a bloodcurdling, nearby scream to the side brought the artillery group to a standstill.

'What's happening?! Status! Now!' Brim demanded.

'We're being flanked!' a distant shout came not directed towards him.

Brim ran back to get a full view of his battalion. He created a ball of fire, throwing it upwards to get vision of the edges. His eyes widened at what he saw as bodies fell at random intervals, either ripped apart, torn, cut, or stabbed by the invisible shadows beside them. How could this have happened?

'Leader? Your orders,' a confused messenger asked, snapping Brim back into action.

'Stealth bestials have gone around the offence group. Stop fire and focus on defending the artillery group; formation eighteen. Watch out from all angles and light the area up,' Brim ordered but, when the scared man stood hesitant, he added, 'We can't have more casualties. Go! Now!'

'Yessir!'

The artillery group formed groups of twenty, defending the central fire elementals that poured oil onto the ground in an oval.

Brim played a freelance role, darting in between the different groups, taking down the stealth bestials. But no matter how much he overpowered the enemy individually, his strength wasn't enough. As he saved a teammate from an oncoming attack, he saw another slashed down without remorse in front of him.

His battalion couldn't deal with the enemy. Half the potential melee combatants went to the Offence group, those that remained relied on their ranged advantage, and all Brim could do was grit his teeth and save as many as possible.

'Leader, formation eighteen is ready,' the messenger called out.

'Light it up!' Brim snapped back, burning another stealth bestial into ash.

The area around the artillery group erupted into a wall of flames. The stealth bestials outside couldn't enter the new domain lest they get burnt while those inside became trapped.

Brim didn't hesitate to rally his troops, dispatching the separated foes on the inside before bringing the melee combatants to dispose of the enemies on the outside. One by one they whittled down the sneak attackers until they ceased to remain.

His heart pounding, his arms heavy from combat, and his lungs begging for a breather, Brim ordered his men to go back to their duties assisting the offence group. *No room for rest*, he thought, glad the ordeal had passed. However, the sinking feeling in his gut still didn't go away. He looked up at the tinoo formation once more.

Still no change.

'Hey. Can you call your tinoo for me?' Brim addressed the messenger, the allied corpses a sickening sight to him, causing him to clench a fist in sheer hatred. 'Report to the utility group what happened with us then get a status report back on their situation.'

The man nodded, whistling for his familiar. He told the order before the bird flew off several hundred metres behind them where the utility group resided. Then they waited, watching the others resume service, throwing the fire and waterballs at the enemy. But soon a minute turned into five, then ten. The messenger grew increasingly agitated. Brim did too, though he didn't show it.

'Should it be taking this long?' he asked.

'N–no.'

Dammit. Dammit. Dammit. How could I have been so blind?! Brim realised, jumping into action. 'Get anyone that can fight melee back to the utility group!'

'Sir? My tinoo hasn't come back yet.'

'Forget the bird! Tell everyone by word of mouth. This is urgent!'

'Understood, sir.'

However, before he could hear the "sir", Brim dashed towards the utility group, his eyes darting left to right, his arms aflame, his body working to its utmost maximum.

Please don't be too late.

32

Maiden Battle Part 3

Why was it so difficult all of a sudden?

The words rang in Jake's ears as he ducked under the armour-crushing swing of the enemy juggernaut. He then leapt from his position, attacking the opening left behind with his flaming fists. However, the fire dwindled as soon as it hit the fur until it ceased to exist.

'Pincer formation!' Jake ordered, allowing the two mages behind him to take his place, distracting the unharmed target.

Jake retreated, dodging another blow in the process. He flicked his fingers to light his hands ablaze once more. The more he thought, the fewer options he found. Though squadron W had the numbers advantage for once, they couldn't peg back their latest challenge.

Again, why was it so difficult now?

The juggernaut turned around to face the pincer attack. A water elemental shot a stream of water at the furry chest before another fire elemental flung a small projectile at the eyes, but the beast deflected both attacks. However, his attentions were well and truly focused on the pair.

Jake went in again, using the formation to distract the enemy, aiming his punch at the pressure points by the spleen, then the pelvis, then the groin and then the backside of the knee in swift succession. The juggernaut didn't react to the first three locations but the fourth led to his collapse. The water elemental took the chance, sending a burst of water right through the eye, rendering the foe harmless as blood and broken bone oozed out of the socket.

We killed one of th-

Not a moment later, another juggernaut, taller, bulkier and furless compared to the first, barged into the space in front of Jake, knocking him aside. It grabbed the water elemental and hurled the woman into the dust before stomping on her, creating a heart-lurching crunching sound that merged with the ongoing shouts and screams. The juggernaut then lunged forwards, biting the woman's neck with its tusked teeth, dealing the death blow before turning to the fire elemental.

'Get out of the way!' Jake commanded.

But the man just stood there, unmoving and shivering, as the juggernaut made its way to him. Jake burst from his spot. He shoved the man out of harm's way but a strong right hook collided into the side of his chest plate, shattering the stone in an instant and knocking him into the floor.

Now the enemy's sights were on Jake. Blood dripped from the tusks that protruded out of the, (now that Jake thought about it), woman's mouth. The only damage to the foe were mere scratch marks on the vest she wore and Jake didn't expect to add to that. Not when his winded and wounded body prevented him from moving up on time.

I'm sorry Brim... he regretted. He closed one eye, half-waiting for the final strike on him.

All of a sudden, a gigantic fireball smothered the enemy. Jake shielded his eyes from the splash of the flames. When he found it safe to look up again, he saw the enemy writhing in agony as the fire burnt through every portion of her body until she collapsed into a flaming corpse.

'I'm so sorry,' the fire elemental Jake pushed said. He grabbed hold of him, getting him back to his feet.

He took the opportunity to look around and realised that the only reason he lived was because each and every mage, from both AAA and squadron W, were occupied with each other. Neither side let up. For every Eurasian team the enemy juggernauts crushed, a team of Eurasians felled a juggernaut. However, with the chaos of people killing, dying and being flung across the desert, he found the relative peace— as he was dragged towards safety — relieving.

'I shouldn't have frozen like that,' the fire elemental continued to apologise.

'It's ok,' Jake accepted. He clutched his sides to find blood oozing out of the wounds.

Another body crashed in front of the pair, this time Eurasian. The person's armour already laid in pieces, pale skin exposed. Despite the condition, he got up, charging back into action. But the man carrying Jake froze once more.

Guess war is not for everyone, he thought, recalling his first battle and how just as scared he was until Brim came and told him to shut up and concentrate.

'Snap out of it! We don't have the luxury to gawk! Get me back to the utility group then return to action as soon as possible. I'll ask a messenger to send more reinforcements from the artillery group if possible.'

'Huh? Oh, sir, but that's impossible...'

'What?' Jake asked, but when the man didn't respond, he barked, 'Why is it impossible?'

'The tinoos. They're...' the man froze again.

Jake looked up. His eyes widened. The tinoos changed their formation again. This time to a crescent. The words rang in his mind once more. Why was it so difficult all of a sudden?

He blinked twice, but the shape didn't change. It only meant one thing:

The utility group was under attack.

33

Maiden Battle Part 4

Syndra watched Michal pace up and down the long tent they resided in. He made sure to avoid the injured that lied down on the ground, their groans combining together into a chorus of pain and agony. There was nothing either leader could do except to help the medics with their duties.

'Here's another one. He's heavily injured, but still breathing,' a couple of mages brought in a deformed body which spasmed at irregular intervals.

'Place him by the others. We'll see what we can do,' Syndra instructed while opening a wooden capsule of gel, rubbing it against a cut on a man she tended to.

Michal jumped at the opportunity to help the mages ease the body down. He gave them some instructions before pacing up and down the tent, deep in thought. He remained silent, not helping with anything. His actions annoyed Syndra, but she kept it to herself.

A shriek outside caused everyone to jump. All except Syndra that is. She knew better and continued to do her best treating the patients, unconcerned by the tragedy going on outside.

'Why,' Michal muttered under his breath. 'Why only us?'

Syndra didn't bother with the man's whims. However, when he kicked some dust that almost fell upon the eyes of the others, she had enough.

'You know full well why. So, if you can stop causing a hazard with the sand, that would be appreciated,' she snapped. 'Better yet, how about you help us instead?'

Michal gritted his teeth, stopped walking and turned to Syndra with a serious expression that she didn't know he had. 'We have people guarding us as stealth bestials rampage through the rest of our battalions, killing everyone. Why are we given special protection? Just because we're leaders?'

'It's precisely because we're leaders that we must be as far away from danger as possible. If we die because of brashness, then we'll go into disarray. The offence and artillery group *rely* on us to do our duty. If a hundred die because we played for damage limitation, it's better than all fifteen hundred dying because of our recklessness.'

'She's been sliced and stabbed multiple times,' some mages barged into the tent with a body lined with streaks across.

'Tsk,' Michal retreated to the side of the tent, chewing as if he ate the words on the tip of his tongue.

Syndra looked at him and sighed. The only thing more annoying than his cheerful optimism was the brooding expression he exhibited. He didn't even lower the near-dead mage to the ground this time. What little help he offered no longer existed.

'Look,' Syndra addressed, finishing applying some ointment on a patient before getting up from her position to face Michal head on. '*We* cannot do anything. I am a familiar type. Nasir is the only one that can fight. I'd just be a sitting tinoo if I went out there. But *you. You* are an *F ranked stone elemental* with *no combat experience.* If anything, you'd do worse than me. You can't think for yourself properly. You let Gin do all of that for you which is why you feel bad when he's not around. He knows his limits and he knows yours but, obviously, you don't. It's why he's fighting while we sit comfortably under the guards protecting us.'

'I,' Michal started, looking away to gather his thoughts. He then turned back with a serious expression that caught Syndra off guard again. 'I know. I'm a deformed stone elemental that could only melt a certain type of stone and tweak it a bit. That's all. But I will say that you're wrong and that I have been thinking for myself. At first, I was content with following orders and make armour but I've been thinking of how I could fight. I tried creating gauntlets and stone blades. I'm close. I'm oh so close. So, no. You're wrong about that.'

Michal breathed a sigh of frustration while clenching a fist. Syndra didn't say or do anything except to send a piercing glare to those that stopped working to watch. However, despite her lack of response, she knew what she thought of the whole situation. This nonsensical arguing, this rashness, this complacency driven by pure emotion; It was as if the danger outside meant nothing to anyone within this tent bar those who already felt the full extent of the enemy.

'But I guess you're right,' Michal admitted with his usual cheerful smile. 'I know I can't do anything at the moment, so I'll ask Gin to train me and then I can in the future. Then I can protect many people next time. Better than me moping, right?'

Ugh. What is with that sudden shift from depression to optimism? Syndra gave a disgusted look. 'If you finally understand that you're acting pathetic then help treat the others.'

'Will do!' Michal obeyed as he went to grab some supplies from the medics. 'Oh, one more thing. Thanks! I needed that.'

'Whatever,' Syndra mumbled, glad she didn't have to deal with his whining anymore.

She returned to pouring gel on wounds, ordering the medics and comforting the wounded. But, every so often, she would glance towards the entrance of the tent. *Wonder when Nasir's returning,* she thought whenever she did so. The cycle of treating, ordering and worrying about her tinoo continued for the next five or so minutes but it felt like thirty.

'I'm here, miss Syndra!' cooing broke the cycle and slowed-down time.

'Ah! Nasir, welcome back,' Syndra whistled back.

Nasir landed on her shoulders, got a neck rub, then flew to the floor to do his signature language of dancing.

'Good to be back at your side too,' he curtseyed. *'I've got the others into a crescent formation.'*

'Awesome! Great work, Nasir. Give the rest of the report. What's the situation so far?'

'It would seem that the offence group are holding up for now. Unfortunately, they can't send reinforcements to help protect us though.'

'Ah. I don't think the utility group will survive at this rate then.'

'No, miss Syndra, on the contrary. Brim and some artillery group members realised we were in danger and are making their way here. They've already dealt with most of the stealth bestials on the outskirts of our group and are just setting up torches to spot them.'

'Oh, thank goodness! No wonder the screaming has stopped. I was so worried that more would have to die. I...'

Syndra stopped whistling, biting her lower lip to stop it trembling. *'I don't want to go through that again.'*

'Neither do I, miss Syndra.'

Syndra let out a sigh of relief that caught the attention of all the conscious people in the room. She glared back at the medics who got the message and continued their work. But Michal remained oblivious. Not only that, he stopped helping out and began fiddling about with the gauntlets while she wasn't looking.

'Is everything ok?' he asked.

'Yes. We got confirmation that the artillery group has merged with the utility group. We're no longer in danger.'

'That's a relief,' Michal sighed himself, going back to his gauntlets.

'Look at him!' Syndra whistled again. *'He's being pathetic and useless again!'*

Nasir looked annoyed, flying up and onto her shoulder, slapping her in the face along the way.

'Miss Syndra, you really ought to be more considerate,' Nasir scolded. *'He's done all he could do. Everyone's had medicinal lotion on put on them. Did you expect him to do the stitches too? Not like you're doing anything better talking with me and all.'*

'Ugh. Hate it when you're right.'

'Just give him something to do.'

'Michal, go and tell the guards to help Brim. Have one or two remain though. The faster we deal with the stealth bestials, the faster the artillery group can help the offence group,' Syndra commanded.

'Huh? Oh, sure thing,' Michal listened, getting up onto his feet and out of the tent.

'Oh, whatever shall I do with you, miss Syndra,' Nasir teased.

'Shut up, will you?' she replied.

A few minutes later, Michal returned, giving a simple "Done!" before going back to his project again. For some reason, he became the topic of debate between Syndra and Nasir. Not that they had anything better to do. As pointed out earlier, all the treatment they could do as non-medics was done, and Nasir needed to wait for the utility group to be fully secured before going out and ordering his underlings to change formation again.

'There are about fifteen minutes until our reinforcement arrives. I'm sure we'll win this battle,' he assured.

'Yeah. I'm glad. We've gotten through the worst'

'Hurk,' the sound of someone vomiting filled the air. Then the clang of a torch collapsing by the entrance, blowing out upon impact with the floor.

Ugh. That was Michal, wasn't it? Just how clumsy is that guy? Syndra scowled to herself before demanding, 'Light another torch. Make it quick.'

One of the medics managed to get a torch alight. Syndra then turned to Michal to give a piece of her mind. But, instead of the brown drivel of digested lunch, she expected to come out of the man's mouth, blood splattered across the floor in front of him. Stains of red seeped out of four distinct areas on his chest as he clutched his gauntlets. He looked on the verge of death. No, he *was* on the verge of death.

'Look out!'

'Huh?'

Before she knew it, Nasir kicked Syndra, causing her to trip and tumble to the floor. Pins and needles throbbed from her shoulders. She glanced at the cause, finding blood trickling out of three, lined streaks. She clutched the wound, trying and failing to stop the pain that amplified more and more.

Squawking made her look forward. Her body stood still, her beating heart and quivering eyes the only parts that dared to move. She watched Nasir fighting against the invisible enemy, floating blood and a shadow the only features visible. She watched his bravery get punished as something swiped across the breast. She watched as her partner and life-long friend crashed into the ground.

'Nasir, no!' she exclaimed, freezing the other medics in their spot, all as equally scared.

But now the floating blood walked towards her. The sound of dripping broke the seal placed on her. Her body moved again but not to escape. Instead of running, she shivered. From her trembling lips to her shaking feet, every organ in her body moved but purely in the sand she sat in.

Blood dripped from the claws the enemy attacked with. Drip by drip by drip it came closer. Why was it so slow? Just to taunt? Just to instil fear? Whatever the reason, it worked. Step by step by step it came closer, until the bleeding nails stood over her, the blood falling onto her face drop by drop.

'Get off of her!' Michal came from behind, grabbing hold of the enemy. He stabbed the enemy with the gauntlets he equipped.

But the enemy materialised, revealing just the everything bar the head, twisting around in a motion much faster than before. The man grabbed Michal, shanking him in the abdomen. However, Michal grabbed hold of one arm. He mouthed something to Syndra before drilling his gauntlet into the enemy's torso back.

The stealth bestial screamed a painful scream in response. He used his other arm to stab Michal, piercing him again and again and again. He didn't stop, but neither did Michal who persevered, digging deeper into the African.

Michal collapsed the next moment followed by the stealth bestial, his head now materialised too. The medics sprung back to life, rushing to treat their saviour. However, it was too late. He became pale, blood continuing to pour out of his wounds.

'Why are the guards dead here?!' Brim shouted, bursting into the tent. His voice quietened down the next moment when he saw the scene. 'Oh no...'

Brim gave some orders but Syndra didn't listen to any of them. She cradled Nasir into her bosom. Tears fell onto her friend. She tried immediate treatment on him but none of them did any good. His wings didn't move. His lungs didn't breathe. His heartbeat hovered just above zero.

'Nasir, don't die,' she pleaded.

'*Nasir, please wake up,*' she whistled, seeing if that would provoke a response.

Nothing.

She embraced her sole friend, weeping into the feathers and wounds. She didn't know how else to react.

'Nasir...I'm so sorry.'

34

Maiden Battle Part 5

Gin scooped sand with his blade and hurled it at his target's face. The enemy deflected the attempt but it bought enough time. An ally juggernaut grabbed the foe by his arms, leaving an opening for Gin. He took the opportunity, using a fallen body as leverage and pierced the mage's chest. However, the enemy's packed muscles clenched the blade, preventing the strike from going further.

Not deep enough, Gin analysed, retracting his weapon with great difficulty. If not for his training, landing jabs after jabs on the tree back home, he would have been left open for a counterattack.

The foe then elbowed the allied mage, breaking free of the hold that bound him. A crunching tackle knocked the Eurasian to the floor, turning his back to Gin in the process.

Perfect.

Gin unhooked the gun INS from his belt, activating the mechanism, and creating the barrel in an instant, aiming right at the heart. He pressed the trigger in the second chamber; The mage collapsed with a spherical hole through him.

'Thanks,' the allied mage said, getting up onto his feet, panting as he did so.

'No problem. Go help team seven, I'll go help team nineteen,' Gin commanded.

'Understood.'

Gin burst from his spot to the next team. As he skipped passed fireballs, friendly fire and foes on the floor, he almost reached team nineteen, a group of three occupied with a juggernaut.

However, out of nowhere, an ally fire elemental crashed into Gin, knocking them both to the floor. He came to just in time to see a behemoth of a mage towering over him, hurling a punch right at his face. Gin rolled away on time, dodging the blow but when he got back on his feet, he realised he wasn't the target as a pool of blood stood in the place of his ally's now faceless face.

Gin didn't have time to stare as he readied his gun once more. He fired at the distracted enemy but the recoil hindered the shot too much as the bullet flew right past its target, dissipating back into nanobots before it hit anybody else.

The gunshot warned the juggernaut who turned to face Gin but that gave an open angle to shoot at. Gin held his arm, this time bracing for the recoil as he fired once more. His aim was true as the bullet pierced the chest and drove right towards the heart, yet the foe continued its attack, charging right at him.

Gin sidestepped then ducked, dodging a right hook in the process. He then skipped backwards, building some distance between the two. He aimed for another shot, clicked the mechanism and – nothing.

'Tsk. Out of ammo,' Gin mumbled to himself, slotting the gun back in his belt before getting back to his stance.

Gin took a few more steps backwards, assessing the damage he dealt while wary of his surroundings. The enemy was at a stand-still. He didn't move from his position. Blood trickled from the hole on his opponent's chest. Then gin's eyes widened as a small, silver pellet dropped from the beast's flesh before the blood stopped flowing, the wound closing instead.

Just how strong is this guy?! A sinking feeling made Gin's gut heavy, but he kept his composure, returning to a defensive stance. His eyes darted looking for any potential back up.

'Nobody's available,' Gin muttered to his dismay. *You're on your own, Gin.*

The mage finished closing the wound then attacked Gin once more. He dodged the first strike; deflected the second with his shield, pain reverberating through his arm. It was almost as strong as Varunel's punch which shattered his bones. Gin knew he couldn't take any direct hits, so he leapt to the side, keeping his distance while looking for an opportunity.

But then water grazed Gin's thigh, leading to a small wound on his calf. He knew where it came from and cursed his naiveté. He was so focused on his opponent, he forgot to be wary of friendly fire. The area throbbed but the adrenaline soon nullified the pain. Now time was against him as he decided on his next plan.

Gin took the initiative. He used his inferior height to duck out of another swing. He struck out, jabbing the enemy's hip. Before the beast could react, Gin retreated a few metres and out of range, watching the wound he inflicted start to close again.

Gin went in for another attack. He aimed for the torso this time. The opponent lashed out but Gin was too quick. He dodged the hook, side-stepped into position then uppercut the mage, piercing the chest area and retracting in one clean motion.

Gin then retreated to a safe distance then attacked once more. He leaned back, avoiding a roundhouse kick by millimetres. The enemy was now off-balance. Gin took his chance and sent a flurry of stabs in return.

The process continued. Retreat. Dodge. Attack. Repeat. Gin slowly built up the damage to the point that the enemy's regeneration couldn't keep up. He infuriated the enemy, like a mosquito that could never be caught. He knew he had no means to deal a finishing blow on a conscious enemy, but at least he slowed it down enough that he managed to buy time.

All of a sudden, the ground shook in a series of tremors. The sand shifted westwards, tripping both ally and enemy alike off balance. The mage in front did the same but Gin remained steady, using his training in the desert room to full effect. He hopped up to the fallen enemy and sliced the neck, making sure there was no chance of recovery.

Then came the news of what caused the tremors.

'Enemy reinforcements. Two Thousand strong!' the words bringing fear amongst the offence group. They only held on for the time being. They knew they couldn't handle more enemies.

However, instead of getting demoralised, Gin smirked. He looked up, noticing the lack of enemy fireballs, then looked back at his disgruntled allies. He took a deep breath then bellowed,

'These are Eurasian allies. Push the enemy back and win this battle!'

The shout sent a shiver down everyone's spines as it got relayed amongst the Eurasians. Morale shot through the proverbial roof as the enemy juggernauts began backing off in despair, getting cut down from

Squadron W from the front and behind with no African fireball in sight.

Gin continued his role, weaving in and out, slicing the juggernauts one by one. The stabs weakened the enemy. His allies handled the rest. On the contrary, there was no teamwork from the enemy; only a bunch of individuals that lost to those weaker than them.

The enemy fell like flies. As they died, the offence group's forces freed up more and more. Outnumbered and outclassed, the AAA's forces depleted until none of them remained alive.

Gin dusted off the sand that had mixed with the blood around his eyes. He stared in front of him. He knew what happened. It was according to plan after all. The slope that the battlefield began with no longer existed. Instead laid a massive chasm where Eurasian reinforcements continued to climb out of.

An emphatic victory would have been an overstatement. They struggled, fought, and some even died. In the end, that didn't matter. It was still Squadron W's win.

'Alright, spread out into formation forty-nine and make sure not a single stealth bestial remains and check if anyone's playing dead,' Gin gave one last order before muttering, 'Hopefully the utility group didn't suffer too many casualties.'

35

Aftermath

The sun rose over the battlefield, leaving a giant shadow where it hit the Eastern walls. The long-awaited battle came to a close. All that was left to do was to stock food for the return trip, clean up the area, and treat the injured before the trek back to squadron W's rezah tree.

However, despite the task at hand, Gin sat in front of the row of bodies, all lined up and stripped naked in rows of ten. He watched; Watching with a clenched fist full of sand and a drooped back, his head poised at one of the deceased in particular. The one with multiple stabs wounds that already crusted over, a sheet covering the rolled-over eyes.

'Hey, Gin?' a worried Joan called.

'Mm?' Gin responded. It was an empty reply; void of any positive emotion as she feared.

'Does–' she paused, figuring out how to bring up the topic. 'Did Michal's death–'

Gin placed a finger on her lips. She got the message, giving up and joining him beside the lifeless bodies. But, instead of being focused on those dead, she tended to the wounds on her patient, tending to the gash on his leg that didn't heal as much, coating it with a healing gel through her index finger. Afterwards, she took off his armour and inspected his back, finding several burn marks and bruises. *No reaction again*, she worried some more as she pierced his skin with her nails. *Was his unresponsiveness mental or physical?*

'I know what you want to say,' Gin spoke up, sighing as he did so. 'And no. I'm just counting our losses. I

have to write a report to send to the colonel, no?
Death is natural and expected, especially in battle. We
just have to go onto the next mission and move on
from all of this.'

'That's a little harsh,' Joan played along.

'Meh. They couldn't defend themselves and died in
the process. I did my best to train them, but it looks
like they couldn't use that. They didn't anticipate a
sneak attack and this is what happens. No point
brooding over the grunts of the operation.'

'And you don't care about them?'

'Why should I? I've seen more. I've lost more...This is
nothing.'

'Gin,' Joan addressed in a stern manner, sending a
shiver down his spine. 'Tell me the truth. Do you
really feel that way?'

Gin lowered his head, brooding for a few seconds
before turning his body around to face Joan. His eyes
contained red and the residue of dried tears lingered
on his scarred face. His lips trembled.

'No,' Gin croaked at last, reluctance still in his voice.
'Of course not. But I still need to put up this façade,
don't I? I'm the leader after all. If I say how I feel or
feel how I say, it just wouldn't be right, would it? Not
in the eyes of the others at least.'

'Huh? What do you mean?'

'Just listen,' Gin's voice turned into a whisper.

Joan didn't understand what he meant but kept quiet
regardless. It wasn't until then did she notice the
slowing down of some mages as they walked past the
pair. A few even stopped just out of earshot but their

glances and body language showed that they referred to Gin in their conversations.

'Wow. Did he really let a thousand Eurasians die?' one of a careless trio of fire elementals said (all of whom Joan recognised were part of the reinforcement team).

'What did you expect? He's a manush!' a second, just as careless, replied to his compatriots.

'Really? No wonder I saw him crying a while ago. I heard the manush get super emotional. Is that why Team A split up?' the first asked while the third looked on.

'Yeah. Apparently, he also drove Rob's battalion out in a fit of rage because they didn't listen to him, leading them to their doom. We could have had a flawless victory if Rob was in charge,' responded the second again.

'What? No way.'

'Yes way.'

The third mage that didn't speak throughout made his move. He shifted his body to face Gin and Joan before speaking in a tone which made it obvious that he wanted to be heard by the pair, 'Can't believe Maria chose him to be in charge of the offence group!'

How do they not realise how much Gin is hurting? Just because they came at the end to clean up and not witness the horrors of war he did? And the fact that he wasn't afraid to tell me he was a manush from the very beginning (though I didn't believe him at first regrettably) proved that it has nothing to do with his judgement and character! He is just like us mages, sheesh! the thoughts rang through Joan's mind.

To put it bluntly, their attitude disgusted her. Through clenched teeth, she stood up to give the deluded trio a piece of her mind. However, before she could utter a word, another fire elemental walked up to them. She didn't know the man, so decided to ignore him and carry on with her planned scolding.

'Oh, will you shut up!' the man bellowed, stopping everyone, including Joan, in their tracks. 'Betrayals, makeshift groups, trust issues; Oh, so much trust issues. Do you know how much we've suffered these past few weeks? I know we were incompetent and lacking order throughout, but we've definitely experienced a thousand times more than you guys who came to the fight to hog the glory without fear of death. So, how about you get back to work? Those bodies won't move by themselves.'

The onlookers grumbled for a moment before leaving the vicinity, while the braided man who caused that to happen walked towards Gin. He stood by him, waiting for a response, but getting nothing in return.

'Oi, help me out. We need to feed the mage-eaters,' he requested.

'Oh? It's time already?' Gin looked up. 'Right. I'll get on it straight away.'

Despite his words, Gin sat in his spot. He didn't move at all, much to the annoyance of the fire elemental who gave him a gentle kick to the shin to show it.

'This really isn't the time for moping around, Gin. This really isn't your fault alone. And this really isn't how a leader should act, though I'm probably not one to talk,' the man's words quietened and quietened as he continued speaking before picking up again for a final, 'Just get up.'

Joan tapped on the man's shoulder, grabbing his attention. 'I think we should leave him be. He's not feeling too –'

'Dammit all!' an exasperated Gin cried out, punching the sand below him and scaring Joan in the process. He breathed deep breaths before jumping onto his feet in one go. With a cheesy grin on his face and an odd spring in his side, he confronted the two. 'Sorry, I just had to release my negativity in one go. Thanks, Jake! Let's get to work now.'

'Ugh. I still don't approve of you,' Jake grumbled, heading off to do the job alone.

Joan stood there blinking. *What did I just witness?* she questioned the sudden change in atmosphere. Gin, the guy who sat down all gloomy and downbeat just a few seconds ago, now stood as if nothing had happened. Was his smile h face? Oh! You probably have more patients to tend to. I'll leave you to it then.'

'No,' Joan denied way too quickly for her liking.

'Hm?'

'No, nothing. I'll help out. The other medics already treated everyone that needs treatment anyway. I'd just be extra baggage if I joined them. Might as well carry these bodies instead.'

'If you say so,' Gin shrugged.

To no one's surprise, he headed straight for Michal's body first. He wrapped his friend in the shaven fur of the lupim, removing any remaining inedible bits of stone that clung onto him as well. Then, noticing the open, lifeless eyes, he closed them before hauling the body onto a stone stretcher, newly made courtesy of the other stone elementals.

'Grab the other side,' Gin instructed, grabbing hold of one end.

Joan obliged without saying a word. She just observed his actions, voice and mannerisms. None of which gave what he was thinking away to her dismay. It made her realise how little she knew of him. Him being a manush with strange objects called nanobots were all she understood about the mysterious man that entered her life. From the very first day he joined squadron W to now, a whole year or so had passed. How did she manage to last this long, watching his time in the squadron, while being clueless about the person's background throughout?

'Joan, what is Syndra doing?' Gin asked, breaking her thought process.

'Huh?' Joan paused.

She didn't realise they already began walking towards the chasm where the mage-eaters were, carrying Michal's body along with them. However, what Gin referred to were the group of tinoos huddling around a woman with no defining feature except for how dark her hair was.

'What do you want to know in particular?' Joan asked.

'I honestly don't know why she's doing it. I assume she's whistling something, but that's about it.'

At least his curiosity is genuine, Joan concluded before responding, 'Those tinoos lost their masters. She's just giving them the choice between staying and looking for a new master or choosing to be free.'

'By free, do you mean that the wild tinoos we see are actually —'

'Yeah, they're likely to be the descendants of the familiars of fallen mages.'

'I see,' Gin said as he watched some of the birds fly into the sky and away from the battlefield. 'That's an interesting custom.'

Joan noted how Gin learnt more of her species just like that and yet, she couldn't do the same. She didn't have the right questions. Where would she even begin?

'Um, leader,' a fire elemental called out to Gin, this time someone much more hospitable to him to Joan's relief. 'Can you help me?'

'What do you need?' Gin answered the woman.

'Sorry for causing you too much trouble but I can't seem to create a spark,' she indicated to an oil–laden enemy bestial.

'Sure, I can help with that. Joan, do you mind?'

'No, not at all,' Joan replied, lowering the stretcher with Gin.

He went over to the body and activated his blades. The branches then entered the second chamber of the INS, creating a spark that ignited the body. The burning flames covered the stench of the decaying body for the most part, but everyone still needed to cover their nose.

'Why couldn't you make a spark in the first place?' Gin asked, a weird nasal sound covering his normal voice.

'My fingers are a bit wet from my sweat,' the meek girl responded.

'Is that so?' Gin understood as his Xernim began to grow a thin sheet of wood out of his upper arm. He split it off and gave it to the mage saying, 'Use this to wipe your fingers. It should absorb most of the oil.'

'Oh, thank you!'

'No problem.'

At least his kindness is genuine, Joan chuckled to herself as she watched the spectacle. *Wait. When did the Xernim grow that far?!*

'What's so funny?' Gin wondered, stopping her from asking out loud.

'Nothing,' she smirked instead, picking up Michal again. 'We're almost at the chasm by the way.'

'Oh, you're right,' Gin said, stopping all of a sudden. 'Woah.'

Joan looked at what caught his attention. An adult mage-eater sat on the edge of the hole with a quadruplet of featherless chicks by its side. It waited for its opportunity, leaning and inspecting those that came close. Whenever someone did, it spread out its wings, showing off their monstrous size in all its glory. Then, when someone threw a corpse into the pit, it dived down, grabbing the body mid-flight before gulping it down in a matter of seconds.

The chicks on the other hand screeched and bobbed their little heads up and down, begging their parent to pay attention to them when it returned on its perch. The adult listened to the younglings, rolling out its long tongue. A reddish-brown sludge rolled down to the tip, dripping into the birds' gaping mouths as they swallowed the mush with satisfaction. *Wait. Why am I watching this?* Joan questioned her interest despite seeing the same scene many times in her past.

'This is all so fascinating. How did we even get to this point?' Gin mumbled as he picked up the pace again.

'Is this how you see the world?' Joan asked, linking her own experience with Gin's words.

'You heard that? Ah, well, ok then,' Gin gave a soft chuckle at his absentmindedness. 'How do you think I see the world then?'

'I don't know. Seeing everything with child-like enthusiasm? You find amazement in the most mundane of things and never hesitate to explore what you don't know. All of which under a secretive state where you lead people on, making them think they know you when no one really does. Hmph!' Joan pouted at the end.

'Are you,' Gin stopped by the edge of the chasm and noticed Joan's expression for the first time. 'Are you perhaps angry with me?'

'No.'

'I'm not *that* stupid, Joan. I can tell you're not happy about something. My guess is that you're frustrated because you know nothing about me, my past, or where I came from.'

'What? How did you...'

'Well, I've been thinking a lot lately,' Gin paused to lower Michal onto the ground. He sat by the body, looking across the chasm. He stared at a fifth chick that joined its family, this one with a complete set of feathers on its body. However, what irked Joan was that this particular chick seemed to stare back.

'And what have you been thinking?' Joan asked, shaking her head to dispel her suspicions about the bird.

'Ever since the attack in the forest, I feel like my past has come back to haunt me. I locked it up or at least thought I did, but I now think that was the wrong thing to do. If I wasn't as insufferable in the beginning – if I wasn't as impatient with Alder – I could be much stronger and the other battalions might have looked on me favourably instead. Fewer people would have deserted as a result.'

'Gin, thought we told you already. All the bad that's happened so far isn't your fault.'

'How about you?' Gin ignored Joan's comments. 'Do you have any regrets? Stuff that you wish you could have changed in the past few months?'

Joan didn't know how to respond. She didn't even expect the questions in the first place. It made her step back to think as she came with her own answer. But, when she figured how she would respond, she joined Gin, sitting down with her legs dangling over the edge of the chasm.

'Yes,' she began, letting out a deep breath to clear her lungs. 'I should have believed you were a manush when we first spoke. I should have asked to join you on your side of this mission instead of using the underground caverns under The Path. I should have been there to keep both you and the squadron in check. But I wasn't.'

'Heh.'

'What's so funny? I poured my heart and soul into that.'

'I know. But hindsight is both wonderful and useless, isn't it?'

Joan looked at the lifeless Michal then back at the ever-pondering Gin. 'Yeah, I suppose it is.'

'But the beauty of it is that we can improve on ourselves today.'

'Huh?'

Gin stood up to Joan's surprise. He picked up Michal with both arms and, with a couple of pre-emptive swings, he hurled him into the pit. The adult mage-eater that was watching them all along plunged and scooped it in its beak, completing the process by swallowing Michal whole before returning to the chicks.

'Did you know us manush bury our dead instead of feeding them to animals?' Gin gave a triumphant exclamation before breathing a final sigh at his friend's fate.

'Where did that come from?' Joan jumped from her seat, almost tumbling over the ledge.

'It's me trying to turn over a new leaf, I suppose. I want to be more open about my past. From my point of view, not even I was thinking about it. I just wanted to learn more and more about you mages, even if I didn't realise that was my aim from the beginning. And you wanted to know more about me and the manush, right Joan?' Gin said with a smile directed at her.

Before she knew it, Joan kicked her legs against the chasm in a playful manner, glee running across her face. 'So, *why* do you manush bury your dead instead of feeding them to mage-eaters?'

'I don't know. Something something tradition something something. We just do it. We don't have the mages' sentiment of looking after the environment. If we were to do something, it's probably because my ancestors did it and no real reason, unlike you guys who feed the animals who in turn feeds nature which in turn feeds you back.'

'Pfft. Yeah, that does sound stupid,' Joan agreed, unable to hide her amusement.

'I know, right?!'

'Let's head back. We got lots of work to do still,' Joan reminded, getting up on her feet and grabbing the stretcher. 'But I'd love to hear more of your customs along the way.'

'Ah, right. You're right as always!' Gin replied, grabbing the other side.

'Oh, by the way, you weren't so insufferable when you first joined,' Joan tried to console, still unsure what Gin's mental state was.

'I think I was.'

'Ok, you kinda were.'

'Heh. Told you!'

'Shut up. You still are,' Joan stuck her tongue out.

'Aaaaanyway, shall we get back to my culture?'

'What about your past?'

'I,' Gin started but stopped, his face drooping back to the depressed mess before. 'I'll...'

'Let's hold it off for now then. Tell me when you're ready,' Joan reassured.

'Ah, yeah,' Gin forced a cough and changed his expression once more. 'I got a good story where we celebrate someone's birthday even though that guy's been dead for nearly half a millennium. Want to hear that?'

'Yes, let's. I want to know how stupid your race really is.'

Gin burst out in laughter. It got so serious he stopped moving to take a moment to relax. But, when he regained his composure, he turned to Joan.

'Thanks,' he said with the warmest of smiles.

Or at least that's what Joan wanted to believe his expression meant. In all honesty, she realised that Gin was still hurting from the losses. He still blamed himself for them. His smiles? Probably an attempt to not make her worry. His offer to talk about his past? She could tell he only scratched the surface of the truth. The sudden change in emotions? Well, she really didn't want to press the issue to find out yet.

But still, Joan couldn't help but think, *at least Gin is someone genuine.*

Book One End

MAP

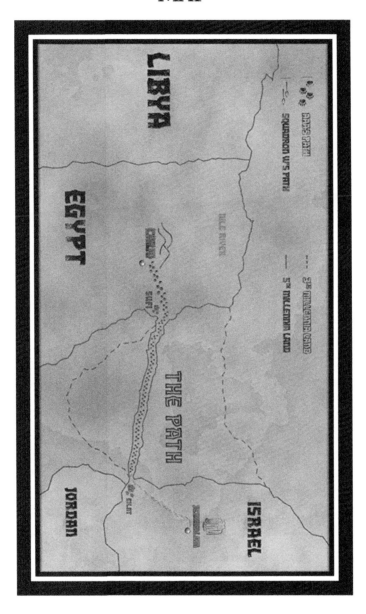

~We Thank The Following For their Support~

These lists include all those who bought the 1st Copies
ever made as well as artwork.

	Panda	
1st Copies	Connie X.	

Kamilla M.	1st Artwork
SS Tanya	
Amanda B.	
Brandon	
Sajid A.	

~We Thank The Following For their Support~

These lists include all those who bought early copies
in print and electronic versions

Kaleb B.
Chhewang T.
Angelina G.
Anthony G.
Robert H.
Caleb C.
Greg L.
Darrel M.
Muhibbul I.
Emu
Patryk K.
Daniel W.
Shawna T.
D. Rednal
Nicklas N.
Joseph K.
Brian G.
Jakob S.
Michael B.
Nishant M.
Haajira A.
Jacob H. H.
Zehn M.

Concept Art

Xernim Gauntlets, designed by Panda (penname)

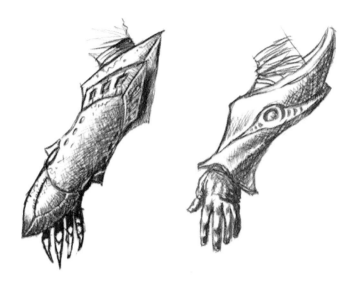

Printed in Great Britain
by Amazon

24435111R00223